Vakho

The Wolf's Cub

Vakho

The Wolf's Cub

Marek Boszko Rudnicki

Chapter I

He stared, disbelieving his senses.

It was not a dream or delusions or the old storyteller's tales by the fire. Not one of my grandfather's many terrifying stories about the Moskales after the uprising, or uncle Vakhtang about the fighting in the Caucasus.

He saw and heard, but he was unable to comprehend the images, process their monstrosities and explain them rationally.

The sight deprived him of his will.

Paralyzed, he remained motionless, unable to make any decisions.

He only watched what was unfolding before his eyes. And although it recorded events in detail, the mind refused to receive them, even though they were taking place here and now.

***

Several huts were on fire. Drunken soldiers wandered around the village, looking for harassment with the peasants, bursting into huts, pulling terrified women out of them and forcing them to drink, dance and romp with them. And when the men protested, they were hit a saber on the head, and it was good if that was all.

In the distillery located next to the village, even before their arrival, on the orders of their grandfather, the vats were filled with fresh mash of apples and millet. Now it was starting to ferment, but the soldiers did not mind. They clung to their contents, swallowed the slurry with ladles like soup, and then, with their legs tangled, went on to conquer the countryside, with singing on their lips. He only caught out the gibberish repeated word Bolshevik and interrupted, incomprehensible: Mudra party of the Bolsheviks...

Who is this? Seemingly Russians, but some other than the ones he knew so far, supposedly tsarist, and yet not like that. And this one word, Bolshevik, inflected with love in all ways, hard, with a hint of some fierce and ruthlessness, completely different from the melancholic notes previously heard Farewell of Slavianka or Prajdiom krasnoje morie. And in behavior, wild inertia, total chaos, as if they had no commanders, which made them more like an ordinary gang, not a regular army.

His attention was drawn to the shouts near the barn, which during the folk world periodically served as a common room.

He sharpened the image through the binoculars. A few drunks were dragging the defending and calling for help Hapka, the daughter of a member of the village council, the wise and calm chairman Kuźma. This one, Janek also saw it terrified from his place, swayed hanging from a rope on an old pear tree that grew in the main square of the village. Not alone, but in the company of the mayor Fedek and Ivashka, whom my grandfather said clearly sympathize with the Bolsheviks and told the granger to keep an eye on him. As you can see, his sympathies did not help him much.

At one point, the girl managed to snatch one of the tormentors out of the hands of one of the torturers and tried to escape, but the other one was faster and hit her in the face with his fist so hard that she fell limp to the ground.

The soldiers laughed, and then two grabbed her legs, stretched them to the sides, lifted them high, and another rolled up her skirt and threw it over head. The fourth from company loosened the strings of his pants, lowered them demonstratively and, amid the mockery of the other companions, lay on her.

After waking up, Hapka tried to defend herself, but she was too weak. They held tight, and as she began to howl, they tucked her blouse into her mouth.

After a few minutes, the first one stood up, greeted with laughter and cheers from his companions, followed by another, and then standing behind him, and a few more who approached. When the line was over, they started all over again. When they got bored after some time, Hapka lay motionless, and the fact that she was still alive was evidenced only by her breasts moving spasmodically to the rhythm of interrupted breathing.

The one who had hit her, the big bullyboy with a scar on his cheek, spoke to her, and when she was silent, he nudged her brutally with his shoe, and finally kicked her. When she still didn't respond, he slowly pulled the Mauser out of its holster and as if nothing, without any hesitation, shot her between her breasts, causing another burst of mocking laughter from the others.

Something died in Janek. Suddenly, without notice. He just felt his body sink into an inertia that he could not contain.

Hapka...

***

They must have arrived relatively recently, because their caravans were just approaching the village; carts unpacked with prey stolen on the way. Cupboards, tables, some mirrors, duvets, even a decorative bed, chairs, armchairs, samovars, clocks, paintings, candlesticks and a whole lot of trinkets thrown haphazardly. These were not items from peasant huts, but equipment from the mansions they passed along the way.

A dozen or so carriages, one after the other, with harnessed horses, judging by their color and figure, also probably taken from master's stables. At the end of the column, there are three empty ones, followed by a four-bay tachanka pulled by a heavy machine gun and several riders dressed in woolen burqas and Tatar hats with a red star. Someone played the harmonica, another sang a song about a mean commander, and his companion shouted next to those who had already settled in the village.

Janek, who saw the death of Hapka in front of his eyes all the time, and guilt and grievances against himself that he had not reacted, that he had not helped and saved the girl, watched it not like reality, but a moving image sometimes shown at a marketplace. Hidden in a nearby orchard among the plump quince trees, he painfully pressed a small pair of binoculars against his wet eyes, which he had taken for hunting, a gift from his grandfather when he was ten years old.

Sudden commotion among the soldiers. Even the drunken ones stopped, their frolics ceased.

The squadron commander probably drove into the village, surrounded by a few horsemen, and surprisingly in the uniforms of the tsarist army. A man in a black jacket sat on a black horse next to him. They exchanged some comments and they probably did not have the same opinion, because they gesticulated strongly.

The stillness lasted a moment. A soldier, probably the one who shot Hapka, ran up to the group and showed the direction of the court. Orders were given, and they rushed in that direction at once.

"Grandfather Sylwester and Vasily are there," thought Janek. "I must let them know what is happening, warn them, or maybe they already know what happened." He thought, terrified of their fate, remembering the stories of those who managed to escape from the occupied territories and told what had been done to the inhabitants of the mansions.

He jumped up, determined, overcoming his weakness, composed only of one, in order to find himself in front of his grandfather as soon as possible and tell him what was happening in the countryside.

Hiding behind the trees, he began to run as fast as he could, overcoming the weakness of his numb legs.

***

A month earlier, German troops had begun to slowly withdraw from their positions, handing them over to the incoming Bolsheviks. Commanders of troops often slept in the manor, sharing with his grandfather his thoughts and negative opinions about the politicians in Berlin, thanks to whom they lost the war.

The tsar abdicated, there was a riot in Russia and various factions clashed in the fight. The imperial army practically did not exist anymore, discipline was gone, and German troops, still strong, occupied a large area stretching as far as the Sea of Azov and Don Taganrog. They did not like the fact that they gave up the conquered territory without a fight. It didn't even help to know that it was a political act that Berlin had made a secret deal with Lenin and that now occupied by the army of Supreme Commander of All German Forces in the East, Ober-Ost, was to be abandoned for the benefit of the Red Guards.

The commander of a separate squadron of the cuirassier regiment, Oberst Günter Alleberger, stayed with them for a particularly long time, because as it turned out, he knew his grandfather from their youth, when they fought together as young volunteers with the tsarist army in Crimea.

Janek, flushed on his face, listened to his stories, how German uhlans clashed with Russian cavalry on the Vileyka, and how they chased them far to the east. And how the entire Vilnius operation was wasted when the chief of the general staff, Erich von Falkenhayn, demanded that their commanders, General Erich von Ludendorff, send troops from the east to strengthen the Western Front.

Names meant nothing to Janek, unlike his grandfather, who inquired about some colonel Wilhelm Bader, the commander of the Infanterieregiment König Wilhelm I regiment, and about other officers serving in it.

What he remembered most was how this Alleberger warned his grandfather against the Bolsheviks and told what the fat, dark hordes and ordinary gangs, which multiplied in the times of universal chaos after the overthrow of the tsar, were sending out in the occupied territory. How they introduce people's power by murdering the nobility, raping women and killing children. When they burn mansions and even murder livestock, they cut down entire parks, spreading the slogan of "social justice". And he urged to prepare to flee west, or at least send Janek's mother there earlier with him and his sister, because when the red fighters arrived, they would be certain to die.

And now he was running to the manor house, terrified, for the prophecies of Oberst Alleberger had become apparent before his eyes. Fear for his grandfather and Vasily gave him strength. He did not think about himself and was glad in spirit that his grandfather, together with the cuirassiers' departure, sent them to a distant family near Lviv, his mother and sister Anna with a few servants. Contrary to her protests, she would not go alone without Janek. Grandfather then convinced her that Janek would be fine, and the peasants owed him so much that no harm on their part could be expected.

***

He noticed the glow from a distance.

"It's over, they killed them, I'm left alone." Terrified, he could not collect his thoughts and rationally assess what he saw.

He felt so much regret that there was a previously unknown sharp burning sensation in his chest and a piercing pain in the area of the breastbone.

However, he did not slow down.

He kept running. "This isn't true, it isn't true," it rattled in his head.

As he passed the hill with the orchard, he paused, panting.

There was a burning shed where agricultural tools, straw and grain were kept. The glow illuminated the entire surroundings, shimmering it with intense red and a bloody glow reflected on the buildings and the ground. The stable building a little further away was partially burnt. An orange and yellow flickering reflection glowed in one place and a gray and white vapor floated in the air where apparently someone reacted and poured water over the beams.

In front of the porch of the manor there were three driveways to which drunk soldiers took the contents of the manor. They did it slowly, staggering because they must have already had their stock of wines. Every now and then, they burst out croaking as they showed each other a tampered detail, the use of which they did not know. They did not care about torn objects, which from time to time escaped from their hands, fell to the ground, which caused a wave of curses. They were not put in carts, and thrown in without worrying about whether they would scratch, break or damage. One heap was filled with furniture, corners and paintings removed from the walls, cords, rows, unobstructed burqas, and even wolves standing in front of fireplaces, or sets of utensils to keep the fire.

It was at that moment that the troop with the squadron commander and the man in the black jacket accompanying him, whom he had already seen in the village, arrived.

The commander stopped his horse, looked around, then gave a short order to the accompanying riders. Without a word, they jumped to the ground and began giving orders to the soldiers. Janek did not hear the content of the words, but after the movements he realized what was going on. The soldiers, who had been sluggish so far, as if suddenly sobered up, sped up and the furniture was brought back into the manor.

He took out the binoculars and began to carefully examine the entire surroundings. With horror, he noticed the corpse lying on the ground by the well. He adjusted the focus and now he recognized the body of Maruchna, no longer the youngest wardrobe mistress, who firmly refused to go with his mother because she had to support her own mother in the village. Admittedly, grandfather had promised to look after the old woman during her absence, but she asked and did not go. She remained, and since she had practically nothing to do, she only cleaned and mended the garments of the other three men in the manor. And now she was lying on the ground like a discarded, unnecessary rag, and Janek only guessed, mindful of the pictures from the countryside, what could happen to her.

Apart from her, he did not notice the rest of the servants, as well as his grandfather and Vasily. It occurred to him that they must have been killed, too, and thrown into the shed before setting it on fire, but he quickly pushed the thought aside as uncontrollable hysteria began to flow with it. He gritted his teeth, but the tears that were already pressing down his eyes could not be restrained.

He just absorbed the images, breathing faster and faster as he fought the panic that engulfed him.

***

This morning, even before dawn, he was awakened by the movement in the court, unnatural for this time.

Vasily was gone, grandfather dismissed his questions and told him to make his own breakfast. Maruchna, whom he tried to loosen her tongue, only huffed something incomprehensible that "they are going," but who, she no longer explained. She pushed him into the kitchen and served him a bread with meat and milk. During the course of Vasily returned, they locked themselves in the boudoir with his grandfather and did not leave it for a long time. And right after that, Vasily went somewhere.

Janek felt that something was going on, but his grandfather disposed of further questions. He didn't like being treated like a little boy, but sometimes it happened that secrets were kept from him. He had once overheard his mother quietly but firmly clarifying something to his grandfather, but he only understood the words when she raised her voice. Just one sentence: "He is still too young, why annoy him unnecessarily, it will be explained to him later." He even wanted to protest that he was not so young at all, that he was already seventeen that others his age went to officer training, but he quickly forgot about the conversation. Even when he asked if they had any news from his father, he was also dismissed with a joke or a shrug.

And this morning, after he had eaten, his grandfather ordered him to go to the forest on the pretext that he had to hunt some capercaillies for dinner. This surprised him, seeing a few crumbling birds and a supply of meat in the pantry.

As rare, grandfather made sure he took a bow with a large supply of arrows with him, not the Darne shotgun he used to go hunting for birds. And to his surprise, he ordered to take a name-day gift, completely useless for hunting, a Rast & Gasser revolver. And a large supply of food, and a burqa, although it was still warm outside and this one seemed completely unnecessary. It then occurred to Janek that officers would probably stay overnight in the manor again, although for some time no retreating German troops had been seen in the area.

Maybe some Russians will come?

When he left the court, scowling that nobody wanted to tell him anything, his grandfather took him in and threw him as if nothing had happened: "Just do well." And then for a moment more, which was also not his habit, he held his shoulders, looked intently in the eyes and added: "You are already a man, almost grown up, you know how to hunt and you are not stupid, you will be fine, as the need arises. Remember, never act like a woman who screams and panics instead of thinking. As if," he repeated, "you can count on the countryside. The peasants aren't bad, sometimes they just are seduced by something, so... Go and come back before evening."

When he had gone a few steps, he suddenly heard: "Do you remember where I hide my shotguns? Come on, go on."

And that's it.

He was surprised by his grandfather's behavior, but offended he did not ask what had happened, why the question about shotguns, because he used to hunt for birds with a bow and another time with a bird's gun and nobody ever asked him what he was taking with him. Vasily made his first bow for him when he was twelve, and he taught him how to shoot. And when he was sixteen he got another one, tough, adult. He always said that the animal must have a chance and the rifle only deprived him of that, but he did not refuse the shotgun either.

"Where did all this nervous excitement come from?" He was still wondering, but he knew that if his grandfather himself hadn't explained it to him, he wouldn't get anything out of it. Eventually, when he came back from the hunt, he would see for himself what it was all about.

***

He hunted five capercaillies, but he had to follow them far away, where deep in the forest there were clearings with a wide stream, and it was not close, because more than ten versts in a straight line, and with bends and dodging, almost twice as many. Along the way, he ate, dreaming about hot food, seeing in his imagination his favorite omelets with rose preserves, which were made the tastiest not by the cook, but by Maruchna.

He chose his way back through the village.

He got to her after dark.

And he saw what before, even listening to Vasily's story about the Caucasus, he could not imagine; drunken soldiers with strange red stars on their caps, what they were doing, the village council hanged on a tree and raped Hapka. Then it dawned on him why his grandfather had sent him hunting with a bow and not a shotgun. Perhaps he was afraid that if happens what happened, Janek would not be able to stand it mentally and would start shooting at the soldiers, and then he would inevitably die. But why didn't they warn him?

"They must have known something," he concluded, thinking about the strange behavior of his grandfather and Vasily before they set him out on a hunt. "Why didn't we run away before this gang showed up? Why did they send me to the forest? What did quiet Maruchna to soldiers? Where are the loved ones, killed or escaped?"

And now, holding the binoculars to his eyes, he was watching the court and trying to figure out what to do. And no reasonable idea emerged. He was scared like never before. He felt the fear and despair paralyzing him. And at the same time, a great deal of regret to his grandfather and Vasily, who did not precede him, abandoned him and said nothing, and now they deceived him.

Chapter II

He dreamed of a mansion in which he did not walk, but he flew hovering above the floor, unnoticed by the household, like a ghost flitting among the living. Carters passed him, hurrying somewhere on the order of Vasily, the guard and the gamekeeper hastily came out, passing the blacksmith in the doorway, and in the depths of the hallway Maruchna went to the room of his mother followed by one of the younger servants, Zenia.

He swam curiously, as if he were observing a strange house, yet familiar to him. First, through a great hall decorated with hunting trophies, on his way to the living area, from which some voices could be heard, he gave up and turned to his grandfather's boudoir, who was sitting bent over a large map spread on the desk. Vasily entered, to whom grandfather sometimes referred to by the strange name Vakhtang, the real one, because the new one, used, he only adopted it at the court, when they returned from the Caucasus together. At that time, they were still very young, younger than Janek's father, who was not even in the world yet.

However, all this he learned not from someone in his family, but from old Yefrosinia. She was father's wet nurse and they practically raised him together with Vasily, when grandmother died in childbirth, and grandfather was unable to recover for a long time after her death. She also called Vasily as Vakhtang and once, when he was still a little boy and she was taking care of him, she told him that Vasily was the Wolf. He laughed at it, but for a long time he looked suspiciously at Vasily, whether he would suddenly turn into a wolf. Only when he grew older did he understand that it was Vasily's Caucasian name. He himself explained it to him later, when he was older, when he told about his native Caucasus, about the battles of the survivors of Shamil's army with the Russians, about the fearless Polish Imam's guard, in which his grandfather served, and about how he saved his life. And then he called him Janek - Vakho, a young wolf who will one day grow into a fearless male wolf. He remembered how proud he was to be a wolf and how everyone would fear him.

***

He woke wet with sweat, his throat dry and tongue stiff. He was recovering for a moment, feeling a tingling sensation in all his muscles. A buzz was pulsating in his head, and an intrusive clock beep on the back of his skull, hitting the hands and causing unbearable pain.

He drank a few sips of water, the dry throat was gone, but the fear was back.

He lay down tired and quickly fell back to sleep. This time he dreamed of Hapka, joyful, smiling, and playful in the meadow.

She had long impressed him and induced a state he did not understand. He was losing track of time with her, he couldn't express himself, and when she accosted him he felt like red and didn't know how to react.

It was for her that he ran away from the court to the countryside under the pretext. And she invariably greeted him with laughter and joked that it was impossible for the master to talk to her for so long, what people would say, so that he would not look like that, and then she snorted happily, like a young foal and ran away, but not too fast, as if waiting for him to follow her.

And now it was like that, when he was running after the girl on a flower meadow, and she supposedly ran away, but not enough to move away. And when she stumbled and knelt, bent low to the ground and massaging her ankle, not for the first time, he stared at the deep cut of her shirt, under which it twitched like two living animals, full breasts moved by a deep breath.

And then suddenly the picture changed, and he saw the gloomy Ukrainian laughing as he got up from her body and pulled out a gun...

He woke up again, this time screaming, and he stayed there for a long time in the dark, unable to keep the recurring image from before his eyes.

He fell asleep only in the morning.

***

He woke up numb, sore, not sure where he was. He was still on the verge of bane and reality; he closed his eyes to return to the vision of a peaceful manor and plunge into the atmosphere of everyday bustle, but the memory of the events came back and brutally brought him back to reality.

Several days had passed since he fled into the woods, fearful that the Bolsheviks would spot him. At first, he wandered pointlessly among the trees, unable to find a place for himself, because each of them seemed dangerous to him. Finally, he remembered a cave he had discovered by accident in a group of rocks two years ago, when a wolverine unexpectedly emerged from the foliage that covered it.

It was the perfect place to hide. The entrance was higher than a man, and the perennials growing here masked it perfectly. It was so narrow that you had to squeeze through it to get in, but the cave was already spacious, almost as big as the courtroom in the manor. It also had an advantage. At its end, in the rock, there was a wide crack leading somewhere else. Once, when a storm caught him during a hunt, he took refuge here, lit a fire and, out of boredom, penetrated its course, curious about where the smoke was escaping.

The crack stretched over a dozen meters, leading into another niche, this time smaller, with a small stream of water throwing out of the wall, which flowed down onto the ground and disappeared into the next crack. Right next to it was another hole, not too big, but wide enough that it managed to press into it. Further on was a low corridor that ended only above the marshes. And what was important, which he checked practically, the whole thing was a chimney, and the smoke from burning fire was flowing through the entire cave and came out just above the water, floating invisibly among the marshy vegetation.

***

The food was over.

While escaping, he lost the majority of the hunted capercaillies, and after that the only one he had left and baked, only bones left. His stomach was growling, but the reluctance to go outside these four days effectively discouraged him from moving. He felt that he had to force himself to move, and the inner voice mocked him, that he was afraid, like a little boy, that he was only fear that had no rational justification, because since no one had found him here so far, there is nothing to to fear.

When he was ten, his grandfather allowed him to hunt alone for the first time. He did not know it then, but Vasily discreetly followed him to the forest. After some time, he hunted a black grouse, and when he was content to jump for joy, he did not notice that small piglets appeared on the clearing, curious about the cause of the noise. When he saw them, instead of withdrawing immediately, he carefully approached them, and they, also against nature, did not run away, but stretched their nostrils towards him, inhaling the scent. It must have mixed with the unknown, human and grouse blood that dominated.

A menacing grunt and the appearance of the sow caught his attention late enough that he only managed to climb a nearby tree when she attacked him. And then fear overtook him. He even imagined for a moment that a pissed off sow would undermine a tree, and he would fall right on her sabers, which would tear him to shreds.

The sow watched him for only a moment, then she huffed angrily at the piglets, and together they hid among the trees.

And Janek was sitting terrified, afraid to go downstairs. It was evening and he could not make up his mind. His imagination gave him images of a wild boar lurking somewhere among the trees. Vasily found him and started joking that he scared him because he thought that a lynx was sitting on a tree. He did not ask a word what he was doing among the branches, and he praised the hunted black grouse that a good shot, and not everyone with a bow, could do that.

Only after a few days did he take him aside and said him the story of his childhood, as for fear of the gori, as the wild boar was called in his homeland, he spent the whole night on a rock, fearing to come down from it. And then Janek reluctantly, blushing and not meeting his eyes, admitted that he had escaped from the sow. Vasily laughed that they had similar adventures and praised the real courage to admit his fear. And to beat him even more, but the time will come for that and that he has already taken the first step. After some time, when Janek returned to that hunt and his retreat, he asked if the sow would have attacked him if he had not escaped to the tree. Vasily just laughed and muttered under his breath that the sow was in the gun sights all the time, but he was very careful about the buckling between the branches.

***

He took his bow and revolver with him. It was his only weapon. In contact with a detachment of soldiers, they gave chances of survival, but probably not victory. But he was consoled that it was his forest. A coniferous forest in which he knows every path, and it will be a foreign territory for everyone not local. Admittedly, he admitted the idea that there might be people of the forest, even poachers among the Bolsheviks, but, he repeated to himself, this was his forest.

First, he scanned the surroundings carefully for human traces, and when he did not find them, he breathed a sigh of relief. Now it's time to decide what to do next. See the village, what has changed and if anything has changed there, or go to the manor and check the same. What if the Bolsheviks had withdrawn, and even better if they had not found the hiding place in which Grandfather kept his shotguns and what they had collected over a year ago, when fights between the Russians and the Germans continued a dozen or so versts.

Then, as soon as it seemed that the front would reach their region, grandfather ordered the inhabitants of his villages to hide their families and their belongings in the depths of the forest. Farm supplies were also transported here.

Just in time, a week after this decision, Russian troops appeared in haste, escaping further east. And then came the German ones. Somewhere further, they encountered a temporary Russian fortification, and a battle ensued. The first ones could not withstand the pressure, but they did not disintegrate, but withdrew backwards. On the same day, when the Germans were not expecting anything and were resting, the Russians returned. They launched the evening assault, forcing the surprised and unprepared opponent to retreat far to the west.

Even though it was far away from the forest, you could not only see but hear the chaos of skirmishes, chaos of fire, attacks and escape of moving troops. Grandfather was especially careful at the court, afraid that one of the commanders would turn the buildings into a place of defense and everything would go up in flames. The manor house was not visible, but the direction was known. Fortunately, this did not happen, and the struggling soldiers headed for the bridge, which, several dozen versts away, was thrown across the river that continued to flow. He explained to the excited Janek when, sitting high in a tree, they watched the far foreground of the fight and tried to see something through binoculars, that they were lucky, however, that these were just the fringes of the main activities taking place somewhere much further.

"If it was a real front, everything would fly in the air from the gunfire and we would certainly not stay here," he explained when asked if any of the soldiers would spot them and shoot them down, like birds.

This scuffle lasted almost two weeks. It was the German units that chased the Russians, the Russians chased the Germans away, and the day after the situation repeated itself.

The inhabitants of the village, hidden in the forest, listened to the sounds of distant battles, blessing grandfather for his caution. And he, along with Vasily and a few young boys who were creating watchdogs on the forest border, saw whether any retreating unit would accidentally escape into the forest.

When the German grenadiers finally successfully chased the Russians away and the shots were not heard the next day, grandfather sent two grooms on horseback to spy on them. When they arrived with the news that no troops could be seen within many versts, he signaled all the peasants to put the carts on. They were supposed to go to the scene of the fighting to collect whatever might be applicable. When asked what was going on, he only told Janek that they had at most one day, or maybe less, to the arrival of the front base, which was progressing through the combat units. When he asked Vasily, because grandfather was ignoring further indiginations, he was busy managing the whole action, why pick anything up, he laughed, but patiently explained.

"There is some equipment left on the battlefield, and you never know when it will be needed in such uncertain times. This is what we did in the Caucasus and it has always worked. If anything happens, we'll arm the peasants..." And without explaining what it meant by "if anything happens", he left to prepare the carts.

The loot was not great, but a lot of rifles, revolvers, sabers, bayonets, a few horse harnesses with saddles, and even shoes, belts and uniforms were taken.

Later, when stabilization returned, and the entire region was already taken over by the imperial troops, which formed the Gebiet des Oberbefehlshabers Ost, grandfather in secret, only alone with Vasily and trusted peasants, they dug a dugout somewhere in the forest and transferred all the weapons there. Janek even took offense at them because they didn't want to take him with them. And when, as always, curious, he asked why and what this place was, he always received only one answer.

"It's for your own good," Vasily explained patiently, and grandfather just shrugged his shoulders and added: "You will have a look, kid, because I can see that this is not the end of this frenzy." And winked at him.

It annoyed him that they both treated him like a little child, he was seventeen after all, but he failed to overcome the conspiracy of silence. However, he was admitted to a secret hiding place in the manor, dating back to the period of the January Uprising, about which he had not known anything so far. It was here that Vasily hid with grandfather several rifles and revolvers along with ammunition, which they brought from the forest to the manor. At the same time, the leaders from the hiding place showed him, an underground corridor, masked and opened by a special lever, which could lead to a group of rocks in the field behind the barn.

Now it was this hiding place that did give Janek no peace. When his grandfather sent him to the forest, he mentioned the place where he kept his shotguns. It was not a handy bay window next to the playroom, but a hiding place, the one underground. However, he decided that he had to check what was happening in the countryside first. The pictures from a few days ago disturbed him and were still vivid to him, and the memory of Hapka's fate was more than painful.

Carefully, he moved forward with his bow and an arrow attached to the bowstring. However, he soon scolded himself that here, in the forest, such a weapon was cumbersome and only bothered him. He slipped the bow on his shoulder and immediately reached for his revolver. If something happens, it's a good idea to have a handy weapon with you. He caught the suspicion that these were symptoms of uncertainty and probably fear, and scolded himself mentally. He inhaled deeply into his lungs and repeated silently again: "This is my forest and I'm almost an adult, Grandpa believed in me", and he moved on, more confidently taking his steps.

***

He chose a roundabout way to the village, carefully looking for human traces, but also for some birds, because his stomach was demanding food and he had to hunt something. The latter were not enough, as if, concerned about the recent actions of people, they had moved deeper into the forest.

Far away, as he reached the forest lake, he noticed several pairs of black grouse leaping up from the trees at the sight of him, but temporarily left them alone. He will take care of them when he comes back. He also noticed traces of hares and made a note of it. At least he won't die of hunger. Breaking through the thick bushes here, he came to a path marked by larger game and headed north through it.

After a while the wind picked up, bending the treetops, but below it, in the undergrowth, it was still quiet and peaceful. You can see the first symptoms of the change in weather were already making themselves known. Summer was inevitably ending.

When the forest began to thin, he knew that it was reaching its edge. He slowed down, looking even more closely at his surroundings. Nothing indicated where people were hanging around. After a few dozen fathoms, among the alders and beeches that are rarely overgrown here, an empty space and the roofs of peasant cottages emerged. He was there. Here, at the edge of the forest, human interference was visible. Broken bushes and even smaller trees that had been cut down indicated that someone was drawing wood for fire from here.

He paused and for a long moment surveyed the entire foreground, carefully listening to all sounds coming both from the forest and from the village. The anxiety returned, but quickly suppressed it, concentrating on choosing the safest way to get close to the houses. He decided to go through the bushes that provided good cover, growing in the vicinity of a large spruce fallout with a few nearby yews and maples.

He started leaning forward, tearing his way through the witch hazel with orange and red flowers, until he came to the place where the dogwood bushes in the group deluded the birds with their fruit, and at the same time grew so densely that they formed a good cover for outsiders' eyes.

He covered the last few meters by crawling.

Now he could perfectly see almost the entire village situated in the depression. He took out the binoculars, suppressing another unease at what he would see.

At first glance, the village was as it used to be. Only three cottages showed signs of fire, which was probably quickly put down; black soot on beams, fresh straw on rafters and minor other repairs. Someone must have realized that if they are going to camp here, you need to keep your accommodation.

There was no trace of the members of the village council hanged on a pear tree. Except for the remnants of one rope, cut probably with a saber, which got tangled among the branches. Now the straps were jiggling to the rhythm of the wind.

On the village council building, where the chairman Kuźma lived and worked at the same time, a large banner hung in gusts with the image of a fat Polish nobleman standing with a whip over a thin peasant harnessed to a plow. The inscription was only partially legible, because the wind was tearing its sheet, making it impossible to read it fully: "Krestianin... polskij pomieszczik chozziet zdiełat tiebia..." And next to it, above the entrance, a large star painted red painted boldly announced who was the master here.

As he stared at the arrogant symbol, Danylo Wolosynchyk left the cottage stretching, but as if different than Janek remembered him before; dressed in a black leather jacket, a cap, a red band over his left shoulder and a cane in his hand. Janek recognized this cane right away. It always hung in grandfather's office, a memento of great-grandfather, who had brought it from somewhere in the distant mountains from some mysterious journey. It seems to be ordinary, made of sycamore wood, but at the top it is reinforced with decorative brass wire with loosely hanging rings. The handle, and this detail prevented it from being confused with another, had the form of an ax, and in place of the head, an eagle's head. He couldn't see it now, but he remembered that there was an engraved inscription somewhere below: "Souvenir from the Tatra Mountains 1868". Once he asked grandfather about her, fascinated by this eagle, he promised to tell him one day, but somehow it happened that Janek was involved in other matters. Now, seeing her in Danylo's hands, his anger overwhelmed him that such a huff and a beggar appropriated her as his own.

Something else has changed. The former beggar, whom the rest of the village community daily muck him about for his laziness, now stood confident, upright, completely different than before. Before the Bolsheviks entered, he was a rotten apple and the last in the whole village. Forever without a job because he can't hit the side of a barn and a total lack of enthusiasm for any work, despite having seven children to support. If it weren't for the neighbors, they would probably starve to death. As soon as he obtained a pair of begged kopeks, he spent them on vodka, after which he became aggressive, and as he did not impress his body, he usually took a beating by accosted ones. And then he would go to the cottage and beat his wife Sveta in revenge.

There was a fire in the square, and a huge cauldron hung above it, guarded by two soldiers. Danylo greeted them, then turned and shouted something angrily towards the house. Another soldier came out pushing Alik in front of him.

Janek reflexively held his breath and strained his eyes.

Alik in the service of the Bolsheviks? It is impossible.

He pressed the eyepiece in the binoculars so hard he felt pain around his eyes.

Alik was as old as he was. He was the son of Pruzyna, and she was the daughter of his father's wet nurse, Yefrosinia. It was grandfather, when he was still young, who ordered her to bring Alik to the manor, so that Janek would have someone to play with. So they grew up together, were friends, sometimes quarreled, and even got hit together from their grandfather, as when, imagining a fight with the Tatars, they accidentally set fire to a haystack and almost would turn the barn to ashes as well. He also taught him fencing in order to convey to his friend what Vasily had taught him from an early age, taking care not only of the archery and shotgun skills, but also of fencing with various weapons. So they waved their sticks fiercely, pretending during trips to the forest that they were scouts and were fighting in an ambush with Moskals, and later, when they had grown up, crossing practice sabers with each other.

Now he was walking slowly towards Danylo, a hunched over, shrunken and resigned. He shouted something again, and when Alik did not react, he lashed him angrily with his stick. The boy covered himself with his hand, so he corrected the blow once more with visible satisfaction. The boy knelt in pain, looking hard at the torturer. Danylo gave the order and the accompanying village leader gave him a kick, said something, and forced him to stand up. And then they moved somewhere towards the end of the village.

Janek breathed a sigh, but it immediately occurred to him that it was selfishness on his part, that Alik's situation was not good, and the Bolsheviks probably treated the other peasants similarly.

He made a mental note that he had to think of some way to reach his friend and free him. He didn't know how to do it yet, but he promised himself he would do it.

***

For some time he watched the village noting the changes in his memory.

Soldiers left some of the huts, while the remaining ones were occupied. He guessed that they had been evicted to others, so that the soldiers had separate chambers.

Three more peasants, also led by a soldier, were led out of the former inn. They went towards the shed, from where he heard the neighing of horses after some time. Three women passed through the village, next to a pear tree, accompanying one hunched over a bundle. They headed towards the cemetery behind the village.

Could...

He guessed they were carrying the dead child, though no man had accompanied them. In the past, when someone fell ill in the village, grandfather sent for a doctor to the town. "Or maybe they brought some disease with them?" It occurred to him, but then consoled himself that he was probably wrong, and immediately doubted it. "Why were they walking towards where there were no longer any huts, and why was one of them carrying a shovel?"

In the same way as he got here, he withdrew carefully before plunging into the forest. Here he relaxed, analyzing the information he had gathered. He came to no conclusions except that he should talk to some peasant from the village about what was happening. And the question that immediately came to him, whether he could trust someone or not give him up, because apart from Alik, he did not trust anyone now. Since Danylo has become an important person under the rule of those from the red star, what about the others?

He reached the manor the same way as a few days ago, from the side of the orchard, because from here he had the best view of the front. In front of the porch, two soldiers were sitting on a straw wagon, talking about something. They were wearing uniforms and he knew from that, that they must have been those who were accompanied by the commander of the Bolsheviks. And if so, that commander of theirs probably still occupies the manor.

Two horses galloped to the west. One man remained on the horse and rode up to the wagon where he talked to the guards, and the other jumped off his horse and ran inside. In less than a dozen minutes he fell out, threw something to his companion, and they quickly drove off the same road they had arrived.

"Something happens?" Janek wondered, wondering at this rush and remembering a completely different picture from the sleepy village.

A man dressed in a black leather jacket emerged from the court. Janek recognized him immediately. It was the same man who had accompanied the commander in the village. He gave an order to the guards, and they immediately jumped off the wagon, dusted themselves off the hay, and stood closer to the porch of the manor. He himself was smoking a cigarette quietly, as if he was waiting for something or someone. Soon another soldier left the stables, leading the horse. The one in the jacket scolded him, threw away his cigarette, jumped on the saddle, and together they walked in the same direction as the two previous soldiers.

"I guess something's going on, but where?" Janek recalled the map of the area from his memory. Far to the west, there was only a large village belonging to grandfather's neighbor, several dozen versts away. This neighbor, Mr. Hryhor Pohorecki, much richer than them, whom Janek never liked, because he made everyone feel that he was wealthy, and in direct contact, which he observed during the official noble conventions in the town, impertinent and even angular. He always tried to impose his opinion on others.

Several times a year he visited him on the orders of his grandfather or Vasily, he left some letters and, waiting for an answer, he talked to his two sons, Anton and Fedor, to pass the time. He was surprised that both of them were so stiff, looking down on each other, as if they had been born to a magnate or perhaps a royal court. Only once in front of his grandfather he scornfully described them as Hooray Henries, but he only laughed: "rich and well-connected", and then seriously added: "Pretend not to see".

As usual in such cases, when his grandfather's casual reply was not enough, he asked Vasily about his neighbors, and he only shed light on the complicated situation with - as he put it - cognatus.

"The Pohoreckis farm on the land that once belonged to your great-grandfather Victor," he explained patiently, and seeing Janek's astonishment, who immediately wanted to ask many questions, he silenced him by tugging his hair on his head. "Relax, I'll explain it to you in a moment. Listen carefully, but you mustn't tell anyone else."

When he had obtained a solemn promise, he took his time to light the pipe and told a story completely unknown to Janek.

When the uprising broke out in 1863, great-grandfather Victor, a respected figure in the district, organized a party consisting of peasants from his villages and friendly noblemen. He equipped her himself and headed for the woods. And because they knew the area perfectly well, they took their toll on the troops of the Moskals. After the fall of the uprising, the Russian governor confiscated property from many families by a special decree. Fighters were often hanged as a warning to others. The repressions also affected great-grandfather Victor, who escaped with his life only because he was not handed over by his peasants or the water boys, which was occasionally seen.

"The know-nothing peasants, in large part," he explained, "succumbed to the tsarist propaganda that Moscow wanted to abolish serfdom and would have done it a long time ago, but the Polish lords did not allow it. Grandfather Victor had given his people rights much earlier, so those from his village were immune to propaganda, and besides, they respected Victor, because they owed him a lot. And those others gave up the insurgents for rubles. This is how it was then. And since the Moskals had no evidence of participation in the uprising, they did not hang him, but he spent two years in prison, because the tsarists considered him a suspect anyway, because he probably helped the insurgents."

Janek wanted to ask about the Podhorecki family, but Vasily silenced him.

"Listen and don't interrupt. What am I done with? Oh, at that time, by virtue of Muraviev's decrees, many properties were taken from the nobility and given to tsarist officers. And traitors who sided with Moscow. When Victor was in prison, most of his property was taken away and only three villages were left. The rest was given to the Russians by Panteleimon Pohorecki, the father of Hryhor, who was a tsarist officer and fought against the insurgents. He came from an old, though poor Russian noble family, but he sided with the Moskals."

"Why," Janek could not stand it and urgently inquired about the reasons for his grandfather's good contacts with the traitor, "if Pohorecki fought on the side of the Moskals, why does he maintain good relations with him?" He could not understand this fact, and in his opinion it was an act of betrayal of great-grandfather Victor.

"You know, fate can be malicious," then Vasily laughed and continued explaining patiently. "It was different at that time. Impudent peasants' ranks, to which the Moskals closed their eyes, attacked noble estates for a long time. And it happened one time that such a pile invaded the Pohorecki mansion, and it was probably about a year after Victor returned from prison. It would be bad for them if he had not gathered his peasants and saved the Pohorecki family."

"But why, after all, he got our property?" great-grandfather's behavior did not fit in Janek head.

"Victor was a very wise and foreseeable man. He knew that simple revenge would do more harm than good in consequence. By saving Hryhor and his family, he gained an ally."

"I don't understand, he was a traitor," Janek was not convinced by such a explication.

"Your father and Panteleimon, as children, later grew up together, became friends, and thanks to the support of the Pohorecki family, they studied at the Nikolaev Cavalry School in St. Petersburg. Father remained in the army, and Panteleimon returned to his estate, because he was only satisfied with the rank of officer."

"I wouldn't expect this from my father," Janek was surprised by this information and indignant at his parent.

He knew his father was a military man, but he never questioned the reasons for it. For him, the Russians have always been the ones who once invaded and liquidated Poland. When he came to the estate, he was always happy, because his father is a father, and despite the love of his grandfather and Vasily, he missed him every day. He proudly boasted to him of his advances in fencing, archery, and shotguns, as Vasyli had taught him. And it was always so bad when his father was away.

"And what do you think," Vasily used an argument that made Janek think about his indignation. "When a new uprising breaks out, who will lead us into battle? Some who only know how to plow and sow? You will need specialists in war, experienced officers, and that's what your father is. Besides, one more thing. Panteleimon and his family had lived in our district for generations. He had to know what Victor's participation in the uprising was. And he probably didn't pass this knowledge on to the Moskals, how do you think?"

Chapter III

Janek spent another week gathering food supplies. There were plenty of birds, and so were the hares. He smoked the stock of meat, he also accumulated a stock of herbs and spices that should last for some time.

He remembered that many of them are useful in winter when health is failing. Not only did he accumulate a large amount of bear's garlic, which was prepared at the court in many ways, including as an addition to meat, as well as St. John's wort, mint, nettle, horsetail, coriander, horseradish, mustard, juniper, rosemary, savory, artemisia, pimpinella and many more, which he carefully dried. He lacked the linen bags, which were hung in the open air in the court, so he arranged them in selected bends in the rock in the cave, making sure that they would not be affected by moisture.

He was aware of the fact that he wanted to postpone the decision of what to do with this hoarding. That he is running away from the actions he should take and the answers to the question that accompanies him all the time, whether he should just hide, wait for some change, or do something for Alik and perhaps others. He was still troubled by what had happened to his grandfather and Vasily and the couple of servants at the court, and he pushed the thought that they were dead after all, and he only hoped otherwise. He knew that the peasants of the countryside could give him answers, but he now had doubts about their loyalty to the court.

***

This time he went along the excavation of the river for observation. In summer it turned into a stream, not more than a few meters wide, through which one could easily walk. It rolled lazily, almost motionless, where it was overgrown with weeds and sluggish on the banks, like a full farmer. In winter it froze, but surprisingly, not entirely. In places where the bottom was heavily washed out, pits formed and the water was always deeper. In these places, when ice appeared in the wells, an ice hole was cut and both peasants and servants from the court drew water.

But in spring, when the snow was melting somewhere far away in the mountains and highlands, there was no one brave who would dare to cross to the other side even in the apparent shallows. The stream turned into a real devil who, like a frightened herd, was tearing somewhere towards the distant steppe, maddened and undaunted, tearing the acquired space from the shores, roaring at any daredevils who would try to tame him. It was this spring nature that carved a canyon a few meters deep in the ground, filled with raging elements after winter, but in summer, when the lazy water receded back into the mainstream, the dry part of the current was a perfect, even route, even for peasant carts.

And it was it, hidden from outside eyes, that he used quickly reaching the place from where he already had a few versts to the court.

In many places, along the banks, leaning downwards, willow trees grew with their long hair, scattering the sand of the steep slopes in the wind. In many places poplars growing among them stood out, and the ubiquitous oyster mushroom with juicy red fruit on long shoots reaching almost to the water, and dormice with similar berries, but mossy and sweeter. Here, at the bottom of the gorge, there were also all kinds of weeds, appearing out of nowhere, probably grown from seeds carried by the river at the end of spring, when the current began to slow down.

Janek was walking boldly, but he was closely watching the high bank and listening. You never know if someone will run away, just to catch delicious bream, roach, rudd, prickly bleak among the draped roots and branches, and often fallen trees, and even, if you were lucky, lost in these in the waters of zander, carp or grass carp. Now, with the Bolsheviks residing in the village, they must have seized all the grain supplies and there must have been a famine.

So he treaded carefully, so as not to tread the dry twigs, and chose the places where the stones formed a path in the sand.

In the place where the lowered bank was only half a meter high, and the clear entrance was made by carts sliding down to the water track, he stopped. He could go to a nearer village or take a few more versts and see what was happening in the manor.

He moved forward. Some inner uneasiness told him not to stop. He walked several meters when he heard a sound coming from somewhere in the distance. And then the snorting of the horses was getting closer, becoming more and more distinct.

He did not think about it, but quickly hid between the dense shoots of the spring, crouched down among them and waited. Somewhere in the depths of his sub consciousness an unease crept.

It wasn't long before he saw horses being driven to the river. There were thirty or more of them. The thirsty ones ran into the stream and lapped the water quickly, as if they had not been watered for a long time. After a long moment, three mounted soldiers appeared, chasing three young boys. Janek had no doubts. The latter were locals. He did not remember the names of two, but he knew the third. It was Joshua, old Mendel's son, who ran the inn. His mother, Rosa, often went out to buy eggs and poultry. He had several siblings, an older sister, Sarah, and four much younger than him, Leah, Miriam, Aron, and Nathaniel. And on the Purim holiday, the whole family appeared in the manor, festively dressed in silk gowns, bringing snacks on silver trays, unleavened croissants and biscuits with honey.

He only saw Joshua when he was in the village, and usually ignored him. Quiet, calm, unobtrusive, but Alik told him that he was not as docile as he seemed at first glance. Apparently, despite his small stature, he stood proud when the boys from the countryside teased his younger siblings, calling them scabs and threw himself into a fight even with much stronger ones, for which he was badly hurt more than once.

He got to know him more closely two years ago after the incident with the young Fedor Ostapko, who, due to his strength, impressed the boys and led a group of troublemakers. He went to the village because he and Alik were going to plan a two-day hunting trip. He heard a commotion from afar. What he saw surprised him. Fedor sat on the downed Joshua, punching him as furiously as he wanted to kill him. Before he could react and run to the scene of the fight, Alik appeared and threw at Fedor. It is not known how it would have ended, probably also beating Alik, if not for Janek. He fell between pummeling fists and, using the teachings of Vasily, he threw them both so that they fell to the ground.

Fedor sprang to his feet quickly, though stunned by the blow, at first he did not know who had attacked him. He had uncontrolled fury in his eyes, and he would have probably attacked Janek, had he not come to his senses in time, seeing the young lord ready for everything. However, his rage did not pass. His fists were clenched so tightly that his knuckles turned white, and his narrowed eyes sent hateful lightning. He was breathing heavily, looking at Janek from under his bowed head, unable to make up his mind whether to throw himself at the lord or to pounce. In the end reason prevailed over fury, and fear of the court did its job.

"He started," he only hissed, pointing to the lying Joshua. "He, I'm innocent, I was just defending myself."

And he continued to stare blankly, but already piggy red eyes began to run away to the sides. Now he was beginning to fear the consequences that might befall him. It is one thing to fight outside the court, which grandfather did not tolerate in his villages, and another thing in front of the young lord and threatening him with an arrogant attitude.

Janek wanted to slap his face so that he would remember, but he reflected. It was not for nothing that Vasily and his grandfather hammered into his head that prestige is not always gained by force. He squinted his eyes, as he had observed with his grandfather repeatedly when he settled disputes, then grimaced with an ironic smile.

"Eh, Fedor, strong as an aurochs and stupid as a partridge. Aren't you ashamed to beat the weaker ones?"

He paused, waiting for the words to reach the Ukrainian, then added:

"I won't tell Grandpa, but let me not hear that you use the power that God gave you to do what the devil suggests. Measure, because not me or grandfather, but God will show you how He did it with your father."

There was an uncontrollable grimace on Fedor's face, neither regret nor worry that must have consumed him from within.

His father, Chawrylo, was also once famous for his supernatural strength. He was able to lift the wagon loaded with wet grain effortlessly when the axles in the wheel parted under the weight and they had to be hastily replaced with new ones. After his wife died, he began to drink and look for harassment. Everyone went out of his way, fearing for their lives. Until he found Moskals from the 4th Cossack brigade, who stayed at the inn at that time run by Joshua's grandfather, Jochvet. When he was well drunk, and the Russians were no worst, a brawl broke out from word to word. Mockery flew, and after them sharp insults, and when one of them, a Cossack, grew like a bear, was already getting up, Tatiana, Chawrylo's sister, came to the inn, who was the only one who influenced him.

It seemed that the row would go away, when the soldier, seeing the woman, snorted: "Woni byliatsa na niej i baczat nosiu". Chawrylo cannot stick such an insult and, without thinking much, he attacked the Moskal. The one, less drunk, and perhaps simply stronger, parried the blow, then hit his head so hard that Chawrylo fell backward, hitting the edge of the oak table. He groaned in pain, his body twitched and he went still.

The Russians quickly left the tavern, because their commanders did not tolerate fights. Chawrylo was helped by the neighbors Tatiana carried to the cottage. It seemed like another brawl was over and there would be a huge bruise the next day. On the next day, however, the Ukrainian could not get up from his bed. He has completely lost all feeling in his legs. The court was notified that Janek's grandfather had brought a doctor from the town, who ruled that his spine was permanently injured.

Chawrylo could not come to terms with the powerlessness for a long time. Once he crawled to the shed, climbed the ladder, climbing only on his hands and dragging the limp lower half behind him. When he was upstairs, he put a rope on the beam, and the other end around his neck.

And so it ended.

Now Fedor looked at Janek blankly, but without any previous resentment. His father's example caught his imagination. And later, whenever he met him in the countryside, he would bow from afar, smile and always treat the young lord with clear esteem. The grandfather found out about the events in the village anyway but remembering the promise he had made to the Ukrainian, the grandson pretended that he did not know anything. Once, only at dinner, he muttered, as if only to Vasily: "Oh, a diplomat are growing here", and they both laughed.

And in Joshua he had made a friend who was always willing to help.

Now he looked from behind the bushes, remembering those events. Out of boredom, the soldiers chased the young, and when they didn't like something, especially the young Jew, they casually whipped their whips, not too hard, more for show, that he would pay more attention to washing the horses' hair.

Janek once again promised himself that he had to come up with a way to free Alik, but also Joshua. The fear that came with the sight of the Bolsheviks has been displaced by anger and rage that he is so helpless and can do nothing.

***

The horses were bathed for over an hour. When the soldiers ordered a retreat, he remained hidden for some time, not sure if any of them would come back. And when nothing seemed to be so, he stepped carefully to the ford and checked how far they had gone.

And then he moved on, keeping close to the weeds and the canyon wall, to hide at any moment if the situation called for it. But nothing happened, so he sped up.

In a bend, where the river had carved a wide curve in the ground, lugging trees and boulders carried in spring from somewhere far away, he went ashore. Hence, it was closest to the orchard at the manor house. Hiding among the tall grass and keeping a close eye on the foreground, it took a few minutes for him to reach it. It was easier now.

He was surprised to find so many leaves on the ground. He realized that summer was ending. The transition to winter was always short, followed by an unexpectedly frosty morning and the surroundings changed beyond recognition. Suddenly, the green disappeared, and all nature took a dusky gray color to finally cover the world with dirty white linen. This fact made him aware that he was not prepared, that he only had summer clothes, and that the burqa with which he went hunting would soon be insufficient. He made a mental note to sew trousers, leggings, a hat and gloves from the hare skins that he carefully collected and treated. He was not very skilled at this, but he helped Vasily while he did, forcing him to sit with him and study. He didn't have the right pelt for a jacket, and he hadn't seen deer or roe deer lately, and he had to do something about it too. Before the frost reaches the ground and the game will be harder to find.

"My young Vakho, you never know what you will meet outside the door," Vasily murmured sententiously, forcing Janek to accompany himself to this boring job and teaching how to make thongs, how to bind them in fat and which part of the bones of the hunted game is best for making an awl.

The place by the rocks, where the underground excavation from the manor house was conducted, has not changed. The soldiers were still watching over here. The makeshift shed they had put together only seemed to be in worse shape than it had been the last time. It made him think that they might be treating this place, or even a stay at the manor, as a makeshift and moving somewhere further west. However, so far there was no indication of this. A cauldron of which was rising over the fire. There was a scent of soup in the orchard, but no scent of meat. Another association - they had a little food, and this raised concerns about whether, when winter came, they would start penetrating the forest to get it.

***

He withdrew. Now he wanted to see what was happening from the main entrance to the manor.

And here practically nothing has changed. There were two soldiers in front of the porch, and their behavior did not indicate that they were particularly vigilant. They smoked some vile wild tobacco, the stench of which even reached the place where Janek was lying.

He watched the surroundings for a long moment and at one point he found himself missing the time when it was a peaceful, safe place and life went on as normal in it.

He backed off, suppressing the sadness that engulfed him and the emptiness he didn't know what to oppose.

After returning to the cave, he was discouraged from any action. He felt like an insignificant cog of a powerful machine of time and history in which no matter what he decides and does, it won't matter.

Depressed, he lay there, unable to bring himself to take any action, head full of pessimistic thoughts mixed with self-pity and complaints to his grandfather and Vasily that they had left him.

He fell asleep tired and dreamed some nightmares that quickly faded into oblivion replaced by another.

***

He woke up early in the morning.

It was still dark outside. He felt much better both mentally and physically. The wraiths of the previous day had disappeared somewhere, and the need to hunt a deer or a roe deer and get a pelt for a winter jacket.

He critically examined the bow and arrows. Poor weapon for a big game. It all depended on the accuracy of the shot and hitting the right spot, and that could be different. He could still use the pistol, but that was what he was afraid of, because the roar of the gun carried through the woods.

The first leaves fell off the trees, creating the first rug of a colorful carpet on the litter. There weren't many of them yet, but they were a harbinger of changes and an announcement that winter is already lurking somewhere behind the tollbooths. The thought came back from the day before that if he only thought about her and did nothing to be prepared, he would be unpleasantly surprised.

He walked brooding and at the same time looking for clues. He felt suspended between duty and the urgency of the moment and the memories of the court how they prepared for the season ahead.

He paused, took a deep breath, and pulled himself together, shaking off the thoughts he knew would add nothing to his situation, and he looked for clues more closely. And these were few. Most of them were only hares and foxes following in their footsteps, and occasionally wild boars and deer, as if the rest were crouched somewhere waiting for the metamorphosis of nature. It encouraged him more, but with poor results.

He decided that he should check the fields on the edge of the forest where the does should be feeding for leftover crops.

Less than an hour later, he reached a place where the arable land had carved a large bay in the forest, where his grandfather sowed spelled and farro for domestic needs. Until the arrival of the Bolsheviks, the field had not been mowed, so he hoped to encounter fallow deer that often forage here.

He was wrong. There were many traces, but no animals.

He sat down on the ground, a bit gloomy, trying to organize in his mind all the places where the game might have wandered and why. For a moment he considered whether by any chance the Bolsheviks had gone hunting, which could scare her and cause her to retreat into the deeper parts of the forest. Probably not, because human traces would have appeared in his eyes, and he would not notice them.

He was about to get ready to go deep into the forest when it occurred to him to try to penetrate the area where there had been fierce battles between the Russians and the Germans. And where grandfather, after the end of the fighting, made a trip to bring as many trophies as possible. Admittedly, most of the access to it was through open terrain, across fields, but as he recalled, in many places there were tranches scattered and dug up by fighting soldiers, which would provide good cover if he saw the danger. He hoped to find some useful items for himself that had been ignored during that trip, but considered useless at the time. He was mainly thinking of cannon thimbles in which to store oil, though a much better find would be an abandoned pot or cauldron where he could smelt this oil. As he remembered, the front in this place changed literally every day, finding something useful had a chance of success.

***

He stepped out into the tree-free space and now carefully used every small hill as a screen from the bystander, and every field of bushes as a natural curtain preventing him from being seen.

He hastened, remembering that the place where he intended to go is not within reach, and has several versts to cover. He stayed away from the dirt track that led in the same direction, though not far enough out of sight. He concluded that if anyone moved from East to West, that would be the use of it, and it would be good to see who was attending it. Probably only the Bolsheviks, he realized in his mind, because the peasants had no interest in going further beyond their villages.

After more than an hour, he arrived at the scene. The trenches felt as if they had been built yesterday and not months ago. They stretched in different places and directions, covered only at the edges with exuberant vegetation.

He spotted the place where the position of field artillery cannons was probably. It was easy to see them, because the ruins of the Russian or maybe German cannons in which the projectile had hit, reached above the tall grass. He remembered from the first trip that the scattered remains of the soldiers made him sick, and he struggled to hold back from vomiting. They were gone now. Only dead iron sticking out into the sky, a witness to a struggle for ideas that the ordinary soldier probably did not even try to understand.

He paced for a moment, wondering what might be of use to him, but found nothing useful in the twisted iron. Only wheels would be useful, but in order to use them to build a makeshift cart, he would have to have the right tools to detach them from the tow trucks. Besides, they were too heavy.

Fortunately, empty, fired shells lay around the place. He found a dozen of different sizes and weights, put them in one place, and began to seriously consider how much he could carry and how many trips to the cave he would have to make to transport them. And then he started searching the tranches for some cauldron or pot. In one line of the trenches he found nothing, except a few old boots with what he guessed were sticking out memories of what had once been a soldier's legs, now more like a dirty branch with scraps of cloth. He also came across German helmets half-buried in the sand, and that pleased him. If the search for the boiler had failed, he could have used it. They were deep enough to serve as a useful pot after gutting their leather interior. One of them still had the skull with the remnants of dried, dark brown skin. He shuddered involuntarily, carefully took it out, but took the helmet with him. The inner voice about the need for a Christian burial for the remnants of man was quickly suppressed. He couldn't afford any sentiments. Not here and not now.

Elsewhere he found the remains of a few soldiers barely covered with a thin layer of sand. He wondered why the Germans, usually meticulous and pedantic, when they had ruled over the established Gebiet des Oberbefehlshabers Ost for quite a long time, had not buried these corpses. He replied to himself that it was one of many skirmishes, somewhere on the sidelines of a more important struggle, certainly not important enough for anyone to bother with it and look for anything here. And the Bolsheviks? The question came by itself, as did the answer. Sure, when they got stronger, they would start searching similar places to get steel for the mills, because something new had to be produced.

He wanted to leave when it occurred to him that he was again succumbing to the sentiment that might take revenge on him in the future. He pulled out a knife and meticulously cut metal buttons from the remains of torn and partially moldy uniforms. With three, he found belts, shoulder straps and pouches in quite good condition, and digging further, he even dug up two backpacks. Surprisingly, the blankets attached to them smelled of mildew, but the material of the backpacks was in very good condition. It was also fitted with two bayonets and that made him very happy.

He kept telling himself that he was not rummaging in the cemetery, that it was not a dedicated place, that if he did not do it today, others would come tomorrow, the Bolsheviks, or perhaps peasants, and would have no moral qualms about using what was still suitable for use. And yet he could not get rid of the doubt that he was violating the sacred, doing something inappropriate, unworthy of a human being, certainly not a Christian, which puts him on a par with wild dogs tearing weaker kinsmen apart and disdainful of carrion.

He gritted his teeth and continued to search the grounds.

After an hour, he collected a few more helmets, additional military and officer belts, bayonets, three backpacks, another harness with pouches and two gas masks in leather containers. He threw the masks away, but he left the containers behind. The loot also included two pairs of high-heeled officers' boots. Others he had to reject because of their size and content. It was with one of them that he got a vomit, when, after pulling out the remnants of the unfortunate man's legs, from which he found only his lower half, a stench so great that he could not make him try them on. The remains were generally only bones now, but those dug out from under the deeper sand often preserved tendons and rotting muscle tissue.

At one point, he gave up on further searches. He did not completely expel the demons from his head and these intensified the thoughts circulating somewhere in the subconscious that, despite explaining what he was doing, he robbed human remains, that he profaned them and that nothing justifies him.

He failed to shake off the thought that he was behaving like Bolsheviks robbing courts, disrespecting anyone or anything. Once again, he threw them into the depths of consciousness and rebuked in his thoughts that he was pitying himself that he had to think rationally, because winter was coming and he didn't know what would be useful to him. And when there is snow and the ground becomes as hard as rock, he will regret not taking something, because he has been tormented by remorse and that depressing thinking is the result of physical exhaustion.

He rested for a while, struggling with his scruples and objections, and when he finally suppressed them and threw them to the edge of his self, he replaced them with a consideration of how the collected objects could be carried to a forest cave. He realized that there were far too many of them for a single walk. He had to hide the rest somewhere, just in case someone also thought to search this so far forgotten shambles.

He set off again in tranches looking for a convenient place. All the shelters, which housed the hospital or kitchens, were collapsed and completely ruined. So he was looking for a hole, a funnel after an explosion, which might be a hiding place. Neither fit, nor it had nothing to replace a shovel and help form a large enough hole in the ground.

He was returning, resigned, to the place from which he had set off, because the sky was already gray and the evening was about to turn into night. When he was almost there, it was only now that he noticed the unnatural topography. What he had previously taken to be the uneven terrain was a remnant of bullet-worn ramparts. During the day he hadn't even seen them, but he was just watching the deep trenches. Only now, as the twilight cast long shadows across the unevenness, did the field show its war wounds.

It was climbing from below to the edge of the trench as it caught a protruding, sharp piece of broken beam. At first he did not pay attention to it. He was angry with himself for not respecting the only jacket he had. He unhooked the flap strung over the sharp edges and wanted to move on quickly, but the other self-started to think. A wooden pole sticking out of the ground and beyond the trench? After all, it did not grow because of a mysterious force.

The phantoms crawling out of the time of day showed what could not be seen when the sun was shining. Among the tall grasses, when he parted them, there were more than enough broken remains of wooden structures, the remains of something larger, now broken into splinters, mostly covered with sand and covered with the ubiquitous corns, cornflower and veils. An explanation came to him, and he had to quickly check the accuracy of his suspicions.

He jumped down the tranche and began digging into the deformed wall of the ditch, which no longer resembled a fortified flank, but rather a bulging sandbank thrown here by unknown forces. The first movements did not bring anything, but after a while, the damaged elements of the structure of the former shelter began to emerge.

After a dozen or so minutes, the hand hit the vacuum.

He breathed surprised at the accuracy of his suspicions, and even though the skin on his hands had already turned red and stung, he began to dig even more intensely. He quickly widened the opening. It was easier now, because the sand suddenly started to pour down somewhere, as if into a hitherto invisible cavity underneath.

He smiled with satisfaction. He was sure that the recess found would fulfill its role. Even if it does not turn out to be large, the opening will be easy to enlarge. He kept digging until there was an opening large enough to squeeze through. He only wondered for a moment if he would be covered with sand when he did. And after that he slipped his legs inside, he didn't feel the bottom, but that didn't worry him and he jumped down.

And he stood surprised. At first, he couldn't see the inside clearly. It was too gray outside, and the little light that reached here only revealed the darkness a little. He stood there for a long time, adjusting his eyes to the half-light. And then he congratulated himself on his suspicions. It was definitely the section commander's bunker, or an officer's bunker, or at least the part that had withstood the missile's detonation. Details still faded in the dark. He carefully checked by tapping on the ceiling beams to see if the whole thing will collapse on his head, but it seemed strong and intact.

He saw the ammunition box, put it under the dug hole, and went outside. Here he wondered what to do next. Go back to the cave at night or move things here and set off with some of the loot only in the morning.

He chose the latter as more rational, although now, after all, he began to feel hungry and thirsty. Tough, he'll suffer through this, and in the morning, he'll decide what to do next. He pulled out a thick echinacea bush growing nearby to mask the entrance to the shelter.

Chapter IV

The darkness surprised him, and at first he didn't know where he was. So he lay motionless, trying to orient himself, catch some noises, but the silence was so great that it was disturbing. It took a while for him to locate some muffled noises somewhere outside, a gentle scratching sound, but they weren't the sounds of the woods.

His memory was slowly coming back.

A bunker or a shelter or whatever it was, partially collapsed, and the exit probably where the now-almost invisible streak of light filtered through the branches of the night before.

He stood up and carefully exposed the masking branches of the echinacea, sticking only his head out.

The morning sun was still low, sharpening the shapes of the surroundings. The grasses quivered slightly in the gusts of dawn gusts. Right next to the entrance, not more than two meters, the weasel, the perpetrator of the mysterious scratching, was busy digging up the ground. Maybe she sensed a voles nest, or maybe she was just looking for some grubs. Her pastel summer fur seemed to have faded and flashes of white appeared in it, a sign that winter was coming. At one point she froze, catching a new scent in the air, turned towards Janek's head, stood there, and then continued digging through the sand.

The stomach said asking for food. He will have to wait until he returns to the cave.

He backed away, and only now, when it had gotten a little brighter in the shelter, did he examine him carefully. Its part, the one directly adjacent to the tranche, was destroyed and partially collapsed, which was probably the result of artillery fire. The surviving fragment, forming a rectangle with sides no larger than four by five meters, did not collapse, probably only due to a partition wall made of thick beams, which used to separate it from the whole. If it was an officer's shelter, then, he analyzed the room carefully, it might not have come from the fighting he and his grandfather had once watched while sitting high in a tree. At that time, the positions of German and Russian troops changed almost every day, and neither side had time to erect such labor-intensive structures. They probably used only the earlier trenches from the period when the earlier front stood nearby and the soldiers had prepared the area for positional combat.

Russian? German?

Undoubtedly, he was lucky to stumble upon this place, and that, after tearing his jacket against a shattered beam, he sensed with his seventh sense that something in the topography of the place did not match. And he searched them. The shelter itself, the remaining part of it did not look like it was plundered since the explosion destroyed the one from the side of the tranche.

He inhaled deeply, as did the weasel just observed. No, he didn't feel the characteristic odor that the dead bodies had exuded even after a long time, and he breathed a sigh of relief. This he subconsciously feared, mainly the fact that he slept with the decaying corpses. The inhabitants of this place must have left it before the fire. If not, they were stuck somewhere under a mound of collapsed ground in a broken part, and he had no intention of checking it out.

He scanned the interior and walked to the far wall, where a metal bowl stood on a wooden stand, and next to it, as if in a hurry, shaving utensils. Not even a piece of soap, dry and cracked, on a piece of some old newspaper that was so yellow it was impossible to read anything. Right next to an overturned shaving brush lay a thimble with a half-burned candle stuck in it. This pleased him more than the dirty razor, but he was also interested in the small brown comb that was used to comb mustache. It will be useful for detangling the formed tangles.

He hadn't touched anything yet.

It was darker in this part than at the opening, he only made a note of what he should take with him when he left. The walls of the shelter were covered with boards, cracked in various places, but still fulfilling their role well. Only in one of them was the longitudinal crack so large that fine sand spilled out of it. Right next to the crack, someone posted a photograph of a woman coquettishly looking towards the photographer. There were dried, crumbling flowers behind the frame.

In the opposite corner, on a makeshift plank table, stood a teapot that caught his attention, along with three tin mugs and one earthenware. And some packages with faded drawings. When he took them gently in his hand, it turned out that one contained coffee, very old and weatherworn, judging by its not very pleasant smell, while the other contained tea. His mouth tasted of a drink he had not drunk for a long time.

He leaned over to the spacious shelf under the tabletop. There were several cutlery and a few plates under the napkin. They reminded him of the court and his stomach tightened. He quickly straightened to shake off the flooding nostalgia, and only now saw what he had not seen before, focused on the details littering the makeshift furniture.

On the wall hung an officer's jacket with the characteristic two rows of buttons, lined with fur. The rush of joy at this find was so violent that he let out an uncontrolled cry of joy. All the things, the helmets, belts, harness, and even bayonets he had accumulated so far evoked no emotion; he knew they could come in handy and just collected them. Like a beggar who ends up in the garbage of discarded material episodes from their lives that are no longer needed by the owners, and for him are valuable because of their practicality, so far inaccessible and beyond his reach.

He took it off the nail hammered into the wall, walked closer to the light and turned it for a moment, checking if it had any damage, abrasions and, in general, in what condition it was. And it was in good condition, with no obvious signs of wear. He took his own and tried on the prey. It was perhaps a little too broad for someone who was as tall as him, but his carcass was a little bigger. Nevertheless, he was glad, he felt the fur of the lining with delight, stroked and purred content with the bonus of fate, unable to bring himself to take a picture of it. And then he caught himself thinking that he must be starting to run wild if he was acting like that. He quickly pulled it off and placed it where he had prepared the things to be moved to the cave yesterday.

He was pleased and was already wondering if there were similar places left on this abandoned battlefield, and what he could do to find them.

For the record, he returned to the dark corner to see the rest of him. In the foreground was a sack tied with a thong. When he undid it, it revealed that there was grain inside. Who needs grain in a shelter? Maybe if it was an officer's shelter, you had a horse. The horse, however, does not feed on grain only, rather on hay.

He shrugged and set the sack aside. And then he saw her and felt a sudden pound of heart.

***

In front of him, on the wall, where the jacket hung, there was a leather, half-exposed cavalry holster, calmly waiting for him to notice it. And in it Winchester Model 1910. As he had not noticed her before, he did not understand, but he did not think about it. He looked happy, not believing what he was seeing.

He remembered this unusual type of weapon that fascinated him because it differed from other military rifles. He knew that he was not part of the equipment of either a German or an Austria-Hungarian officer. It had to be a weapon captured from the Russians. While the tsarist troops were still operating in their region, the commander of the Leib-Guardian Regiment of His Majesty, Count Mikhail Vasilyevich Ridiger, stayed at the manor for a few days. His soldiers were armed with just such rifles.

Grandfather was able to hit the commander's taste with his drinks, so relations with the soldats were almost friendly. Janek talked to the soldiers who kept watch around the manor, asked about their strange weapons, and they talked to him willingly, boasting that the elite units, and their regiment belonged to them, had the best weapons, including the Winchester M 1910.

After their departure, he was fascinated with telling his grandfather that the regiment's adjutant, always smiling and full of serenity, Lieutenant Stepan Demienkov, whom Janek immediately liked, even let him shoot a target in the orchard and praised him for his hawk eye. Grandfather only laughed at his fascination with the unusual weapon, which - he announced mockingly - is not Russian, but purchased for special guard units from the Americans. It towered over the popular Mosin, and even the French Lebel or the English Lee Enfield.

"Whether a weapon is good or bad does not depend on its design, although partly yes, but most of all on the skill of the shooter who uses it and knock it down once and for all," he said then, extinguishing Janek's fascination.

And now he had this rifle before his eyes, and his former infatuation had returned, not in the mind of his grandfather's warnings. He carefully pulled the weapon from its scabbard, admiring it in awe and stroking it, like the fur of a found jacket. He checked the operation, then began looking for cartridges. They hung next to them in belt pouches, four magazines in each, which when he found the rifle, he was not happy with the jacket he found. This small amount troubled him and restored his clarity of thought. He found the candle he saw at the pelvis, lit the matches lying next to him, and began searching the room meticulously. In the flat cabinet, he found only an empty pistol holster and tow for cleaning weapons, but there were no Winchester cartridges and no pistol.

He moved quickly to the collapsed part of the bunker and, despite earlier fears that the sand might hide the remains of buried people, he began to nervously move it around and drill a hole. He was indifferent to what he would find, only those bullets he wanted. Hand after hand he plunged in, finding nothing. At one point, when a beam creaked ominously and collapsed, he was kicking more carefully, observing with fear that something might suddenly fall on his head. He had already selected so much sand that the pit was large enough to fit in it. Exposed beams and planks began to dangerously signal that they existed.

He was already backing away when the vertically undermined part of the sand suddenly collapsed, and part of the ceiling with it. He felt gravel pouring down his back and head. And suddenly he cooled down, terrified by the vision of being buried.

He felt himself sweating, and panic was building up in his mind.

The ceiling fell, but only partially. He stopped with a strange scratch and groan on the side reinforcements of the structure.

Janek did not move for a moment, fearing that the whole thing would fall down. Nothing happened, so he carefully stepped back. And then he noticed that the corner of a sturdy cupboard had emerged from the sand. He looked at him fascinated, not knowing what to do; go back to digging or give up. Fate clearly mocked him. He went to get the bayonet and, stretching his hand forward, he began to dig up the sand and free it from the piece of furniture. It was going slowly and reluctantly, but he was consistent. Every now and then he checked the wooden wall to see if it was still holding up and if it would hold on when there was no more sand underneath it. And he kept digging, panting more and more, this time more with emotion than exhaustion.

The painstaking and careful work took him almost two hours, but eventually part of the cabinet was exposed. There was a metal hook on the side, and they made him think that he could hook the uniform harness he had in his collection on them and try to pull the piece of furniture out of the rest of the rag without unnecessary risk of being covered.

As he thought, he brought the idea to life so quickly. And then he denied it and, drawing more and more, prayed that it would work. For a long moment there was no sign of it. He was gasping, choking, his throat was getting most of the dryness, but only in the blink of an eye he gave his hands a breath and continued to tug the harness alternately, then pulled with all his might, jerked and pulled again just to move the cupboard.

And finally it worked.

The cabinet must have been heavy in itself, and while standing, covered with not the lightest sand, it probably sank a bit into the floor planks. Now it groaned, surrendering and shifted a few centimeters, and then another and more. He did better with each stroke, because the sand on its parts fell off and began to act as lubricant on the ground.

Eventually, the sweating body pulled it far enough for him to think it safe to get to its contents.

It wasn't a cupboard.

He had just seen it now. It was a large trunk that opened from the top.

It wasn't locked up. There was a blank space where the padlock's eyelet entered between the staples, and it hung with the keys inserted on a special handle next to it. He put his hands on the lid and slowly, holding his breath, tried to lift them up. It did not resist. He lifted it upright and looked inside uncertainly.

The chest was full of its owner's personal underwear. But only in one part. In the other there were small boxes stacked on top of each other, and in them, when he opened the first one from the top, the coveted Winchester ammunition, and the 401SL cartridges. It touched him so much that he sat down next to it and for a long moment he rested staring at the much desired find. Excited by it, he said a short prayer of thanksgiving to Saint Anthony and continued looking, unable to move.

***

He sorted out the collected items, focusing on the three courses to the cave. What fit, he packed into backpacks. He decided that he would take a rifle with him every time, although he was aware that in the event of a meeting with the Bolsheviks, and such a possibility existed, it would end in shooting. If he did not have it with him, there was always a chance that they would take him for a poor peasant collector who tries to forge his poverty by accumulating what others have despised.

It was almost noon when he set off towards the forest with the first packages. As with the trip to the tranche, he walked carefully and avoided places where he could be seen from a distance. The closer he was to the forest, the joy of returning home, although a temporary one, but his own place, which he himself had found and made a substitute for a lost court, grew in him.

As he crossed the sand courtyard, he carefully examined the tracks. And these did not indicate that anyone had followed him recently. The horse's hoof marks were so weathered that no one had passed this way for at least a few weeks. Similarly with the least visible human and characteristic depressions of horse carts.

Before setting off, he searched the area looking for something that could well mask the opening to the shelter and discourage a potential curious person. He masked the hole itself with a few logs that he found among the grass, but that was not enough. He was very afraid that someone would come to this place by accident, like himself, but he also explained to himself that it was irrational anxiety, because who would think of wandering around here. Finally, on a small hill, he could see a growing barberry bushes with bright red fruit, almost two meters high and most importantly, with very sharp spines.

He made a bit of effort to tear the bush out of the sand and not injure his hand at the same time. Satisfied, he forced it to enter the shelter and thrust its lower part into the crack between the splinters, and then covered the place with sand. The effect was more than satisfactory. Looking closely, everyone would think that the bush just grows here.

He was already climbing among the first trees when a sound came from a distance. He hid behind bushes and reached for the binoculars. Now he regretted that he had left the wax binoculars with a case and changeable filters in the shelter, which he found in the chest under underwear. He examined it carefully then, intrigued by the two unusual emblems on glasses. The first was an eagle and the inscription Tirol, and the second, with an element of a stylized eagle, some vegetation and a transverse, stylized sash with the inscription: Kufstein. On the side, it was engraved with the inscription that it belonged to the equipment of the 20th Regiment of Mountain Riflemen C.K. "And what were they doing here?" He wondered and came to the conclusion that since he found an American rifle from the armament of the Russian special regiment here, then binoculars from Alpine troops should not surprise him. In war, various strange things happen, and there was also the possibility that this section was defended by some troops moved here so far away.

He did not hesitate any longer, because riders on horses appeared on the road in the glasses. They were Bolsheviks in their distinctive topped caps and a large red star on the front. The same were shared by those who protected the commander at the manor. There were eight of them. They rode quickly, but without any apparent rush. They talked about something, bursting out laughing every now and then.

"Well, that's nice," he thought. "If they came faster like that, they would not miss me." He felt a thrill seep through him, but not of fear, but more of emotion. He waited motionless for them to move on, and only then got up and continued on his way. This time, twice more closely observing the forest and catching the sounds of nature. They, more than his sight, could have warned him, if somewhere in the depths of the wilderness some soldier was hunting. He remembered his earlier suspicion that the Bolsheviks were running out of meat and might be trying to hunt something in the forest.

He reached the cave unhindered. There were no human traces near her, and that reassured him a little.

***

The grotto welcomed him with its unchanged interior. It was here that he felt the tension that accompanied him when he was out of her begin to ease off him. And fatigue comes, slowing down your movements and bringing you an aversion to everything except to lie comfortably on the pelts he has gathered, close your eyes and fall into a blissful sleep.

He hardly succumbed. He ate only smoked meat and washed it down with water. He really wanted to make himself a cup of tea, because he had also brought a kettle from the shelter, but he also fought this temptation. He had to come back, that was the most important thing. He can move the third part some other time, but he had to come back today.

He took a shotgun and a cartridge belt with him. Had it not been for the riders he had noticed, he might not have done it, but the sight of the Bolsheviks was very convincing and it broke something about it. Somewhere in the consciousness, or perhaps deeper beneath it, a stronger and stronger desire to confront them, a desire to face them, to punish them for the countryside, for the court, for grandfather and Vasily, for those people who had been murdered, for the captivity of Alik and Joshua, for the loss of their home for all the harm he has suffered.

He felt an inner irritation and determination. Maybe this rifle was the cause, giving him a sense of power, or maybe the whole day full of excitement he didn't care. He walked faster this time, though still alert and tense again, ready for any surprises. By the track, he carefully inspected the entire foreground. There was a silence broken by birds with their trolls, the light sound of grass swaying in the gentle wind, and nothing else.

He reached the shelter as fast as he had crossed the forest.

He mentally praised himself for the masking with barberry, it was worse with removing it. The roots caught somewhere below and he had to struggle with them for a while to get the bush out. He surveyed the area once more. There was still an almost bucolic idyll of wild, now unworked fields. Somewhere in the distance he saw deer running towards the forest, and nothing else.

Quickly, this time without delay, he prepared the things of the second throw, which he pushed out through the opening. As he picked up a stuffed backpack, something caught his attention; some dim flash in the heap from which he had previously extracted the trunk. The sand must have slipped further, revealing something. Carefully examining the condition of the ceiling, he reached out and felt it.

Metal.

He brushed the sand away with his fingers and he knew. It was the shining fitting crowning the saber scabbard. Quick question: alone or with content? He gripped it tighter and pulled it out easily.

There was a saber in the scabbard. He took her to him, unable to contain the emotion and the wetness in his eyes, and hugged her tightly to his chest. "It was a really good day," he thought, and once more silently whispered words of thanks to Saint Anthony. And he promised himself that during the next or another visit he would try to make even makeshift stamps and support them with the uncertain wall of the collapsed part of the shelter, to fumble further in the sand. Maybe there are more surprises.

Chapter V

He went to the shelter for the third time after two days. This is because the next day he found a few deer grazing near the forest on his way. He had only a rifle with him, he gave up hunting because he admitted the possibility that someone could hear the roar of a gun.

He went back to the cave, left Winchester, and returned to the same place already with the bow. He was afraid the animals would move somewhere, but the herd was still there, just a little further. He waited patiently until evening. He knew that at dusk they would return to the thicket, seeking shelter here for the night.

The hunt was successful. He targeted an old, large buck. The shot was good, and corrected with the second arrow knocked the animal to the ground. His meat might not be as good as the goat's, but he meant mostly the pelt for his pants.

He dragged the animal deep into the forest and just dressed it here. It took him a long time to clean the pelt. He had finished the rest in the cave. Once it was stripped of fat and meat, he pulled it over a makeshift branch frame. He knew from experience that otherwise it would shrink and lose its flexibility. Later, he boiled hooves in one of the helmets, and when he got - as his grandfather called - neat's foot oil, he smeared it on the whole thing. At the same time, he hanged the obtained meat over the fire to make it well curled. He wished he had salt, and in the absence of it, he used ash from the fire. He hoped it would fulfill its role at least partially.

***

When he returned from the third trip, he began to wonder what to do next. He was drawn to see if anything had changed in the countryside. Or perhaps the Bolsheviks had moved out of the court, though he realized it was unlikely.

First he finished the skin tanning. He cleaned the places where the meat was left over, then rubbed it with oil.

When he ate after work, thoughts circulated about securing the entrances to the cave. For some time he had been haunted by the thought that it was unprotected, that anyone could accidentally end up here as he once did. This thought bothered him especially after he saw the Bolsheviks in the road. He wasn't sure what to do. He decided to use what he did while securing the shelter among the tranches, but this time using a different method.

He found the thorny bushes of Ruscus and Holly in the forest. He took out their rhizomes and planted them on straight approaches to the cave. He was counting on wild plants to grow in the spring. Maybe not all of them, but if only some of them grow, it will be a success. He masked the whole thing with cut off branches. After that, he found wild blackberry bushes and planted them, too, but on the outskirts of the first. With clipped vines, it obscured enough passages between trees that it should discourage everyone from traversing them.

He realized that he was deliberately delaying visiting the village and the manor, looking for additional works. At the same time, these masking actions stem from the obsession that haunts him, that if he does not do anything and does not protect the habitation from possible disclosure, he will be punished for laziness, that failure to take revenge will be quick. He explained to himself after each day of work that it was only the fear resulting from the situation he was in that suppressed him, but he returned with the dawn of the next day. It was only when he finished his gardening work that he calmed down, muted internally, satisfied with the work done.

Now he could go to the village and the manor.

***

Nature was clearly changing.

The morning no longer greeted with a pleasant chill, but with a piercing, sharp cold. There was a long shimmer of moisture on the bark of the trees, which did not dry out with the first rays of the sun. And it stood low on the border of heaven and earth for a long time, as if refusing to rise above the horizon. And it did not immediately illuminate the surroundings with a glow, but stained purple for a long time, reluctantly giving the earth a warming breath.

He left the cave almost at dawn. He directed the steps to the river, to walk along its edge to the vicinity of the manor. He wanted to check that the outpost at the rocks was still in place and that the guards were alert not only during the day but also at the end of the night.

The water in the rapids also changed. It had acquired an apparent density, and the depths of frost were carried, brought here from far away, where the first winter shows its claws.

At the bend, he noticed, among the old logs, which still remembered previous springs, a sack tucked between the branches. He couldn't see exactly from a distance. He surveyed the high cliff and the ford nearby and went to see what it was. He rebuked himself in his thoughts that he was turning more and more into a real old man, who would not ease off and would look at every garbage dump. He shrugged and was about to turn back when a detail intrigued him in this swaying bag.

"No, it can't be," suddenly a cold chill chilled his thoughts and his body.

He came slowly.

Then the blood drained to his legs, which suddenly buckled and he dropped to his knees as he recognized the contents.

It was a body.

Not one, but three tangled with each other.

He stared in horror at his swollen, rope-bound hands and rotten, disintegrating faces, already partially devoid of fleshy tissue.

And he felt a stench unlike any other, pressing into his nose, settling almost physically on his clothes, swirling over the "sack" like a swarm of invisible death.

"Who did it?" A naive question flashed through his mind, although he subconsciously knew the answer. Judging by their clothes, they were not peasants, but representatives of the intelligentsia or nobility, or perhaps the richer townspeople. Two men and a woman in ragged, torn covers. One of the woman's legs was broken at the knee and protruded unnaturally to the side. Whether it was nature or the work of the torturers, it was difficult for him to judge.

He was speechless with horror, breathing rapidly. He had already forgotten what the Bolsheviks were doing in the village and what he himself had seen. Now those images have returned with all their clarity and sharpness, opening the wounds of memories. He shifted his gaze further to calm himself down, and then he found a black log protruding above the water level, and another corpse pressed in by the swirling bend here. Also men, also women, he didn't even count them, because one of them… He rubbed his eyes because squeezing tears blocked the sharpness of his vision. It was a teenage child, a girl, judging by the braids.

He had had enough.

He stayed on his knees for a long time, then he got up and struggled to put his feet back on the trail.

Thousands of thoughts flashed through his mind, each with the words "kill", "kill", "kill" in it. He came to a place where the cliff of the rapids had dropped to just a meter and a half, broken by large piled stones. Close to the edge, the river's current was smoothing in the spring, the water darkening and creating deep holes. Sometimes she draped fallen trees like the ones on the opposite side. Now the place was overgrown with summer vegetation that turned yellow and brown with the passing of warm days. He took refuge in it with the remnants of his former caution. Here he was invisible from the shore.

And so he persisted, trying to throw the images out of his head, to calm down and arm himself with a firm resolution that he added them to the already long list of crimes of this hate-smeared mass that despised everything that was not like it and murdered otherness to the glory of the proletariat's homeland.

***

He did not know how long he was hanging on the edge of the self. The tears had long since dried, but inside he could feel a fire, where nothing would grow for a long time.

He was roused from his stagnation by a sound on the shore, above him, still distant but still approaching the water.

He felt fear, but it quickly turned into an awakened, sudden hatred.

He checked the saber attached to his back, the blade sticking out over his shoulder for easy retrieval. Vasily taught him that too. He took his bow off his shoulder, drew the string on the shaft, and placed the quiver beside him. He did not take his shotgun this time, and perhaps good, because otherwise, in the first instinct after what he saw, he would probably have run to the manor to take revenge for these innocent people, regardless of the consequences of a blind abomination.

After a while, he could see the distinct hitting of hooves on the ground. It was a single rider. What was he doing here and what was he looking for? Who was he?

He was clearly taking his time. It was coming from the direction where the court stood. Maybe he's one of those who protected the commander? Janek felt his hatred towards this Bolshevik commander and towards everything he represented was growing.

He stepped back and made his decision, rejecting his hesitation and fearing that if he considered the situation he would be overcome with fear and would do nothing.

He positioned his bow so that he could reach it easily, and the quiver slung from the side of his belt to keep arrows at hand.

And then he continued to listen to the sounds.

The horse stopped no more than twenty meters from the river.

"What is he waiting for?" Janek analyzed the situation. "Maybe the others? But why here and not elsewhere, closer to the manor? Has he made an appointment with someone?"

He looked over the edge for a few seconds.

He met the horse on which the Bolshevik rode. It was his Sewek, who had been raised from a foal, and who was his most favorite of all his grandfather's stables. Now, however, that might have been a hindrance, he might have betrayed him if he had whined when he met his master. He also wore his favorite saddle, made by Vasily.

He digested it all, waiting a moment for the grief that had flowed from somewhere deep within his soul to pass. He leaned out of the pit again and very slowly climbed one of the large boulders. Using grasses and other fringing plants, he carefully stuck his head above the edge to see what was happening in the foreground.

Now he also recognized the rider.

It was the soldier who first started the rape of Hapka. A large man with a characteristic scar on his cheek and a Mauser ostentatiously tied to his side, from which he later killed the girl.

Something broke in Janek.

Any doubts that were troubling him suddenly vanished somewhere. Never before he has been so determined as he is now. There was no trace of uncertainty left, only a cold calculation of how to get to this Bolshevik.

He waited for what the soldier would do. And he got off his horse and sat down next to him. He rummaged in his pocket, pulled out a tobacco bag and made his cigarette, then set fire to it slowly.

He was clearly expecting someone.

After a dozen or so minutes, in which nothing happened, the rattling of a moving carriage sounded from the side of the village. Janek was familiar with this sound and he was surprised where it came from and who was driving it. It belonged to his grandfather and you could recognize it from a distance by the sound of tiny bells placed at the backrest. They made a soft sound that was so perfect as they drove across the fields to visit their neighbors.

The carriage approached.

He recognized her driver. It was Danylo, that loser in the service of the Bolsheviks. He was bursting with pretending to be someone he wasn't, clumsily leading not from the trestle but from the passenger seats. Had it not been for the gloomy situation, Janek would have burst out laughing. So ended an inept attempt to imitate someone you weren't.

Danylo pulled up, turned with difficulty, and stopped the carriage.

"У вас есть?" Soldier did not engage in unnecessary conversations with him.

Danylo, under the influence of a sharp question, clearly shrunk. He just nodded and reached for the box attached to the couch. He opened it and handed the soldier four bottles probably filled with vodka, probably not with water. He took them, opened the saddlebags and, without saying a word, slipped them inside.

After that he turned to Danylo, waiting for something else.

"И теперь это более важно," and he added ironically, "зверь."

The peasant, without a word, reached under his jacket and took out a large package carefully wrapped in a colorful scarf.

"Это было не случайно, более?"

"Это действительно все, признал, где они спрятали," he assured eagerly.

"Просто заткнуться, потому что я убью," he threatened.

Danylo shrank, nodded eagerly, and waited only for a sign that he might be gone.

The soldier looked at him carefully, perhaps for a deception in his assurance, and the peasant visibly cringed in fear, his eyes flickering to the sides.

"Что еще? Возьмите," the soldier tossed contemptuously and turned his back to the carriage. And Danylo jumped, this time on the coach-box, and rode away as quickly as the whip-whipped horses would allow.

Janek felt his hatred towards this Bolshevik growing in him.

Quietly, he reached for the bow and put it on his arm, then, flexing his muscles and avoiding the noise, slowly rose to the shore.

The soldier heard nothing, busy untie the knot in the received scarf.

"Get up, bastard."

Janek's words, hardly thrown out by his clenched throat, sounded low, but they did their job anyway.

The soldier quickly turned, clearly surprised. Seeing a stranger, not a peasant, but someone of the hated lords, holding a tight bow in his hand, he did not know how to react. His eyes only widened, shooting sideways, whether he was alone or with the company.

He jumped to his feet, reached for the pistol, but his nervousness was unable to unhook his holster.

Janek drew the string tighter and directed the arrow straight into his eyes, now wide with fear.

"Помилование… Господи…" The Bolshevik changed tactics and now began to drool and mumble while repeating "Я невиновен, я просто простой солдат…"

You can see that he had such lines practiced in the past.

Janek watched him closely. He did not miss that he was only pretending to be frightened, that the soldier was tense and tense all his muscles. He maneuvers his hand at the belt for no reason, checking how quickly he can reach the saber. And gibbering his "*я невиновен*" he is clearly plotting whether the arrow will prevent him from jumping to Lach, who appeared out of nowhere, before he releases the next one.

A moment of uncertainty hung between them.

The Russian continued to investigate whether to jump on this smaller and probably weaker opponent without drawing a saber or to do it by jumping on lord pup. And Janek felt that his hatred towards his opponent was fighting a battle, knowing that he hadn't killed anyone yet, even though he had played war with Alik many times.

With the memory of his friend, the scruples subsided. He remembered Vasily's words: "Hesitation can kill as easily as bravado."

He released the arrow, but the nerves did their job.

The Russians jumped to the side and the arrowhead only split open his forearm. He cursed and, without thinking of his wound, he rushed towards Janek. Simultaneously with the skill of the thugs, he quickly drew his saber, raising it to deliver a blow.

Janek did not reflect.

He dropped his bow and immediately reached from his shoulder for his saber.

When the man swung, he made a quick feint, then delivered a long, dragged cut through the Bolshevik's chest. The other groaned again, staggered, and tried to strike again using his height and strength. Janek easily escaped from the line, beat his weapon, did not let the blade slide over his, he withdrew smoothly by half a step and before the Russians realized he reached with the blade of his throat.

And that was the end of the fight.

Blood gushed from the wound, the head swayed, and the hand with the saber, suddenly deprived of power, fell to the ground.

The Russian stopped, leaned forward, then his legs buckled and he fell to the ground, dead.

***

"During the war, there is no time to consider what is being done," this was another sentence by Vasily, which Janek remembered as he stared at the corpse. "You do what you have to do and it results from the moment, and time will tell if you made a mistake or chose the best solution and what the consequences are."

He grimaced, the sentences had a different overtone when you sat in a quiet court and took on a special meaning in the situation in which he was now.

He took a deep breath and walked over to the Russian. He thought quickly that he had to do something to the body quickly, because if someone found it, the consequences would fall on the countryside.

He walked over to Sewek, who was standing calmly, smelling a more familiar scent than a sight, and screamed happily. He patted his neck, brought his face close to his mouth and gently puffed on the noses, to which the horse responded with a neigh again.

He reached into the panniers, curious about what the Bolshevik had hidden in them. He found a monogrammed shirt, probably from a robbery from some mansion, and he tied it around the soldier's neck to stop any blood that was leaking. He didn't want anyone to find the traces of what had happened. He returned to the saddlebags where he could see the straps. He took them out. Now they will come in handy. He forced the horse to lie down, then secured the corpse behind the saddle, ordered it to rise, and fastened the Bolshevik's arms and legs to the saddle girths so that it would not slip while riding.

"Go to the forest and hide the body there, or maybe, on the contrary, go towards the Pohorecki manor and get rid of the carcass somewhere," he wondered considering all the pros and cons of both solutions.

The latter had the additional advantage that it would pass several ponds along the way, where it could easily get rid of the corpse. And no one will think to look for the perpetrators of the Bolshevik's death, since no one will find him. By the way, he will see what's wrong with the neighbor's court. It would take a long time to go on foot, and there was a danger of being spotted. Horseback riding is another matter.

He settled himself in the saddle. He has not felt so well for a long time. Even when he was a boy, his grandfather or Vasily would put him on a horse, specially selected so as not to prank. And the protests that his bum hurts, that he wants to get down, he had to ride at least an hour a day to no avail. When he grew older, apart from learning fencing on the ground, Vasily also paid attention to saber fighting with a horse. Sometimes he had had enough of these hours and the pain in his muscles, but the old Caucasus was stubborn and would not let go. He had to practice his practice almost every day, and he did it when Sewek grew up, on him.

He reached into an elongated holster strapped to his saddle and took out a Gewehr 98 rifle, probably also captured, from inside it. He checked the operation of the lock and the cartridges stuck in the chamber. He reached for the right saddlebag again, seeing the spare magazines there. Eight cartridges, five bullets each. "Anyway, enough, though it could be more," he thought, pleased. Now he was ready for any surprises, or at least he hoped so.

He started the walk, leaving the open field. He headed towards shrubs and single trees growing here and there. He took out his captured mountain binoculars and scanned the surroundings without changing his pace. Reassured, he hung it on the thong around his neck and accelerated.

The fields shimmered with varieties of yellow and brown. Where the haymaking had failed, rye and wheat bent to the ground under the weight of the grain, and other crops, which usually grew only after the harvest, shot up between the ears of corn. So much wasted good - it occurred to him, and he felt an additional aversion to the invaders that they even squandered it.

After an hour of fast driving, he reached a place where low rocks and clumps of trees jutted above the field. Behind them was the first pond, overgrown with calamus and sparse salvinia and willows, often washing their hair in the depths where large leaves of aquatic plants reigned.

He chose a place where the shore was heavily overgrown. He searched for stones, weighed them down on the Bolshevik's body, broke through the bushes and dragged the carcass into the water. He felt no regret or remorse as he sank into the water. After a while the place returned to normal, only those large leaves swayed slightly on the excited waves.

Something died in him.

This fight was to overcome the uncertainty and unconscious fear of the Bolsheviks that had haunted him from the beginning. With the blow of the saber, he hardened inside, and his inner determination overwhelmed his fears and dilemmas. He was alone, which does not mean that he is weak and that he will give up. Now he knew why Vasily and grandfather attached so much importance to his exercises and why his father, when he came to the estate, enjoyed the most his skills, which he boasted about, proud of what he had learned.

He got on his horse and moved on. He still had to travel a few versts to the Podhorecki estate. He will arrive just when the evening starts and the gray light will make it difficult to see the lone rider.

***

The mansion was only partially burnt. Only the black beams protruding from the site of the fire remained from annex, as was the case with the cart shed. The main building has been preserved, which seemed intact, although here too, the tongues of fire left dark, sooty marks on the walls and empty eye sockets without glass.

He put down the binoculars, wondering if he had missed anything. The place seemed deserted, but it might have been appearances. There was no sound of human presence, no sign of life. Only high in the sky did pairs of screaming kestrels and hawks circulate.

He noticed a pair of foxes heading towards the manor, but at one point it stopped sniffing carefully, then turned back and changed its direction.

He had to make a decision.

Why have the foxes changed direction? What did they sense?

He took out his rifle, rattled off, put three cartridges in his jacket pocket, checked the pistol, took a deep breath, put the binoculars to his eyes once more, then headed towards the slight hill and the place where there used to be a shed at its base. From this side it was not visible from the front.

"Maybe," he thought quickly, "the devil is lurking somewhere behind the walls, and he just didn't notice him, because he didn't have the smelling gift that foxes do."

He stopped his horse by the shed. From this side he saw what he could not see from the previous place. A rope swayed to the rhythm of the wind in the large walnut mansion at the rear. If something had hung on it, now it must have fallen and be hidden amongst the grass over a meter high. The rope ended with a loop.

He got off his horse, gripped the rifle tighter and, leaning, began to move towards the court. Still no disturbing sound. He breathed reassured. The fears were in vain. So he straightened up, and at the same moment he heard, somewhere on the verge of audibility, the snort of a horse and its hooves hitting the ground.

He fell to the ground.

The sound came from the side of the manor.

So he was wrong...

He quickly ran to the corner, partially covered by tall grass.

He waited patiently for the sound to repeat.

Second after second and minute after another passed.

"Охуел ты, ёб твою мать," suddenly it came from somewhere in the depths, the horse's nervous snort, the sound of a whip strike and the whine of a complaining animal answered.

Someone was inside, he was sure of that. Certainly not the former owners and certainly not a stray peasant here.

He was still waiting. The sounds from the court suggested that something was beginning to happen there, perhaps preparations for the trip. Single insults thrown into space: *"придурок... тупица... дубина..."*, no longer left any doubts. Three different voices and that characteristic guttural tone of vodka-eaten throats. He had heard similar ones in the village.

His hands tightened on the buttstock.

He made a decision.

Slowly, carefully taking his steps, he ran to the next corner, crouched down, and glanced quickly behind it.

A shaky man in a fur vest was leading his horse outside. He turned around, hooked his saber on the frame and the angry shouted something inside, and from there came an incomprehensible answer.

The Bolshevik let go of the bridle, reached under his puffer jacket, took out a small pouch and began to roll a cigarette. Meanwhile, he went out, also leading the horse his companion, and following him, cursing under his breath, another. They were all dressed differently, but each had a pointed, helmet-like felt cap with a red star on the front.

The first one gave an order, stretched, and grasped the bridle.

Two decisions fought each other in Janek's head: "let them go or shoot them." After all, it rattled on his head, "there are people, can I kill a man?"

He closed his eyes for a split second to recall the pictures from his village.

He felt that no matter what happened, he had to do it. To break through once more, using the same methods as the Bolsheviks.

"Куда спешите товарищи?" He came around the corner and silently tossed a question in an undefined direction.

His calm words impressed them more than if he had screamed.

They froze motionless.

Only the two who left as the last one quickly looked at the first, you can see their commander. There was no panic on the faces, but rather astonishment and surprise. The vodka did its job and the understanding of the situation slowly reached their heads, but from the shifting eyes he could see that they were trying to quickly judge whether he was alone or others were around the corner. They were not, he understood it quickly, it's one thing the scared peasants it's another thing experienced soldiers who were not easy to frighten despite the rifle pointing at them.

The former only tilted his head, as if he had suddenly seen a strange, unknown animal or, more importantly, he had met a long-lost acquaintance who was presumed dead. He took the cigarette butt out of his mouth as if nothing had happened, and he did so ostentatiously slowly. He looked skeptical at him, shrugged, and threw him to the ground. His mouth twisted in a grimace that mimicked a smile, then his left hand pointed to something on the roof of the manor house.

Janek pretended to be fooled by the gesture that distracted his attention, but out of the corner of his eye he was carefully watching the Bolshevik's right hand.

And she quickly reached for the Nagant tucked in his belt.

He did not have time to draw it when Janek squeezed the trigger.

The bullet hit the Bolshevik in the chest, and the next two knocked back the other two.

And there was silence.

Only the horses shook their heads violently, as if checking that the bullets could not reach them, then lowered them again, waiting quietly.

Janek did not allow himself to consider what had happened. His adrenaline was still buzzing as he walked over to the first one to be shot. He was dead. Likewise, the second, but the third's chest was moving rapidly. He knelt beside him and forced him to meet his eyes. Life was draining from him, his eyesight slowly blurred, and his throat was breathing more and more hoarse.

He asked him what unit they were from and, surprisingly, he had no trouble getting an answer. The other was losing consciousness, not knowing who he was talking to. There was even a crooked smile at the memory, God knows what. They belonged to Budyonny's Cavalry Army, specifically from the Cherezhabitki regiment of the sixth division sent here from the Caucasus. They were commanded by Lieutenant Colonel Leonid Kluyev, the political officer was Isaac Babel, and the regiment consisted of about a thousand sabers.

The Bolshevik's face changed, becoming ever paler.

Janek continued asking about the prisoners and the direction of the march, and whether the burning of this manor was their doing. The soldier nodded. He gave the time when they came here and Janek associated it with a quick patrol leaving his manor.

"Комендант приказал..." the soldier gasped more and more, breaking his sentence. "Не берите в плен… "

"And women, children, after all..."

"Дети… и женщины также… являются военнопленными… они только задерживают марш..."

The lying person's eyes sparkled. Perhaps he thought he was being questioned by the regimental political commissar, the one named Babel, and he was pleased with the well-given answer.

He had to hurry. Soldier breathed his last. The body twitched, the hands convulsed, and the hands closed and opened as if they wanted to tell something too.

"And this court," he quickly mentioned the name and place of his family home, and when he did not see understanding in the eyes of the Bolshevik, he specified and indicated his direction and asked about the detachment stationed there.

"...Это... специальное... разведывательное... подразделение... чрезвычайная комиссия по борьбе с контрреволюцией... " the neck tensed, the head lifted a few centimeters above the ground, then fell limply.

He was dead.

He looked at the dead Bolshevik without regret.

At least he knew what was happening in the area now. A special unit of some strange service, the political police, was stationed in the manor. The Bolsheviks did not take prisoners as they rushed east, and they considered the murder of ordinary civilians, even women and children, something normal that served the cause.

Near the manor house there was a pond where carps were bred.

He dragged the bodies over here, weighed them down with stones and drowned them.

He remembered the lines at the back of the mansion, though he didn't have to check it, he figured out what it was used for. Debris lay beneath it among the tall grass. Judging by the remnants of the clothes, they belonged to the hanged one, probably Hryhor Pohorecki. Time made the cervical vertebrae and rotting muscles of the corpse's neck fail under the weight of the body and broke, and it landed on the ground. Three meters away, he found other bones, probably belonging to one of the heir's sons, Anton or Fedor. There was a saber cut mark on the skull. He figured they had hung the father for fun and made his son look at it, and maybe even kick a stool from under his parent's feet. The piece of furniture was lying next to it. And then they killed him. He did not know what happened to the second son, and he did not find any other remains. His first instinct was to bury the remains of both of them, but he restrained himself. This might draw attention if the soldier, who had participated in the execution, appeared here again, although - he realized - that it was rather unlikely. Let them lie, the burial will not help them anymore.

He turned and went to look at the ruins of the barn. Among the ashes, he found many bones. They had to spend the household there, close the gates and set fire to them. Was he among the second of Pohorecki's sons? The fire consumed everything but bones, equalizing the status of the inhabitants of the court.

He went outside to breathe some fresh air. Despite the passage of time, the stench of burnt meat and all that associated with a fire still wafted in the barn.

He looked at the manor house, which he remembered from his visits here on the recommendation of his grandfather.

He looked nothing like him now. The work of destruction was complete; a peculiar document of the culture of the wild, which took the world into proletarian possession. Furniture and paintings cut with sabers, some burned in the middle of the living room, where the invaders set up a fire. The collapsing remains of broken trinkets and the ubiquitous, broken shells of earthenware vessels. In a broken porcelain potty lying against the wall, apparently considered a useful container for food, leftovers, judging by the dried beans and greens, some food eaten in it. Even the tiled stove showed signs of being severed with sabers. The remains of the cornices were scattered around, littering the floor.

Straw was brought into one room that had once been a bedroom. Probably the proud winners kept their horses here because they left behind their droppings. In the side room that had once been occupied by Fedor, he found a cauldron for boiling water buried in the ash in the fireplace, and he took it with him. From the sideboard in the next room, where the tableware was kept, only shells and pieces of furniture were left, which they probably also chopped up for the purposes of the fire. He also looked into the kitchen, but it showed a veritable mess of broken colanders, vegetables, sieves and strainers, which in the eyes of black had no value because they were "full of holes".

He went out to the threshold of the court, rested on the stairs and for a long time digested what he saw. These were not people like the peasants in his grandfather's villages. Or at least he grasped at the vision and did not allow the thought that it could be otherwise. And immediately he remembered Danylo Wolosynchyk, faithfully serving the new power, and at once his faith shrank, like a skin hung in the frost.

***

He went on so lost in thought and torn apart, even more lonely than before, without faith that whatever he did, made any sense.

He clung to the thought, remembering Alik that at least he could try to help him. Just how?

A snort of one of the horses brought him back to reality. "What's next? What to do with mounts?"

He stood up with difficulty, as if he had been working hard. The sabers taken from the village leaders were tied to the saddles. Only one of them, the one he shot first, was armed with a revolver. Attached to the saddle of his horse was an ornate holster, also probably a lot from a robbed manor, and in it a Mosin rifle, its shorter version. He pulled it out and examined the condition it was in. Surprisingly, even in good conditions, it can be seen that the Bolshevik at least cared for weapons. Maybe it was not a rifle as reliable as the two already obtained by Janek, only with four bullets in the magazine, but always an additional weapon.

Now he remembered the bundle he had received from a murderer by the river. He reached into the saddle but gave up. He'll see him in the cave. Probably lard and a piece of bread for the road. There were also some papers in the purse, but he had left these for later.

He delayed the decision what to do next all the time. He had four horses, but nowhere to hide them in the forest, and more importantly, how to feed them there. "Or maybe?" He remembered that deep in the forest, though quite far away, there was a lake with an island in the middle, called Buchak Lake by the locals. "No, it doesn't make sense," soberizing came soon. At any moment frost will come, it will cut the surface on which the wolves will easily pass and that is what the horses will be left with. He had to let them go. However, before that he will hide the saddles somewhere in the forest, because you never know if they will ever be useful.

Making the decision restored his balance of thinking and the goal strengthened his spiritually.

***

He took the return path slightly to the south, where there were no roads, only arable land and wasteland, as well as clumps of trees and rocks protruding above the ground.

The entire surroundings took on the color of intense yellow due to the ubiquitous, uncontrollably chamaecytisus that now covered every free space of the earth. Here, too, in the formerly fertile fields, no one has harvested, and the only trace of interference was left by the steppe animals. He glimpsed wild donkeys among the bending to the ground, and in the distance he saw even a grazing herd of timid jerians feeding nearby suhaki. Neither of them even looked up. Perhaps due to the distance, and perhaps not disturbed for a long time, they did not pay so much attention to their surroundings.

He wanted to see the village of Zarubynci from a distance, where one of the Pohorecki tenants had a manor house, a dilapidated nobleman, a certain Lazar Churylow, burdened with a group of children and his corpulent wife Zofia. Sometimes he would visit his grandfather on business. Janek liked to listen to him, because he always joked, always keeping his serenity and cheerful disposition. He hadn't expected anything good, but he decided that since he was here, it was good to know what the situation was even in this further area.

He drove there longer than he had expected. He had wasted too much time choosing the way that he would be invisible from a distance, from a tuft to a tuft of trees, between bushes and where the grass grew up in the tangle of horses, and often above their heads. He approached the village cautiously, not straight ahead, but in a large arc to the north, sheltered by the trees of a large orchard.

As he approached Zarubyncia, he noticed from a distance that the church tower, usually looming above the huts, had disappeared. And then the picture became more and more expressive; what remains of the temple are only half-ruined, burnt ruins and two side walls protruding like the ribs of a fallen mythical animal. It was similar with the houses closest to them, which were also consumed by fire.

He took out a pair of binoculars, scanning every place for a long time, especially preserved huts.

No traffic.

He drove to the tollbooths, tied horses to a half-fallen fence, and on his own he drove onto the main road. The silence in the usually bustling village was poignant, it literally screamed with dead space.

Near the well opposite the ruins of the church, three bodies rested side by side, or rather what was left of them; faded rags and the bones of the owners not completely chewed by wild animals. A little further, around the corner of the inn, several more resting against the wall, suggesting a mass execution here. However, they were not shot because there were no traces on the plaster, but probably cut with sabers to save ammunition.

The manor house, located just outside the village, was not even as dilapidated as he subconsciously expected. For some reason, the fire set here consumed only part of the roof, soaked the walls, and went out. He stepped onto the porch, stepped over the threshold, and almost tripped over what was left of the house of the master. His ragged clothes, speckled with dark brown stains and cut with the strokes of sabers, were silent testimony of how he died. Further in the corridor two small, dry bodies of Alyosha and Misha.

He looked away.

It seemed to him that he had gotten used to such views that they no longer impressed him, but no, the sight of the dead children made him stop and soothe his inner trembling for a long time.

Once his emotions were subdued, he moved on.

Invoked the rational part of thinking to search the house. There was always something the Bolsheviks could overlook or dismiss as unnecessary and useful for him.

In the nursery, next to the two bedrooms, lay the body of the tenant's wife, Zofia, still holding the two bundles after her death. He guessed that they were the youngest of Churylow's five offspring, twins, one-year-old Daria and Sonia. They must have starved to death when their mother was struck down by a sword blow, almost chopping off her head. Nowhere to find the body of the tenant's son from his first marriage, sixteen-year-old Igor. Had they taken him? For what? As a helper? Rather not, and judging by what the soldier told him before his death in the Pohorecki manor house, there was an order not to take prisoners.

He found nothing useful. He also looked into the futkamera, where the feed for the animals was being prepared, but there was nothing here either. On the other hand, in a half-collapsed forge he found abandoned pliers, a few hammers and files, and - what pleased him the most - not yet fully processed, thick and solid blades, which were supposed to be used to make plowshares, and in other processing, scythes. Judging by the violet color of the rainbow, they were only initially hardened.

There was nothing else to do here. He threw the finds in the saddlebags and, without getting on the horse, walked back to where he had left the three. He wanted to absorb the images of destruction in order to throw out of his mind even the slightest pity for the murderers, those here and in every place where the Bolsheviks appeared. He only wondered why the grandfather's village had survived? And he quickly found the answer. Commander Cherezustomki made his home in the manor, and someone had to provide food to the detachment stationed in the village. Paradoxically, the peasants saved their lives thanks to this presence. Maybe not all, but most.

However, why this special unit did not move further, behind the front lines, remaining in its deep rear? Were the Bolsheviks getting ready for a major operation? Or maybe they were securing the place where the staff was to be stationed?

Thinking this way, he almost hooked his head on a pitchfork stuck in the wall of the house. He bent down and froze.

On the teeth of the tools, almost huddled to the logs of the house, hung the decaying remains of a child of a year old.

He had had enough.

He swallowed the lump in his throat and picked up speed.

And then, almost coming out from behind the hut onto the road, he heard distant voices.

Three others stood by the horses they had left behind, and three soldiers next to them, examining his bags, arguing over their contents. They shouted to each other, cursed and wrenched a Mauser pistol probably discovered in a saddlebag.

He didn't think twice, just quickly backed up to his horse and reached for his rifle. He assessed the distance and set a Gewehr sight, calibrated from 400 to 2000 meters. The others stood no more than three hundred meters away. He crawled and looked around the corner.

They were still arguing.

He evened and calmed his breathing. He rested the gun on the corner of the hut and tracked down the first, closest to the horses. He squeezed the trigger slowly, considering how long the other two would be shielded for a moment after the shot before they reacted, cooled down, and sought shelter.

He should be able to set them on fire.

He took a deep breath, then slowly let it out.

Calmly, not to break the shot, he squeezed the trigger.

The echo of the shot had not yet subsided when he already had the second in his sight, and he looked around in confusion. Before he could understand, a bullet hit him.

A third reacted, but too late. The impact of the bullet threw him backwards.

He reached for his binoculars and scanned the place carefully, looking for any movement or companions of the three.

There was nobody.

Without laughing, he got on his horse and rode up to the dead.

"Three again, why exactly so many," flashed through his mind, but found no answer.

He got off and walked over to the lying ones. Neither showed any signs of life.

He reached into the saddlebags of their horses, but found nothing interesting in them, except for a small sack with a few silver, feminine ornaments, probably carefully hidden for the future, the loot of the brave Red Army. He tilted back the saddles one by one, under the leather of which some important documents were often carried. Under one of them he found a letter, sealed in thick waxed paper, addressed to a commissioner.

"Well, couriers," he concluded the find. He put it in his saddlebag and decided to read it only when he will be in the cave. He already had one package with a letter found on the scarred guy, who started Hapka's rape.

There were sabers attached to the saddles and only one Mosin rifle. "This one must have been the commander," he thought. He found himself throwing back the thought that flashed into his head by force of his will, causing panic that he had killed people once again.

He recalled the murdered children and dealt with the Bolsheviks.

He had to stage the events because he had no intention of looking for another pond to get rid of the bodies. He took three rounds from Mosin's magazine and put them in his pocket. Then he pulled out one of the sabers, slashed the other with it, and placed the weapon in his hand. He did the same with the second and third, a potential commander, who had a rifle in his hand instead of a saber. He looked at his work for a while. It looked plausible, but not quite. He looked through the eyes of whoever finds these dead bodies. Wouldn't he wonder why the third one was also shot? He took the rifle out of the commander's hands, stained it with blood, then cut it over the butt with his saber and threw it on the ground. He assessed the fallen ones once more. He took the first saber from his dead hand, plunged it into the wound and twisted the blade, masking the hole, then threw it to the ground as well. He took one bullet from his pocket and reloaded the Mosin's magazine. The saber of the second fighter ran across the hand of the third.

He looked critically and did not come up with anything new. Was the sight more likely now? He hoped so, but what those who found them would think was their concern. He reached for the jewelery pouch and gripped the dead commander's fingers around it. This should draw attention to and suggest that they fought for silver.

And after that he mounted a horse, took the ropes of those with whom he had come, leaving the Bolshevik mounts next to the corpses. Once again he looked at the whole, remembering the Latin stuck in his head by his grandfather and the words of Virgil about succumbing to passion. With complete satisfaction he said it aloud: "Trahit sua quemque voluptas", then added philosophically, wondering at himself that he was so calm: "Tres faciunt Collegium."

Chapter VI

The return took place without any surprises.

Being in the forest, he reloaded the items he had acquired and the saddle made by Vasily into his cave. He knew it was irrational, because he needed them in the cave, but sentiment won. And then, riding bareback on Sewek, he headed for a nearby group of sand rocks, heavily dented by corrosion.

He chose a niche that guaranteed no water to fall into it, even during rain or spring snow melting. He hid the other three saddles here. He masked the opening with loose stones, additionally covering them with thorny bushes, again with rock fragments, and finally pressed clay into the gaps.

All that was left to do now was to let the horses go.

He rode to the forest line, got off the Sewek and shouted at the horses to move away.

They did so right away, but then stopped and began nibbling at the grass. Only Sewek did not react, looking surprised at his master, putting his ears straight forward and not wanting to part.

He walked up to him and stroked his head. The horse looked at him, curious as to what was going on and why he was going to go away. However, at the same time the bloated nostrils showed concern that they had to break up. He spoke gently to him as he used to, then patted him again and pointed to the other horses.

Sewek seemed to understand something, though he did not seem convinced. He stood hesitating for a moment, rocking his head up and down, then snorted and slowly walked away.

Janek felt something tighten his throat, but he quickly took a deep breath so as not to fall apart, turned and quickly headed for the forest.

***

He returned to the cave and only now felt overwhelming body and mind exhaustion.

He needed a good sleep this day.

***

He woke up with a headache. He put it on a barely smoldering fire, ate his breakfast, and settled for the luxury of making himself a cup of tea. While waiting for the water in the kettle to boil, he looked outside and was amazed.

The entire surroundings changed color overnight. The trees, bushes and grass were covered with a blanket of fluffy snow. Its whiteness was interspersed with threads of delicate purple in places where the temperature was still slightly above zero, and the warm earth caused it to melt and turn into delicate, icy tongues.

The whole forest was asleep. Even the birds were silent. The silence was broken only by creaking boughs moved by the wind somewhere in the upper parts of the trees. Down here, even the gusts were imperceptible.

He covered the opening and made some tea. He considered for a moment whether he should lie down and take another hour or two, but he fought back the tempting thirst and reached for the writings he had found in the saddlebags.

He began with the one from the first of the Bolsheviks. The sealed package was relatively thick and placed in a leather bag. He cut it gently. Inside there were three smaller ones, addressed to some commissioner, and the rest to two commanders with names that, like the first, did not tell him anything.

He started with those aimed at the military. These were orders to dislocate the troops, to move them to another place in the direction of Lviv. The first to the regiment commander of the sixth division of Konarmia Budyonny, Lt. Col. Leonid Kluyev, and the second contained amendments to previous regulations. He glanced at the dates. They were separated by three months, which was not the best proof of the efficiency of the Bolshevik communications services.

The third was intended for the own hands of the political officer Isaac Babel and concerned the initiation of secret preparations for the regiment to return of the 6th division to the 1st brigade. With an additional note, in a separate sealed note stamped "Top secret". He was to highlight the Jewish Red Army soldiers as potentially insecure, ready, under favorable circumstances, to betray the People's Revolution for the benefit of the white lords. Emphasizing that one should especially be careful with members of the old middle class, teachers, merchants, shopkeepers and the like, representing the bourgeoisie, because those - as there have been cases before - only pretend favor, and are in fact plotting against the proletariat. At the slightest suspicion, without playing in court, be shot immediately.

Then a personal note to Babel to act carefully but firmly. And explaining that many "our trusted companions from the Politburo, like Grigory Yevseyevich Zinoviev, formerly known to the commissioner as Hirsh Apfelbaum," are willing to forgive "theirs" no matter how they acted. This is an unforgivable mistake - underlining the writer, a certain Kliment Voroshilov - which may have an impact on planned hostilities. Although the intelligence agents, left especially on the Polish side, fulfill perfectly well, and their reports are valuable to the revolutionary troops, nevertheless one must remain sensible in these critical times for the proletariat. He concluded with the example of "imitating" a trusted comrade, Semyon Budyonny, who completely eliminated the "potential threat" in his troops. And a meaningful, underlined sentence: "For us in the present situation, the merits of Comrade Budyonny and his Cavalry Army count for the revolution, and accusations of massacres against the Jewish population, not disseminated by enemies.

Janek wondered for a moment what this Voroshilov, probably some important Bolshevik, meant. He didn't consider it long, leaving the puzzle for later. Letters taken over from subsequent messengers, also stamped "совершенно секретно", were also addressed to Commissioner Babel and it interested him. Why so much for this one? What are the Bolsheviks preparing that the majority of the letters were addressed to a political commissioner, not to the military?

In the first, quite short, information appeared that caused the heart to beat faster. It was actually a message sent by some commissioner Bronstein about the disturbing activity in this area by a nondescript Feliks Jaworski, a former officer of the tsarist hussars, who formed a large unit. "He is attacking the members of the "Revcom" and terrorizing peasants," he wrote. A further warning is that this Jaworski "shoots whole revolutionary committees without mercy, where they take away from Polish bloodsuckers what is rightfully owed to the peasants." Further the supposition that his squad consists of "trained veterans of the Great War."

At the bottom, a loosely drawn remark, already added by another, a certain commissar, Jefim Shchadienko, that there are probably several ordinary gangs in this area, sometimes cooperating with Bolshevik troops, and this should be used in intelligence operations. And further that it is necessary to "urgently", the word underlined twice, to send a special unit to the area, preferably a whole well-armed regiment, to neutralize the actions of this bandit as soon as possible, because a great offensive is being prepared and until it starts, which will soon take place, the backup must be absolutely clean.

Janek thought about it. Until now, when the front changed and the Tsarists were stationed in the court alternately with the Germans, for him it was a fight fought by strangers. He did not care at all, although the comments between grandfather and Vasily showed that it was good for Poles when their oppressors got to fight with themselves, because there would be a chance for the revival of their homeland. He did not know what they meant and could not even imagine what this Poland could look like, about which the world was talked about so much, but brought up on love for what was long gone and what he had not experienced himself, he was happy himself, although he didn't really know what to do with it. But he was more interested in hunting expeditions with Alik than overheard reflections.

However, now things had changed and he had experienced personally what the Bolsheviks were, with whom he had never dealt before. The Tsarists and the Germans did not come as friends either, but they did not commit such crimes as they. Maybe Moskals once, after the fall of the uprising, about which there was a lot in family stories, but that was a long time ago, and the Bolsheviks arc here, now, at your fingertips and he has seen what they are doing.

He opened the last letter. It was actually a short note with the order that Comrade Babel should immediately report it to Cavalry Army's staff as soon as he had any information. It was about the "Kazakh gang". Apparently, they works somewhere in the region, complements himself in action with the "Jaworski gang" and is as ruthless as the former, or even more so.

The letter stated that the intelligence did not have any information about who this "Kazakh" was, it only knew his pseudonym and so far it has not even been established who is part of his gang and how many sabers are counting. One thing is certain, that it is very dangerous, because it has already broken up three large detachments of trusted "Cossacks" sent for intervention, which in itself makes you think about his military experience. "He sows terror among his peers' comrades" - underlined sentence. And another: "All information is a priority here." And another one: "There are assumptions that he may have a relationship or work with Ataman Kherson Grigoriev, and his actions raise suspicions in the Politburo as to his intentions." And then an attached report of an unnamed commissioner: "The villages are going up in smoke when this bandit appears, and he hangs the ringleaders of burning of courts on roadside trees, which discourages ours from setting up Revcoms. For our righteous actions of punishing bloodsuckers for the years of tyranny of masters, fear spreads with its cruelty".

"You have to want to understand and not pretend to understand," he remembered one of his grandfather's sayings, because he did not understand anything about these orders and their suggestions. However, he understood one thing, that somewhere someone had organized an armed resistance against the Bolsheviks and was responding to their crimes with the same. Unfortunately, the writings did not specify exactly in which area.

***

The snow was pouring down intensely all week, and after that it still hadn't stopped, but it was just a tiny fall of fluffy powder lazily circling in the air and littering the ground like a delicate carpet of dandelions. Moved from place to place during stronger gusts of wind, it created momentary drifts, leveling depressions and creating hills where they had not existed before. The trees, shrubs, and earth took a uniform color, enveloping all the nooks and crannies of the forest with white. Even individual branches are no longer visible, hidden in thick gloves that make up winter fur.

Janek tried several times to go outside from the other exit, the one from the lake, but immediately gave up on his further trip. Each step made a visible mark, and the fact that it was immediately covered with a new layer did not change the situation in any way.

He knew he had to leave in a while to get some fresh food, but so far, even in the swamps, he hadn't noticed any traces. All animals, including birds, waited for a time when rainfall would become regular, not so frequent, when temperature fluctuations and snowfall formed an outer layer on which to move, and for the smaller ones, dig corridors underneath so as not to throw face hungry predators.

Fortunately, remembering the change of weather, he had accumulated enough wood in the cave, and the thick rock walls, heated by the fire, kept him warm for a long time. He was especially glad that he had provided himself with tarry pieces of larch, perfect for lighting and keeping a fire alive. During the night he did what Vasily called the best. Already in the past, while during hunting you had to stay overnight in the forest, he used it with success. He split the pine block in two lengthwise, put a glowing piece of larch in the middle, and that was enough. The fire did not go outside, but spread over only the two inside walls. He kindled them to the heat and kept them like that, slowly digesting them until dawn, and often longer, giving them more friendly warmth than any kind of wood stove.

He devoted his free time to sewing leather trousers, which turned out to be not as easy as he imagined. He had no needles, the thongs he made were not always of the quality he wanted, and the laborious sewing of individual pieces with them strained his patience. Were it not for the fact that there was such and no other weather outside, he would have left it for later, for an indefinite period of time, as long as he would not tire himself. However, in the end, common sense prevailed, but only after a few days he finished the work, and although he was far from the production of an expert furrier, he was very proud of himself. Fur pants kept warm and did not restrict movement, and most of all, protected against snow.

After that, he sewed leggings to protect his boots, and hat and gloves. Here, the experience of sewing trousers came in handy. When they were ready, he started snow skis, which he constructed from previously prepared flexible spruce branches, joining them with leather and straps for fastening.

He was ready to go into the snow, no matter how much it was.

***

Winter, as if after too long absence, did not intend to break the down blanket covering the ground. The next week the snow fell slowly, it swirled violently, and in the breaks it cut with hail needles, compacting what had fallen earlier.

He waited a few more days, killing his free time working on a primitive javelin rather than bear spear, having more fun with the work itself than with it. However, every now and then, he would deviate from this boring activity, allowing time for the bone-resin mixture to dry in the places he was strengthening. And then he was happy to do another one in a row, because he did it every day, cleaning captured rifles and even polishing cartridges, and then he did the same with the pistol and revolver.

He felt some inner excitement as he took the weapon apart and then closed his eyes and tentatively folded it back, faster and faster each time, without making a mistake, reflexively, without thinking and wondering which one to fasten on. The touch of the weapon gave him a sense of self-confidence, increased his value, and when that was not enough, he drew his saber and maneuvered it, inflicting blows, evaporating an imaginary opponent, countering, minimizing unnecessary movements and inventing economical, combined with fast cutting, shifting the weight of the body from one to the other the leg, balancing and above all combining the movement of the wrist with the forearm and tilting the body.

It was difficult because the size of the cave did not allow for freedom of movement, but at the same time this minimalism of movements forced non-standard movements, which turned into quality. There was no possibility of making any lunges, jumps, going sideways, only precision.

And later, tired and content, he returned to bear spear and continued to create it more to pass the time than he needed. After all, why would he need her if he had rifles?

***

He woke up with a scratching sore throat and a dry mouth. He felt an unpleasant throbbing in his temples, and his muscles seemed to scream so he wouldn't make them move. He downplayed it all on the account of staying too long in the cave and near the fire. He decided to go out and hunt something.

He changed into a new outfit, glad that he made it. He took his bow with him and walked outside from the side of the swamp.

At first he did not recognize a place now resembling a landscape full of hills and ravines made of snowdrifts.

He strapped the rackets to his feet and tested that they stuck to the surface of the snow. He did not collapse, although the first steps were not secure. However, it did not take him long to remember how he was running in the fields on those made by Vasily.

He moved slowly, crossing the frozen swamp in meanders, looking for traces.

He didn't have to look long. The icy crust was covered with a blanket of fresh rainfall, and numerous intersecting tracks were clearly visible. But it is one thing to see them, and another to know how long they have been imprinted. In several places, the tracks of the grouse crossed with the characteristic prints of the fox's paws, which suddenly twisted and followed the first ones. He chose the ones, unspoiled by the trail of predators, but after a long journey and thrashing in different directions, he did not come across any bird.

He hung around like that for a while longer. He tried to listen to the forest music to hear the sounds, but the silence was almost perfect, broken only by the creaking of trees under the weight of the snow and the soft whining of the wind that rose as unexpectedly as it disappeared immediately, as if discouraged from frolics.

At one point he found traces much clearer, wolf, and he examined them more carefully. He realized that meeting a few could have ended tragically when he only had a bow. He carefully examined the place they passed and the surrounding area, trying to count how many there were. He might have made a mistake as to the number, because the footsteps of the first, as was the pack's custom, were followed by another. But if he had analyzed the crumbling snow around each depression well, there were five or six, but still many for one.

He rested for a moment, feeling that his well-being is not as he would like it to be. He was having a hard time, sweating over his body and feeling general discouragement. He decided to drive a bit more and return to the cave.

He turned to the side, making some way to avoid walking in his own footsteps. Admittedly, it was difficult to recognize them, which he noted with satisfaction, because again small, slowly spinning petals began to sprinkle from heavy, low-hanging clouds. However, he remembered that a good hunter could follow tracks, even obliterated by rainfall, as well as leaving signposts. And he did not know, and this thought was constantly circulating in his mind, whether there were no forest people among the Bolsheviks.

Busy taking long strides, he almost ran into partridges buried in the fresh powder. They hid under the protruding stems of tall, frozen grasses.

He froze so as not to frighten them off, but it didn't do much. They literally burst out of their cavities, flapped their wings, wondered for a few seconds, spinning in circles, and then not noticing the immediate danger, though still alarmed, they walked away unhurriedly.

He waited motionless, carefully following the direction they were headed. And when they were distant from him, that he could barely see them, he took off his bow, shifted the quiver to one side, took out three arrows and put one on the bowstring. Now he followed the herd slowly. He knew they certainly hadn't gone very far, because it was not their way to do so. It would be different if they panicked and had no reason but to change places.

It wasn't long before he saw them again. This time they crouched next to a clump of jasmine, whose snow-covered branches formed a natural umbrella.

He approached slowly, several paces away, drew his bow and fired the first arrow. The hit cockerel flapped its wings, sprang to its feet and fell dead. Others, concerned, began to shake their heads as they checked what had happened, but did not move. After a while the second, third and fourth fell.

He wanted to kill a few more, because it's good to have a supply of meat, but suddenly, somewhere in the distance, on the verge of listening, he heard a wistful howl.

He froze and fears returned. He shook his head worriedly. The wolf pack must have been hovering somewhere nearby, and God willing, they would not find his tracks. He quickly tied a strap around the chicken legs and threw them over his shoulder, then headed straight towards the swamp and the cave.

This time he was stretching his legs without playing with careful foot placement.

The wolf was dangerous, especially when it was hungry for winter, which Vasily warned him about more than once, giving him many good advice on how to act if he happened to meet him in the forest. He remembered his murmuring adages, which he did not know what to match, although he sensed that they were talking about something: "You want to eat meat, follow the wolf's tail" or, more understandably: "A wolf will not be satisfied with flies". However, his stories of these predators imbued with love for Vakho, from which he was given his name. He never spoke of them with fear or hatred, as others did, and how not infrequently he heard at hunting meetings of the nobility where his grandfather sometimes took him. Once, remembering Vasily's remarks, he interrupted the conversation in defense of the wolves, when the company of mead had already emptied many kettles. And then he was only answered with laughter and mockery, lest the wolf's cough not choke him, because he is young and knows nothing about life.

But now he sped up as he began to sweat even more. He was breathing faster and faster, feeling tired in his legs and looking closely behind him to see if he could see dark spots slipping by against the white snow. And laboriously, persistently, he continued on, regardless of the increasingly felt fatigue and numbness of the muscles in his legs.

He calmed down somewhat when he reached the edge of the swamp, now recognizable only by the characteristic snowy caps hiding the bowed alders.

He would stop to rest and get his breath back. He concluded that he had been in the cave too long, which had a negative effect on his well-being and condition, and that brought him like an unprovoked panic. He smiled, mocking himself that Vasily was wrong to call him Vakho sometimes. He is such a wolf as a hero of a hare.

He only got up after a long moment, feeling that sweat is flowing from him like a rushing stream, which was already a clear symptom of something more than a common cold. He remembered to make himself a strong infusion of herbs, honey and garlic as soon as he got to the cave, and to sweat well by the fire. He couldn't afford to be ill now.

And then, almost only from the corner of his eye, he saw that he was being watched.

***

There were six of them. As he previously guessed by examining the tracks. He had not made a mistake, and now he was not at all happy about it.

They stared at it in complete silence, examined the smell, placed in a semicircle, only a few dozen meters away from it. They stood motionless, doing nothing to betray their intentions.

"How could I not notice?" He was angry with himself for approaching so imperceptibly. He panicked that it was all over and he couldn't help but stifled it. He had no time to fear. He had to do something, but not to provoke an attack.

He remembered all of Vasily's remarks sharply, then slowly and cautiously turned to face them.

He quickly calculated that if he ran away, they would be faster and catch him by the time he got to the cave. So this version was out of the question.

He took the arrows from the quiver, holding them with his fingers, and placed one on the bowstring.

"Do not run away, retreat very slowly, showing them ignoring," Vasily's warning sounded in his ears. "They must feel that you are not afraid of them, and they feel fear from a distance. They must feel respect, even though you will be alone. However, when they attack, target the main male wolf and don't miss."

Well, Vasily had a shotgun in mind, and he only had a bow.

"Wait... wait..." It was only now that he realized that he had a Mauser by his waist under the fur coverlet. The fact that he had forgotten about him was blamed on the fever that was overwhelming him. The pistol is not a rifle, but it is better to have than just a bow.

"Concentrate," he repeated to himself. "For now, they are just watching you and clearly examining what's in front of them. It's not an animal, because it's smell deer hide mixed with the juice of a grouse, rather than something else, something like a creature because it moves on two legs. They are cautious, they will not take any chances unless their hunger has clouded their mind. Or maybe," another reminder of Vasily's advice, "one of them has already met a man and knows the sound of a gun?"

He reached under the fur coat with his right hand and pulled out a pistol.

The wolves moved slowly towards him. Taking their time, as if they were sure they would not miss a meal anymore.

He was still standing, though some thought made him run away.

He stabbed the arrows in front of him into the snow for easy reach, the bow beside him, and as they continued, paw by paw slowly approaching, Mauser reacted violently.

The crackle of metal rang out like a gunshot, tearing the silence to shreds.

They stopped in surprise, their mouths stretched out towards him and intensely catching the scent in the air.

It meant they knew the sound of the gun. The only question is what they will decide.

They and he remained motionless for a long time, watching each other. Finally, the male wolf at the front began to move to the side, and a youngster stood in his place.

But they still waited to see if anything would happen after the sound.

Only the mouths stretched more towards him.

Janek wondered if he would keep them, at least for a while, when he abandoned the hunted partridges. This thought of getting rid of food caused an inner anger, which, paradoxically, gave him strength and, with determination, restored his clarity of thinking.

He watched them carefully, trying to read the speech of the taut bodies as they were thinking. But the thought of getting up and running was echoing in head, and she was getting more and more obtrusive.

Male wolf growled and the pack moved forward again.

When they covered a few meters, Janek remembered another advice from Vasily.

He jerked his arms out above him to make him look bigger, made a sound of a howling or a roar from his lungs, and took two steps forward while stamping his feet violently. This is how the bison scared enemies.

The pack stopped and jumped back, but only a few steps. The maneuver also clearly surprised them. This "something" was not afraid and warned.

Janek stomped for a moment, then slowly, step by step began to retreat backwards. He scooped up arrows and a bow, holding a pistol in his right hand, which was unmanageable. Now was to be decided what they were going to do. He deprived them of their self-confidence, but they were hungry and probably will not give up the hunt easily. However, he gained a point for himself. They will not throw the entire pack, but they will still be careful.

Backwards step by step, looking in their direction all the time.

They followed him, keeping a constant distance.

Time lengthened disproportionately and at some point Janek thought that he was going backwards, but as if he was standing still.

Minutes passed, one after another with the careful placement of feet, which was not easy with the forward-only rackets strapped on.

At one point he glanced back. He breathed out. The cave was close now, so close he hadn't expected it. Just a few steps away.

He suppressed the urge to throw himself into her, and that saved him.

The young wolf, walking in front, could not stand the tension, sprang up and threw at Janek.

It seemed to float, barely brushing the snow as it approached its destination quickly.

If the others had done the same, Janek would have had little chance in this clash.

He picked up the pistol and when the wolf was in the air, not more than a few meters from him, he fired aiming at the head.

Once, twice and three times.

The speeding body shuddered as it tried to turn back, then plummeted into the snow, already limp. Only his paws twitched for a moment longer, then he stopped.

Janek immediately moved the weapon towards the next one, but the rest, clearly surprised by what had happened, stopped and turned their heads towards the main male wolf. This moment he stood still, as if analyzing the situation, then slowly turned his rump to the mysterious and dangerous animal and, taking his time, began to walk away.

Others followed him.

***

Before returning to the cave, he skinned the wolf, leaving the rest outside. He did it on purpose. The fur might be of use to him, although he did not have good conditions to tanning it as in the summer, but he mainly wanted the remains of the carcass. The meat will surely disappear very quickly, and the small predators that come for it, attracted by the fresh scent, will trample all traces of its rockets.

Outside, he also tanned partridges so as not to clutter the cave.

With only his will, he lit a fire, put a cauldron of water on it and threw pieces of meat and herbs into it to make broth. He had to eat something full-bodied so as not to throw honey and garlic on an empty stomach, and these were demanded by the body, clearly being digested more and more by some disease.

And then he rested in the lair, waiting for the food to boil, and before he could put his head to the fur well, he doze off into nothingness.

***

He woke up, not knowing how long he had slept.

His head was cracking, he felt a large chunk of something in his throat that made it difficult even for swallowing, and his nose was completely blocked with a runny nose.

He took the ready-made soup off the fire. Its scent was in the air, unable to escape, filling the rooms, suffocating the remnants of clean air. Waiting for the broth to cool down a bit, he went to the exit into the swamp and revealed the exit.

There is no trace left of the wolf and partridges, only the numerous traces of the predators that feasted here and the blood that soaked into the snow.

He took a moment to savor the crisp air, its coolness flowing pleasantly over his sweaty face, then closed the exit again. He did not want to tempt fate.

He came back, gulped down his soup, ate the meat, and then nibbled on it with garlic and honey.

He lay down again. The eyes closed themselves.

***

He dreamed some nightmares, woke up, drank some water and fell asleep again.

He was tormented by further nightmares, terrifying images full of monstrosities, interspersed with the vision of thousands of corpses floating down the river on a caws.

Awake, he opened his eyes, reached for a cup of water with difficulty, took a few sips and fell on his fur to see almost immediately more visions, full of disfigured faces with gouged out eyes. And then more; Headless hulls, ripped breasts, and bellies with entrails. He could smell the sweet, rotting flesh all over the space.

Overhead, against the background of the black clouds, almost merging with them, hovered hundreds of ravens, circling over the carrion, screaming in their own way until the entire sky turned black, cut only by bloody scars of lightning.

***

When he opened his eyes, he felt a little better. From the barely smoldering querns, it had been hours, maybe a whole day, or, most likely, he had slept even longer.

He crawled out of bed with difficulty and stood up. His head immediately felt so dizzy that he had to sit down quickly so as not to fall.

He rested for a moment, gathered his strength and the will, not having the slightest desire to do so, because the body violently protested and refused to exert himself, to get up again and approach the fire. It was only two steps away, and he felt as if he had taken a verst.

He cleared the fire of unnecessary ash. Only two barely hot coals remained. He added small splinters to give him a chance for the fire to return, then sat down beside him and waited, so he was napping. When he smelled fresh smoke, he woke up and added larger twigs, and when they got fire, he covered them with large pieces of wood.

He was dozing again, and when the body felt the warmth emanating from the fire, he put on the pot with the broth, waited for the soup to warm up, poured himself a solid portion, adding pieces of meat.

The stew tasted so good that he made a correction, ate it slower, and when he was done, he covered the fire with logs and with a sigh of relief, he fell back asleep in the lair.

Chapter VII

He woke up a few more times, added wood to the fire, drank water and ate a piece of meat. After he had finished his soup, he put on a new one and continued to sleep.

***

He didn't know how long this cycle of sleep, eating, and recovery lasted.

When he woke up this time he was sore, but not from illness, but from lying on the hard bed for too long. The gathered brushwood in the lair was so trampled with his body that it only gave the illusion of softness.

The disease is gone, but has left a strong weakness. He also felt that it was much cooler in the cave.

He overcame the urge to lie down further and sprang up against what his body was telling him to refuse to leave the lair. At first, the pain in the back of his skull made his head dizzy.

He struggled to balance, leaned against the rock and had to wait a long moment until his body returned to normal and the spots in front of his eyes disappeared.

He forced himself to bend a few times to improve blood circulation. He also tensed the numb muscles as he leaned forward and to the sides, causing another pain.

After such a warm-up, he did not feel better, because immediately the stomach remembered about himself, and the intrusive craving manifested itself in an increasing burning sensation around the upper abdomen and waves of painful intestinal cramps.

He wanted to eat something, but the cauldron was empty and only empty pegs were sticking out where the meat hung.

He knew he had to hunt something down quickly and replenish his meat supplies. Without food, he will not return to full health and form.

But he felt a marked lack of the will to fight for survival, still present some time ago. Common sense dictated going outside, and the whole body going back to the lair. Only somewhere to the side of this struggle did the thought supported by the desire to fill the stomach with something, anything even weed. Can he only make herbal decoction?

He mastered and forced himself to think and plan wisely.

The fire was almost extinct. He repeated the lighting procedure, and once he had obtained the fire, he pulled a few logs and carefully placed them. He chose the wetter ones. It will take some time for the wood to dry, and then the heat will slowly digest it without unnecessary flames and smoke. When he comes back, the cave will be warm again.

He went to the exit from the marsh, opened it slightly and surveyed the area carefully. Nothing disturbed him, so he left a small crevice to create a cug.

He came back and considered taking anything besides the bow. Remembering the adventure with the pack, at first he wanted to take the rifle, but found that this time he did not go too far. And the roar of the shot carries far, so he didn't want to risk it. Someone can hear.

What if you happen to encounter something larger than a tiny bird or small rodent? Bow? It may not be enough. He would take the Mauser with him, of course, although the pistol is not a rifle, but he knocked the wolf down. He noticed the inconsistency of his deliberations at once, but he did not change his mind.

His eyes fell on the primitive javelin he had been working on in his spare time, more to pass the time than to need it. It resembled bear spear, although it was far from the original. He took it in his hands and thought glad that he had done a good job after all. He chose a soaring hornbeam branch on the shaft. The wood was difficult to work with because it was extremely hard. Elm wood was used for the crossbars behind the potential blade, because these were very flexible, and this was needed to stop the pierced body sliding along the spar.

He had never tried it before, because it wasn't a handy weapon to run around in the woods with, and besides, he didn't quite know how to make a blade. Doubts were dispelled by a coincidence when, during one of his trips deep into the forest, he found several rocks with a spring. At the base, the water washes the ground, revealing sand and pieces of flint with characteristic stripes, sharp at the edges like a grandfather's razor. He picked up quite a few of them to pick out the ones that could replace the knife. He was especially pleased with one of them, because nature had created the perfect blade. All that remained was to attach them to the spar. After returning to the cave, he labored for many days, carefully breaking the beginning of the spar, then soaking it for a long time in water, then rubbing it with resin, carefully binding with thin lianas, lubricating again and applying another layer, and finally drying slowly. In total, he obtained a solid weapon, although so far unproven and a bit heavy.

Later, when he got to the old trenches and took a few bayonets with him, he even thought about changing the blade, but he didn't want to. He then got a rifle and put his trust in it. He did not expect bear spear to ever be practically used. Until now.

He broke off his thoughts, aware that he was deliberately leading them with him, to put aside the decision to go outside. "Buck up," he thought.

***

He unveiled the original entrance of the cave, and not without difficulty, because everything was frozen outside.

It was cool outside, but as there was no wind, it was not very penetrating.

He came out masking the entrance, mostly with snow.

He put his feet carefully where there was little white powder, because the temperature had cut his surface into ice lumps all over the place, and he was not sure how thick the top layer was. The question came again if he wasn't leaving too clear traces, and the fear of spotting the cave. He quickly convinced himself that only a good hunter or tracker would spot them, but an ordinary peasant, and among the Bolshevik soldiers, simple peasants and workers predominated, who rather did not walk in the forest and probably did not even venture into the forest.

Dark clouds could be seen between the treetops, heralding imminent snowfall. He had to hurry up.

For a moment he wondered whether to choose the direction towards the river, village, manor or deep into the forest. He chose the latter. There are always fewer traces to be found, if by chance among the ever hungry soldiers one finds one who, however, had to do with a forest and, besides, had to hunt something.

He walked cautiously looking for traces. He came across them over and over, but he couldn't tell which ones were fresh and which were made some time ago.

Hunger made itself felt again with a pain in his gut. He ignored it, trying to occupy his mind with the analysis of the traces.

Where next? Maybe to those lonely rocks with numerous caverns? He was no more than half an hour away from them. There was a chance that some small animals were looking for protection from the cold in the caves.

He moved on, also looking through the branches of the trees to see if he would see a bird. He was also looking for signs of movement in the thick grass. He wouldn't even despise a little bird, not even dreaming of hitting the traces of partridges or black grouses. It reminded him that there was a small lake near the rocks to which he was going, probably frozen now, but it gave him a chance to meet some ducklings, goldeneyes or even white-throated hummingbird he had already seen. He knew they liked to spend the winter here, because they even had enough food in winter.

The hope that something could be hunted improved his mood. He sped up.

The stomach felt like a sharp pain spreading through her entire abdomen again.

The lake was surrounded by peat bogs and numerous streams fell into it - he recalled the topography of the area - so it was a place where there was a chance to meet also capercaillies. He also remembered from his grandfather's stories that the capercaillie searches for water in such an area, because in the stream not all of the water is frozen, and he does not despise the fine gravel, which he swallows to improve digestion. And since there were also mounds of ants in the area, which the birds eagerly fed on in winter, especially their young, he comforted himself that he would not return to the cave empty-handed.

For some time he was walking, not finding any fresh clue, when at one point he caught a sound difficult to interpret, as if violent scuffling combined with screeching and droning.

He stopped listening.

He felt the fear involuntarily that the Bolsheviks had appeared in the forest, that they had found his trail and only waited for them to emerge from the trees and attack him.

He knelt tense, gripping the javelin tighter.

The sound was back.

It's not a human sound.

He breathed as a whine heard him.

Are they wolves again? It wasn't a good idea. Although he had not noticed any trace of a pack so far, the previous adventure did not exclude it, and the hungry wolf can travel several dozen kilometers a day. Today it is gone, tomorrow it suddenly appears penetrating the area, and the next day it is already very far away.

He listened attentively, still not moving, contemplating whether to withdraw or to check what was going on in front of him.

Crouching, he felt the recurrence of an attack of an empty stomach, and a sharp stab spreading not only over his stomach, but further down his back and even reaching his lungs. This restored his thirst for food and reluctance to return empty-handed.

He had to make a decision, he couldn't stay that way any longer.

He rose slowly.

Somewhere ahead there was the sound of scuffling in the snow, as if someone were running breaking frozen grass, constantly repeating itself and mixed up with the whir of an unknown animal.

Sucking below the ribs strengthened the decision. If he did not go further, he would return to the cave even more hungry and weakened. He will move forward and check, but maybe these sounds are just a noise amplified and exaggerated by winter silence. It occurred to him that it might always be a mobile wolverine that has caught something and is now fighting foxes for prey, or even a wolf, which wouldn't be weird either. And if so, he does not need to be afraid, and a spear or even a bow slung over his shoulder are a sufficient weapon against even this agile and formidable creature.

He took a step forward, carefully putting his feet down so that the sound of breaking frozen grasses would not reveal his presence too soon. And then another and another.

Now he was sure, hearing voices in front of him, that it was a fight between two predators, and certainly not only for the prey, but mostly for life. If it were summer, or even spring or fall, one of the parties would give up long ago. But now it was much harder to get food.

There was a screech combined with a whine, followed immediately by a deep, furious roar.

Wolverine doesn't roar like that, neither does the wolf.

He stood undecided, but immediately convinced himself that he too was a predator, so he couldn't back away when he heard noises that were difficult to interpret. If they are struggling, they are weakened and therefore his chances against them are, if not equal, even greater.

He moved decisively forward. The temperature seemed to have dropped and he felt more and more tingling on his face and a chill attacking his fingers and toes. He knew that the weakness of hunger was also a factor.

He passed two grated hornbeams and an elm leaning towards them, the branches of which joined with its neighbors, forming a dense tangle of branches. Below, overgrown junipers grew right next to them, creating a green and white embankment so dense that it would be difficult to overcome if someone thought to tear across the terrain it occupied.

He had to pass by the side, on their edge.

He glanced at the slope of the elm for possible escape up the tree should the need arise.

He lingered a moment longer before moving as a mighty, triumphant roar broke the momentary silence of the forest. It trembled in the air for a moment, modulated by a guttural sound, sweeping the entire space and announcing who was the master and only winner.

Subconsciously, he already knew who had made it, but in desperation caused by hunger and cold, he decided that he would not run away, turn back, and not be overwhelmed by fear. He needs to eat tonight too. "I'm also," he repeated in his mind, "a predator."

He hit a sharply descending bend, climbed the opposite bank and slowly opened the branches of the fallen fir trees that grew here.

The space behind them created a space free of trees, like a mini clearing, only a few meters high, crowned on one side with white snow-caked rocks with a black chasm cut off.

It was a bear's lair.

It was from there that something provoked the bear, the lord of the forest who usually sleeps at this time. And he was the winner.

The battle-torn area was no longer white. The snow feathers were gone, and now it looked more like a field driven by a madman's plow. And it wasn't entirely black either, but a mixture of gray that clearly distinguished patches of dark red gore. Certainly not a bear, but a breathless she-wolf with a bloody, torn abdomen, from which still smoking guts were pouring out. The fact that it was not a male wolf but a she-wolf was evidenced by three small bloodied fur scattered nearby, bear victims. It was in their defense that she attacked a much stronger opponent, regardless of his size, powerful claws, opposing only her agility and fangs that were unable to chew through the thick skin and long hair.

Maybe she provoked him and woke him up by entering the lair, maybe her little, or maybe he woke up alone, as it sometimes happened to replenish the organism demanding water. One thing was for sure, that in front of the lair he found puppies playing and before they managed to react and escape, he killed them, furious that they had interrupted his sleep. The she-wolf had to be nearby, but by the time she could reach the place of the slaughter, the three bloodied furs were already out of breath. And she pounced on the murderer of children, seized by amok, and they are in charge of revenge. And although smaller, her fury had an effect; the bear had a torn mouth, a torn or bitten off nose, and instead of one eye, a burning cavity in the skull.

Now he stood still, exhausted, panting, cradling his head right and left, recovering and shifting from paw to foot. Jan could see why. One of them also suffered and was running aglow. She-wolf did not dedicate her life for nothing, she fought to the end, as if continuing without puppies would no longer make sense to her.

The scent of fresh blood circulated in the air, the stench of rotten grass extracted from under the snow, and the stench of the torn guts of the she-wolf.

Jan moved and the bear stopped. Perhaps he noticed the slight movement, because a torn nose should not signal an unnatural human odor. Whatever the cause, he suddenly froze and stuck his head out in front of him. There was something like a growl, or a snapping of teeth against each other, from the throat.

The animal wasn't sure about the information that gave him his senses. He looked at the she-wolf lying in front of him, then he shifted his eyes to the carcasses of the puppies and raised his head in alarm, trying to sniff. When that was no use, he shook his head, twirling it left, right, and finally like a horse, from top to bottom, making a guttural grunt. Finally he roared, shaking his jaw, repeated, lengthening it in time, and hearing no response, he growled, then suddenly stood on his hind legs and roared again.

He pricked his ears for a moment and looked around to see if his roar would have any repercussions. He continued like this, then dropped on four legs and headed towards the fir trees.

***

Janek froze.

If the bear catches even a speck of his scent, he will not hesitate and will attack with all his fury. He couldn't move, though, and only hoped his scent would dissolve into the stench of the field from the recent battle with the she-wolf.

The bear stopped no more than four human steps in front of the fir trees. He kept trying to catch the scent, but the remnants of his nose wouldn't allow it. His eyesight did not help him much, because he was by nature weak and was based mainly on smell and hearing. But nothing in front of him was moving, and with an obvious effort, he again stood on his two legs and once again with a loud roar, he shouted a summons to the invisible opponent.

Janek tensed up in himself.

This was the moment he had to take advantage of, and quickly. Somewhere in the background lurked the thought that he was risking that no one in his family would go to the bear alone, that the stupid javelin pretending to be bear spear was only a substitute for those in the family house. And most importantly, a flint blade may be hard and sharp, but it does not retain the flexibility of good steel and, when struck badly, it may snap like a match, or its mount simply will not last and will fall apart like a rotten stump.

The beast repeated the roar, starting with a high-pitched tone and ending with a guttural bass, a tone quieter but all encompassing the surroundings.

And he took a hesitant step forward.

Then he rejected considerations.

There was no time for that anymore.

He leapt forward, aiming his blade where he hoped to be a bear's heart. It was his only chance.

He hit his shoulders with all his strength, feeling the flint blade pierce through the thick skin and plunged into the chest of the roaring monster. Almost a fraction of a second later, taking advantage of the fact that the surprised animal froze, bent the spars towards the ground and rested them firmly against the protruding roots of the fir.

For a moment, a very long moment, or maybe it just seemed to him, the bear was motionless, surprised by the attack and the pain in his chest. Time has stopped. Man and animal remained suspended in the void of time, waiting for something that would burst the bubble of space, deciding the fate of one of them.

The roar that escaped from the bear's throat, pain combined with helpless rage, was so powerful that it seemed to Janek that the whole forest shook from it.

The beast tried to knock the javelin out of its chest with his paws, and when he failed, he desperately moved forward, thrusting it even deeper and deeper, until the flint reached his heart, tore it, taking all Mishka's strength, which after a while fell in its body onto the javelin, which broke with a crash.

His body hit the ground with a thud, and after a few convulsions, it went still.

And then there was only silence.

Neither of the paws twitched, no gurgling escaped from the throat, and only bloody gore, leaking more and more from the mouth, formed a dark spot where the mouth had plowed the ground.

Janek waited, panting and taking control of his body trembling with emotion. He knew from Vasily that the bears often pretended to be dead, and when a careless hunter inadvertently approached them, they suddenly attacked.

So he waited a minute, two and more, watching the still body.

But nothing happened.

He plucked the second part of the shaft from the ground and brought it closer to the bear's mouth. He did not react. He stabbed him where the front part had digged into his chest. Nothing too. He swung and hit the head. No reaction.

Now he just breathed out.

He sat down on the ground, feeling how weak he was. The muscles in the arms and legs continued to twitch with emotion, and perhaps with exhaustion. He stared at the dead animal wondering what to do next. Subconsciousness ordered further action, but at the moment he did not have the strength to take it. He closed his eyes, falling half asleep.

When a sharp pain flowed from somewhere deep inside his belly, he woke up and struggled to get up.

The first snowflakes were already spinning between the trees. It seemed a tone brighter, but the low gray clouds were a harbinger of an impending snowstorm. He waved his hands to warm up and pulled out a knife. He had to skin the bear quickly, cut out the meat and fat. Such a second opportunity to get such a large amount of food will not happen a second time. Vasily taught him skinning during the hunt, but they were usually smaller animals, and sometimes deer, and even wild boars, but never bears.

He set to work.

It took him longer than expected to peel off the skin and then cut off the flesh and fat. When he finished he was panting hard, barely keeping to his feet. He wrapped everything in fur, tied it with bear intestines, and placed it all on two skids made of branches. He tried to pull the heavy package. It was not easy, but he was satisfied with the work done. Will do the trick.

He looked at the remnants that were left. He wanted to quickly return to the cave, but common sense persuaded that you shouldn't leave so much meat for the inhabitants of the forest. By the next day, even the smallest dice would have been carefully chewed.

He overwhelmed himself, took out a knife and divided what was left into pieces, then tied it with intestines and hung them individually on the branches of trees. When he finished, he didn't have the strength to go to the cave.

Before he sat down, his eyes fell on the dead she-wolf. Before he thought he couldn't do it, he walked over to her and skinned her. It was easier than skinning the Mishka. And the extra fur he will definitely use.

He threw them on a prepared makeshift sled, picked up the ends of the branches, and some movement was registered in the eye.

He quickly grabbed a part of the spear with the blade and turned around, ready to repel an attack from any potential animal.

No movement in the clearing. He must have mind slip, and the strained nerves had caused hallucinations. But he was still watching his surroundings vigilantly. He saw nothing and was about to bend down to grab the shaft when the mind registered something again. It was already so dark that he had to strain his eyes to find out that they were not hallucinations.

"Could some puppy survive," crossed his mind.

He studied the carcass for a moment, then walked towards it. When he took a few steps, the fur moved and showed little teeth.

It wasn't a dead puppy. It was the fourth wolf child who had somehow escaped death and probably had been sewn up and scared under one of the bushes so far. The bear didn't see him, and neither did he. Now he knew why she-wolf had fought so much with

Mishka to the end. For the life of this little one who now cuddled up to his dead brother or sister and trembled with fear.

He came closer. The puppy curled up, but showed its teeth.

Janek crouched down. He had to make another decision. Leave puppy or maybe take it with you. In the manor house he liked the dogs, wandering with them in the fields and going on trips to the woods. It was a wolf though, not a dog. Admittedly, Vasily had heard stories of how small puppies were extracted from wolf pits in the Caucasus and domesticated to fight their kinsmen as an adult to protect the herds, but it was somewhere far away, and he had not heard of similar cases here.

He looked at the quivering fur and made up his mind. With a quick movement, he grabbed it by the skin on the back, then pressed it against his chest. He skinned she-wolf, so her scent was still fresh, though probably mixed with the bear's blood. The puppy tried to pull away at first, but later, when it caught the smell of his mother, it calmed down and began to softly complain.

"Relax, kid, I won't hurt you," he said to him softly and gentle.

He carried it to the sleigh and put it under the she-wolf's skin. The puppy was not going to run away. The smell of she-wolf calmed him.

"Maybe I got a friend," Janek muttered to himself, who felt that today something had changed in his life. He has overcome fear, his own weaknesses, and a bear and will have a companion in lonely days.

Chapter VIII

When the tension associated with the meeting with the bear was over, the energy that had been driving him passed away with it. He was still proud of what he had done, but the inner complacency was different, and the condition of the muscles, which showed reluctance to any movement with every movement.

He was recovering at a slower pace than he had originally imagined, and he would have wanted it. The fever hadn't come back, but he felt a general breakdown inside, showing itself to be dull and not even a hint of the old vigor.

***

The wolf was slowly getting used to the new place.

On the first day, he slept on the skin of she-wolf and moaned in his sleep. In the morning, Janek chopped meat and served it on a piece of leather. At first he did not even glance at it, but after a while he carefully sniffed, finally overwhelmed himself, ate, washed down with water and, twisting into a bagel, fell asleep.

The next day the procedure was repeated. This time, however, he no longer showed his teeth while he was serving the food, but followed closely what Janek was doing. Once he saw the food in front of his nose, he demonstratively turned his mouth the other way, for a while, then slowly got up and pretended that he was doing it just to stretch his bones. He was spinning around his own tail, he was walking around the lair as if looking for a new place to lay down, and when Janek did not react, he approached the dish, sniffed it carefully and ate it without hesitation.

Janek wondered if such a toddler was still drinking his mother's milk and if it wasn't too early for meat. However, he had no choice, he would not get milk from nowhere. Besides, he was probably too big for milk, because he judged that he was probably several months old, so the taste of the meat is not unknown to him. He never asked Vasily about such puppies. He was no longer a tiny glomerulus, but he was still far from being an adult.

The next day and the next, the ritual was repeated. At first, wolf cub pretended that he was not interested in the food being offered to him, and when he saw that Janek was not interested in what he was going to do, he eagerly jumped up to her and only looked carefully if he was suddenly taken away from him.

Until one time there was an unexpected breakthrough.

When Janek woke up in the morning, he felt something soft against his face. It was a wolf nestled against his neck, sound asleep and clearly pleased with his new place. The barrier is gone. Now he just had to deal with his upbringing. He remembered Vasily's stories that the wolf would never become a dog, but when he was accustomed from an early age to such treatment as is done with domesticated quadruped puppies, the evil part of Vakho's nature would disappear, or at least be minimized. And he will become not only a faithful companion on expeditions, but also a very intelligent helper.

But will he manage to train him without any experience?

***

The days passed slowly, without special events, divided into sleeping, eating and playing with a new companion. At first, the wolf cub took the caresses with distrust, not really knowing what they meant. He was cringing, his ears twitched, his eyes clearly worried, but when he realized that it might be something pleasant, he quickly liked it.

He played, jumped, chased his own tail, and accosted Janek, inviting him to play, nibbled on wood, slept and played again. The barrier of distrust disappeared irretrievably and he probably treated him like a mother who strangely changed shape, but was still caring, cared for him, gave him food and a sense of security.

At one point, while playing, Janek noticed that it was not a male, but a female, which surprised him a bit, because he was somehow strangely convinced inside that it was a male puppy. And only then did he realize that he hadn't given her a name, and that he had to be called somehow. Name, but what? At first he wanted to name her Vakho, which seemed natural to him, but quickly changed his mind. He had the idea that the cave was his living room, so maybe Salun? It sounded pretentious and somehow silly. He decided to sleep with the idea. That same night he dreamed something, he did not remember what, but he remembered the name of the Queen of Sheba that scrolled through the bows.

And the wolf cub became Sheba.

When he first spoke them, the puppy looked at him carefully, shook her head when she heard them again and probably wondered what was going on. She checked if it was not an invitation to play, jumping joyfully, standing on her paws and licking Janek's face, but she quickly realized that it was something else. She changed tactics and kept checking. She brought her skin, on which she got food, then she torn a pine bough, and when she realized it was not it, she lay down on her back, showing her stomach and wagging her tail furiously as if in apology that she did not understand.

In the end she caught it, probably sensing the intentions in Janek's voice more than the word itself, and as soon as "Sheba" was said, she move her ears and ran quickly. However, this was only the first step in learning. Another, perhaps more difficult, could be responding to orders for a specific behavior.

Janek started with the simplest, such as "sit down", "lie down", and "charge", "watch" and a few others. Sheba liked the "by the leg" order the most. As they circled the cave, she stared at him happily, punishingly following the rhythm of his steps, wagging her tail happily and treating it as another game. The next step was to translate verbal commands into hand gestures. And she caught it almost immediately, without any difficulty. But the real test of science was to be the first step outside.

He chose the exit from the marshes and the lake. The one on the main side was devoid of any traces, while the latter was full of traces.

The snow surprised Sheba.

She sniffed the space distrustfully, not wanting to leave the cave. And when she did that, she put her nose in the white fluff, tasted it with her tongue and only after tasting it for a while, she realized that the new environment could be a field for another fun. She started to run, wallow happily in it, mutter something to herself, rush to Janek, inviting him to run together, head diving and sniffing fiercely, intrigued by many, unknown to her smells.

As she walked away, he called her and she ran quickly. She complied with other orders with as much joy as in the cave. And when it started to pour fine snow, flakes swirling in the air, she looked at Janek with a silent question if she could go away, and when he allowed, she jumped, chasing individual petals and snapping her teeth in the air to catch them, she accelerated and braked sharply, clearly happy. Every now and then the trail intrigued her, she followed him, and when she realized that she had moved too far away from Janek, she quickly returned and jumped again, catching snowflakes in her mouth.

They didn't go very far that day, but it was just a test of what the cave lessons had done. They spent no more than two hours outside. When they got back, Sheba was fed, and when she finished her meal, she didn't feel like having any fun. She quickly lay down comfortably on her skin and fell asleep with a sleep so hard that when Janek quietly called her, she only opened her sleepy eyes, and when he did not repeat the call, she immediately closed them and continued to sleep.

Janek, having nothing to do, once again reached for the correspondence taken over from the Bolsheviks. Who were those ordered to locate and kill? Where did they operate? What has changed in the world, what is the new balance of power created, what power do these Bolsheviks have? Unanswered questions that intrigued him more and more. Perhaps, he thought, the people in the village know the answers to some of them, because after all, they deal with soldiers on a daily basis. However, if he goes there, don't the traces reveal his hiding place? Do the Bolsheviks hunt?

***

The next few days they went out together, venturing further and further.

Janek was closely following the tracks, fearing that he would notice wolf and human footprints, which could be even more dangerous. He also wanted to see in practice if Sheba remembered difficult orders, including "attack", spoken verbally and with a gesture in the form of a fist and sharply stretched fingers. The command was difficult because the direction of the hand was pointing to Sheba. In the cave she understood them, but here, outside, where there was so much new to her, he did not know how she would react and whether, regardless of him, she would throw herself at the first game she encountered.

He came across a herd of capercaillies only after a week, when they moved far away from the cave and reached the frozen lake. Right next to it, the dug up mound of ants was the first trace of them, and the second was ice on the edge of the stream that flowed into the lake. Sheba, feeling the birds, was clearly trembling all over her body, every now and then glancing at Janek with a silent question, what is it, what to do. She was all about rushing forward and checking the leads.

They plunged into the forest on clear, fresh tracks. They didn't have to go far to find the herd. It was sitting in a small clearing, only several meters long, half buried in fresh powder.

Sheba was standing by Janek's leg, sniffing the scent of chanterelles, raising her head silently asking what to do.

He held her for a long time to see if she would remain penalized.

The birds have not noticed them yet.

He showed Sheba to keep down and she lay down, trembling, awaiting further orders. And when he stretched his fingers pointing at the herd, in a split second she turned into a real lightning. She literally burst into the air and, barely touching the snow, dashed towards the herd. The birds, the largest of which, the males, were as big as the good-looking geese, were the first to step out of the snow and straighten their black-feathered heads, necks, and rumps, twirling their yellow, curved beaks, frightened to the sides. The smaller females reacted a little later, showing a different coloration, dark brown and fawn imitating dry grass. Similarly, the young ones, not really knowing what to do, scattered to the sides.

Sheba, not much larger than the males, attacked the closest one, gritting her teeth against his throat. She jerked, looked at Janek for a moment, and when no order was given, she took the next one with one jump, and then she did the same with the two others.

"Leave it!" Janek threw at her, not sure if she would hear and react in the heat of the fight.

She was already flying to another one when the order arrived. She pressed the bird only to the snow and froze.

"Let go!"

Another second and Sheba, with obvious reluctance, opened her mouth and released the bird. This stunned moment shook his head and brown crop, then mobilized himself and began to run away. Sheba looked longingly at Janek, hoping that he would change his mind, but he repeated the order with a gesture and summoned her to him. She hesitated, looked again in the direction where the birds had run away, then joyfully ran up to him.

He praised her, more happy than she was that she had passed the exam. She leapt with two legs on his chest and smugly licked his face happily, then a quiet, satisfied howl came out of her throat. First time.

He sinned the capercaillies on the spot, and then set off on his way back. Fed their entrails, Sheba happily circled him, making regular circles and occasionally signaling that she had found new leads. And when he did not accept the call, she ran on, panting happily with her tongue out, for it was her day, the moment of initiation as a hunter.

***

They went hunting together every day for the next few days, and now he found out what kind of helper he had. She felt the forest better and better, and awoke to her true hunter nature and to her ancestral senses.

Sheba had always warned him in advance that they had some game in front of them. She paused taut and looked at him if he noticed, then pointed her mouth in the direction.

He, too, had to learn her body language.

It was she who found the rabbits he had not noticed, but which were rummaging in the bushes. As soon as he showed that she was supposed to hunt, she jumped into the bushes and came back satisfied with herself, dragging the sturdy king laboriously.

When he heard the sound of hooves in the distance, she was ready to give chase too, but this time he refused to let her go. She was clearly disappointed, but obeyed.

The whole forest was covered with snow, hardened in the frost and only sprinkled with fresh rainfall. It shows clear traces of many animals that had to come out of their hiding places to get food. This dispelled his concerns about whether he would be able to get fresh food during the winter, and that for Sheba's sake he needed much more now.

As they passed the small litter trampled by the larger animals, the bushes in front of them jerked violently and parted. Two dungeons appeared on the path, as surprised as he was.

He froze, because the boar is no joke in winter. And the sight of the dungeons is almost certain that they will attack.

One was clearly older, the other was younger. They froze, and their brown fur, covered with snow, trembled slightly. They began to whistle nervously, pulling their snouts forward and taking in the scent strongly. They probably couldn't identify him, and the smells coming to them were deceptive.

The fact that he had soaked up the scent of the cave probably saved him from an immediate charge.

At first he couldn't tell if they were alone or in the company of others, but after a while he knew the answer. Snow poured from the bushes and a dozen piglets appeared behind the females. They sensed that something was happening and immediately stopped, tassel the stubby tip of the tail almost vertically, stretching it like little antennae.

A ripple rippled through the sows' bodies, a muscle spasm that could only mean one thing, attack.

Janek suddenly wondered whether to withdraw at once, without haste, giving way to the field, or perhaps not to reflect and quickly take the scratching post back, hiding behind the nearest tree, without waiting for the charge. Because the fact that they would rush to him in defense of the piglets was more than certain. It was just a matter of seconds.

At the same time, he cursed himself for not maintaining the vigilance so necessary in his situation.

The sow was the first to move forward, though not as surely as is the custom of the exasperated old wild boar. The smell of him disliked her and urged her to be careful.

And then it happened.

Sheba jumped out from behind, slightly to the side of the place where he was standing, so far rummaging in the bushes somewhere in the back.

It was too late to give her any order.

She braked on stiff legs in front of Janek, and a menacing, hoarse growl emerged from her throat.

The boars braked sharply, surprised by the appearance of the wolf.

It was no longer just a strange animal with an even weirder smell, but a concrete enemy, a forest killer to be feared. Maybe not as big as them, but its scent was the highest warning in the forest and an order to escape.

The sow snorted, stopped by the subconscious force and at the same time the fear that had overcome nature, almost instantly turned and threw herself into the thicket, forcing the younger sow and the piglets to do the same.

For a moment you could still hear the beat of hooves and the ever quieter sound of fleeing wild boars.

And the original stillness reigned around again.

Sheba stood taut for a while, then relaxed and ran to Janek, tucking her mouth under his hand and demanding praise. And now he felt sweat trickling down his back and his legs tremble uncontrollably.

***

The following days were spent on trips to more and more distant areas. The forest lived its life, and Sheba grew fast, became brave and they got on better and better with Janek.

There was no shortage of meat. Janek brought grouse from each outing, but more and more often he caught himself thinking that he had to check what was going on in the manor and in the countryside, whether something had changed and how especially the peasants were able to cope with the winter, since they had to support the entire squadron of Bolshevik soldiers.

When he decided to go out, a snowstorm came, and the heavy rains lasted over a week. After that, the dark sky, hanging almost above the treetops, turned pale blue, the wind blew the clouds somewhere, and the sun took over the world. Pale at first, but occasionally bursting with heat that melted the top layers of snow, coating them with a silvery coating. And then, unexpectedly, winter let everyone know again with all its might that it had not left yet and was sprinkling wet and heavy snow again, and after the next days only light, circling in the air like a down eiderdown ripped in the wind.

This interlacing continued for a few more days, after which the weather normalized, the sun showed only occasionally and for a short time.

Then he decided to go for a trip, which made Sheba especially happy, who was clearly fed up with sitting in the cave. She fell outside happy, diving into fresh snowdrifts and sniffing for traces of animals.

He directed his first steps towards the manor. Breaking through the snowdrifts was not easy, but the rockets helped, but not always working where the powder was fresh and did not freeze.

At the forest line, he carefully scanned the foreground looking for human traces. He did not find it, which convinced him that no one was trying to venture into the forest. This, however, wondered why the soldiers did not, and neither did the peasants, because, he considered, they probably did not have too much food, unless the Bolsheviks were supplied with supplies. He had to check it out.

He resigned from the further journey to the manor, fearing that he would leave traces too fresh and that light snow would not cover them quickly. He turned towards the village, and when he reached the edge of the orchard sleeping in the white buffer zone, he chose a place for observation, not visible from a distance, under tall bushes covered with a thick white quilt. He crawled underneath, pushed out the unnecessary snow on one side and through the window he created he carefully surveyed the countryside through his binoculars.

Nothing happened for an hour. Nobody left the huts outside as if the village was asleep. He distinguished only huts with smoke rising from their chimneys and those as if no one lived in them. He was tempted to check it out, but common sense prevailed and he continued, growing more and more bored that nothing was happening.

After some time, from the hut, where he had previously seen the propaganda slogan displayed, two soldiers came out, turned a corner and peed, and then returned inside. Now he noticed the snow-cleared area in front of the entrance. He turned the glass towards the other huts. To the place where smoke rose from the chimneys, it was similar; a few meters ahead, leveled terrain, packed snow and drifts of dug paths leading to one larger one in the direction of the far manor.

"What about the peasants?" He wondered, rejecting the thought that they had been murdered. They were needed by the Bolsheviks for cleaning work, but probably no one worried about their condition, even the wood was not taken care of, as evidenced by the dead chimneys.

He lay there, thinking about everything, planning some actions and dismissing them as unreal. He wondered which hut Alik might be in, where Joshua lived, probably not in the family inn, over which the smoke from the chimney was rising, and which of the huts was now occupied by the salesman Danylo Wolosynchyk.

He was about to retreat when a woman came out of the hut without smoke, scooped snow into the vessel and quickly returned inside. This confirmed his earlier presumption that the peasants were fine, but their condition is probably not the best, because the chill outside and the lack of food had to do their job.

***

He didn't come back to the cave. Being in the fresh air was doing him good, and so was Sheba, joyfully patrolling the area and circling it in its bends. From time to time she stopped, showed the direction where an animal should be, and when he did not react, she continued circling, but did not chase.

They walked around the cave in a large arch, going out into the frozen swamps and further towards the place where the forest ended and the steppe began. It took a long time, but he did it with joy, feeling tired in his legs, but also remembering where the snow fell the most, where the tracks cross, and instinctively looking for human traces.

He was coming to a place where the forest had thinned as Sheba growled softly, unlike usual, signaling a large animal.

He took the Winchester off his shoulder. "Could it be wild boars again, or maybe wolves?" It flashed through his head, and the laziness on foot and with the weather disappeared quickly. This time the anxiety that accompanied him during the previous meetings did not arise, but rather the curiosity. The rifle in hand gave confidence, although somewhere in the depths of the subconscious came the standard question whether a possible shot could be heard in a distant manor or in the countryside.

He was looking at Sheba, and she was sniffing the air strongly, raising her head high, and even from time to time standing on two paws to better catch the scent floating higher. She wasn't sure what she was feeling, it was clearly visible in her, because she changed places every now and then, but this time she was only walking away a few steps. Finally she caught the direction, froze, showing it with her mouth, and waited for Janek's order.

He chambered, but the animal the wolf sensed did not approach, and probably did not move away. Against all reason, he decided to find out what it was and why Sheba was acting a little different from what she usually did. She did not show anxiety, on the contrary, she was intrigued by the new fragrance. He ordered her to walk by foot and step by step they headed for the clump of trees and bushes growing in the foreground of the forest line, because Sheba had indicated this place. At first glance, there was no indication that there was anything inside; no visible footprints on the snow covering them, no movement, no sound.

They walked a few steps from the clump.

Then a soft sound came from it, like hoofing on a hard ground.

The animal probably sensed them, understood that they were approaching and reacted nervously.

Janek must have already known what he had in front of him, although it seemed almost impossible to him. He remembered the characteristic stamping of the front legs, the protest that showed that he didn't like something, that the animal didn't accept something.

It had to be a horse.

No other ungulates, deer, roe deer, or wild boar responded like this. But where does the horse come from? Or maybe - it suddenly occurred to him - it was a lurking soldier who had spotted him from a distance, hid to suddenly attack? Suddenly, another sound came to the original sound, resembling a sharp flap of its tail on the sides. Now he was sure it was definitely a horse, and it was exasperated, unsure of those who approached. And if... It occurred to him that the scent of Sheba, dominating his scent, could have such an effect on any animal whose natural instinct is fear of predators.

He had to check it, find out, he could no longer stand still and deliberate endlessly whether it was as he suspected or otherwise, without making any movement.

He ordered the she-wolf to remain in place, which she did not like, and he began to circle the tuft looking for a place where the animal could get inside. Everywhere the snow thickly covered the bushes and the low-hanging branches of trees, but in one place the layer was disturbed and only fresh fluff, the one from the last rainfall, the layer of which was still not thick enough, suggested that something had passed this way some time ago.

His hands tightened on the rifle. He parted the branches and, ignoring the falling snow, cautiously moved forward. At the same time, he listened to the sounds. Now there was silence, no hoof pounding or tail slapping on the sides.

He must have been heard by now, but that's something, that horse, if right, stayed where it was. One step forward, a fraction of a second to catch a movement and another, stop and then forward again.

He had traveled a few meters when, through less frequent bushes and branches here, he saw an animal.

It stood still, as if to hide its presence in this stillness.

It was indeed a horse. Severely scared, unsure of his fate and, judging by the sunken sides, for a long time without proper food.

"Sewek, good horse, do not be afraid," he said these words softly so as not to scare him.

He recognized him right away. It was him. As the other horses departed, this one had to stay waiting for his master's return.

Something in Janek's soul hissed with joy, but also with regret. That was why he let the horses go free to give them a chance for survival. In the forest, he thought then, there was no place for them, and no food. It was especially difficult for him to part with his horse, but then he considered the decision rational for both of them. And now fate played a trick on him, and Sewek's attachment surprised him so much that he did not know how to react and only repeated with a lump in his throat: "Sewek, Sewek, Sewek..."

The horse was still standing with his back to him, motionless, only his ears twirling in all directions that he could hear and analyze. The initial rapid movement of them had stopped, and now he only clipped mute, clearly calming down. At one point, he snorted softly, screamed, and slowly began to turn to Janek.

They stood there no more than three meters away, looking into each other's eyes, then the horse took a step forward, then another and another. He recognized him. It was evident from all his behavior. In those large, dark brown eyes, Janek noticed, or maybe it was just an illusion, a mute reproach, that he had left him alone for so long.

Sewek took one more step, until his mouth almost touched him and then his lips delicately nibbled at Janek's face.

He reached out and began stroking his head, then over his neck, and again over his head. The horse screamed, this time louder and happier, and then tucked his head under Janek's arm, happy that his master had been found.

***

Convincing Sewek that the wolf was not a danger was difficult. He tried to turn his back to Sheba all the time, even kicked a few times and was still nervous. He was afraid and Janek knew why. His rump had a wound that was not completely healed. Only one animal could do that, a wolf. The fact that the horse survived the clash could only be explained by the fact that it did not come into contact with the entire pack, but a single individual, perhaps strongly weakened, perhaps already old or very young.

Likewise, Sheba, seeing the unknown creature next to her master, didn't quite know how to react. Something told her she was safe, and at the same time she couldn't be neutral. So she circled because it was the first time she had seen such a large animal. Perhaps this, as well as the fact that Janek was speaking quietly to him, and in a clearly friendly tone, made her finally ostentatiously ignore him, which at the same time partially calmed Sewek.

***

Where to hide him and how to feed him - Janek kept wondering, not finding any good idea. He did not want to leave the horse to himself again, although the thought flashed through his mind that only such a solution was rational.

Eventually he came up with a half way out. The area around his house was blocked off before the snowfall with various thorny plants, although only possible access paths and with people in mind. Now he decided to use it.

When they reached the vicinity of the cave, he searched for a not far off spot among the trees where the fall of the fallen ash and its vast roots now sticking out in the air formed a natural wall. He remembered that such places were often used by deer and elks, and even wild boars to breed their young. It took him a long time to construct the remaining walls and roof, supplement them with thorny branches of bushes, and mask the whole thing with snow.

The work was completed in the middle of the night. Just in time, because the first, sleepy petals began to fall from the dark sky. He was so tired now that he could barely stand on his feet. The horse, led inside, remained calm. Now all that was left to do was get him food, but where, he had no idea of it.

He blocked the entrance to the makeshift stall and returned to the cave, exhausted. He wanted to calmly consider this new problem, but his exhaustion prevailed and he fell asleep and sat down in the lair.

Chapter IX

He dreamed something, but he couldn't remember the details. Only one, a painting from the trenches and an open shelter where he got so many useful items, including the Winchester. After all, there was a bag of grain, considered by him at the time to be completely useless. But now he was more valuable to him than if he had obtained another rifle. Sewek may not get the hay, but it was better than grass shoved out from under the snow.

Satisfied, he quickly prepared a modest breakfast. And then the horse went. There was a joyful neighing at the sight of him. Sheba, just in case, did not go inside, but when he was leading Sewek outside, she started wagging her tail against nature, like a dog. The horse only glanced at her, carefully studying her behavior, but this time he showed no concern. Apparently, he also decided that the young wolf was not a danger, especially since the master was nearby and showed a clear sympathy for the predator.

Now he congratulated himself on the little bit of sentiment that he had taken the horse's saddle, his saddle, to the cave.

He saddled Sewek, who took it very calmly, even with joy. And then he led him by the bridle through the forest, not wanting to tire the animal, because he was weak and so thin that he wondered whether to get on it at all.

He took the longer path before reaching the edge of the forest. Here the snow was hardened by the wind and the track was close, so he hoped the horse's hoof marks would not be noticeable. Besides, soldiers probably drove along the road, leaving reflections in the snow with those left by the sleigh.

He still didn't get in, guiding him for a while, until he got to where he decided to turn, because the snow was packed hard here, creating a hard shell slicked off by gusts of breeze. The fine fluff that had fallen all night was now blown from place to place, effectively masking every trace.

The trenches had changed since the last time he was here, and it took him a long time to recognize where the officer's shelter was hiding. Now the whole thing was covered with mounds and snow mounds, winded snowdrifts and leveled places where, until recently, trenches had been carried out.

The entrance was frozen over and he was getting tired again trying to get in. He was sweating when he finally revealed the entrance. He left the horse outside with the wolf. There was silence inside, and the darkness was lit only by the glow emanating from the entrance. He did not intend to be here long, although the peace and quiet urged him to rest and breathe after work.

He found a bag of grain, pulled it outside, masked the entrance again, and poured the grain into the panniers he had prepared. Sewek felt the food, because he was nibbling at it with his lips, demanding something. He only gave him two handfuls so that the horse's cramped stomach would not suffer from the excess of new food.

The wind had ceased, a pale sun emerged from behind the clouds, and the whole area in its rays began to sparkle with sharp flashes of light glaring at the eyes.

He had done the task and now he wondered whether to go back now or try to go further. The second thought was tempting him, because he was fed up with hiding in the woods, and the ignorance of what was happening in the region tormented him more and more.

A dozen or so versts to the east was the medium-sized village of Малинів, called the Monkey by the locals. It had about two hundred inhabitants. It belonged, like several others, to Konstantin von Mershejdt, a former tsarist officer, decorated for the January Uprising. The previous owners, the Demidecki family, were driven to Siberia. There was an inn, a large farm with stables, a large granary and a small manor house where a tenant, a nondescript Bekir Tarkowskij, lived, about whom he heard from his grandfather that he did not love both Ukrainians and Poles living in the village. Just what it will do for him. The bad side of snow was that he couldn't hide anywhere from the view from afar, and a possible escape from the Bolsheviks, who probably had well-kept horses in view of the possibilities of the emaciated Sewek, was more of a wishful thinking than reality. But were the Red Army horses really well looked after? Winter probably took its toll on the Bolsheviks as well. The thought comforted him.

He decided. He got on the horse. Sewek snorted happily. The rider's weight did not bother him. Which didn't mean he should push him. He felt the joy of being on the horse's back, but he didn't rush him, walking slowly, enjoying the moment. Sheba rummaged making large circles around them, checking the tracks visible only to herself, as pleased as the horse.

***

After some time he got off the saddle so that Sewek rested. The sun was still shining, and the rays reflected off the snow made it warm.

He walked happily, inhaling the frosty air, surrendering to the feeling of joy, not thinking about anything concrete, only instinctively scanning the surroundings and the distant horizon, or noticing any movement.

At one point, running Sheba stopped. Something clearly disturbed her. She got up back paws and tried to catch the top scent. She growled and ran to Janek signaling that she would feel something, but she was not sure what it was.

The laziness faded away at once.

He took out the binoculars.

There was a dark spot at the edge of the road's end.

He couldn't see well yet, but he quickly led the horse behind a large snowdrift and summoned Sheba. All he had to do now was wait, following the movement of an unknown but constantly approaching point. And this slowly became more and more visible, and it didn't take long for him to make out the details. It was a sleigh surrounded by two riders. For a moment he wondered if they might have noticed him too, but decided they didn't. He took his rifle from the olstra and chambered. He just had to wait now, he couldn't go anywhere further, because they would surely see such a move even from a distance.

So he waited patiently as the others grew closer and closer.

When they were no more than a few hundred meters, he could already tell that there was only one man sitting on the horse-sledge and, unlike the riders, he was not a soldier. The others wore sheepskin coats and fur hats, while the latter was dressed more than modestly, clearly chilled in a thin coat that did not suit winter. He sat huddled as if trying to save some of the warmth he had left.

When they approached the snowdrift that covered Janek, one of the horsemen, he noticed it now, drank from the bottle he held in his hand, and then gave it to the other soldier. He guessed it was vodka and they were sharing it while shouting something at the coachman. When he did not react, the soldier rode closer to him, grabbed something from him, and when the hauler did not react, he took his leg out of the stirrup and kicked him. The body tilted limply, then straightened with difficulty at the command of the soldier. He laughed happily, took the bottle from his companion and drank a lot.

That moment, when the coachman straightened up to curl up in himself again, was enough.

Janek recognized him right away. He had no cap on his head, he was changed in his face, but it was him.

Alik.

Suddenly all the nonsensical plans he had made in the cave to contact his friend came back, which had nothing to do with the possibility. Until now, he had been convinced that the villagers did not leave the village that they were sitting in huts starving from hunger and cold, used only for services for soldiers. Now it turned out otherwise. And at the same time, for a split second, he saw pictures of those murdered in the village of Zarubynci and the Pohorecki corpses.

"What to do?" He thought for a moment, unable to make up his mind, and at the same time felt his anger and hatred grow in him.

When the soldier driving closer to the sledge shouted something and approached Alik again, and he did not react, pulled out his whip and lashed it at the coachman, he decided. He no longer thought about the consequences of the intervention. He jumped on Sewek, squeezed the rifle tighter and rode out of the snowdrift.

Drunken vodka slowed the reaction of the soldiers. Busy with the conversation, they did not notice Janek until he was at a distance of not more than a dozen meters. The sun was behind him, and perhaps its rays also contributed to the delayed reaction of the Bolsheviks. When they finally noticed him, they fell silent, pulling the reins of the horses sharply and stopping in place. They were clearly surprised by the sight of Janek and they did not know how to react. They were confused and surprised by the clothes of an unknown rider, dressed in an unknown military jacket. Or maybe one of them had dealt with an Austrian uniform before and now his memory was making up for it.

Janek came a little closer and stopped Sewek.

He didn't know what to do next. Disarm and let go or wait for them to react.

He hasn't made his decision yet. He hesitated and left her to the further development of the situation.

They still just stared at him, and the moment dragged on.

"Where are you going?" Finally, he asked a short question in Polish, and when they did not understand, he repeated it in Russian.

They were still silent, and the only answer was a shrug, and the former shrugged, which prompted Alik to understand that they were not dealing with theirs.

The sledge moved away, but at some point began to slow down. The horses harnessed to them, not feeling the presence of those on which the Bolsheviks were riding, also stopped. Alik on the coachbox did not move, did not even turn to see what was happening. He was probably so cold he didn't care what the reason for the stop was.

Sheba appeared at the rear of the soldiers' horses. She did not come near, clinging to the ground, but the animals sensed her and began to twitch their legs restlessly.

The tension in the air grew from second to second. One side had to make the first move, and each side waited for what their opponent would do.

Janek involuntarily looked at the road to see if other riders would appear on the horizon. And what he saw, a small black spot, sped up his decision. Someone was riding the track, although for now, without the binoculars, he could not see if it was a single rider or several.

Just then he noticed, beyond the horizon, black smoke rising up into the sky. At first, it was only slightly gray, indistinct, like a random cloud, but more and more distinct as the seconds pass.

The soldiers tried to calm the horses, more and more nervous under the scent of the wolf lurking behind, throwing their rumps to the sides and snorting anxiously.

In the end, the first one, tightening the reins tightly, forced the horse to calm down. Being turned sideways to Janek, with his right invisible hand he quickly reached under his puffer jacket. He drew his revolver and fired a shot almost immediately, without aiming. He didn't have time to aim and the bullet flew out somewhere.

The second time he did not manage to pull the trigger, because Janek, noticing his nervous movement, immediately picked up Winchester and when the latter fired, he also shot him straight in the chest. And immediately he aimed the barrel at the other, who had already pulled the rifle off his shoulder, repeated it and before he could pull the trigger, another bullet from the rifle knocked him off the horse.

Everything happened in literally seconds, though time seemed to have stopped and stretched into minutes.

He checked whether they were moving and at the same time reached for the binoculars.

A small dark spot turned into four riders. They were still more than a verst away, but suddenly they stopped, looking back. They, too, must have noticed the smoke probably hovering over the distant, but not visible from here, Malinova. Or maybe they heard something too. Suddenly they turned back and after a while they disappeared below the horizon.

He breathed out, though he still felt the tension inside.

He jumped off his horse and walked over to the lying Bolsheviks. Neither gave any sign of life.

Go to Alik or do something with them, he considered quickly and decided it was more important to get rid of the tracks.

With no little difficulty he placed the corpses on their mounts, then headed for the steppe. He drove about a kilometer, found a depression between the drifts and threw it there. He was in a hurry, because he was growing anxious about the fate of his friend. Before he left, he stripped off the soldiers' sheepskin coats and caps, and from the gunner a holster with a belt. And then, in his haste, he merely covered the carcass with snow. The rest of the masking, he hoped, should be done by the blast that usually comes in the evening. There was not much left until dusk, and the first gusts could already be felt. The wind usually brought with it a fine fluff, which by morning should cover everything with a new snow coat, and, as God willing, level the ground beyond recognition.

He returned quickly to the track, carefully examining the road and the horizon. It was still empty, and the smoke drifting in the distance was already creating a black wall that spread over a long distance. For a moment he wondered what was causing him, but he gave up. Alik was more important.

He drove up to the sledge. The friend was asleep, but it was not a normal dream, but a visible fever that took his senses. He shook him, but didn't even open his eyes. His forehead was covered with sweat. He tucked one of the caps on his head. He threw one of the sheepskin coats on the sleigh and placed it on top of him. He still did not respond to this action. He covered him with a second sheepskin coat. And then he tied the bridles of the soldiers' horses to the sleds, sat on the trestle himself, and forcing the horses to effort, he sped them towards the forest.

Sewek trotted after him, as did Sheba.

For a good half an hour he went through the trees until they were so thick that it was difficult to drive between them. He stopped and cut a dozen bushes. Then he reached into the sleds to see what they were loaded with. It turned out that, apart from meat, they were loaded with crops, grain and hay, which pleased him more. He checked Alik's condition, then reloaded the packages onto the Bolshevik horses. He disengaged the towing sledge and drove it away. They could not be of any use, enough trouble with the Bolshevik mounts, with whom he did not know what he was going to do either. With difficulty he managed to get Alik on Sewek. He wrapped the sheepskin coats on him and prayed silently that the life of his friend would not disappear. He roughly masked the sled with branches, and he attached one to the horse so that it glided through the snow, although it masked the fresh hoof marks a little.

He headed deeper into the forest.

***

He lit a fire in the cave and put on the broth. Later, he herded the horses to Sewek's pen and fed them. He masked the entrance and returned. The soup was already warm, he poured a little into the plate and he worked hard to give a few spoons into the mouth of the unconscious Alik.

He put him comfortable, covered with a sheepskin coat, then returned to the horses. He searched the bags of the Bolsheviks. He found jewelery hidden in them, but he didn't care much for it. As before, he found letters in a special pocket under the rug of one of the mounts. He took them and came back.

He boiled water and made himself a cup of coffee. He decided that he deserved the luxury, then reached for the documents. There were two, each in a waxed envelope, the other additionally in a sealed leather case.

The first one contained an order from Lieutenant Colonel Leonid Kluyev to a commandant Anastasius to give provisions to the sent Cheka officers, mainly for horses that were starving. At the bottom, a handwritten note of the addressee to Klyuyev, what he passed on and how much. And note that there are some strangers in the area, although he did not see them personally and he obtained the information from one of the local peasants he trusted. And the request that the commander send a few officers, because the dozen or so soldiers who guard the supplies may not be enough if the peasants, forced by starvation, rebelled and tried to steal them. Besides, the behavior of the local politician seems very strange, as if he had a deal with some military who visit him at night. Besides - he reported - he is greedy, which undermines the good name of the communist, because he searches the village collecting jewelery stolen by the peasants in the farm.

The second letter, with the inscription "confidential", was addressed to the political officer in Klyuyev's unit, Isaac Babel, from the political officer, Abraham Rosa, probably the one to whom the commandant had written the denunciation. This one contained more details and also a denunciation, but on Anastasius. In it, he created his own revolutionary committee and ignored political orders and even rebels the peasants. Admittedly, when winter began, the commander hanged a dozen ringleaders for the first symptoms of the revolt against hunger, but only Poles, because he did not move the Ukrainians. What was so strange that the peasants of Polish origin sit quietly, do not rebel, and the Ukrainians, whose do not like everything, sauced. His man from the group of Anastasius's soldiers informed him that he had secretly received highly suspicious envoys, and according to his discretion, they could have been the people of Hetman Nestor Ivanovich Makhno, commanding the Revolutionary Insurgent Army of Ukraine, whose commitment to the idea, however, seems highly doubtful.

The sentence is further underlined: "Now, there are screams against us everywhere that we are fighting the people instead of slaughtering the Poles to the last one, which would bring savings in food supplies, and these are shrinking. This could cause more riots." It ended with a request to send a squad of trusted officers to keep the situation under control.

He put the papers aside, trying to figure out what was happening in the area.

They showed that somewhere in the region there was a hetman Makhno, whom the Bolsheviks did not trust. The previously intercepted letters indicated that they also had trouble with two units, called Jaworski's gangs and the latter, Kazakh, about whom they knew nothing.

He reached for those letters to remember what was in them about this Kazakh. It has not been established who is part of his gang and how many sabers he counts. Compared to the information about the former, Jaworski, this one seemed to be a more mysterious figure and probably was much more agile, since the writer emphasized: "All information is a priority here." And he added, although these were probably only his assumptions: "He may have a relationship or work with Ataman Kherson Grigoryev, and his actions raise suspicions in the Politburo as to his intentions.

No, he didn't understand any of this. Not only some hetman Makhno, but also ataman Grigoryev. Sure, he mused, they must go far away somewhere, or else he would have met its consequences. Although - he remembered the smoke on the horizon that had caused the riders coming from Malinova to turn back - maybe that was what they had done? Or maybe, after all, a revolt of hungry peasants or the result of the games between this commander Anastasius and the political commissar Rosa?

He figured he wouldn't come up with anything sensible, and that only Alik could be the only source of information, when he recovered. Then he would question him. The only good news from the correspondence he had read was that since the Bolsheviks was at loggerheads with themselves, his exaggerated caution in hiding the dead was completely unnecessary. And so probably the responsibility for their deaths would be attributed to these mysterious groups.

***

Alik woke up after three days. During the course, Janek tried to pour the broth into his mouth, but he couldn't do too much, because he choked and only swallowed some of the food.

When he opened his eyes, still bloodshot and foggy with fever, and when he saw his friend, he was so exhausted that he did not even have the strength to rejoice. Or perhaps he even suspected that it was just a vision or a fever-born dream. He only grabbed his hand and tightened his fingers on it, and a moment later, as if the sight were too much of an experience for the body, his eyelids closed by themselves and he drifted off to sleep. This time he was more calm than in the previous days when he was throwing himself, mumbling and warning someone against something.

He woke up after nearly twelve hours. He wanted to get up right away, but still didn't have the strength to even sit down. He wondered where he had come from. He tried to fight the tangled tongue, but Janek wouldn't let him ask questions. And wasting no time, he poured a large dose of broth into him, and then, although he refused to do so, furrowed him with garlic, herbs and tea for fear that it would not be only a temporary improvement in his condition.

Alik, as soon as the meal was over, almost immediately fell back to sleep despite himself.

This interweave of waking up, trying to find out where he was, eating and falling into nothingness continued for a few more days. He woke up, ate and went on sleeping. His fever had dropped, but he still needed time to fully recover.

During the course, Janek went out to feed the horses. The changes in Sewek's condition were more visible than in Alik's. The horse gains more body literally overnight.

Later, he and Sheba circled the area looking for human traces, but when he did not find them, it made him feel better and better. He hunted by stocking grouse. Once he went to the edge of the forest, where he hid. Nothing remained after the skid marks, because the snow masked them effectively.

***

The solstice of winter was becoming more and more visible. The snow was still falling, but it was different than at the beginning, more dense and wet, not letting the whips of the wind.

And there were more clues on it, you can see the hunger was driving more and more inhabitants of the forest out of their hiding places. The tracks were clearer now, like their owners' signatures, but stamped with tiny paws. Hares flashed in search of food, foxes following them, and even ermines wherever they were, leaving tracks in the snow resembling small dwarf skis. He did not notice only the wolves ones, which calmed him because of the horses. On the other hand, wild boars made their paths, collapsing in the wet snow, leaving tracts of last year's bedding torn to the ground in the feeding grounds. And deer, using the already shoveled hard permafrost, digging up the last year's grass to the last, and small bushes that can be eaten. You could also hear, though not as loudly as in summer, the screams of bullfinches, nuthatches, quickies and all this small stuff, hiding so far in basins or hollows of boughs.

Long icicles formed on the branches of trees and shrubs, shedding around noon when the sun was warming the longest, juicy drops of water that gathered just below them, forming puddles, freezing with the onset of evening and the lowering of the temperature.

Somewhere far, beyond the horizon, spring was already getting ready, still sleepy and slow to live, but felt every day.

***

After a few days, Alik gained so much strength that he did not fall asleep after eating, but leaned on his elbows. His face was still pale, but already with slight blushes, still haggard but with a broad smile.

He looked at Janek with admiration and asked nothing. He wandered with curiosity around the cave and its interior, fur coats, hanging hens, rifles, saddles and military general hanging on pegs stuck in the cracks of rocks.

"What are you staring at?" Janek broke the silence, happy that his friend is on the right path to regain strength.

He handed him the tea and sat himself on one of the saddles.

"Because, you know, I don't know, I don't remember anything, only the terrible frost and the soldiers who kicked me so I wouldn't sleep. And then nothing. And only some images when you gave me soup and nightmares that I was going somewhere, that... What about them? And what about you because we thought you were murdered when they came?"

Janek smiled. They had so much to say to each other, but now he didn't know what to ask first. Information was important to him, which he wanted to connect with what he read in the Bolshevik writings and about the situation in the countryside.

"As you can see I'm alive and I'm not bad at all," he laughed and, spreading his hands, added ironically, "This is my court now."

"What about the soldiers? You bought me out?" Alik was clearly bursting with the emotion he awoke when he saw a friend he was sure had been killed by the Bolsheviks.

Janek looked at him attentively, debating whether to tell the truth.

"Bolsheviks? They are dead," he said, trying to be indifferent.

Alik jerked his head up, he was silent for a moment, then a broad smile lit his face.

"It must be good, because they are bad people, not even humans, some beasts. Do you know what they did in the countryside?"

"Partly and only what I saw."

"When? How did you get away?"

"Grandfather sent me to hunt, and when I returned, they were already in the village and in the manor. I saw Hapka and what they did with her, and the same with Maruchna at the manor."

"I know," the smile faded from Alik's face. "Not only with them. Old Mendel's Sarah was also raped."

"And they killed her?"

"No, after that she hanged herself, she couldn't bear the humiliation. You know how proud she was, but it destroyed her. Mendel took his own life a few days later. The kids only stayed with Rosa."

"And Joshua?"

"He lives. Maybe because he is a Jew, and a political commissar is also a Jew."

"Sarah is also Jewish."

"Seems like that, he even punished the Bolshevik who raped her and had him trained, but... I don't know, I don't understand what they are doing. In Malinova, there they went for supplies, murdered the master's family, even his children, two boys, and raped his wife and daughter, and later hanged them. They robbed the entire manor and smeared shit on the walls when they got drunk. And then their commando exchanged blows with the political commissar and they hanged a dozen or so peasants, but only Poles, and they made the Ukrainians their more power."

They were silent, each digesting the words they had spoken in their own way. Alik experiencing what he saw, Janek analyzes it and compares it to the content of the documents.

"Have you seen in Malinova, apart from the soldiers residing there, any strangers?"

"Only once when we stayed the night. I went out to pee and then, their political commissar talked to two new ones."

"How do you know it's an alien?"

"I went there a few times and I remembered the faces, and it was none of them. They also had other uniforms, short sheepskin coats, like the Russians when the war was still going on, similar to the Cossack ones. And better armed. Everyone with a saber and a rifle."

There was silence again.

Janek remembered what was in the letter of the Bolshevik commander and what he wrote in a confidential letter from the political commissar. Who were these strangers?

"Do you know if they are in the village?"

"No, they were gone this morning."

"How many times have you went there and was it just you?"

"Mostly."

"And why did they choose you?"

"Because I repaired their sleigh, they decided that if they would fall apart on the way, I would put them together. You know I have a flair for carpentry."

"I know, but who else has ridden?"

"Sometimes they took Fedor because he was strong, but once they loaded sacks with millet on the sled, the skid broke on their way on the moguls and they had to go to us, to get me, to repair. And since then, most often I was the hauler."

"And what side is Fedor on?"

Alik smiled.

"He pretends to love the Bolsheviks and thus he can help people."

"And he loves?"

"He hates them more than I do."

"Why?"

"Because they raped his Fedka, you know, the one with braids up to the ass, such a bundle of laughs. He imagined that he would sneak into their favors and take revenge."

"Did he do it?"

"There was no occasion, but he probably will, you know him. He only respects you, and he is insane after his father."

"So you can contact him and he will not betray?"

"Certainly not."

Janek considered whether to ask about his grandfather and Vasily. The mere thought that he would receive an answer of their death held him back, but now he overcame himself and he did it.

"And mine? What about them? I haven't seen any graves."

"I don't know. It's a strange thing. As soon as they entered the village, a few went straight to the manor. Danylo led them. He probably had contact with them before, because he greeted them like his own. No shots were heard, and only later found out that they had killed Maruchna. I don't know what happened to your grandfather and Uncle Vasily and the servants."

"Nobody saw anything? Heard nothing?"

"In truth, everyone was afraid of these Bolsheviks and only looked not to expose themselves. Except for Danylo, because he immediately announced that he was creating Revolutionary Committee, that now new orders have come and the lords have to be cut. And he immediately pointed out to the soldiers the chairman Kuzma, the mayor Fedka and this Ivashka as the courtiers, and they were hanged on the pear tree. Ivashka screamed that he was also a Bolshevik, but nothing helped him. You know, he had a conflict with Danylo before, when he stood up for his wife and fired him. He got his revenge."

"How's the food? I saw a woman carrying the bundle towards the cemetery. Any disease?"

"Yes, a disease called hunger. A large proportion of the youngest died at the beginning. These robbers took all our food. People were cooking even the old belts when the dogs ran out, and when someone found one potato it was a feast for the whole family."

"How is it now?"

"They hardly leave the huts, they are so weak. They drink hot water or make soup from pieces of bark and wood, but it doesn't help. Hunger killed a few elders as well, and one, this grandfather Lyshko, went crazy with hunger and they had to tie him up so that he would not murder anyone. And so he gone."

"And you?"

"I had it better, because before going to Malinova I got a plate of soup. Not that they loved me, but their commander, that captain at the court, ordered it when he found out that I was a carpenter. And I mended their sleighs, because they are stupid, none of them could do it. And when they gave the swede, I pretended to eat it and carried it to my family."

"How's your mom? What about wet nurse Jefrosinia?"

"God saved them, both lost a lot of weight, but they hold on. Maybe thanks to my help."

Janek tossed it on the fire. He already had a picture of the situation, but still not complete.

Exhausted from conversation, Alik lay down, but followed his friend with his eyes. He was curious about the story too, but he didn't dare to ask. He was still tired and exhausted, but his curiosity prevailed and he was losing the fight against the overwhelming sleepiness.

Janek noticed his friend's condition, but he wanted to learn about a few more issues that troubled him.

"Where does Joshua live now?"

"No longer in the inn, because there..." Alik chose his words with difficulty. "This is where their rev-com resides, Danylo and a few more important Bolsheviks live there. The rest of the soldiers took from the peasants better huts, and they chased them out. Now they nest together, but maybe that's good, because it's warmer, and the firewood is not allowed to be took from the forest."

"Why? Are they afraid of the forest?"

"No," Alik sneered ironically. "They are afraid that the boys would run away and they are forbidden under the penalty of death."

"And nobody tried?"

"Two, old Latych and his son, but they caught them right away, because they did not hide far away, and made a shelter about a few hundred meters from the edge of the forest and immediately lit a fire. They spotted them, caught them and hanged them on the edge of the forest. For fear that no one would try anymore."

"I didn't see anything, and..."

"Because," interrupted Alik, "when the winter began and it was blowing hard, the ropes broke and the game did its job."

"And Joshua," Janek returned to the topic, "in which hut is he?"

"The one on the edge of the river, at Pantiflon's. Together with the kids and Rosa."

"What if we got him out? Would he come with us?"

Alik thought about it, then firmly agreed, then added hesitantly:

"You know, if he escaped, they would get their revenge on everyone in the cabin. They come on strong with everybody. I don't know if he would do it."

"You're right, but something could be made up."

"You thought about it, because I can't help. It would be good to have him with us, I feel sorry for him, after his sister died, he broke down, and you remember how close they were."

"I remember, but he is a Jew, maybe he has a fondness for those Bolsheviks, there are many of them."

"Not Joshua, although there are many Jews among the Bolsheviks, but not all of them. Do you remember what he once told us when we talked that they stick together and that is why they earn money faster than others?"

"Not really."

"That the greatest enemy of a Jew can only be another Orthodox Jew. And he hates all of them, those who serve the Bolsheviks. And he wouldn't betray us, I can guarantee it. Not after he lost Sarah and his father."

"And the other peasants in the village? Cooperate with them?"

"All they have to do, follow orders, and fear. You don't know what happened in other villages. And when these bandits indulge each other, they boast about it. I'm telling you, Janek, these are devils. Almost a third part of our village is dead. Killed, raped, starved to death. Nobody loves them except Danylo, but they are afraid."

"So who's in this rev-com if the boys are scared? After all, not only Danylo himself?"

"Well, no, he chose the more intimidated ones, but he only gives orders."

"How about the soldiers? Are they listening to him?"

"Their political commissar who lives in the court made him his deputy, but it's a sham. He is important to those stationed in the village, but those in the court are different. They don't care about him. It's Cheka, they are the most important. Everyone is afraid of them, even soldiers."

***

Janek would question Alik for a long time, but at one point he noticed that he had not answered the question because he fell asleep. He covered him carefully with a sheepskin coat and stared at his friend's calm face for a long time.

Various thoughts flashed through his mind, memories from before the invasion and those he had happily spent at the court, unaware of what was happening in the world. Probably his grandfather and Vasily knew it, but they never talked to him about it. Where are they now? What are they doing?

His eyes were starting to stick by themselves, so he got up, dressed, and went outside with Sheba. If he's going to save Joshua, he has to figure out some way. And fast. So far, however, he couldn't think of any.

He walked towards the village. Maybe there he will think of a way to take him to the forest.

***

At the rocks near the manor house of the former post, there was only the construction of a shed for guards protruding in the snow. And it's not whole. Probably some of the wood was burned in the fire, or maybe it ended up in the fireplaces in the manor house.

He cautiously crept up to them and examined the place where there was a boulder that had to be moved to enter the shallow well.

There was another one down there. Behind him there was a trench to the manor. He was probably frozen now and Janek didn't even try to go downstairs and move him. He didn't want to leave any traces.

He went back to the trees in the orchard and between them he came to the village. On the way, he saw traces of chopping apple, pear, plum and cherry trees. It was from here that the Bolsheviks took wood for the mansion's fireplaces. Now he knew why, even at the edge of the forest, he hadn't noticed the tracks. The forest was farther away, and the orchard was close.

Smoke was rising from the chimneys of the huts probably occupied by soldiers. The others looked uninhabited, but he knew from Alik that the Bolsheviks did not allow wood harvesting. Were it not for this smoke, the village would look abandoned. Before the advent of the Bolsheviks, even in winter it felt like the village was teeming with life. Dogs ran and barked, the sounds of animals could be heard, someone was going somewhere, someone was leaving, others were entering their huts, kids were running around playing, and now there was dead silence here.

He walked around the village to the east to see the hut on its edge where, as Alik had said, Joshua would live with his mother and siblings. Single tracks in the snow from the hut's doorstep ran towards the village, and some towards the fields. He guessed that the latter, much rarer than the former, leading to the field where the cemetery used to be, continued to the river.

He made a large bend and walked in that direction. He was right. The trail reached the still frozen river and a large ice hole cut in the middle. It was probably where they got fresh water from. Only them or the whole village?

He looked carefully to see if anyone would come accidentally and examined the tracks. They mingled with each other; horses, boots and... He thought it was an illusion, but no. As he bent down, he could see clear reflections of bare feet. Who walks on snow without shoes?

"Or maybe," it occurred to him, "the Bolsheviks punish a peasant for some imaginary offense, out of anger or to show who has the power and is allowed to do everything, and chase without shoes?"

It didn't do any good to belabor the point. One thing was for sure that the water was drawn in this place and maybe that is the way he was looking for. He had to think it through.

Chapter X

Alik quickly recovered.

Janek showed him everything that could be useful and the areas where he most often saw wintering grouse, the pit after the windthrow, where he killed the bear, the place where he last met wolves and a clump of trees where Sewek hid, who did not go away with the other horses.

Together, this time on horses, they went to the officers' shelter on the way, checking the place where the sleigh was hidden. There were no human traces in the forest, which they found only on the road. There were not many of them, which meant that the route was not used very often.

The masked shelter aroused additional admiration from Alik for Janek. He couldn't believe that you could discover something hidden in the ground among the trenches. And to tame the wolf, which was the terror of the peasants. "You should have had a gift," he thought, "that God bestows on only a few, and there was no doubt a young lord among them." Although they grew up together, and Janek's grandfather did not make any difference, he was equally oppressive of both of them for their offenses, there was an invisible and unspoken border between them. In the countryside, his closeness to the court meant that they treated him as one of them, but standing much higher in the social hierarchy. He was sometimes made to feel it with jealous comments, especially when some of them got drunk, but in the lining of the comments it felt as though they would all like to swap with him.

He himself felt this thin, invisible line, although Janek always treated him more like a milk brother than a stranger. He felt it especially when, on the orders of the elderly lord, they were going to the Pohorecki estate, where they met Anton and Fedor, for whom he was only one of the peasants, although better dressed than the others.

And now, when Janek showed him all the places, and told him how he was doing, his admiration for him grew with each new place.

"Why are you so pensive?" Janek interrupted his considerations, laughing at his gloomy face. "Look here," he pointed to where sloped sand blocked most of the shelter. "We'll have to somehow protect the ceiling beams and continue digging. Here I found a saber, maybe we can find something else that will be useful to us."

"And what if we dig into the corpse?"

"Then we will say good morning to him and talk about what it was like in the war."

"Don't be kidding, after all..."

"Alik, you have seen much lately, come on."

"It's not that, just somehow awkward."

"Oh yeah, I remembered. Remember when my grandfather and Vasily and the peasants brought back what they found here after the battle?"

"Sure, later I helped them move it all from the carts to a pit in the forest and mask it."

"That's what I mean. Maybe you know by accident, maybe the peasants were gossiping something, where did grandfather and Vasily take everything from this pit later?"

"Ha, ha, and why should I not remember. The women gossiped that we were hiding some treasures, but the village administrator, Kuzma, and the head Fedka, only rebuked them, so that the gossips would not spread. Wiser peasants also laughed at the women that there was missing only devil there, but no treasures."

"They didn't know?"

"Well, no, because the lords transported it themselves. Only Kuzma and Fedka were admitted to the secret, they helped them, but they were hanged by the Bolsheviks."

He paused, then added:

"I think that Danylo must have whispered something to the Bolsheviks about it, and those, when they got to the mash of spirit, were both on the rope at once. And there was no longer any way to get out of them where these supposed treasures had been hidden. And the next day I heard this important political commissar from the court, how he shouted at Danylo, that he told the soldiers instead of him, and the secret was lost."

Janek pursed his lips, wishing he knew the location of the place. Although they had two weapons in abundance for the time being, the ammunition had to be saved, because there was not much of it.

"There is one more place left, and luckily I know where it is," he finally said.

"What are you saying, some treasures?" Interest suddenly flashed in Alik's eyes. "Gold, jewelry..."

"You are stupid," Janek laughed amused. "Will you make bullets of gold? Would you like to shoot diamonds?"

"Well, no, I just said this. What do you know about?"

"I know where the shotguns and ammunition are, but there's a problem."

"Do you know, or you don't know?"

"I know but..."

"You can't tell me? I understand."

"You don't understand. It's a hiding place in the manor, we must..."

This time it was Alik who started to laugh violently, hitting his thighs with joy.

"It's impossible. You know who is sitting in the court."

"And that's the problem, but it can be solved."

"Forget Janek, there is Cheka there, we will not be able to make it, even if there were even a few more of us. These are not those lousy soldiers, but real fighters, with experience. Do you know that their commander is a former tsarist lieutenant colonel? It's not just anybody."

"How do you know?"

"Once, when they got drunk with this political commissar, they remembered the old days. And I overheard, because I was doing reinforcement at the rafters in the attic, and it was good to listen through the window. And I know."

Janek thought about it. The writings he had intercepted showed that the regiment sent from Budyonny's army was commanded by a Lieutenant-Colonel Leonid Kluyev, and a political officer was Isaac Babel. If the tsarist and experienced officer, the Bolsheviks had not been promoted to general, it means that the leadership of the All-Russian Extraordinary Commission for Combating Counter-Revolution, Speculation and Abuses of Power did not trust him. How did they know this political commissar Babel? The latter, judging by his name, was a Jew. And why were they sitting in the manor, since most of the troops were farther west.

"What were they talking about? Maybe they were saying something. Where does their knowledge come from?"

"I don't know, I didn't exactly eavesdrop on it. I was afraid that if they realized that someone was hearing them, they would shoot me. It just happened that they were doing something together in Odessa, some sort of trading with military sorts, but nothing more."

"That's something, they must have liquefied their stocks on the left. Their commander had to have access to them, and the political commissar exchanged goods for cash. Nice deal."

"But why do you need this?"

"I'm trying to find out who our opponent is."

"These are real devils, they are very dangerous, Janek," repeated Alik with all his might, clearly scared by his friend's ideas. "Do not plan, because it may end badly for us."

"Why don't plan?"

"I know you, I can see that you've already figured out something and now you just match the cards to the deck."

"Not really, Alik, not really."

"And you know, there is young boy there, I mean, like their writer."

"And what?"

"Well, because this one does not look like a peasant, more a tsarist. A familiar face, as if... I don't know."

"And...?"

"Sometimes I got food from him, when no one saw it. He doesn't quite fit this bunch."

"Maybe a soft-hearted Bolshevik," Janek sneered.

"No, no, really different. He even confessed to me once that he knew me because he was here once."

Janek suddenly became interested in the story. From his observations so far, it did not appear that any of the fighters seemed familiar to him.

"Do you know his name?"

"Kind of like Demenkov, if I don't twist it."

"You sure?" Janek was looking in his memory and immediately remembered the young, smiling adjutant of the regiment, Lieutenant Stepan Demenkov, when the commander of the Leib-Guardian Regiment of His Majesty, Count Mikhail Vasilyevich Ridiger, stopped at the manor. Now he wondered intensely what such a man was doing among the Bolsheviks. Was he forced or did he do it voluntarily?

"Stepan Demienkov?"

"I don't know the first name, but I think the last name is correct. Really decent, and their commander always mocks him that he doesn't fit in with the revolution, but I don't know what's going on."

"And that's good news, as long as it's good." Janek summed up the information philosophically.

It was a new asset to the plans that slowly matured in his head. He still had to digest them and test his guesses.

***

Winter was clearly ending. It was getting warmer every day, although the frost still returned in the evening and chained back what had dissolved during the day. The surface of the snow hardened, forming a crust that made it easier for smaller animals to move around and at the same time made it all the more difficult to hunt.

This condition also made human traces more visible, as well as horse traces. When Janek was leaving with Alik, they steered them so that the hooves reflected in the permafrost did not lead directly to the cave, but to the depths of the forest. Many times, wasting a lot of time, they looped the route so that any unauthorized person would get lost.

"I don't like that at all." Alik was more skeptical than his friend as he looked back and assessed the clear footprints left by the horses. "There is less and less snow, bad snowfall, they can track us."

"It's possible, as long as they enter the forest."

"They can do it if we provoke them."

"They can, but will they?" Janek was optimistic, although deep down he had similar fears.

"You're up to something, I know you."

"We'll see, for now we have to get the horses moving."

They only left the forest almost half a mile from Malinova. Alik showed the huts, the farm and the tenant's manor visible in the distance. After the latter, there were ashes and they associated it with the smoke on the horizon when Janek took Alik from the hands of soldiers.

"If we got so closer, maybe I will spot someone I know," Alik forgot about his earlier doubts, he gained confidence in excitement and was now ready to take the risk.

"Don't overdo it, slow down, nothing by force, we will always make it," Janek reassured him, toning his friend's aspirations.

They drove even closer, but only far enough that they could possibly be spotted from a distance, but without details of who started. Janek did it on purpose. If one of the soldiers spotted them, the small figures far on the road would not arouse interest. And if he did report the commander, the commander would start to wonder if, by any chance, Lieutenant Colonel Kluyev or the political commissar Babel were checking those in Malinova. Certainly, he would not send a patrol to investigate what kind of riders they were, let alone send a deliberate one to a commander to ask why he was doing it. The commander in Malinova probably had no idea that the letters had not reached the manor and he would be in the uncertainty as to who the horses were patrolling somewhere in the distance. On the other hand, he considered, if there was any truth in the letters, maybe that local political commissar had dealt with the commander or vice versa. It would be worth checking, but showing up in the village in the light of day would be an unnecessary risk.

They left the road and Janek steered the horses further south to circle the village on the other side. After some time, they came across a part of the road further east. Judging by the traces, he was more frequented than the one leading to their village. Who was visiting Malinova? Another unanswered question.

From this side, they saw better what had burned down. What remained of the tenant's court were only the stumps of tanned and blackened beams protruding into the sky. Alik did not remember if anyone had lived here after the renter was murdered with his family. So why was the building set on fire?

***

This time they returned to the road from the north, when it was already dusk and gray covered the whole surroundings.

Only then did they come closer to the village. On its edge there was a huge shed, in the old days a warehouse for grain, hay and gardening. Janek was glancing at Sheba all the time, but she showed no concern. Was it not being watched by anyone anymore?

They drove close enough to be no more than twenty paces away. Only then did Sheba begin to stop and sniff to let know that she felt something disturbing.

They held their horses listening to the evening silence. So far, nothing disturbed her and it was difficult to tell what the wolf felt.

They dismounted the reins, throwing them onto the frozen bush. Then they went on foot. Janek pulled his bow off his shoulder, threw the rifle on his shoulder, and Alik gave his action and huddled up to the walls of the barn. Still nothing disturbed the silence. It wasn't late enough for everyone to be asleep, and yet there was no sound coming from all over the village.

They slowly made their way around the building until they came across the closed gates. They opened it gently and slipped inside.

Sheba growled softly.

Someone was inside.

They waited for a sound that would reveal whether it was an animal or a human. They did not catch anything for a long time, and only after a while the snoring on the second part came to pass. Strongly muffled, probably by the beam wall dividing the warehouse into two halves.

Visibility has dropped to almost zero. They stood waiting for their eyes to adjust to the darkness. Only the overhead skylights gave a bit of light, and you still had to be careful where you put your feet.

"Еб твое мать..." Suddenly there was an incomprehensible gibberish.

They stopped listening to see if they woke someone up, but then they heard only louder snoring.

Janek gave a signal and slowly, step by step they moved on. As they slipped into the second part, they saw two figures half covered with straw and sheepskin coats. Both were fast asleep, and there was a stench of raw alcohol and vomit all around.

They slowly withdrew and went back to the first part. Here, along the walls, there were sacks with grain and edges. Janek pointed to them, letting them know that they had to be used and - he pointed on his fingers - to take one.

They approached them when suddenly a menacing gurgling came out of Sheba's throat, and at the same time the gate opened and a boy dressed in a long sheepskin coat stood in them, with a rifle on his shoulder and an oil lamp in his hand.

"Swolocz, shto wy dielaietie?" He blurted out.

At this point, he realized that there was probably no locals in front of him.

He froze in surprise, shook his head as if in disbelief at what he was seeing, then threw the lamp onto the threshing floor and reached quickly for the rifle.

"Charge," Janek said to Sheba, reached for the quiver, and before the soldier could grab the gun well, he fired.

"... Shto..." The other man still grunted, not comprehending what was happening. The arrowhead stuck in his throat effectively prevented him from acting. He staggered, dropped the rifle, grabbed the arrow with his hands trying to tear it out, but when another pierced his eye socket reaching his brain, he slumped with a groan on the floor. Convulsions shook his body, then he went still.

Everything happened so quickly that Alik did not have time to react. He didn't even raise the rifle, just stared paralyzed at the unfolding scene.

Sheba trembled all over her body, sensing the fight, but obeying the order, she slightly crouched down, tensing all her muscles and slightly lifting her tail.

"And it's all over," Janek carefully surveyed the Bolshevik, feeling his blood bubbling up. He couldn't show his emotion, fearing for Alik that he might not stand the tension and do something stupid. In the second part, the drunk soldiers were asleep, they could wake up. He ran to check it out, but still they slept.

He came back, asked Alik how he was feeling, and as soon as the latter nodded that he was fine, he whispered softly that he would be back soon and went outside.

There was still silence all around. The horse of the one now lying dead stood just outside the gate. He listened to the silence, but there was no sign of any more riders. He ran to their horses and led them to the shed. He opened the door. He motioned for Alik to help him and they threw the soldier over the saddle. Then they loaded their bags and two more on the one with the corpse.

Only now did Janek notice that the flame from the broken lamp was licking the spilled paraffin. He looked at the remnants of straw scattered across the floor. They had to hurry because when it exploded, it was sure to be noticed. He urged Alik, who still couldn't get over it, looked around, to get in. Accelerating quickly they drove away to the east. Janek wanted to get to the road leading somewhere further, which impose roads and created a danger that someone would notice them and raise the alarm, but also distracted from the direction of the actual escape.

After half an hour they threw the dead man into the bushes, and when the village was completely covered in darkness, they turned back west. There was still silence. Nor did it indicate that the fire had spread, or at least it was not visible from their position.

***

Alik's first baptism of fire went well, but when they entered the forest his body rebelled from the excess of emotions and he vomited. He apologized to Janek for his weakness that he was so paralyzed when he saw the Bolshevik that it was stronger than him, but the latter only waved his hand and dismissively stated briefly:

"Everyone has to go through this."

And immediately he added, seeing the wretched face of his friend:

"At least you didn't pass out like a woman and get hysterical," he laughed, encouraging him.

They did not go straight back to the cave, but took a roundabout way heading east, then turned north, and when they had gone far enough from the village, they turned south, reaching the forest.

Another horse came to them and Janek decided that the next day he would lead him to the edge of the forest and let him go. They did not have much fodder, despite the provisions they had gained, he had to decide to get rid of him, although in truth he felt sorry for him because he liked horses.

That night, Alik slept restlessly, lunging, waking from time to time in fear, then fell asleep again and dreamed again. It wasn't until the morning that the nightmares departed him, and only then did he fall into a deep, restful sleep. So strong that when Janek got up at dawn, he didn't even wake up.

Chapter XI

The horses snorted softly, clearly pleased to be out of the woods. It was still half an hour before dawn, so the sky was still dark, though with lighter, dark red streaks of the sun breaking over the horizon.

For a long time Janek had been concerned about the situation in a distant town, where they would go shopping every now and then, or on the occasion of some meetings that his grandfather had. He decided that they would go there to investigate the situation at least from a distance.

He was also wondering why the so important command of Cheka was stationed in the manor, not in the city. Did, he thought, Lieutenant Colonel Kluyev, commanding a regiment and a thousand sabers, according to the information of one of the killed Bolsheviks and his companion a political commissar Babel were fighting their own war under the pretext of serving in the All-

Russian Extraordinary Commission for Fighting Counter-Revolution, Speculation and Abuse of Power? It was convenient to be on the side, and at the same time in the center, as long as they set themselves up for loot in the mansions plundered along the way. And perhaps it was likely, given that the first of the Bolsheviks with whom he fought and whom Danylo used while observing his superiors also tried to get something for himself.

Before that day they went on a trip to the town, Janek decided to somehow protect himself in case of a meeting with a red squad. To Alik and himself, he sewed a star on chest, stripped of fur hats obtained from soldiers, and they put on such hats on their heads. He kept them not because of these stars, but because of the prosaic reason, cold. They were practical, and the stars were eye-catching and unambiguous.

They drove across the frozen ford and made a long bend to the west before they set off straight into town. After the events in Malinova, Alik shook himself long ago and even boldly announced that this time no sight of a Bolshevik soldier would paralyze him.

Janek enjoyed his attitude, the more so as he subconsciously felt the risk of going so far into the open area. He felt safe in the forest, he knew every path there, and here you could see them even from a distance. It was possible to come across a large unit, although on the other hand they could always turn back, and besides, he consoled himself, who could ride on horses, if not a Bolshevik?

They saw the church spire far away. There was no sign of mindless arson here. Apparently, every house or building was carefully used by soldiers. The only question is how many were stationed in the town?

They paused, watching the suburbs carefully through binoculars. No traffic. They drove closer. Now a single car flashed across the block and disappeared behind the walls of a two-story tenement house. Besides, two or three passers-by showed up somewhere in a hurry. "Maybe it is too early, but if there is an army that does not sleep until noon, the traffic should be bigger," wondered Janek.

They drove close enough that they heard shouting from the vicinity of the market square. They couldn't make out the words, but there was nothing menacing about their tone. Emboldened, they entered a side street to get to the main square with the back of the houses, where the town hall and pub used to be, the mayor and a dozen of the wealthier inhabitants used to have their house, and where once, even during the war, every Friday there was a market for which local peasants and often the nobility came.

They carefully examined the windows of the houses they passed, holding their rifles unlocked through the horse's pylons. They both felt a tension that increased with each step of the horses.

"Or maybe they are sleeping off drunkenness." Alik looked around carefully.

"Maybe, but it is unlikely, a drunkman wakes up early."

Sheba, sensing the tension, ran right next to Sewek. Janek even wondered if he should leave her in the cave, but with her whistling and choking sounds, she forced him to participate in the expedition. He succumbed to her, although he knew it was not wise. She was sniffing now, but was more focused on how her master was reacting.

The street on which they were going had no cobblestones. This one only covered the main street. So the horses' hooves did not echo in the silence that reigned over this unusual morning in a now strange place.

They stopped the horses at the entrance to the main road. From here you could already see the buildings of the market square, from which every now and then came some laughter and shouts.

"What we do?" Alik asked softly, as if the tone of his voice depended on whether they would be noticed.

"We got here, let's check it," Janek was not sure that he wanted it, but it was he who made the decision and said it more to himself than to his friend.

However, he did not move his horse and continued to stand listening to the sounds from the square. These escalated, fell silent, and exploded again. They heard only single words muffled by the walls of houses, curses and dirty jokes, guttural orders rather than commands, more like the sounds made by a drunken company that did not quite know what to do with a well-started day.

In the end, Janek made a decision.

They couldn't stand like this forever.

He let his friend know, they drove onto the pavement of the road to emerge a few dozen meters further between the first houses of the market square.

Red flags fluttered in the town hall, and a large banner covering some of the windows said: "Do not regret your life in the fight against the enemy of the working class." Next to it there was also a huge, inept drawing of the globe, Lenin standing on it, who was holding a broom and sweeping various monarchs, officials and rich people into space.

In front of the town hall, a dozen or so armed soldiers were drinking vodka standing in small groups of two or three or sitting on a few peasant carts lined with straw, shouting gibberish slogans as if they were at a social party. Several women circled between them, shoving bottles. They laughed loudly at their jokes and willingly let themselves be caught by anyone who wanted to slip their hands under their blouse or skirt.

Nobody even noticed when Janek and Alik drove up closer.

"What's going on here, comrades?"

The first question eluded them, but when Alik repeated it in Ukrainian, hitting one of the Bolsheviks with a rifle butt, now only some of them noticed them.

"Who's asking?" The big red-faced man pushed his companions away, leaned on his hips and looked at the riders proudly. He had to be the boss here, and that's what he was demonstrating.

Janek mentally thanked himself that before his departure, this time he had read the intercepted Bolshevik correspondence in great detail. There was a small mention of the Revolutionary Red Warsaw Regiment, which comrade Lenin appreciated and gave others as a model of revolutionary attitude and ruthless treatment of opponents. Some anti-Bolshevik uprising in Jaroslaw was even mentioned, which the regiment bloodily suppressed and then shot several hundred people from among those who surrendered. And what was very strange for him, it was mostly made up of Poles. Now he decided to use it. What was the name of the red warlord who commanded him?

"Western Rifle Division, political commissar Zbikowski, commander of the Red Revolutionary Warsaw Regiment," he drawled coldly, looking into the man's eyes. "There was a question, comrade, I am waiting for an answer. Or maybe life is not nice for you?"

Out of the corner of his eye, Janek saw that suddenly all eyes were on him and an unexpected tension hung in the air. Had they heard something about this "Warsaw" regiment?

The Bolshevik suddenly lost his confidence, lowered his hands and tried to stand at attention.

At that moment, a stout woman appeared next to him.

"As I live and breathe, Vasily show you the papers, if you are so important. What is this regiment, I have not heard."

"Quiet, stupid, it's Warsaw."

"So what, for me..." She did not finish, because the man hit her face with his fist. He straightened up again quickly and, despite the vodka he had drunk, submitted his report relatively smoothly.

"Forgive me, comrade, famous regiment, I did not recognize it, and a stupid woman tells rubbish, but she is a good companion, but..."

"I asked what was going on here," Janek unceremoniously interrupted him without changing his tone.

The man straightened even more, and the others, who had so far only watched the exchange, sprang to attention.

"Well, we are to shoot a few rebels, they will bring them."

"On whose orders?"

"Well, comrade, political commissar Danylo, who does replace Comrade Babel from this village?" He indicated the direction somewhere to the east. "Yesterday he came with his comrades from Cheka and they chased away some who talked badly about the revolution. And a few others from that village over there..."

"What village? You don't know the names?"

"Somehow I don't remember, and the other one is like..."

"Malinova," the woman lying on the ground, rose to her feet, wiped the blood from her nose and, trying to redeem herself in the eyes of the unknown officer, quickly added: "I'm from this village, and they, those boys, they set fire to the tenants' palace."

Janek looked at her, then made her feel the mockery in his voice.

"You say the palace, but they are bloodsuckers, and thanks for burning them down."

"No comrade, it's not like that," the woman was suddenly scared that she was speaking so directly, she bowed her head and in a broken voice explained: "The palace was empty, and they agreed with some counter-revolution and the local commander, too, plotted together and a shooting took place."

"Who with whom?"

"With our political commissar and his men, and these traitors from the commandant."

"This political officer of yours is here? And this Danylo?"

"Sure, they finish the interrogation, because it is time to send a report to comrade Babel, what happened."

Janek quickly considered what he heard. It was prudent to leave. There were more of them, and if there was a firefight, things might turn out to be unfavorable for them. After all, there were only two of them, and a dozen of others, drunk, but always more than them. He had to think up something hastily, taking advantage of the fact that the Warsaw regiment had a good reputation with them.

He looked away from the woman and turned to the bearded Bolshevik.

"Are you in charge here?"

"Yeah, me."

"Then listen to me carefully, comrade. I have other information about what happened in Malinova and who was the ringleader. And I have separate orders related to this Danylo. He's a white spy. You understand?"

It was evident that the calm, confidential words made an impression, but the soldier still digested them, not quite knowing how to react in a new situation.

Janek decided to help him in this.

"I was not going from Kharkivsk so far ahead of my people to play some shit here," Janek stressed the last word, looking carefully if the name of the place invented by chance would attract someone's attention. It did not attract. So he added:

"From now on you come under my orders. Is it clear? How many are you in the city because there is some silence?"

"There was more comrade, but two days ago an order came that the regiment was to be somewhere and only we stayed and our command, I mean," he began to enumerate using his fingers, "ours, Commander Jewlenski and political commander Harpan, the one from Malinova, probably Rosa and political commissar Danylo."

"They left already? I was still hoping to find them. How many soldiers in the building?"

"Well, the commander, the political commissar, this Danylo and Rosa, and two of our guys, who are guarding the others."

"Rebels?"

"Well, the imported ones."

"We will like this, Comrade Vasily. Get organized with your men, because they've gotten drunk as a skunk. I'm going to the building, and when I get back, you should be ready to go. This," he emphasized by stressing the word "this", "would be short-lived. The revolution doesn't like traitors, and we don't have time for interrogations. Is that clear to you?"

The Bolshevik analyzed the words he heard for only a second and you could see his face reaching him with the phrase "Revolution doesn't like traitors." And the fact that this important newcomer has no objection to him, but to the officers. He straightened even more and saluted.

"As you ordered, comrade."

"Well, better be like that."

Janek nodded to Alik, who was holding the horse a few meters away, to have all the soldiers under the gun. Sheba stood quietly next to Sewek, but her spine showed that she was all tense. The soldiers looked at her, some of them recognized the wolf, but that she was standing calmly, only bare her teeth, you can see that this was the will of this foreign commander.

The first part of the game has been played. It remained the other one that could have been more difficult.

The Bolshevik saluted again and gave orders to his men.

***

They tied horses to the ornate hoops of the entrance to the town hall. They pretended that they did not care about what was happening in the square, but Janek closely followed Vasily's actions. The man, apparently taken over by the orders and trust that he had been bestowed with, was quick to pull his people together. The more drunk were submerged in a water trough to sober up, others prepared carts for the road, and women ran around the houses carrying various items.

"I think they believed," Alik watched the actions of the soldiers with a certain disbelief. "What's next?"

"We play va banque."

"It means?"

"We go for broke. We have no choice. You heard what I told him, Danylo is a spy, and the others are suspects."

"I heard, I'm not deaf, but..."

"Danylo has to answer for what he did in the village, for the dead."

"You want him…"

"He'll recognize me, and you too, we can't give him a chance to raise the alarm."

"You want…"

"I want. And the others, we'll see, don't talk, come on. You probably know the peasants who brought them here, at least from our village."

"Probably yes, and from Malinova, I'll see."

They went inside. Hall was dark, lit only by two windows, now obscured by some rags with more slogans.

Janek stopped listening. Somewhere upstairs, muffled voices were probably heard from the mayor's office, but it was certainly no interrogation, as this Vasily was saying, or rather an argument. What now? To the basement where they probably keep the arrested or upstairs? What to do and in what order so as not to arouse suspicions in the soldiers?

He considered for a moment, and Alik and Sheba looked at him more and more nervous. He could not show his friend that he did not know what to do, that he had no plan and was reacting intuitively.

He could feel the tension in him grow, though he tried with all his will to remain calm. He was aware and it was a positive side of the situation that his officer's jacket is associated with a certain difference from the Bolshevik costumes, and at the same time the version that he was the commander of the Warsaw regiment made him credible. He must also learn something more about this regiment, because it probably arouses respect not only among the Bolsheviks, but also fear in ordinary soldiers. And that could only mean that they were worse than they were and probably had a lot of blood shed on their hands.

He couldn't go on like this and decided.

He motioned to Alik and pointed down the stairs. There used to be a door here, but now there are bare hinges. Maybe they were burned in the winter, or maybe they were taken out on purpose, now it doesn't matter.

He started walking downstairs, putting his feet firmly on him to be heard down there. Such a demonstration of confidence and strength.

They hadn't really come down yet when a soldier appeared downstairs and looked at them, curious but uneasy.

"You keep an eye on these counter-revolutionaries?" He asked him a question in a sharp tone that suggested he was important.

The soldier looked at him and you could almost see his galloping thoughts and uncertainty about who it was.

"Nu, scoundrel, talk, till I'm good."

When asked, he looked timidly at the unknown officer with a wolf by his side and began to be afraid.

"Are you deaf comrade or do you prefer to switch with them?!" Janek pointed behind his back without lowering his tone.

"No, your bliss..." the soldier crumpled the old tsarist army phrase in his mouth and quickly corrected himself."Niet, comrade, they are there, locked up and there are two of us, by order of Commissioner Harpan, we are waiting for orders and..."

"Enough," Janek signaled that he should stop and ordered: "Lead to the prisoners."

The latter was still hesitating, but seeing the newcomer ostentatiously shifting his hand to the butt of the revolver, he quickly nodded and walked along the cellar. Its darkness was lit only by the skylights of small windows overlooking the square and the few smoldering torches stuck in the cracks of the wall.

A second watchman emerged from the darkness, but said nothing. He glanced apprehensively at the wolf. Just in case, he took a basic stance.

"Here we have them, separate from this village, and here from the other," the Bolshevik pointed the door.

"Open up."

"They are not closed, there was no need, Commissioner Harpan..."

"I will get square with him separately," Janek grunted.

He opened the door a crack. It was dark in the basement, only the stench emanating from the darkness.

"Get some light."

The second soldier disappeared around the corner and brought a burning torch.

"Light it up."

Figures lying on the ground emerged from the shadows. He quickly counted five. They didn't even raise their heads. The fact that they had been subjected to a brutal interrogation was immediately apparent. Battered and scarred faces with dried blood, all swollen with tumid blotches, broken, spasmodic breathing. He acquainted with some of the peasants."

"Second cell."

Here the image repeated itself. There were seven of them. He didn't know any of them, though one of the faces seemed familiar to him, but it was so mutilated, covered with blood and earth, that he couldn't remember who it was.

"These ones from Malinova?" He made sure.

"Yes."

How did he know this face? There was no time to wonder, he had to order these soldiers not to think.

"Outside, your commander, Vasily, is preparing the carts for departure," he directed the words to the first of the soldiers. "One should go to him, get someone to help and take them outside. Two carts for this bastard, I must have them alive. Hurry up."

The soldier did not argue, but beckoned the other one to go to obey the order.

"Let's go," Janek commanded Alik, not looking back.

They went out to the vestibule of the town hall. It was here that he allowed himself a deeper breath. He looked at Alik and saw that he was very moved by the sight of his friends from the countryside. He did not show it by behaving like Janek; for the Bolsheviks they were tough officers, who were nothing surprising, and had a mission to fulfill.

"In the other basement where those from Malinova, did you meet someone?" He asked softly.

"I think three are Poles, one Ukrainian, I worked with him, a good boy, they murdered his father and brother, I think there is also a German, and the other two are probably Russians, but I'm not sure, although the most massacred one reminds me of someone, but I not associate."

This peasant's face resembled someone to him too, but he left it for later.

"We're starting the game, check the gun." He pointed to the stairs to the first floor. "And don't hesitate."

Alik just nodded, pursing his lips in determination. It was no longer the same man from a few weeks ago that the mere sight of a soldier had paralyzed him.

***

They entered cautiously, ready to react immediately if the situation called for it.

There were still arguments from behind the door to the mayor's office. Judging by the tone, the stormy conversation was watered with alcohol.

They were already at the top of the landing when the door to the building opened and several soldiers, led by the one who had followed them, entered. They headed straight for the basement. Janek noticed that neither of them was armed. Apparently, his orders were being carried out exactly as he wished.

They climbed the rest of the stairs and stood at the door.

"And I tell you, you stupid Jew, that your Babel is a clever guy and can guess, so it's time to move elsewhere," came from behind them.

"He's right, he and Lieutenant Colonel Kluyev have been up to it for a long time," that was clearly Danylo's voice. "If it weren't for the security guys, we could have been take care of them, they've already accumulated so much..."

"Scumbags, you only have gold in your head, and this is about the party," argued a voice, but further arguments were muffled by the laughter of the others.

"And where is that Cossack, Danylo, for whom you worked?" It was a different voice. "Suddenly he stopped coming."

"I'm also wondering, because when he got a cut from me, he left somewhere and the trace of him broke off..." a loud belch, "...Kluyev was also worried, because he was his trusted one, and he even suspected that he might have been taken care of by some local. It's been two months or longer."

"You're raving," laugh of the overcrowded voice. "This is such a Cossack that you fear to oppose it. No man would be able to cope, even if he was tied up, he would win..."

"Da, the colonel was, nevertheless, worried. They'd let him know if they stopped him."

There were sounds of prisoners being led outside. If someone from behind the door looks out the window, they will see what is happening and raise the alarm.

Janek made a sign to Alik. He took the Mauser from its holster and chambered.

"Ready?"

The friend nodded.

"And you wait here," he said to Sheba. "Charge."

He put his left hand on the doorknob and gently opened the door.

Four men were seated at the table. There were a few bottles of vodka on it, and a large pile of jewelry, gold bars and ten-rubles gold Nicholas II on the spread napkin.

"Get out!" One of the men, sitting with his back, did not even turn, recognizing that one of the soldiers had entered it without permission.

The others looked up and froze at the sight of the gun pointed at them.

Danylo struggled with the alcohol that darkened his self, but not so much that he would not immediately recognize Alik. When he looked at Janek, his eyes widened, not believing what he was seeing. His face, red with vodka, suddenly turned pale, and his lips twitched as if he wanted to say something, but he ran out of strength. He was terrified.

The others watched without a word, trying to understand the situation.

The third one, who had been sitting so far with his back, turned and it was he who kept his cool blood. You see, he was used to giving orders. He was wearing a black leather cap, glasses on his nose, and a thick beard and mustache framed the lower part of his face. Judging by his sharp Semitic features, it must have been a political commissar Harpan. Now he narrowed his eyes, in which ill-concealed anger flashed, but he asked cheerfully, as if nothing had happened, and greeted old friends.

"And you, comrades, with a visit or orders?"

"Jakimski," Janek invented his name, not wanting to use the commander's name this time, because they might have known it, and added ironically: "Commissar Jakimski, Western Rifle Division, and Revolutionary Red Regiment of Warsaw."

Harpan, because it must have been him, twitched his lips and the relief was clearly visible on his face.

"And what's up with my friend, Commissioner Zbikowski?"

"All right, he sends you his regards, as long as you're Harpan."

"Da, that's me," the commissioner turned to face them. "And is Zyramik still there?"

"Who?"

"You must be new, because he composed a regimental song," the political commissar laughed and began to sing: "Do not use your lords, do not support them, the Red Regiment of Warsaw wants to defend the freedom of the people. We will not be dazzled by the words from the palace or the pulpit..."

"Silent, scumbags!" Janek shouted, not moving from his place, because he realized that the other was trying to distract him.

Danylo, who had been sitting huddled so far, his head bowed low, as if to hide his face, suddenly straightened with determination in his eyes and reached into his puffer coat pulling out a pistol.

He hadn't had time to direct it at the arrivals when Alik, carefully examining the seated ones, pressed the trigger of his revolver. The bang sounded much louder than normal, because, magnified by the closed room, it bounced off the walls like a thrown metal ball in a glass ball. After being hit by a bullet, Danylo was thrown from the chair. He fell to the floor, with one leg hooked on the seat, which was hanging for a moment, twitching, and then it dropped as well.

The faces of the two, so far silent, showed terror, only this Harpan remained calm, or at least pretended he had nothing to do with the excesses of his companion. The fact that it was different was evidenced by a single drop of sweat that ran down his cheek.

"Would you like a drink, comrades? This Danylo was also under suspicion. So what, pour?"

"What's next?" A disturbing thought flashed through Janek's mind that he did not know how to play out the situation. Somehow he couldn't kill these three for no apparent reason.

"And this, Comrade Harpan," he pointed to the jewelery with the end of the barrel, "is this in favor of Commander Budyonny?"

"Oh yes, just for him," the Commissioner suddenly clung to the thought. "And this Danylo," he pointed the corpse, "tried to convince us that the gold should be given to the commissar Isaac Babel, because his authority is here, and Kluyev's regiment is from Cavalry Army."

He looked at Janek, examining his reaction, pleased with himself that he had created a credible fairy tale, and when he was silent, he added:

"And you comrades, with what orders?"

"We got news that you, like those bloodsuckers, oppressors of the people, gather gold for yourselves."

"No, that's not true, it's for a revolution," Harpan suddenly began to explain himself, and his calm so far began to fade away. "Comrade Zbikowski can testify for me, I'm a faithful son of the Bolshevik party, we together, on the orders of the People's Commissar, Comrade Lev Trotsky, suppressed the rebellions of anarchists and Socialist Revolutionaries in Moscow and Yaroslavl, he can..."

"He can do nothing, comrade, you have betrayed the idea, you are stealing the property of the communist authorities, and for that there is one punishment, you have used it yourself, I suppose, in Yaroslavl."

There was silence.

Harpan was suddenly sweating so much that his face was now wet. Fidgeting in his chair, he tried to think something up quickly.

He did not know who had sent the strangers here, and that of the Warsaw regiment enjoying the bloody fame. Who reported? Maybe this Babel, trying to distract from himself, and yet they had a separate arrangement, only between them. Or maybe Babel has already been killed?

Unable to think of anything in sudden desperation, he yanked the pistol out of his coat and, without aiming, fired at Janek, amok in his eyes. At the same moment Alik's revolver spoke and the police officer, with a hole in his head, was thrown onto the table, from which he fell to the floor.

Janek knew that the shots were heard outside. He was concerned about the soldiers left in the yard. Admittedly, he had suggested to this Vasily why he had come here, but you never know what will come in his head. He motioned for Alik to look carefully and see what the moods were down there while he looked at the two remaining alive, now cowering in fear.

He waited for Alik to come to the window, and when he nodded that everything was fine, he asked:

"Commissioner Rosa and Commander Yewlenski, am I wrong?"

They both nodded eagerly, following the movement of the Mauser barrel.

"What happened in Malinova? You, Comrade Yewlenski and you, Comrade Rosa, enlighten me."

They started speaking over each other, outdoing each other in testimony and giving facts. They showed a clear picture of the game between the farm commander and his commissar. The former relied on peasants of Polish origin, the latter on Ukrainians. And the first one lost. He and his men were exterminated, and the manor of the former tenant was set on fire to justify an external attack.

"If I'm not mistaken, Comrade Rosa, you were in touch with emissaries from Hulaipol, from this Nestor Makhno and his Revolutionary Insurgent Army of Ukraine."

The interviewee paled even more.

"Answer me kindly."

"It's not like that, comrade, I... they were... I had no choice..."

"Did they come to you or not?"

"It's not like that, comrade, I'll tell you everything as it was. Envoys from Pyotr Alexeyevich Kropotkin arrived, who, despite being a great lord and aristocrat, joined Makhno and the anarchist movement. And Lev Trotsky did not believe them, but he ordered to cooperate with the Ukrainian troops, I received an order directly from my comrade Iosif Unshlikht, a special order straight from Petrograd. But this my commander, Anastasius, started to suspect something, and he had dealings with someone else, maybe with Petliurian. I sent this intentionally asking Unshlikht what to do and I was ordered to liquidate the commandant immediately. What was I supposed to do? An order is an order."

"And this gold?"

No answer was given to this question, and there was silence.

"Why did you want to kill those peasants you keep them in the basement?"

"It's his idea," Rosa shrugged and pointed at his companion. "They wanted to kill them, to have an explanation for this Commissioner Babel, because he is a smart Jew and has been cooperating with Lieutenant Colonel Kluyev since before the war, when they were engaged in some common business. Supposedly he was given command over the regimental Cheka, but Commissioner Trotsky ordered to keep an eye on and watch over him."

"And what do you say, Comrade Yewlenski?"

The confused shrugged his shoulders too, but he gives as good as he gets from his companion.

"He is lying, bastard, because he try to deceive himself, there is always like that with these Jews..."

"You bastard..." Rosa tried to interrupt him, but the unequivocal movement of Janek's Mauser made him silent, only he stared with hatred at Yevlenski, who continued undeterred.

"It was he who sniffed these anarchists, because it was the Jews themselves and even a republic in Hulaipol and ours, when they caught it, it was straight to the sand, I had reports. And this Babel is also an Orthodox Jew, but it only cares about collecting gold, he will probably run away to them, before our people go to the Polish mess, because they are already getting ready. And he doesn't give a shit about a revolution, just like this one," he pointed with his head at the person sitting next to him, "these Jews are like that, only business, they would sell a mother..."

He didn't finish because Rosa couldn't stand the accusations and suddenly something inside him boiled over. He yanked the revolver out of his jacket and before Yewlenski could react, he shot his companion straight in the face.

This time Janek, in which the tension reached its zenith, instinctively pressed the Mauser trigger and shot the commissioner. Alik did it almost simultaneously. By the time the shots faded out, the two dead bodies fell to the floor, joining the others.

There was silence. It was still ringing in their's ears when Janek ran to the window to see how the soldiers in the marketplace reacted. Some of them looked curiously at the windows, but the guns remained on their shoulders. They clearly did not want to find out what and how the tasks were done by the commandery. It calmed him down; the fairy tale sold to Vasily still worked. He noticed two carts ready for the road, on which the peasants transferred from the basement were imprisoned.

"Pick it up and we take to the woods," he said to Alik, and now he heard the scratching at the door violently. He guessed that it was Sheba, concerned about the shots, who couldn't stand it and tried to get into the room.

Chapter XII

They left the town hall with their rifles slung over their shoulder as if nothing had happened. They refrained from ostentatiously glancing at the soldiers and examining how they behaved, but from the corner of their eyes they could see what was happening and whether the events in the town hall, and the shots were heard here, did not make them react.

"I think it's okay," Alik said under his breath, and Janek only confirmed his observations, then straightened up and called Vasily with his hand, who was clearly waiting for this sign.

"Comrade Vasily, all these traitorous four are dead," he said briefly, as if talking about the weather, watching the soldier's reaction. He remained calm, although he showed nervousness. "I'll show you something and you'll report it in the staff of Commander Budyonny."

He reached for the bundle Alik was carrying, untied it and showed the contents. Vasily's eyes widened at the sight of so many valuables, unable to take his eyes off them.

"This scumbags betrayed the ideals of the revolution and used it to collect gold for themselves. There had to be only one penalty. On the orders of Comrade Trotsky, we commande it to the benefit of the Western Rifle Division of the Revolutionary Red Warsaw Regiment. Do you remember?"

Vasily continued to stare at the valuables, unable to make his voice heard.

"Comrade..."

"Sorry, Commander, but I've never seen so much goods."

"I asked if you remembered what I said."

"Why I was not to remember, but comrade, perhaps you could give me a receipt, a letter to Commander Budyonny, I'm a simple soldier, they may not believe it."

"You'll just report back to the staff. And you will say how much gold it was, you saw for yourself. It's enough. Now hit the road."

Vasily's hands tightened on his hat, you can see that he couldn't make up his mind and something was bothering him, but finally he persisted and asked.

"You, comrade, aren't you coming with us?"

"New circumstances have arisen, related to the dealings with anarchists, and besides, they are waiting for me in the regiment.

The suspicions of the interview were confirmed and I did my job here. I'm taking the peasants with me to the Warsaw headquarters. Probably we will meet anyway when our people attack the Poles. And good luck in the name of the just struggle of the proletariat."

"Da tochna," Vasily stood for a moment, as if he wanted another question, but resigned. He saluted, then turned and gave the order to his coachmen.

***

They watched the carts departing until they became tiny points in the distance. The wheels in the melting snow left a clear mark, and that worried Janek. Their carts will leave them too, and it will be necessary to take a detour and drive long enough to discourage any curious people who would like to see who was going, in what direction and what he was doing here. There was no longer any chance to count on snowfall, because winter was ending and the sun was taking over the land more and more.

Another problem was the peasants, whose condition was not the best. Alik has penetrated several houses and brought the quilts so that they could cover themselves with something and they would not die of overcooling.

Let them go or take them?

So far, none of them said, although Janek saw their curious glances and the question of what would happen to them, looming almost in the air. They certainly saw a difference in the treatment of them by and by the Bolsheviks. The peasants from the countryside, he could see in their stealthy looks, must have recognized them, at least three of them, for the condition of two was such that they reckoned with the fact that they might not survive the way. And that meant that they had to get to the forest as soon as possible if she decided to help them.

The thought of letting go or taking care of began to win in him, although he did not know yet where and what to do next. Twelve people that was a problem. Releasing them to the village would certainly result in another interrogation and death. Give them a clear path, let them go wherever they want, the effect would be similar.

Now, looking at them, he remembered that the face of this one of Malinova was familiar to him. He walked over to the cart. The peasants avoided his eyes, tilting their heads, and this one...

Only now did he recognize.

Previously, it was dark in the basement, and his swollen, beaten face did not bring any associations, and besides, he was so busy with events and tense that he did not even try to strain his memory. But now he was looking, and he was distrustful.

"Alik, come over here."

As the friend approached, he pointed to the unconscious.

"Does he remind you of someone?" He still didn't believe it, he thought it was just someone similar, and the swelling and numerous wounds on the face had so distorted the face that it could resemble anyone.

"And how?"

Alik stared at the peasant, then shook his head in disbelief.

"Young master Fedor Pohorecki, but as if changed and thin as not him."

They looked silently at the unconscious when suddenly one of the peasants said shyly:

"They, my lord, had brought him somewhere long ago from some manor house, because only he knew how to operate the machines, because it was master... I mean, a thresher and others, and they were not able to start them."

"Then why is he like this?" Janek felt his agitation growing in him and he struggled to restrain himself from asking the question in a sharper tone.

"Because, sir, when the Bolsheviks started to clash among themselves," he glanced if he did not say something cheeky, "and when the people of this commissar Rosa killed the soldiers of Commander Anastasius, they killed some of the Polish peasants and arrested him as well. That he kind of fueled a rebellion among them."

"Did he do that?"

"No, sir, he is a good man," the peasant tugged his hair in frustration, not sure if he had done right, that he broke away with the answer and kept looking at the red star on Janek's chest. "If he could, he brought us food, a bit of turnips, potatoes, and even millet, because you can also cook soup. And it made no difference whether a Ukrainian or a Pole. Even this German," he pointed to an equally battered man sitting opposite him, "when they killed his brother and father, and raped his mother and sisters, and wanted to kill him, he defended him from the bullet that he was like a good helper and knows machines."

Janek just shook his head.

"What's your name?"

"Igor, my lord, Sedenkov."

"Then tell me what would you like to do now, where to go?"

The peasant looked at Janek with an expression of surprise as if he had seen the lord god himself.

"You are a Bolshevik," he glanced once again at the star on Janek's chest, "I don't know. You have your orders, I heard what you said to this Bolshevik. That, as if to some Warsaw regiment, I do not know, I..." he stopped irritated.

"Take it easy, Sedenkov, you will be safe, and neither will the rest of you. What did you do before, because you are more talkative than the rest."

"I..." He paused and you could see that he was struggling in his thoughts whether to tell the truth or lie.

"I'm asking you, so?"

"I helped..." he fell silent again, then decided not to hedge. "I helped in the parish at pope until the Bolsheviks hung him on the tower."

"At Father Parafiniuk's?"

"Da, at his place."

"He was an Ukrainian, why did they hang him?"

"Because, sir, he shouted to this commissioner that there are wicked ones, like those Jews who hung Jesus, they also hanged him."

"People didn't riot? It was their priest, as I remember well liked."

"Loooord..." The peasant stretched, surprised that it was obvious. "When Rosa himself shot three people who wanted to protest, the rest were silent."

"So, where do you want to go? You are free, you can choose."

"You're not taking us to this Warsaw regiment?"

"No, I don't even know where that regiment is."

"But..." the peasant's face suddenly lit up as he understood that this star does not necessarily mean what it symbolizes. "You aren't theirs, but different?" He asked how it seemed to him, tricky, but immediately he curled up involuntarily, as if he had committed some kind of sacrilege. "Forgive me, sir, I didn't mean to, forgive me, I'm stupid."

Janek laughed for the first time since coming to town.

"I don't have time to chat with you, Sedenkov, what would you like to do now?"

"I don't know, my lord, we will not go back to the village, because the soldiers of this commissioner have stayed there, I don't know, they will beat us up when they see us."

"You can come with us to the forest, I will hide you there."

"Please, my lord," a shy smile appeared on Sedenkov's face and he quickly corrected himself. "But what we are going to do there, they are barely breathing," he pointed at the barely breathing companions. "The closer to god than to the forest."

"Zastrielit'?" Alik cut in on the conversation, and the scared peasant immediately shrank even more, but quickly assured:

"Niet, niet, maybe they'll survive, they... we haven't eaten for many days and that's probably why they're weakening."

"Don't grumble and listen to what the master says," Alik said shortly and added mockingly to Janek: "You can see that he is from pope, because he doesn't shut up. He will be good." And to Sedenkov: "And how are you, your family?"

The peasant's face darkened.

"No, sir, they slaughtered my father, mother, sister and two brothers."

"I mean, you do not love the Bolsheviks, or maybe they are right to fight for the people?"

"Niet, my lord, I hate them like any of us, and they don't think about people."

"We'll see."

Janek listened silently to this exchange of views. On certain occasions, Alik knew perfectly well how to address the peasants, and he did so now.

"Alik, we're going, first like the soldiers, and then we'll turn into the forest. We've been here for too long."

"Sedenkov, can you walk?"

"Da, my lord, I can."

"Then come with me."

He returned to the town hall, and the peasant followed, still scared but also curious.

Janek went upstairs, to the room where the dead bodies were lying.

The peasant in the doorway stood in surprise and only listened to how hard he was breathing.

"Don't stare, their clothes may be useful to you, rip them off."

He collected four pistols with belts and holsters, and sabers hanging from the chairs.

"Sedenkov, can you shoot?"

"My lord, I was in the war, but only officers had revolvers, we had rifles."

"Can you do it?"

"Sure, sir, both of them shoots."

"Here you have a revolver, a belt, a holster, and with these clothes, hurry up, time is running out."

Janek, when the peasant was tearing shoes and clothes off the corpses with undifferentiated joy and some wild satisfaction, penetrated the room. He found some staff maps, some papers stamped "confidential", washing utensils, and extra coats in one of the closets. The latter he pointed to Sedenek to take them too. He took the gun and wrapped the uneaten flesh and unfinished vodka in paper.

After a dozen or so minutes they were downstairs.

Unanswered, the Ukrainian separated the uniforms, ordering the more conscious to wear them. He left it for himself, with real joy putting on the jackets taken from one of the commissioners. He took Janek's food and distributed it fairly to the peasants.

Janek recognized among those from his village Ivan, the son of a miller, who was friends with Joshua, and sometimes, when there was more traffic in the pub, he helped old Mendel. He seemed as fit as Sedenkov. He motioned for the Ukrainian to give him one uniform, boots and coat and ordered him to drive on the first wagon. Cause of surprise, he also handed him a pistol and showed the reins of the second cart to the Ukrainian.

"Let's go, and anyway, you know what the weapon is for. We've been here too long."

***

It took a few hours to get to the forest. They covered part of the way using the still frozen riverbed, although the ice has become almost transparent, you can see that any day it will let go and the floe will start flowing down somewhere lower, as it used to be here every year.

Janek and Alik penetrated the road going far away to check if there were no strangers in sight. The tension from the town was gone, but still its trace remained in the organisms. They felt tired, they would have liked to shorten the way, but safety was more important.

On the way he asked Igor if they had noticed the townspeople, but it turned out that when the peasants were brought here, they were gone, and neither were the troops.

"I only heard from one of the soldiers that when the Bolsheviks came to the city, some were killed, merchants, officials, and others were rushed away," he said shortly.

It was already dusk when the carts drove into the first trees. Janek led them to a distant lake with a small island thickly covered with bush and trees. The ice on the lake was still passable, but the wheels fell twice into places where it was already brittle. It took time to haul out, and they reached the island once it was dark.

Janek did not allow anyone to lie down. He showed the healthier ones what to do, and those in the middle of the thicket built a hut, first bending the branches of the trees, threading them with evergreen boxwood, as well as with the common ivy and scarlet fire. On top, and to cover the whole thing, they added creeping, very dense branches from Irga and Ligustra.

It should be warmer for the sick here, the more so that he put the horses pulling the cart between them, so that they would additionally give their bodies warmth. At the end he ordered silence, promised he would come back with food and at the end he dragged the unconscious Fedor onto his Sewek with the help of Alik.

When they got to the cave, he was so tired that he doubled over on his feet. However, he could not afford to rest. Likewise, Alik who, unanswered, prepared a supply of meat, honey and herbs with garlic, and went to the peasants. He was commanded to kindle the fire as Janek had taught him; without smoke, small, warm for a long time. He also took the pot to brew the herbs and make soup in it. Janek was afraid that the hungry would throw at the meat, which exhausted organisms would not stand up and would return everything.

And himself, after Alik had gone, prepared food and herbs for the unconscious Fedor, as he had done for Alik when he had escaped him from the hands of the Bolsheviks.

***

For a week Fedor's condition, like the two peasants from his village, did not improve, but neither did it, which gave rise to hope, it did not worsen. The breakthrough almost simultaneously for the entire trio did not come until the following week, but they were recovering very slowly anyway.

Time passed for Janek and Alik to look after the sick ones, to hunt, because there were now a lot of mouths to feed and on short trips to the village and the manor house to check what was going on in them.

Fedor, as Alik previously did not believe, that he was alive and that it was not a dream. He wanted to know everything right away, he asked what was in his court, although he had no illusions that he would hear any good news. Janek silenced him, told him to rest and promised that they would talk to him as soon as he regained his strength.

When he returned from hunting one day, he found Fedor in a much better condition arguing lively with Alik. They both suddenly fell silent when they saw him, as if ashamed to find them so amused. He didn't ask, pretended not to notice their confusion, and started making the soup, somewhat surprised Alik had forgotten about it. He was intrigued by how this comity had come about, since Fedor, the one from before the war, not so much despised Alik as the whole Pohorecki family, believed that everyone in society must know their place and treated his friend like everyone else in the court.

They ate the ready-made dish and Alik under the pretext of looking into the others and checking the health of those most affected, disappeared.

"You know, I have to tell you something," Fedor began, and when Jan tried to say no, he silenced him with his hand. "I have to, I thought it over. I understood something when the Bolsheviks invaded our village. I saw them dragging my father and Anton somewhere into the garden, how without any warning they murdered the Birski family, who happened to be staying with us, and before that their three daughters and their mother were raped and then drowned in a cesspool while still alive. I saw how peasants who refused to participate in their killing orgy were killed, but before that they nailed their children with pitchforks to the walls..."

He paused, and the memories of those moments must have been so strong that he began to gasp, gasping for breath.

"Stop it, Fedor, tell me another time," Janek tried to interrupt him. "You're still too weak, you have to..."

"No, Janek, I have to get it out of my mind," Fedor was silent for a moment, then continued. "Thought I was going to lose my mind. I didn't know why they didn't kill me. I found out only later how they took me to Malinova and told me to start the machines. I wanted to die, I even refused, they locked me in a henhouse and didn't give me food or water, and even took my clothes. I don't know how many days I was dying so naked until they broke me. I stopped thinking about the crimes, kills, rapes. All I could see was water... When they released it, I had no strength for anything. And I started working as they wanted. I saw what they were doing while drunk. And - this is what I wanted to tell you - I understood something else. I don't know why, but then you and your friendship with Alik kept coming back to me. There, in Malinova, I was helped by such a boy, Andrei. And yet he should, like others, despise me, a noble, and yet..."

There was silence.

Fedor's face, shriveled with memory, almost turned gray, and tears ran down his cheeks.

Janek wanted to react somehow, but he restrained himself. He waited for Fedor to calm down.

"And when I woke up here and saw you, Alik and that wolf, I wasn't surprised at anything anymore. All my pride was long ago killed by the Bolsheviks, and only hatred with which I can no longer fight remains. I hate them so much that I'm afraid of myself."

"What about this Andrei? He stayed in Malinova?"

"Someone reported that he was helping me because I was working with machines, but they continued to abuse me, and he would come and explain that the paths of suffering, the paths to God were unexplored. He was going to go to the seminary when the war broke out. He was very religious and very spiritual. And when they reported that he was brother with me, they dragged him out of the cottage, tied his legs to two horses and tore him apart... And the mother, who threw herself in his defense, hung by her legs on a branch and then practiced saber strikes on her..."

Another silence was prolonged, and then Fedor, gathering himself together, added softly:

"I envy you very much that you first understood the things that I had to come to when I experienced everything on myself. And thank you for saving my life."

***

Three weeks passed and spring broke out, literally overnight. From moment to moment, buds appeared on trees and shrubs, the forest began to turn green, and all the birds, until now speaking sporadically, were now trolling powerfully. The bird cherry trees were covered with flowers releasing a suffocating, sweet scent heralding aromatic berries, as did the blackcurrant bushes that grew almost everywhere.

Janek went to the river several times admiring the view, which always made an impression on him. The ice cracked, and where it was thinner it broke the bond with winter and created large blockages of accumulating ice floes, not infrequently several meters high. Another time he watched these icebergs crack, fall on thin ice, break it, create smaller pieces, and together they rush down the river, pushed by the water piled up beneath them, tearing off new and larger chunks, all the way to the place where the thicker the ice had not yet surrendered, and the mountain of the last breath of winter was rising again.

One time he saw that the whole river was flowing rapidly, and there was a faint stench above it. At first he thought that the moved clay soil smelled so bad, but as he got closer to the shore he was shocked. In a large crash in many places he saw frozen human corpses, partially rotting, dismembered, insulting the image of death and human dignity. A sign that where upstream the massacre began and the Bolshevik troops began moving west.

***

A few days later the frost briefly returned and cut the river down again. Heavy, wet snow sprinkled from the dark clouds. It was probably the last spurt of this winter. Even the birds fell silent, surprised by the rainfall, and the animals crouched somewhere, waiting for the weather to change.

Janek instructed Alik to start training healthy peasants in the use of weapons. He handed out spare rifles, no ammo so far, and had them practice aiming, disassembling the rifle, clearing jams, lubricating, and maintaining. Later he also added sabers to teach them the basics of fencing.

"You want to make soldiers out of them?" Alik had doubts. "They're country cousins, common to the harrow, not the rifle. Only this Sedenkov was in the army, the rest are..." He waved his hand, not ending.

"Let them earn our protection. They may still be useful. I remember my grandfather telling about my great-grandfather that he made a strong party out of peasants and commoners that took its toll on the Moskals. I just made up my mind that times different, Moskals changed its name to Bolshevik, but that does not mean not to try."

"But, but... Peasants are not ordinary..."

"And what do you think, the Bolsheviks made soldiers from whom, their bandits?"

"Yeah, right, are you sure of them?"

"No, but I think there is so much hatred in them, they suffered so much, they murdered their families, and you can probably carve them into soldiers. They are no worse than those red fighters."

"If you want so..." Alik was not convinced, but he started training.

After a week, Alik announced that he must have been wrong. He was surprised by the determination of his charges, who patiently repeated the instructions for hours; they stayed with their rifles at their shoulders, playing the bow-tie with the rear sight, changed positions from standing to kneeling, and then they did the same while lying down for many hours every day. And when it comes to marking shooting while on the move or while rolling on the ground with a rifle, making an apparent shot and further changing position, it even bursts with enthusiasm and joy. They did not complain, showed patience and great determination to carry out every order well, to convince Alik that they deserved their trust. At the beginning, they treated riding a horse and using a saber with some distrust. They often fell, they were afraid, but as the hours passed, their perseverance brought results, and the desire to be proficient in learning everything was so great that even Alik felt tired of learning.

"I think they adore you," he laughed, giving Janek the training report. "I even heard once that they composed a song about you, and you are like an ataman in it, leading them to fight and revenge."

"Stop it," Janek was not used to such praise. "When the time comes, we'll go somewhere else and they'll start shooting hard. We will see how much enthusiasm this gave results."

In his soul, however, he felt glad that he had decided to train peasants and that he was kindly flattered by vanity, that they had a positive opinion of him. And he remembered the words of his grandfather, who assured his mother who was leaving with cuirassiers to a distant family near Lviv that the peasants from the village liked Janek because he had no fancy airs, he did not stand above them, and if there was a problem, he tried to resolve it objectively, despite that he is still so young."

"Mom, what about her," joy faded as he remembered the family he had not seen in a long time. He remembered his sister, Anna, who was always smiling. How are they? Have the Bolsheviks got there yet?

Feeling that he was overwhelmed by sad nostalgia, he nodded to Sheba, went to get Sewek and headed towards the court. Alik was with the peasants, Fedor was asleep, he did not want to sit so idly in the cave.

The snow still slickered, heavily circling the air. There was a smell of spring, although the wet air was saturated with damp and despite the temporary lowering of the temperature, it lacked the winter sharpness and former freshness. The branches of the trees and bushes were covered with a white eiderdown that dragged them to the ground, bending them sharply, as if they were carrying a weight beyond their measure. Occasionally, he noticed only a few traces in the snow, a sign that the game was carefully hiding in the holes, waiting out the time when the trail could be dangerous for them.

***

The manor house visible from a distance has not changed. Smoke was coming out of the chimneys, not rising, and lying low, unable to fly higher. Nobody was around, even the neighing of the horses from the stables could not be heard. Were it not for this smoke one would get the impression that no one lives here and has been abandoned.

He observed the area for a moment, then returned to Sewek and Sheba patiently waiting for him, and went to the village. He circled it in the forest and went out onto the road, found that there were no new traces on it, so no one had followed it for a long time, and only then did he go towards the hut where Joshua lived.

He stopped at a distance, but there were no signs of life here either. Only somewhere in the center of the village could there be any shouts or chants resembling the sounds of a happy libation.

The sight of fresh tracks in front of the hut, including horse tracks, reminded him of the ice hole and the place where the water was drawn. He thought about checking who was going there, scolded that it was not prudent and, contrary to his internal warning, directed Sewek towards the river.

He felt the pleasant feeling that the nostalgia had disappeared somewhere and a well-known tension arose that sharpened his senses. He was himself again, as before, when he wandered around the village alone, not knowing what was happening with his friends and family. He even smiled to himself, because the new situation he had found himself in since his stay in town was starting to make him feel lazy for a long time.

The sound of hooves in the snow was like shuffling along the shore as your feet sink into the wet sand. He slowed down to make the sound quieter.

He watched the tracks on which he was driving. The footprints of two horses and one pedestrian were very clear. A sign that they were moving recently, because the falling snow not only did not cover them, but they were as clear as if they had just been created.

"Why are you pushing there for?" he thought over and over again.

Then he paused his horse for a moment, but curiosity quickly won out and he moved on.

He drove up to a hill rising up here, behind which a river flowed in a canyon. There was no sign of the riders returning, they must have been by the river, but he heard a vague, gibberish scold interspersed with insults and curses.

He pulled off Ewek's reins.

He plunged the Winchester, unbuttoned his jacket and pistol holster, then removed his bow from his shoulder, unbuckled his quiver, checked for easy access, and pulled out two arrows. He was ready to meet. And although he still thought it was stupidity and unnecessary bravado, something pushed him to see what was going on there. The image flashed from memory involuntarily when the ice cream started to rise after the temperature increased; the terrifying sight of decomposing bodies on the flowing crash, silent testimony of the cruelty of the conquerors.

Sheba showed nervousness, showing him with all her attitude that she felt strangers. He motioned for her to run away and gestured up the hill. The wolf hesitated only for a moment, then quickly ran towards the bushes overgrowing them and disappeared between them.

He took a deep breath, peered towards the rooftops of the outlying village houses, and slowly moved forward. The closer he was, the sounds were clearer.

His muscles tingled.

He rode carefully up the hill. Mentally, he once again became convinced that he was doing well, that the time of hiding and panicky fear for the Bolsheviks was over, and he gently chased Sewek away.

He drove to the top of the hill.

At the bottom of the river bank, not more than twenty or thirty meters, there were three figures. One was kneeling at the ice hole, and next to it lay a wooden sling with two overturned water jars. On horseback, soldiers were circling, mocking him and occasionally slapping him with their whips.

"Get up, you scumbag, you pig... Suddenly you ran out of strength... Move, Jew, because we will beat you, you lousy pig-fucker, scab..."

Janek did not move. He just watched the drunken soldiers torment the kneeling man, who was trying hard not to fall. They had a great time. Even when they struck their whips, it was as if casually, to confirm their words, not to kill him.

After a while, the sobriety of judgment returned with a fierce surge of anger and hatred towards the two. He moved Sewek's knees, put an arrow on the bowstring and began to approach them. He felt the adrenaline level in his blood rise; all the senses were put on high alert.

When he was no farther than ten paces, one of the soldiers lashed the kneeling man so hard that a blood streak remained on the boy's back.

The second Bolshevik, provoked by this, also raised his whip.

Janek was fed up with this sight. A little more, and they would take his life.

He tautened the string and shoot.

At that moment the other rider saw him.

The astonishment on his face struggled for a split second with the attempt to understand what he was seeing, and his raised hand was motionless. He only managed to open his mouth to get his companion's attention as an arrow hit him in the neck and paralyzed him, reaching the nerves of his spine. A contraction jerked his head back, tilting it back. And it continued for a fraction of a second, on the verge of life and death, after which the body began to lose its balance with the escaping breath and slowly slide off the saddle.

The second, with his back so far to the shore, only now noticed what was happening. This one seemed more sober and his reactions more coordinated. Without thinking, he turned his horse around and began to pull the rifle off his shoulder. Perhaps he would have had time, had it not been for Sheba, who could not stand it and ran down the hill. At the sight of her, the Bolshevik horse snorted in terror and flung it sideways, trying to turn its back to the wolf.

Janek's second arrow hit the soldier when he was trying to take control of the mount and at the same time focus the rifle. The arrowhead stuck into one of the sockets, sank into the brain and caused almost instant death.

He fell to the ground like a sack of rye thrown from a wagon.

There was silence.

The kneeling man did not move. His body was still twitching from the pain and the chill. He did not notice what was happening around him. He waited for more blows.

Janek jumped off the saddle and ran to him.

He distinguished the boy before he started shooting.

"Joshua, it's me," he blurted out, touched, touching the arm of the kneeling man.

The man cringed, terrified.

The words did not reach his consciousness.

"Joshua, it's me, for Kaduk! Look at me!" Janek shouted trying to reach his consciousness.

He still didn't respond.

It was only when Janek shook him strongly that something hit him. He looked up, looked, his eyes widened in disbelief, then consciousness refused to cooperate.

He passed out.

Janek wasted no time in getting it back. Sheba did not let the horses move away, and those terrified by the smell of the wolf almost cuddled up to Sewek standing calmly.

He tied the pommels of their saddles with a strap. He took the sheepskin coats off the corpses, threw one over the saddles, took the weapons, hung them from the saddles, thought for a moment and took off their long boots from the Bolsheviks and put them in the saddles of his horse. He looked at the soldiers. He couldn't leave them there. He quickly pulled the bodies to the edge of the ice hole and lowered them into the water. The current under the ice quickly pulled them deeper.

Only now he had lifted Joshua resting on the snow and placed it on the connected saddles. He was surprised that the young Jew weighs so little, almost nothing.

He did not give in to his emotions, although they tugged at him. He felt he had to hurry. If suddenly, for some reason, someone appeared, and God forbid the riders... He dismissed the thought, additionally tied Joshua to the saddles so that he would not slide down and cover him with a second sheepskin coat. He started off. Not too fast, but just enough to leave this place immediately.

This time he did not come back the way he had come. He chose the shorter one, between the village and the court. It was more dangerous, but he hoped none of the soldiers would stick their noses out of their warm huts when it was snowing.

Chapter XIII

"You did it, you did it, you are crazy." Alik rejoiced like a little child, nurturing and feeding Joshua who only ran his eyes around the cave and showed that he still didn't believe what had happened.

When Fedor saw the young Jew, Janek was concerned about his reaction. The Pohorecki family never tolerated the Orthodox Jews, and even when a trader tried to sell something, they chased him from their lands, often letting their dogs run. Grandfather once hinted that it was the result of a conflict with a Jew, also an officer, during his service in Hryhor's army, when they both liked a young girl. She chose the latter, and the trauma remained and passed on to the family. But now, as Fedor bustled about trying to help Alik, he was relieved. Apparently the experience with Malinova really changed the boy.

He went outside. From the time when the cave, not the largest, despite the second chamber, the one with the spring, became a dwelling place for several men, it was tight. Months of solitude and freedom did their job. He had to change it, just how? Maybe a permanent camp needs to be built in the place where the peasants were staying?

He went to Sewek's stables, took new horses and went to the island. It was not a long time since he left all training duties to Alik. Time to see what the results are.

He wondered, and the thought kept coming to him that security had been compromised. It was beginning to be dense in the forest, there were people and horses, and it was enough, he reasoned, for the Bolshevik command to make a decision that the forest should be searched. And this could happen when their commander, Kluyev or Commissioner Babel combine the facts, the disappearance of soldiers and it will come out simply, that a Polish party must be active nearby. And where can they hide? Only in the forest. He had to clean up this too.

Meditating like this, he quickly reached the lake. He got off with Sewek and carefully surveyed the island through the binoculars. There was no indication that anyone was on it.

"Okay, he taught them something," he thought about Alik's training. "The first task was to live there in such a way that no one would notice any human interference. The second - masking with branches and creeping wicker so that the surrounding area looks like one green wall, visible from the shore. And the third - maintaining absolute silence.

There were two fords to reach the island, invisible, hidden under water, covered with a sheath of slurry, but with hard, non-collapsing ground at the bottom. Elsewhere, the silt from the very shore created a treacherous trap impossible to cross.

He left Sewek and only with the watchful Sheba moving by his side, he crossed to the island. Before he could put his feet on firm ground, the wolf's low growl made him realize they were being watched. Another point for Alik. The ford was guarded.

He didn't stop, just turned back and softly whistled his horse. This one was just waiting for it. In a moment he was with him. Sheba stood taut pointing in the direction where the guard was hiding.

"No strangers?" He asked aloud turning to the supposed guard's hideout. He didn't see him, but he sensed surprise in response that this one had been discovered.

"All right, Commander, no one, but how did you see me?"

He waved his hand and made his way deeper into the island without answering. Let them think that nothing can be hidden from him - he allowed himself a bit of vanity. And the fact that he got the information from the wolf was his secret.

He was surprised, however, to see Sedenkov emerging from the thick bushes.

"Hello, Commander," the Ukrainian saluted, standing in a basic position. He saw his surprise and uncertainty as to why it was not Alik who had come, but him.

Another point - Janek did not allow himself to show his astonishment, but he felt inner satisfaction that in just a few weeks his friend turned these peasants from passive victims into quasi soldiers. "We'll see what else he managed to get out of them."

"Everyone knows I've arrived?"

"No, Commander, but the guard let them know by te.. le... graph" he spelled the newly learned word with clear satisfaction.

"What?"

"Well, this is what wachtmeister calls it, such strings from the guard to the camp, a green ribbon up, it's ours, if black it's a danger and grab a weapon, and if it's red it's something uncertain and you have to be vigilant."

"Wachtmeister?" Alik's term astonished him.

A lot has changed in these few weeks.

"Well, yes, wachtmeister Alik taught us everything."

It was close and Janek would have burst out laughing. He could hardly remain serious. Even during the idyll, before the war, Alik's favorite book, which he almost knew by heart, was "The Deluge", and the model of conduct was wachtmeister Soroka. How vividly he transferred literature to peasants, which he did not boast to Janek. Wachtmeister? Commander? It is all right if it is easier to train. He congratulated his friend mentally.

"Colonel..."

This next nomenclature surprised and amused Janek so much that this time he laughed, making Sedenkov visibly embarrassed and suspected that he had smacked something wrong.

"Speak, speak, I remembered something," he reassured him.

"I mean, Commander, that is, Colonel..." Sedenkov was not sure if he was making good use of the charges instilled in him. "And because I am mistaken, but the wachtmeister spoke once of you as a colonel, and once as a commander, then I don't know how to say," he pointed back towards the camp. "And he also said that," he interrupted and took the missing words out of his memory, "a deluge and the plague must be eradicated, so I think that the plague is the Bolsheviks and the colonel is better suited. And he told us about such a colonel Kmicic, who also defended the peasants against some Swedes for our grandfathers, that he saved Czestochowa... it was very interesting..." He broke off, embarrassed by his talkative talk.

However, it was evident that Alik's stories made a great impression on him.

"Speak as you like, and now lead me," Janek briefly said so as not to show amusement.

And it was big, and he was amazed at his friend's ingenuity. The Swedish Deluge adapted to the present conditions, which seemed to him an interesting idea to reach the imagination of the peasants. And apparently it worked. What else did he come up with?

After several dozen meters, they approached a seemingly uniform wall of greenery, when it rose to reveal an entrance reinforced with a thick palisade.

He paused, even more amazed. The masking with different plants was perfect. And behind it was a real fort. The whole thing must have taken a lot of work. Now he understood why Alik had traveled with Sedenkov and Ivan to the old war-time fortifications to look for abandoned axes, saws, and other junk. It seemed risky and pointless to him, but Alik assured him that he had a plan and would be careful. They even took three additional horses with them. Now he understood.

"If you would educate him, he would be a good builder," he summed up his observations in his mind.

The entire camp was surrounded by a palisade of thick tree trunks. On the opposite sides were two roofed towers, near which he noticed lights with colored tapes. It was probably thanks to them that the guards sent information from their posts. In three places, ladders led to the treetops, disappearing among the foliage.

The Ukrainian was proud to show the details. Janek did not comment, but nodded his head approvingly. At the same time he was catching the attentive glances of others standing almost at attention. He was aware that they were waiting for his reaction, maybe even praise, because a lot of work was put into this place.

"Nice, ingenious, but let's see what you already know," he said quietly. "Have you been practicing?"

"Yes, sir," was the reply immediately.

He looked at them with curiosity and thoughtfulness, wondering how they would prove themselves in direct confrontation with battle-hardened soldiers. I remember my own hesitations, doubts, and yet they were representatives of the people whose freedom the Bolsheviks allegedly fought for, proclaiming it to all and sundry. On the other hand, they experienced the practical side of ideology on themselves and their families, and when they were brought to the town, where they were to be shot. He believed in their peasant, sober reasoning and interpretation of reality. And now it's them...

He broke his thoughts as he stared at the faces, now serene, with laughing eyes, clearly waiting for him to check them out.

"Okay, let's see what you already know." He reached for his saber and pulled it out of its scabbard. "Who's first?"

They looked at each other, not so sure anymore.

"Sedenkov, come on," he ordered the Ukrainian. "Don't think, come on."

"Because, sir..." The peasant suddenly reverted to his usual nomenclature, which was a sign that he was not at all confident in his abilities, which he suddenly doubted.

Old habits had to take over. After all, Alik was his guy, and here stood a young lord who, admittedly, snatched them from the hands of the Bolsheviks, but always the one from the court."

"Come on, Igor, do not grumble, you are probably the first charge after the commander-in-chief," sneered Janek, amused by his resistance, although he sensed it, but understood it. He had to overcome this natural reflex and quickly overcome this distance. "I won't hurt you. Now, take an attitude, no Bolshevik will wait for you to think about it and only break your guts out."

The other slowly drew his saber, unsure of the command, and waited to see what happened next.

"What are you standing there? Attack, it's not a stick, it's a weapon."

He saw a flash in the Ukrainian's eyes and the blade flashed through the air. It bounced without problems. Another attack. Block and repetition. He parried a blow and laughed.

"It's not a flail, Sedenkov," he rebuked the Ukrainian. "Think, concentrate, this is what the wachtmeister taught you..."

He mark an attack, testing his skills and reflexes. He felt stubborn, only able to cut a few basic cuts, but the thinking was worse. The peasant reacted intuitively, as if he were hitting with a rail rather than a weapon.

"Sedenkov, do you remember how they killed your family?" Reminded him to trigger a more lively reaction. "You have a Bolshevik in front of you, kill him."

This time, Sedenkov attacked with real fury, putting all his strength and hatred into the blows. Still, it was flail, not fencing.

"Where did you serve?" He parried the blows without any problems. "Not in infantry or cavalry, is it?" He jumped back and waited for the hatred in the eyes of the Ukrainian to pass away and for the old Igor to return, talkative and cheerful by nature.

"I was at the artillery," Sedenkov breathed deeply, restored to reality. "I'm sorry, as I remembered..."

"Nothing happened, but in the fight you have to think, and not get carried away by hatred, and now hold tight and watch yourself," Janek turned, than unexpectedly for Igor, he easily knocked off his saber, which flew high into the air.

Sedenkov looked surprised, not comprehending what had happened, and the rest just groaned in surprise and envy.

Janek shook his head.

"Who's next? Who better than Igor?"

Silence answered him. They rolled their eyes to the side. After such a show, neither wanted to stand.

"I think it's just me," Ivan, the miller's son, turned out to be bolder than the others. "It's difficult, sir, because the hand is untrained, but I think we're better at shooting."

"Without bullets?" Janek sneered, but took a quick look so as not to intimidate them.

"Yes, because Alik told me to stand motionless for hours on end and aim, a bead, rear sight, front sight, rear sight, so that the rifle would not twitch, even if hands fainted. And he hung a stone on the barrel for everyone, so that we would get used to the weight," Ivan said it now with conviction, but also with clear satisfaction. "And he showed how to shoot while rolling on the ground, how to kneel, and how to hide so as not to get..." He paused for a moment, but seeing that Janek was listening carefully, he continued. "But there was no way to prove ourselves, we aim at flies, birds and all the time a bead, a peep sight and so all day long, and sabers..." He fell silent again and just shrugged.

"So take yours rifles in hand and aim."

"For what, my lord?"

"For anything."

He watched as they more confidently reach for their rifles, taking them from the trestles, how each one targets an imaginary object and how they freeze motionless, and later they quickly change to another, and only the crash of the dropped taps interrupted the silence.

He watched everyone closely. They mastered dry shooting to a much greater extent than using a saber. In practice, however, it will turn out what they can do. He watched carefully that the ends of the barrels did not vibrate, how they regulate the breathing each time the trigger is pressed, how they concentrate when changing position.

"Okay, guys, this looks much better to me," he interrupted the show. "And with the sabers I will not let go. You have to exercise, but preferably not with them, because you will only chip them. Put it down and find a heavy stick. And hurry up, boys, I don't have time for learning."

They scattered in search of. A few barely brought sticks, so he dismissed them and ordered them to look for the heavier ones.

Only these could be used to show maneuvering the wrist, and not by simple force. He also found the right one for himself, not too long and not too fat.

When they were ready, he arranged them in a semicircle, and then he showed each of them the various secrets of fencing.

"A saber, guys, it has a blade on one side, and that should be used," he said, slowly demonstrating each word with the motion of an imaginary blade. "Curved, so not stabbing like a bacon pick." They reacted with laughter; a sign that they are listening carefully, relaxed now. "It must be ready to cut, attack immediately, without making any swings, because a swing is a waste of time and a better opponent will be faster and cut you like a threshing machine. It is best if you have it erected. Then the cut may go on several sides. It's one thing and the other is the wrist. Power in your hand, but it's the wrist that gets the blade where you want it to hit."

He demonstrated a slow cut from above, paying attention to his wrist movements. He repeated again and again. And then he told them to do the same.

He watched how they put into practice, with what determination they do, trying to show him that they are diligent and want to learn.

"Without strength, practice precision, it will be time to strengthen the blow, now only this move and the next one," he corrected the more rash.

After an hour, he showed the importance of steps and feet in the fight on the ground. He also discussed the difference in

272

maneuvering the weapon from the horse. He took a saber and explained how to use a handguard's whiskers to make a precise cut, and how to use the strike technique to deflect a blow, and if you unbalance an opponent, put it on the blade. And how, instead of force, to use the weight and bend of the blade, so that the effect grows from the rounding and movement of the weapon, not the muscles, and to use it also to counter thrusts.

***

It was already dark when he returned to the cave. Alik was concerned about his disappearance for several hours, but made no comment. Instead, under the pretext of showing something outside from the swamps, he led Janek there.

"Something happened? Fedor and Joshua?"

"No, they're fine. There is nothing left of the pompous lord, and Joshua dozes more than talks. Where have you been?"

"With your peasants on the island."

"Something's wrong? You disappeared so suddenly, you usually say where you are going."

"We felt tight in the cave, I wanted to get some air."

Alik looked at him frowning.

"I noticed it myself, but what should I do? Take Joshua and Fedor to the island? I don't know how the peasants will take it. You know, kind of... Fedor, he's always a lord, maybe Joshua and I will move over there, just let him recover completely."

"It'll have to be unraveled somehow, you can't isolate them, but why are you dragging me here? Anyway, congratulations on this fort and training, especially on fortifications. You have a knack for such a job."

"Eh, only basic rules, you know, as Vasily told us, and a lot of water will flow before they learn something."

"I noticed that sabers are still flails to them, but maybe they are better when shooting. You will have to go somewhere far away and shoot hard. We will then see how efficient they are. And how, because I haven't checked it, they stay on horses?"

"They are not Cossacks, but quite well."

"What are we here for?"

"Joshua told me about the village and the manor house, because he regularly carried water there. I think we need to do something."

"It means?"

"It's about that lieutenant Demenkov we talked about once. Bad with him."

"Is he sick?"

"No, that's not the point. His commandant whipped him and then locked him in a basement."

"Anything more? For what?"

Joshua only knows what he overheard. It was about some calculations, but what, he does not know. The commander was only screaming that there was supposed to be more that he had not noticed that he was shit, not a scribe, that something else, but what the row was about, he has no idea. I think it's a pity, but how to get him out, I don't know."

"He did not hit in the face, but whipped, somehow strange."

"Not himself, his people. Joshua says he saw them dragged bloodied and unconscious to the basement."

"In the basement, you say, are you sure there?"

"Yes. Oh, there's also the Fedor case."

"You said it was alright."

"Not younker, Fedor Ostapko. Apparently he walks with madness in his eyes, drinks and threatens to clean up."

"Where?"

"Not where, and with whom. Joshua says he may want to kill the commander, that's his target, but that's a guess. For now, he is still limiting himself and weaving around the village, because the manor was informed soon enough, but if he goes on like this, he will be lost."

"So, we have a problem."

"I know and that's why I'm telling you here. You have to think of something, you are after all..."

"Colonel?"

"They already told you," Alik laughed happily. "You know, when I told them about Kmicic, about his adventures, they listened as at the best service. So you became a colonel. In fact, they themselves suggested it, and I didn't deny it."

"And you became the wachtmeister."

"They really liked it. They were fascinated. And they had an unequivocal association: Kmicic and Soroka, a colonel and a wachtmeister."

***

Despite the darkness, Janek went to see how things were going at the court. There are still no posts around, as it was at the beginning. This could prove, although it did not have to be, that neither the commandant nor the commander had ever fully associated the facts.

He returned to the cave on the way, devising a plan of action. He could enter the manor only by using the old tunnel. He could only use Alik for the operation, but he also thought about the role of the peasants as security should the situation get out of hand.

As soon as he drank his coffee, he initiated his friend's plan. He immediately expressed his support and enthusiasm for Janek making his decision so quickly.

"Just tell me what tunnel this is about," he asked quietly.

"You don't know it, you'll see it there. Once upon a time, great-grandfather Victor, when there was an uprising, dug it up so that there was an alternative way to escape from the court. They never used it, or maybe I don't know, but the tunnel has remained. It leads to the hideout in the basement where the weapons were stored. I hope they didn't discover it, because it takes a coincidence to find it when the wall is opened. There is such a special security there."

"It might work."

"Maybe, that's not enough. We must protect ourselves for this. We're still going tonight. Now run to the peasants, give the ammunition. And that we do not have the opportunity to check what their actual skills are."

"I don't understand, what are they for? The two of us will quietly get the lieutenant out. And may it be worth it."

"When the commandant's people notice something, hear something... A lot can happen, we must be secured. If something will go wrong, the peasants will fire at the mansion to distract attention. We risk. This lieutenant colonel has a dozen experienced thugs under his command, and we are amateurs. We must have an alternative, and I am counting on a surprise here. And the night, because at night all devils are black and courage is dying. Understand?"

Alik asked no more questions. Excited by the expedition, he only rubbed his hands with joy and left.

Fedor approached Janek. He sat down, was silent for a moment, and then looked into his eyes.

"I also want to go, Janek, I heard that you are making a trip to the manor."

"You're too weak, and besides, I must have someone I trust here," Janek touched on his ambition, hoping that it would be a convincing argument. "Someone's got to keep an eye on Joshua and look after him in case something goes wrong. You are unlikely to be found here in the cave, but if you do, you can escape through the swamps on the other side. And then Joshua needs the help of someone stronger. Too weak yet and doesn't know the forest."

"I don't know that either."

"But you have more strength and sense, and he never went to the forest, only in this father's bar. You hunted, the forest is no news to you. Do you get it?"

Fedor looked at him aware of the arguments, although internally everything in him spoke in favor of taking part in the expedition.

"Let him go," came Joshua's weak voice from the corner of the cave. "I don't wanna be a burden."

Janek pouted.

"My gentlemen, for the time being, I'm in charge here and it will be as I said. Two weak men are no help, they're ballast. You got it?"

They looked at him, and this time they just nodded their heads without saying a word.

"And I like it," Janek smiled, softening his previous statement. "Fedor shoots well, and you, Joshua, would sooner shoot yourself than use a gun. I don't anticipate that they will discover you here, we will mask the entrance, but I want to take care of it. If I took Fedor, I would have to leave Alik here, because for now I believe these peasants, but time will tell if they are worth it. I know only those from our village, and those from Malinova... You understand?"

Only the last words convinced them.

Chapter XIV

They left well after midnight. Janek in the front, Alik behind him, and one by one, there are other riders.

At the height of the manor, Janek placed the peasants among the last trees of the orchard, opposite the front of the building, carefully choosing each position. He appointed Igor as commander.

"If nothing happens, you retreat to the horses and wait for me or Alik," he gave the last instructions. "But if something unexpected happened and the soldiers ran out of the court, you should shoot. Only without bravado; aim, fire, don't panic, as in exercise. Don't let anyone else think of yelling, though you'll probably feel like it. Remember, if you keep silence, they will fear you. Again, remember, fire and change of place."

"Yes, sir." Sedenkov was excited and proud to command the rest. "It will happen as you ordered; no showing off, just practice, a bead, a peep sight, a shot and a change of place. Maybe the commandant can rely on me. And on them too."

Had it not been for the seriousness of the situation, Janek would have laughed at his proud demeanor. He was also aware that he was endangering people who did not take part in the fight, except for Igor, who served in the army, but spent the rest of the war in the village. Now they were going to prove themselves. Not so much in front of him as in front of each other.

He took two with him, including Ivan.

"Would you go to the island?" he asked him.

The boy scratched his head, unsure of himself. "I think so, but I'm not sure. There are so many trees in the forest..."

The reply made Janek laugh, but he remained serious.

"Okay, let's see, you're going with us for now."

The four of them carefully withdrew, and when they were no longer visible from the court, they got on their horses and drove towards the rocks. Janek stopped at the end of the orchard. Here he ordered the peasants to guard the horses, and he and Alik came closer to the rocks. Hence, Janek watched the dormant manor house for a long time through binoculars. The night was dark and the visibility was bad. A light flickered in one of the windows; probably lamps, where the duty officer was on duty.

They set off, and Janek was closely watching the wolf. Sheba ran alongside, carefully penetrating the air. She showed no anxiety; a sign that she did not smell the danger.

The night was dark, moonless, and the best time to act, the hardest hours of sleep. So he counted that the soldiers in the court were sleeping like a log. And the guard? He's probably dozing too, at least he hoped so, and he's not very interested in what behind the window is.

He gestured to Alik because he was following him. At the top of the mound, he pointed to a large rock that partially obscured the chasm. The snow has long since melted here. In order not to make a noise, they gently and effortlessly pushed it to the side. Janek pointed down and whispered softly that there are protrusions on the stones, it is easy to go down after them. Even before the expedition, he had described this natural well to him in detail, but nervousness ordered him to repeat it again.

It took longer than he expected to cover the four meters downhill. He knew the schedule of transgressions, Alik did not, and with that in mind, he secured his friend. Little by little, performance after performance, they slowly plunged in.

At the bottom, he breathed.

Sheba stayed outside. Anyway, it would be a distraction if any of the soldiers thought of walking at night. It was unlikely, but he had taken that into account when he had the wolf stay awake at the entrance.

He groped in the darkness for a moment, and when his hands found the right boulder, he resisted to move it to the side. He couldn't. Winter debris clogged the stone. Alai came to his aid. They tried again and the stone jerked, then turned to reveal the entrance to the tunnel. It was so dark that if Janek had not known its location, he would not have noticed the opening.

They slipped inside. The corridor was not high. Just enough to allow you to move freely with your head bowed.

He reached into his backpack for a small signal kerosene lamp, which he had taken with him, and had previously found it in the old bunker. It had the function that the width of the beam of light could be regulated, and in addition, it was possible to cover them with colored glass, blue and red. This made it easier to move further, but her light was only visible at a set distance.

Now they were moving rapidly forward. As a result, Alik, forgetting himself, straightened and several times scored a blow against the transverse beams crowning the ceiling. He just hissed in pain, cursed under his breath, but remained silent. It happened to Janek too, and he only mumbled, suppressing a shout.

Not much time had passed when, before the end of the corridor, Janek stopped and carefully illuminated one of the walls. The tunnel ended about ten meters away in a collapsed ceiling and protruding, broken beams.

Alik pointed at the place, clearly worried about the view.

"It collapsed, we will not pass," he whispered in excitement.

Janek shook his head.

"It looks like if someone got here, such a deception," he reassured him and continued to illuminate the side wall of the tunnel.

It took him a few minutes to find what he was looking for. He breathed a sigh of relief, slipped his fingers into the gap between the beams, and pulled hard. With a barely audible creak, part of the wall swung open to reveal a side corridor.

"Come on," he whispered, but, amazed at the ingenuity of the builders, Alik stayed in place for a while, admiring what Janek called the deception.

Finally he followed the dying deep blue light, and his hesitation resulted in another confrontation between his forehead and the ceiling.

After a few meters, Janek stopped, showed him to be quiet and screwed on the wick of the lamp. Now only a narrow beam of light, like a glowworm against the black sky, showed where it had been turned; doors made of rough boards, reinforced with three bars of metal, forming the letter "Z".

"This is the entrance to the hiding place, and behind it are the cellars," he whispered directly into Alik's ear as he approached. "Check the gun."

Each of them took two revolvers and pistols on the expedition. They left the rifles with the horses; it would not be easy to use them in such a narrow place.

Janek listened for a moment longer, but no sound reached their ears. The silence here was so great that their own breaths felt like hard working machines.

He reached for the door and gently opened it. They made no noise, indicating that grandfather needed to keep lubricating the hinges. The memory of him made him feel regret in his chest. He quickly chased that feeling away as he concentrated on the task at hand.

Increased the light.

The room was no bigger than four by four meters, less than two meters high.

There were crates against the walls. Janek guessed what they contained. It was a weapon that grandfather and Vasily had once hidden, and it was found on the battlefield of the Germans against the Moskals. Not all, but only a small part, as Vasily used to say, "a handy storage room". Here, too, he kept a few rifles and melee weapons that they used on hunting. And now for him the most valuable thing, ammunition. He wanted to open it right away, but left it for later, if there was an opportunity and time. Finding this lieutenant was more important.

He walked over to the place that hid the wall lock actuator. Very simple but effective; a thong was stuck in the gap between the beams, which when pulled up, lifted the blockade.

He pulled and then slowly swung the moving part aside. Outside, the darkness was not brightened. He directed the lamp into the corridor and listened to the silence for a long time. No sound.

He carefully swung the entrance open and entered the corridor. The basement was not large; one corridor and a few small rooms where things not of use were kept, and a handy store of liqueurs and mead.

He listened to the silence, but still nothing disturbed him. He realized that he should hurry, but too much haste could bring some surprise, and this he wanted to avoid. He could feel Alik's breathing behind him and that calmed him down.

A few steps towards the stairs and exit from the basement. The lamp light went up. The door to the ground floor of the manor house was closed.

He returned and opened the first of the boxes. Nobody. Second; similarly. Third and fourth, also empty. Only the last one has resisted. The staple was locked with a broken saber inserted into it. He was surprised they hadn't used a padlock, but maybe they didn't have it, or maybe they thought it would be enough.

He pulled it out carefully. The sound of metal scraping against metal made him audible throughout the court, but he knew it was only an illusion of his oversensitive senses. He opened the door a crack.

A figure was huddled on the ground. He came over and illuminated her face. It was all covered in clotted blood. On the back there were traces of a whip and long, now dried brown stripes.

"This is Demenkov?"

He flinched nervously as Alik's unexpected question sounded over his ear.

"Buck up," he reminded himself, nodding only in reply, then knelt, turned the Russian on his back and checked that he was breathing.

He was alive but passed out.

"Okay, the two of us take him, just quietly and carefully."

They raised the lieutenant. The inert body felt heavier than it really was. Little by little they carried him out into the corridor. Here they placed it on the ground, and Janek closed the staple again with a broken saber.

There was still silence. From above, no sound came from inside the manor.

They moved Demenkov to a hidden room. Janek closed the wall. Now there was a question of getting him in a dungeon. The two of them couldn't, because it would be too slow and burdensome.

"Put him on your back," he said.

Alik knelt down, Janek picked the Russian up, and when his friend grabbed his hands, they set off.

Covering several dozen meters of the corridor this time took them longer than the original road.

Janek looked outside. The sky was still dark.

He took a rope from his coat and fastened it on Demienkov's chest, then he climbed with the tips to the top of the well. Alik joined him immediately and together they dragged the lieutenant upstairs. He was still unconscious and that made Janek nervous. However, there was no time, he had to be taken away quickly.

Alik ran to get the horses, and he, with the Russian on his back, started towards the orchard.

They came faster than he had expected. They quickly put him on the horse in front of Ivan.

"Go to the forest. If you get lost, the wolf will find you, just go farther away."

They just nodded, concerned with the mission entrusted to them. He saw their commitment and it pleased him. It was confirmed once again that weeks of training and previous experiences had turned meek peasants into soldiers. He probably could rely on them.

***

"And we for weapons?" Alik was trembling with emotion, eager to act immediately.

"Relax, we can't make any mistakes, but we go again."

This time they led the horses to the rocks. Sheba stayed upstairs again, and they entered the corridor once more.

After opening the boxes, it turned out that, as Janek had assumed, they contained weapons collected on the battlefield of the Germans with the Russians, ammunition for rifles, pistols and revolvers, as well as sabers, uniforms, jackets and coats, as well as backpacks, canteens, even binoculars and other equipment elements. It occurred to Janek that grandfather and Vasily wanted to have the full equipment of a small unit on hand, if it had to be formulated quickly. But what for? Did they anticipate the course of events, or maybe - it occurred to him - they planned, like great-grandfather Victor, to form a party after the end of hostilities and resume the guerrilla struggle?

He left this consideration for later. He only wondered, but for a moment, why he didn't have the entire hunting collection, rifles and other rifles that grandfather kept here. If someone took them, only they, before the evacuation, before the arrival of the Bolsheviks, and this...

He felt a tightness in his chest that made him breathless. Was grandfather with Vasily alive?

He pushed his thoughts away. Not now, he'll wonder later.

He motioned to Alik to tie the weapons with straps and to pack ammunition and other things in sacks. He also set to work, chasing his friend, who turned every weapon in his hand, admiring the good stored in the hiding place.

It took them several turns to get them all to the rock well. When they finished and the boulder rested in place, they began to heave the packages outside and later fasten them on their horses.

As they were about to move, Sheba growled, but signaling only that someone but theirs was approaching. Janek reached for his revolver and waited. Less than a minute later, a rider emerged slowly from behind the orchard trees, carefully surveying the countryside. Only now Janek noticed that the sky had already cleared and that the dawn was behind them.

"It's Ivan," Alik recognized the rider first and waved his hand at him.

The happy one drove up quickly.

"What's happening," worried Janek asked quickly, already directing Sewek towards the orchard. "Are you back already? Where's Demenkov?"

"Well, nothing, Commander, but we were concerned that you were not coming back and I sent this Russsian with another, and I came back myself."

"There was an order that you..."

"I know, sorry, we were afraid for you, if you did not fall into the hands of this Bolshevik, sorry, because this..." he stopped embarrassed.

Janek felt grateful for their anxiety, but at the same time he realized that he had omitted in his plans to appoint a liaison between the group in front of the court and him. There is still a lot to learn. But now, instead of scolding the newcomer for not following his instructions exactly, he smiled.

"You did well, you thought, but follow your orders in the future."

"Yes, Commander, it won't happen again."

"It's not that it would not happen again," Janek quickly caught his word. "An order is an order, but there are situations like this now where thinking and anticipation are more important. You did well. And others?"

Ivan glowed with pride.

"The rest in their positions, as was ordered, only in the manor house has already started to move, they must have stood up, but none of them has climbed out yet. There were only some screams, but we did not understand what exactly. Like fight."

"We're going after ours and go back..." Janek ordered quickly.

They rode on in silence, but Janek sped up his horse. Something was bothering him. Where did the shouts at court come from? Were they holding someone else? Or maybe they quarreled?

***

Upon reaching their destination, he checked their positions by approaching each one individually, asking if they were cold, and praising them for remaining patiently in position.

He remembered the memories of his grandfather and Vasily from the fighting in the Caucasus, and among them there was a message that every soldier must feel the protection of the commander and should be exchanged with each one, at least a few sentences. "It binds soldiers and ties them, and gives respect to the commander," their explanations were vividly remembered by him.

He asked Sedenkov about the screams Ivan had mentioned, but he did not know who was shouting.

"So suddenly, and then there was nothing left," he just said.

He quietly ordered him to withdraw the people from their posts, one by one, so that there was no noise.

He started doing it when suddenly the door of the court kicked from the inside with a bang and Fedor Ostapko literally flew out, falling to the ground. Behind him, Lieutenant Colonel Kluyev stumbled, whip in hand, clearly furious because he immediately waved angrily and hit the man lying. Right behind him, the political commissar Babel moved on his soft legs, bottle in hand, croaking and cheering for the commander.

"And kill this carcass... I warned you not to trust... Practice and killlll..." his tongue was tangled.

He leaned against the doorframe, barely keeping his balance, and tilted the bottle.

The situation was so unexpected that Janek fell to the ground and only showed with his hand not to react, because a few had already pressed the rifles, ready to open fire.

None of Kluyev's bodyguards had shown up yet. Apparently it was a matter of these three. Immediately Janek remembered what Alik had said about Ostapka. Was he going to implement his threats? How he got here.

He crawled to the one lying next to him.

"Did anyone come to the manor?"

"Well, yes, this Ostapko," came the soft answer.

"Why didn't anyone tell me about this?" Janek was angry and expressed it.

The peasant was frightened silent.

"Talk for the kaduk, Sedenkov didn't mention anything, just calm."

"Well, sir, because it was calm," this tried to explain. "And this is Ostapko, the one from our village."

"I know that, but..."

"Lord, he's supposed to be red, but he's angry because they desecrated his Fedka, so we didn't say anything, and you didn't ask, but whether they were leaving the court and not entering."

Janek did not have an argument for such a explication, and further inquiries and showing anger would not change anything. The peasant logic was sometimes incomprehensible to him.

Ostapko tried to get up. He propped himself up on his knees, then, with visible effort, rose to face the lieutenant colonel. His face was covered with blood. It was obvious that he didn't care about life, because he laughed madly in his eyes.

"We will play with your girl one more time, and then I will give them to the soldiers," sneered Kluyev, provoking Ostapko, and when the peasant moved towards him, he lashed him with a whip, leaving a bloody streak on his chest, repeated and again.

"You are stupid, now all the women will be shared," the commissar, whose legs did not hold, chuckled from the threshold and now he collapsed on the ground, enjoying the situation. "Stupid, comrade Ostapko, a lot of women in the world..."

The lieutenant colonel's blows took effect. Ostapko took just one more step with his last effort, then his legs gave way and he fell to his knees. His eyes still blazed with hatred, but visibly dimmed.

"What to do," thoughts in Janek's mind galloped faster than the answer to them. He orders to shoot, soldiers will fall out, and the fire exchange does not have to be in his favor. The night is different, the day is different. At night, surprise worked in his favor, now his people are hidden in the bushes, but there are more of those and they are more experienced.

He made a decision.

Now he couldn't back down. He had to show that he was the commander, that he was not afraid to set an example.

"Be ready," he gave the order softly, not even sure if everyone heard it.

He got up and when the lieutenant colonel whipped the kneeling man, he left the bushes. He did not notice him and only when Babel's warning shouted: "Леон!, еб твое мать!..", he turned and froze. Only for a fraction of a second, because the next time the whip flew to the ground, a saber flashed in his hand.

"Who the fuck are you?"

"Gold will be of no use to you anymore," just such a sentence came to Janek's mind to throw the other man off balance.

"Who..."

"You stole for the Tsar, you stole for the Bolsheviks, maybe you will also steal something in hell..." Janek, without waiting for his reaction, attacked Kluyev, who carefully parried the blow.

"Who the fuck are you?" he repeated and at the same time he attacked, cutting across, but Janek, observing the movement of his saber, dodged and cut with his one.

The lieutenant colonel did not have time to react this time. The blade cut through his neck, and blood spurted almost immediately. He froze, stood for a moment longer, then fell to the ground without feeling.

"Еб твое мать!" The political commissar blurted out of his mouth as he watched what was happening.

He tried to get to his feet quickly and at the same time pull the bastard out of its holster.

Janek jumped up to him and at that moment the door opened and a soldier ran out with some papers in his hand with the words: "Шеф, я..."

He did not finish seeing the stranger standing with the saber, the commander lying in the blood on the ground and struggling with the commissar's revolver rope.

Janek was a few steps away from these two.

The soldier was closer.

He jumped in his direction, while still in the air, he slashed the surprised face, landed on his feet and at the same time with a half turn of the blade on the bent commissioner. Another spin and a blow from the bottom.

The soldier fell straight down with his neck split open, the commissar straightened for a moment, but then the body went limp and hit the ground with a hollow blow.

Meanwhile, Alik, without waiting for orders, ordered Ostapko to be taken outside the yard, and he ran to the door with three others. Here, seeing that no one had raised the alarm in the manor house, he signaled the others to join. They ran, crouched, and waited for further orders. No nervousness, punitive, as in training.

Janek saw it out of the corner of his eye. He called Alik right away and in a few words he distributed the people. There was no time for detailed planning. The surprise should have been used.

Four sent to the rear of the court and ordered an attack from that side. Two to the sides, where the windows also opened, and the rest behind him.

A long time seemed to have passed, when in fact not even a minute had passed.

He sheathed his saber, took out the Mauser, and nodded to Alik that they were coming in and to stay close behind him. He opened the door ready to open fire immediately if someone appeared.

Nobody was there. He walked quickly down the hall, listening for voices deeper in the house. At the same time, he wondered how it was possible that no alarm had been raised, and what had happened at court had not disturbed any of the commander's guards. Could they feel so confident? Where's the guard in the room they had spotted the light earlier? Maybe it's the one who ran out into the yard?

Behind him he heard footsteps. He glanced back.

Behind Alik, clenching their hands on the rifles, a few people moved in silence. Their faces were calm and they only looked carefully at the sides. He noticed their pursed lips in determination that they were not here by force, but by the will to fight those who had suffered so much harm. Janek's lonely attack on the lieutenant-colonel in defense of Ostapko and the demonstration of what he had done to the political commissar and the soldier, without calling them for help, did his job. They had a role model and now they wanted to prove themselves.

He pointed at the door to the living room and the next room, tiptoeing at two people. The rest of the stairs to the first floor where voices were heard. Now it was all about surprise. He remembered someone saying that the commander had a dozen or so soldiers with him, but how many exactly, no one knew.

He waited, giving his own time to climb the stairs. Now it all depended on the simultaneous attack on all rooms. He showed Alik the sitting room with his barrel, and without waiting for him to understand, he quickly walked over to the door leading to him.

He could feel the tension in the air.

There was a scream from above, followed by the roar of gunshots.

He kicked the door open and, before it even swung open, he jumped inside. Several sleepy soldiers, reaching for weapons, sprang up from the lairs spread out on the floor. He didn't give them a chance. He squeezed the Mauser trigger, and Alik behind him did the same. Before the shots ceased and the bullet-torn soldiers fell, he ran into the corridor, from where the roar of a rifle gun could be heard. The same thing happened in the rest of the rooms. He noticed the swing of the closet door next to the kitchen, fired through the door, and then opened it. The soldier's body fell out.

He ran quickly from room to room, but the others were empty.

On the second floor, the shots stopped and he ran up the stairs worried about it.

Beaming faces greeted him.

"Twelve, dead," Sedenkov reported shortly.

The court was under control.

According to the reports of the others, 22 soldiers constituted the protection of the commander. They were all dead. At the time of the attack, apart from the one that went outside, the rest were still asleep. Judging by the musty stench of alcohol, he hadn't evaporated from the fighters as the shooting began. Janek concluded that they were incredibly lucky, thanks to which none of his people was even injured. If a typical military discipline reigned in the court, the attack could have ended tragically. Apparently the Bolsheviks felt very safe. Maybe they got some information that their troops attacked to the west?

Now it was time to decide what to do next. And fast, because the roar of the shots was certainly heard in the village. How will they react?

He went outside.

He noticed Ostapko, who with the help of Ivan changed his shirt to one taken from one of the dead soldiers. "Tough fellow," he thought. "He recovered quickly."

Beside him, he noticed a young woman, probably Fedka, who was gently washing the blood from Fedor's injured back.

"She, where was she?" Asked one of the peasants who was taking the weapons of the dead to the court.

"They found her tied up in that cell, where the commandant shot the fighter through the door. The answer was supported by a broad smile. "It's good that she was lying, because she would have got it too. A brave woman, she immediately asked about Ostapko."

He walked over to them.

The girl, frightened by the sight of him, looked away. Fedor, on the contrary, straightened up to meet his eyes, but then bent down; the wounds must have been burning too much.

"Master, I'm with you..." he blurted out, grimacing.

A bloody streak, now causing puffiness, running from his forehead across his cheek and mouth made it difficult to speak.

"I'm ready... I was just pretending to be a Bolshevik to make this," he pointed to the corpse of the commander," to get... I failed, because they drank until the morning and they noticed, and I..."

Janek saw him fight the pain and once again it occurred to him that he would not like to have such pure hatred and determination as a peasant.

"You don't look good," he assessed, but Ostapko immediately denied:

"It's nothing, my lord, it will heal, and there are about fifty Bolsheviks in the village, if we move right away, we can break them."

"Few of us, more of them, we may not be able to cope."

"These bastards are strong in a group, and when shots are fired, they will run away, my lord, they are cowards," he argued.

He changed the subject and began to question Ostapko about their location and weapons. He planned quickly too. The surprise might indeed have been an asset for them, and he liked the suggestion more and more. The others didn't know what was going on, they only heard the shots. In the end he had almost made up his mind, but he still had doubts. In the euphoria after a victory, it is easy to become a victim.

He got everyone together. There was also a peasant, probably Yuri, who was supposed to be taken by Demiankov to the island, together with him.

"He woke up, Commander, and insisted on bringing him to you because he has important information," he explained, not sure if he had done the right thing.

"Where is he?"

"Well, in the bushes, bring him?"

"There's no need to."

Demenkov, guarded by one of the peasants, sat where the gunners guarding the main entrance to the manor had previously held positions. Janek thought once again that Alik's training had brought results and they leave nothing to chance.

At the sight of Janek, the Russian rose and staggered at once. His body revealed the urges were stronger than his physical condition.

"Thanks for saving me," he said shortly. "They probably would have tortured me, because their loots did not match."

"About this later, sit down, because here you will die here." Janek joked. "How did you come to join them?" He started to address by first name showing that he decides here.

Demenkov sensed it, but made no comment, only smiled understandingly in reply.

"You grew up, you survived, my congratulations," he also started to address by first name. "But why? The lieutenant colonel was in the Preobrazhensky Regiment of His Majesty's Yegers. Here we met, but not close, just friends. When the Bolsheviks overthrew the Kerensky government and this ruffian took power, he almost pulled me out from under the wall, where they shot prisoners. He was already on the side of the Bolsheviks and was up to something with them…" He broke off and started coughing spitting out blood.

Janek was waiting patiently, seeing his condition. These few sentences showed that he had no idea what was going on in Russia. What Kerensky government? This tsar has nothing to say? He gave up power? Indeed, his orientation was zero. He had come across only the Bolsheviks so far, and what was happening in Russia was a real tabula rasa for him. He wanted to keep asking Demenkov, but he realized that not right now, because he did not know what was going on in the village. If he attacks her, what's next? Some of his men may die in combat. Does he have the right to put them at risk? Assuming the optimistic scenario of surprise and the surrender of the Bolsheviks, what after that? You won't get to shoot the prisoners, let them go, maybe they'll hit their own people and come back to take revenge.

He summoned Sedenkov.

"I need to know what's going on in the village," he explained to him. "Who can be sent to spy?"

"I don't know, I know the local people as much as Ivan, the local, probably knows better."

"Then call him."

Ivan appeared almost immediately. Sedenkov had to tell him what was going on, because, when asked, he offered to go alone.

"You just have to be careful, because if they catch you, you know what awaits you."

"I can do it, lord, this is my territory, the guys will tell me what is going on and warn me, as if what."

"You're going without a gun," Janek looked carefully at the boy, considering once again whether to let him go, and then signaled to him to move.

He left Demienkov and approached Alik, who was talking to Ostapko.

"He says that in the village, among the Bolsheviks, there are two or three strangers who came yesterday."

"Aliens?" Janek addressed the Ukrainian directly.

"Well, yes, sir, I think they were those who had already traveled to the lieutenant colonel, and because they got some girls they got drunk, they did not go straight to the manor, drank and probably wanted... I don't know, but for sure only one went to the manor yesterday and right back. So I think that this attack on the countryside may be withheld?"

"You were just persuading to attack yourself, what has changed?"

"I know, but he thought it over, he urged him nervously, but he can wait and spying."

"I've already sent someone."

"Oh, that's good, but I would do it myself, after all, they have me for theirs."

"Too late, Ivan has gone."

Ostapko scratched his head, grimaced, then sighed.

"If you would let me, I would also go. Ivan will find out from the peasants, I will find out from the soldiers."

"And if they ask, where have you been?"

"And who would be curious what I was doing. I just have a request to take care of Fedka. I'll talk, see what's going on and come back."

"You look like a herd of horses run over you."

"It's even better, I have an excuse, I got drunk and fell out of the attic and I bruised myself."

"I don't know..."

"I'm asking for permission, I can do it, and they are not so inquisitive. I have a new shirt," he pulled the fabric, "and you can't see the whip blows, only this face," he winced, pretending a smile.

"Okay, go, just be careful, it would be a shame to lose you."

"I can do it, sir," Ostapko brusquely straightened, then returned to his former position. Fresh wounds had to let know.

He quickly went to Fedka and exchanged a few words with her. She tried to protest, but Ostapko just laughed, took her face in his hands, kissed her forehead lightly and walked away.

***

Janek looked after him, analyzing the situation, which suddenly became complicated.

"Alik, what do you say?" He turned to his friend.

"I think they can handle it. They are both locals, this is their village, they know them."

"So we are going, I will not think of anything else, give a sign to the people. Go to the village, hide in the bushes and wait for me and them. I still have a few words to exchange with Demenkov. Leave the extra rifle and horse for him."

"What about the rest of the weapons of these Bolsheviks and ours, which we took from the hiding place?"

"Refill the ammunition, hide the rest in the forest, assign two, the rest are to go with you, let them join you later. Oh, send someone for Fedor, a good shooter will come in handy. Leave Joshua, he probably still hasn't recovered."

He returned to the Russian, who seemed to be regaining strength after an attack of weakness.

"Tell me, what about the tsar and his troops?"

"You sewed up here, you don't know what happened there. The Bolsheviks, when they took power, and the weak were at the beginning, but strong in their mouths, had to show who was in charge and immediately set about murdering everyone they considered potential opponents. They broke up entire families, from eldest to children, without mercy. This tactic of theirs spilled over the whole country," he fell silent, as if gathering his thoughts on how to talk about the events in a few words. "Before we came to your court with my commander, Count Ridiger, we previously stayed in Sławuty, at prince Roman Sanguszko. It was your great Polish patriot, respected even at the tsarist court. The commander told me that the prince was a descendant of your king, this Lithuanian, Jagiełło..."

"You're starting to talk crap," he interrupted. "What does that..."

"I'm not talking the crap, Janek, patience... I just want to make you aware, on a specific example, what the Bolsheviks unleashed and what they are capable of. Otherwise you will also find it difficult to understand my situation."

"But..."

"Please..." He began to cough, and when he calmed down, continued patiently. "A reserve infantry regiment, faithful to the Tsar, was stationed in the vicinity of the Sanguszko Palace. Sent there to protect the old man whom, as I mentioned, even the tsar respected. At one point the Bolshevik agitators reached the regiment and then the devil entered the people. It was they who convinced the soldiers that the officers had to be killed, that this was the order of the government, and they did it. They ran amok, smashed the distillery, and got drunk and, prompted by slogans, burst into the palace. The Prince, and remember that he was already over eighty years old, was not afraid of this drunken blackness and went out to meet them. He tried to speak to them as he was, gently, like a father to frisky kids. Maybe he thought that when his peasants loved him for his exceptional kindness, the drunken crowd would respect his gray head."

He fell silent again, recalling the images from his memory.

"But the exemplary soldiers, under the influence of vodka and agitators, turned into howling, thoughtless mass, which did not want to listen to him. When someone gave the word, probably one of the Bolshevik agitators who led the emotions: "Zaczem tuda?! Zdieś s nim pakończym!" the mass threw bayonets at the prince, and stabbed him like an ordinary pig, and then the manslaughter of the palace began... from courtiers who managed to hide and survived."

"The prince was murdered? But for what?" Janek did not reach the words and he subconsciously opposed them.

"You really nothing..."

"I don't know, although I've seen a lot already, but why so much hate in the soldiers?"

"The war did its job. There was a shortage of food, speculation, prices went up, people started to rebel. An army revolt broke out in Petrograd and do not ask who provoked it, because I don't know. The tsar had taken possession of him and dissolved the Duma, but its representatives agreed with the newly formed Petrograd Council of Workers and Soldiers Delegates, and this juggernaut demanded the tsar abdicate. Perhaps he would not have abdicated had it not been for Kerensky."

"Oh, who is he? Some prince hungry for a crown?"

"No, a member of the Duma, a very ambitious activist of the Party of Socialists - Revolutionaries. He took advantage of the situation and, as he was also vice-chairman of the council of delegates, he sniffed the opportunity. He persuaded the tsar that only his abdication would save the country and end the riots. Nicholas II was naive and laid down the crown. A Provisional Government was formed under the leadership of Prince George of Lviv, but Kerensky quickly took power from him and became prime minister himself."

"And the Bolsheviks?"

"Cunning beasts. They sensed that this was an opportunity for them and began to rebel simple workers that Kerensky is the bourgeoisie, and the bourgeoisie had to be murdered, then the country would be great. The brawls began, not with the participation of ordinary workers, but with spooked criminals, and that was the beginning. They swept Kerensky quickly and they..."

"Wait, my head is confusing. After all, even the simplest people can not be told something that does not exist, such stupidity."

"Sorry, Janek, but I will repeat it again, you are really naive. People, especially the hungry, can be told anything, and the Bolsheviks spread visions of the paradise they would make in Russia. Of course, there were some who did not believe, tried to make the people realize that these promises were empty, but they were immediately declared enemies of the people and murdered under various pretexts. Fear became so great that people were afraid to leave their homes and they preferred to die in their homes rather than look for food. Armed gangs roamed the city, piles of corpses lay in the streets, and no one was supposed to bury them. The omnipresent slogans that you have to take revenge on the gentlemen and take everything away from them, including life, did their job and...." He fell silent once more, tired of the long speech.

He breathed deeply for a moment, calming his breath, then changed the subject again.

"You know, this Kerensky even announced, and this should make you happy, an appeal to Poles to appoint the Polish state in their territories. Revolutionary groups began to form in Podolia and Volhynia, and in larger cities."

"It's probably good, Poland..."

"I told you, naive," Demenkov shook his head and began to explain. "Peasants', workers' and soldiers' councils already functioned everywhere, and each such gang considered itself the most important. Every fool strong in his fists and mouths felt himself a master, and as a result, the mansions and houses of the townspeople were plundered. Chaos reigned in the country, the peasants themselves began to divide the court lands, and later murder became the rule.

"I still don't understand," Janek felt that Demienkov's story had so confused him in his head that he could not collect his thoughts. He did not grasp this amount of information, and here people waited for him to give orders for the microworld in which the game was also played, some fragment of what was happening in the country. "Let's leave it, tell me how did you get in the hands of that lieutenant colonel?"

"You must know that many military men, in order to save their lives, and often also for their careers, switched over to the Bolshevik side. Some caught the well-worn slogan that the homeland is under threat and must be saved from German troops, which, taking advantage of the mess in the country, pushed unstoppable forward, practically meeting no resistance."

"Okay, you have told me about that, what with the lieutenant colonel?"

"He and that Jew with whom he stuck with, they were already working together before the war. I don't know exactly because I inferred it from a few comments they mentioned, but I think they were robbing military resources. When this Kluyev pulled me out from under the barrels, he immediately made it clear: I have to work for them, because I'm educated, I know accounting, I'm not supposed to see anything, but the accounts are to be clear to his superiors. If not, they will murder my wife and parents. He was already the commander of the special regiment of Cherez habits and probably has a high-ranking relative, because he asked to send them to the front. Later, I figured out that it was difficult for him to plunder in the city, because they were doing it more importantly than he was. And the pristine plundering grounds are the lord's mansions in the provinces. And so I got here with them."

"I know that they robbed, but why, the Bolsheviks preached..."

"What they preached they preached and what they did was another matter."

"Leave it alone, you had some important information for me."

"Exactly. They kept other contacts secret, and I wanted to warn you about that."

"Not with the Bolsheviks? With Germany?"

"No, with the leadership of the Ukrainian Revolutionary Insurgent Army and with someone else, but I don't know who."

"God, what the hell are they again?" Janek did not admit that he had already heard about Huliaipole, Nestor Makhno and his army of Ukraine."

Demenkov grimaced again, but made no comment, just patiently explained.

"In two words, it is led by a Jewish revolutionist, Nestor Makhno. Sometimes it is in an alliance with the Bolsheviks, and sometimes not, and they probably do not like each other with Trotsky, the military chief of the Bolsheviks. This Makhno created a state and army independent of the Bolsheviks."

"I'm more interested in this Trotsky."

"Not enough time to explain it, such a major one from the Bolshevik army. What is important to you now is that the commander and the political commissar were in contact with the man Makhno, the nondescript ataman Grigoryev, and that they were to meet his men for days. It was to him that they were to transfer part of the accumulated gold and go to the Makhnovist side."

"When exactly?"

"I don't know, but soon."

Janek tried to draw conclusions from the story and immediately remembered the information about the three strangers. Three, it's not a lot, but it could only be couriers. Maybe they brought information when the rest would come.

"You're staying, you're not fit to fight," he decided, stating that he had been chatting too long, and his people were waiting for him there.

Demenkov protested.

"I don't have the strength to run, but I shoot well, I can lie down and guard the foreground. Now every single eye will be useful to you."

"I'm not convinced, but... I really don't have a lot of people, if you want to."

He showed him the horse, helped him to get on it, and then Sewka was mounted.

They moved towards the village, where his people must already have been. Only Fedka remained in the manor.

Chapter XV

He scanned the village through binoculars trying to find out what was going on. The soldiers ran as if aimlessly, argued, pointed to the distant court, gathered in groups and dispersed. Clearly, without someone in charge, they didn't know how to behave.

After half an hour, Ivan returned and reported. The peasants heard the shots too. Nobody knows what happened, and uncertainty reigned among the soldiers. After several minutes, Ostapko appeared and brought more precise information. The strangers tried to take control of the soldiers, and they succeeded more and more, although still no one had any idea who was shooting and why no Chekist had come from the court with orders.

"They talk to each other that it might be result of drunk, and others that they shot someone, and even that it might be an attack by the Poles, because it is impossible according to the majority, the front is too far away," Ostapko tried convey the atmosphere among the soldiers. "They reason that since they are behind, no Polish unit would break through here."

Janek listened carefully, quickly analyzing the chances. He still delayed giving orders. He involuntarily noticed that for his people he was the commander, but with his right hand Alik, now formally called the chief. And Sedenkov, Alik's right-hand man, was acting as a sergeant. He even liked the hierarchy born in battle, if not for the fact that they were distrustful of Demenkov, though they tried not to show it. They'll get used to it, he thought, and if he proves himself in combat, they'll treat him as theirs.

Behind him, from the woods, he sensed a movement. It was Fedor, the soldier sent for him, and Joshua, greeted warmly by the others. He immediately crawled to Janek's positions.

"Sorry, I couldn't leave you here. I don't know much about shooting, but if I hit blindly, maybe God will direct the bullets and I will hit one," he smiled smugly, as if he would tell a good joke.

Janek looked at him critically, but did not comment. He had to make a quick decision and decide how to play the attack, and he still didn't know that.

"Go to Alik, let him give you a place, preferably near Fedor, and send me Ostapko."

He raised the binoculars to his eyes and carefully studied the behavior of the soldiers. They still had no plan of what to do. Some got on their horses, then jumped off, got into quarrels with others, got on again, and their companions stopped them, shouting something and pointing to the side opposite the court, to the road to Malinova. Three soldiers, distinguished by regular uniforms from the tsarist army, circled among the Bolsheviks and tried to control their disheveled emotions. They succeeded in part, but not entirely, because the uncertainty was all too visible, and as soon as they calmed down the emotions in one group and went to the other, quarrels and be at each other's throats began again.

"These are from ataman Grigoryev," Demenkov crawled over to his position. He pressed a pair of binoculars to his eyes, which he must have found among the loot. "Pay attention to their uniforms, neat, uniform, the ataman pays attention to it."

"You know a lot about him," Janek found himself catching Demienkov out, not fully convinced that Kluyev forced him to serve with the threat of killing his family.

"As much as I overheard Kluyev's conversations with Babel. When the war with Germany began, the ataman created a partisan and took its toll on the imperial army. And then he hooked up with the Michniowce and began to help build a regular army of their republic. From what the Lieutenant Colonel said, he is not an idealist and will join anyone with sabers behind and not very inquisitive about what Grigoryev is doing."

"Did he have any information or just suspicions?"

"The lieutenant-colonel and the commissioner maintained regular correspondence with their superiors, they knew more. Once upon a time, Babel became furious after reading a report he received. It showed that Hrigoryev's troops had murdered the entire Jewish regiment, and in the town where they were standing, they hung out all the Orthodox Jews, including children. Kluyev laughed that this news was good news for them, because nobody here is sure of theirs, and they create Cheka here. There was something else he was raving about, but I didn't understand."

"Do you have any idea how to play it?"

"You are here for the commander."

"Stop it. You've been to the war, you've seen the fights, and you've got an idea ofthe tactics."

"I was with the commander, scribe and adjutant, you think too good of me."

Janek shook his head, then summed up in a few words what he was up to.

"It can work, though risky," said Demenkov. "On the other hand, this mass has no idea what happened and that could be your advantage."

"An asset is an asset, it's time to try it out," Janek crawled back and presented Alik with a plan he had just conceived.

"And who will go except Ostapko?"

"I have to taste what I have done myself, although I admit that I'm not sure that it will succeed."

"Janek, it's too risky, let something happen to you..."

"Then you take command, you are their chief, they listen to you."

"Stop, I'll go," Alik was not persuaded.

"Do not whine, just protect my back," Janek stood up, gave him the last instructions and called Ostapko, initiated him into the plan, and then they got on the horses.

***

At first none of the soldiers reacted, and more likely that they were busy arguing, they didn't even notice them. Only those three from the ataman Grigoriev, who had been circling among the Bolsheviks so far, noticed the foreign riders and quickly headed towards them.

Janek, watching them from the beginning, decided that they would be the most dangerous for his plan. He signaled to Ostapko to be ready. His hand tightened on the Winchester, placing his finger on the trigger and slightly raising the gun.

"Who are you?" The first, apparently in command here, stepped forward in front of them, demonstrating his function. His hand moved in an unequivocal gesture to the butt of the revolver. He surveyed the newcomers distrustfully, and his two companions quickly lined up in the vicinity, assuming a similar position.

They were professional soldiers, used to react quickly.

The other Bolsheviks only now realized that something new was happening, and the quarrels in the groups slowly began to die down.

After a while the tumult died out, and only in silence a few dozen pairs of eyes followed those of the ataman and strangers. They expected the mysterious shots at the court to finally be cleared up, and these two on horseback gave such hope. So they watched with interest rather than fear what was happening.

"Who are you, comrades?" The ataman ringleader repeated the rebuke slightly, pulling out Nagant of the holster. He showed no fear, on the contrary, he demonstrated with his whole self that it was he who had the right to ask questions.

Janek felt the tension. A moment longer, the other will draw his gun and surprise will turn into a limp shooting. He had to react, and immediately. No verbal fairy tales that have worked elsewhere have had no chance of success here.

Only one thing remained.

"Ready..." Fedora warned, then swiftly aimed the barrel of his rifle at the man in front of him and fired without warning, and then at his closest companion.

Ostapko reacted a fraction of a second later by sending a bullet to the third of Hrigoryev's men.

The surprise was complete.

Three bodies falling to the ground, followed by even greater silence.

The wide eyes of the surprised Bolshevik soldiers were the only reaction.

Janek raised his hand up, which was an agreed sign for Alik. The rest of his men emerged from behind the trees, positioning themselves every dozen meters with rifles raised to their shoulders, aimed at the Bolsheviks. They had not shook themselves yet, only stared in surprise at the strange riders, not knowing how to react. Someone had to be first, neither had the will or the will.

Only somewhere further, near the old inn, there was a movement and someone shouted: "To arms, comra..."

He did not finish.

From the side of the trees, where Demenkov had been left, a shot rang out and the soldier, thrown back by the bullet, fell against the wall, then fell to the ground without saying a word. The rest were still motionless, and their fear of the unknown made them unable to make any decisions. Until now, someone always ordered, directed and indicated what to do, and there was no one from the command here.

"Comrades of the Bolsheviks, we are the Polish army," Janek threw into space in Russian, and Ostapko repeated it in Ukrainian. "Give up or you will die."

No reaction, just sidelong glances.

"Who wants to end up like these ones?" Janek pointed to the lying ataman's people, and when there was still no reaction, he fired into the air.

It touched their imaginations.

First, one pair of hands went up uncertainly, then another, and after a while, a few dozen Bolsheviks, without changing their place, stood with raised hands, staring with obvious horror at the strangers.

Janek made a sign and his men started gathering the Bolsheviks and then pushing them towards the central square. Here they were ordered to sit on the ground and still keep their hands in the air while several jumped down and searched the soldiers for hidden weapons.

"Ostapko, give me peasants from the village, not enough of us," he instructed the Ukrainian.

He was afraid that if the soldiers did not see other Polish soldiers in a moment, whom they probably expected to emerge from behind the trees, surprise would be finished and they rush to flee, and then he would not control the situation.

***

Someone had gone to the other part of the village and now the peasants, initially timidly, and later more and more boldly approached the kneeling Bolsheviks.

When they recognized a few of their own among those who watched them, and later surreptitiously pointed to Alik and Janek, self-confidence and hatred emerged in their eyes. Not yet the desire for revenge, but at its limit, which was evident from the change of attitude, quiet remarks thrown under his breath and proudly raised heads.

Janek saw this instant transformation and began to fear lynchiness. Until now, he had not made up his mind what to do with the prisoners, and every idea seemed bad to him. Let free? Rush somewhere towards Malinova? Imprison?

He called for Alik.

"I have no idea what to do next," he said briefly, pointing to those sitting on the ground.

"Look at the peasants, as they clench their fists, they are about to pounce on them."

As if in response to guesses, several men led by one approached the captives, carefully looking at each one of them, then jumped inside and began to take out some of them.

"And we have, do something," Alik looked around uncertainly, watching what their people would do, ready to react if the situation got out of hand.

These, however, only silently watched the situation, but they did not move aside. They waited for orders.

"Get me the ringleader," Janek ordered.

Alik started his horse towards the captives. The peasants noticed it at once and froze. Fear returned. Momentary courage and the desire for revenge, just as it was suddenly born, now it has flown away just as quickly. Now they waited to see what would happen.

He was not the youngest. A scar ran across the left side of his face.

"And you..." Janek quickly tried to remember who had started and suspended his voice on purpose. What is his name? He remembered the face, but without that distinct scar. "Tymko, if I remember good? The brother of the chairman Kuźma?"

The peasant, hearing the calm tone, raised his head.

"Yes, my lord, but the brother is dead, they hanged him at the beginning."

"And you?" He pointed to the side-stretched Bolsheviks.

There was silence for a moment. Janek waited calmly. He was aware of the pressure under which he was being questioned. In the end, he overcame himself.

"Because they are the worst, sir, they have a lot on their conscience."

"You mean? What did they do?"

"The one with the black-mouthed disgraced our women, and when we defended them..." He waved his hand, it was a pity for the words and only stroked the scar. "And the one with a red ribbon around his neck killed Zubko as he refused to let him into the cabin. And the other," the hand went to the third, "had no mercy even towards the kids and beat Kostek, Horpyna's son, so badly that he did not survive.

"For what?"

"He defended his mother when this robber approached her."

Janek looked at him carefully, trying to read from his face how much truth there was. It was stone, the eyes were motionless, only the corners of the mouth trembled.

"What do you suggest?"

The peasant looked up as if he did not believe the question had been asked.

"I, lord, I would judge them, let the peasants decide..."

"You don't have your opinion?"

"Because, my lord, if I was angry, I would..." He paused and lowered his head.

"Tymko, as I can see, you are the oldest among your people. After brother?"

"Yeah, it just turned out like that."

"They're the only ones?"

"Two more, they're sitting there," he indicated the ones trying to hide behind the backs of others. "One, the one in the black sweatshirt, killed Ivaszka, Kłyczko's brother, when he wanted to save his wife from rape. And the other one, when he drank too much, wandered around the village and was reaching out to every woman, even the youngest, without restraint."

"Then give them and aside," he signaled to one of his own to help him, and to Alik: "The rest behind the village and there to bind with ropes. Get some peasants to help."

***

Almost everyone was willing to join the People's Court. Janek appointed Tymko as chairman and chose eleven more for him. They sat on stools taken from the rooms.

Separated from the rest of the soldiers were brought. They scowled, not knowing what was coming.

Janek appointed Alik as an observer. It had to play out within the village and its inhabitants. He left him four horses and assigned the rest to guarding prisoners outside the village.

Only now did he remember Demenkov. He noticed him as he sat on a rock some distance from the others. He rode up to him.

"You shot?" More stated than asked. "Thanks."

"You're welcome. It was one of the lieutenant colonel's guards. I recognized the uniform and face. I saw them every day. I don't know what he was doing here, but I made sure he did not something wrong."

"And he pulled it out, but how did you spot it from a distance?"

"I didn't see much from my position, so I climbed a tree."

"A good idea. Tell me what you think, I want to rush the captives towards Malinova, let them manage there."

"If they were you, they would have smashed you right away, so ask yourself if it's the right thing to do."

"Somehow I can't. It's not..."

"Christian? Janek, they don't believe in god, they don't believe in anything, and they probably don't believe in the proclaimed Bolshevism either."

"What to do with them?"

"Smash."

"Not everyone deserves it," Janek indicated the court that was taking place. "As you can see, only a few are selected, the rest are stupid guys."

"Stupid or not, they would murder their own mother on orders."

"After all…"

"The decision is yours. If you let go, you won't find understanding even in your own people. They wouldn't forgive them. And these great deliberations of yours are just…" He didn't finish and just waved his hand in resignation.

Janek did not want to continue the topic either.

He looked at the trial underway. The first of the Bolsheviks, the one Tymko called him "the black mouth", stood in front of the seated. A woman was standing next to him, telling something. When she finished another one, a young one, maybe sixteen years old, approached and she only shook her fist at him, then she cried and without a word returned to her own, from where another one, this time an older one, came out and began to talk loudly, the words full of hate.

He wasn't listening.

He did not want to hear this list of complaints and regrets anymore.

There was nothing to change from watching the trial. He gave consent to the people's court and knew how it would end.

He turned his horse and told Demienek to accompany him.

He summoned Ostapko.

"Take a few peasants and have all the huts occupied by soldiers look through. Preferably the husbands of these wronged women. Let them not hear what the women testify. Put all the weapons in a pile, and put all the Bolshevik stuff on the other. Let no trace of them remain in the huts. Oh, don't forget the court, too, Fedka is probably worried there. Those dead bodies to the edge of the forest and bury them. You can do it?"

"I can, Commander, and with these peasants, you are right. Better not to listen, it hurts," he saluted and was about to leave, when Janek had another thought.

"Ostapko, do you know the peasants, which of them would be suitable for the detachment?"

The man thought as he scratched his head.

"In fact, probably everyone would follow you now."

"Then choose me ten who know that a rifle is not a flail and have a little idea of a gun. Only with caution. Can you do it?"

"Yes, Joshua will help me, we will choose the best."

"That's good. I'm going to the prisoners."

"Yes, sir," happy with the task, Ostapko left quickly.

Janek had the impression that he, too, did not want to listen to the accusations in court.

***

The captives sat on the ground with their heads down. Around him horses, and a few peasants nearby.

He drove up to them and told them to come back to the village and contact Ostapko.

He saw Igor among the guards, talking to Fedor.

"What are you two talking about?" He asked.

"Igor says and I agree with him that a reconnaissance must be sent," Fedor pointed in an undefined direction.

"I thought of that, too," Demenkov said. "Remember what I said, they can come any moment."

"Who are they?" Fedor asked.

"Some of the Ukrainian People's Army."

"What the hell is that? Bolsheviks?"

"Not really, but that's the Commandant's business."

They looked at him. There was no time to explain. If ataman Hrigoryev's people were really going to appear, it would be better to spot them sooner."

"The three of you, and Lieutenant Stepan will explain to you on the way what the devil he is," he purposely used the old Demenkov rank and combined it with his name. Let them know that he is a potential commander of the three and the name that he trusts him.

After they turned their horses back, he started to tour the guards with each one of them, exchanging a few words. Only one, apparently bolder than the others, asked if the trial was taking place. When he confirmed, he nodded, pleased.

"Okay, sir, they do it," he said shortly. "They have suffered a lot, let them try, in fairness."

"Wouldn't you like to be there right now?"

"I'm now a soldier of your colonel." His eyes showed joy, confirming what he was saying. "The order was to watch these robbers, I watch them. And the boys can do it on their own and without me."

A horseman, accompanied by two women, was approaching the village.

"Is it all over?" Janek was surprised.

It turned out not to be.

"Commander, these women talked about two more who like them and want to take them."

He waited for the women who were out of breath came closer and calmed their breathing.

"What's up, who do you want?"

The first of them, apparently more daring, spoke up first.

"Because, my lord, Nastasya and I saw them hanging old Mendel, because he wouldn't tell them where he had hidden the reds, and then it was rumored that he hung himself, and that's not true. We were afraid and now we told the chairman Tymko, and he ordered immediately told you, and here we are."

"It is true?" He turned to the other, probably this Nastasya.

"Yes, sir, we served together in the inn," her voice trembled, but she persisted and continued. "That's the one they converted at their command. We were in the attic to get some rye for the families, because they kept there and we could see everything through the gaps in the boards, that's honestly true," she struck her breasts to confirm.

She paused and added after a while:

"There was also a third, large man with a scar on his cheek, who killed Hapka, Kuźma's daughter, right at the beginning, but after some time he went somewhere."

He saw their eyes blazing, and it occurred to him that recently his gaze was beginning to flow into his blood. A large man with a scar on his cheek. He remembered him and how alive his death had come before his eyes. If he had doubts so far, they were gone.

He called two guards and ordered, together with the women, to find the wanted ones. Seeing the women, they tried to hide among others, and when dragged outside, they shouted that they had not hurt any of them, that it was a mistake, and finally that the women were taking revenge on the innocent, because their legs themselves were spreading and now they want to get rid of the witnesses.

He rode up to them.

"Comrades, who hanged that old Jew, the innkeeper?" He asked when they noticed him.

The only answer was surprise and lowered heads. Neither of them suspected anyone had seen it.

He signaled for them to be led to the village.

***

He dismounted and took a moment to rest and analyze the situation.

The sky was covered with bright clouds. There was not much time left until evening and dusk.

If he was going to send prisoners to Malionova, he had to do so before darkness fell. But what next? How to play it? Let them go on the way or escort them to the village itself? He doesn't know what happens there after their most recent charge has departed; who was he? Rosa. Who replaces him, because he would not have left his soldiers without someone to look after them. What will happen when the captives arrive and notify the others what happened? Will they be scared or will they retaliate?

He remembered the impression that two words, Polish Army, had made on the local people. You could see their insecurity as he spoke them and the fear on their faces. This gave rise to further considerations, whether somewhere further, in the west, there were any units that appear as the Polish army? More insurgents, like in 1863?

He stretched, his muscles tired.

He mounted Sewek when a rider appeared in the distance. As he approached, he recognized Fedor.

"And how?" He asked as soon as the latter arrived.

He saw the weariness on his face, but - he thought in his mind - he chose to go on scouting himself.

"Nobody, but Demienko and Ostapko went further east, towards Malinova, to look there."

"Then we wait, and you get off your horse and rest. You look like a living dead."

"I feel so, but my strength is returning."

"Yeah, probably from Moscow and they can't get here," Janek sneered. "Don't grumble, just lie down and wait for them."

***

Before they arrived, Alik had come from the village. He had not yet arrived when he shouted, pleased from afar:

"They've finished."

Janek looked on without saying anything, but he heard no more.

"You mean, the end of the judgment, and how's the sentence?" He asked looking at the satisfied face of his friend.

"The kind you would expect."

"Alik, should I pull teeth?"

This one stretched the smile even more.

"No, but I don't know how to say it. They fairly questioned everyone who wanted to talk. Women above all, but also a few peasants, and even allowed the Bolsheviks to defend themselves, but they, apart from denials, had little to say."

"Which is?"

"They are waiting for you and your verdict."

"For me? It's their judgment."

"Yes, but you know how it is. Formerly, the court was a court, but the court approved it."

"Alik, man, look what's happening. Times changes."

"Well, okay, but it can get into their blood and it will be difficult later..."

"What later..."

"Don't get angry, but sometimes you have such... unreal gaze..." Alik interrupted him and to confirm what he thought, he only shrugged his shoulders, and seeing Janek's expression he did not develop his thoughts any more. "And there? They are sentenced to death, but they don't know whether to hang them or shoot them, but there are also those that want to hack them with sabers..."

"Enough, we will not resemble them," Janek felt angry and struggled not to show it. "Shoot and bury the bodies somewhere near the forest so that there would be no trace. Oh, wait, when we'll take those," he pointed to the prisoners, "away so they won't hear. Better that no shadow of suspicion would fall on the countryside if some red troops were likely to reappear. Now go."

"One more thing, they found a machine gunin a tachanka."

"Finally something positive. Anyone know how to operate it?"

"It turns out that the two older ones, Alexei and Semyon, were still in the war with the Chinamen and volunteered."

"God, how old are they?"

"Enough, but I didn't ask. They unfolded it efficiently, cleaned it, and it looked like they knew it. They will train the younger ones, for now they have to be enough."

***

Alik had not yet disappeared among the buildings when two riders appeared on the horizon.

Demenkov was returning with Ostapko.

They placed the horses in front of Janek and the former gave a quick report. "There weren't any soldiers in the village. Some strangers had come the day before, gave orders and set off together somewhere east-south, of which the locals are not sure."

"You know who these strangers?"

"From the description I can conclude that these are from ataman Hrigoryev."

"And yes, at the behest of strangers, and how many were there? Suddenly obeyed their orders? It's weird."

"I thought so too, but scared guys quickly explained it to me. First, as soon as they appeared, they had the people gathered in the square and explained that it was on the orders of Commissioner Abraham Rosa, who would later join."

"This one, that we..."

"Yeah, they played on spec, or they had it agreed in advance, I don't know."

"And they went?"

"No, a few, their charge, they had doubts. They openly requested written orders from Rosa."

"This one probably left some commander while he was away? He wasn't stupid."

"They were commanded by a rota commander and he had a few chiefs to help, and they did not believe the strangers."

"So they let themselves be convinced?"

"And yes, when they got a bullet, and the rest was already polite."

"So how many of these strangers?"

"Small squad, fifteen. They also took a dozen or so Ukrainians with them, which the Bolsheviks used the most. That they must fill the ranks for those who had doubts or something like that."

"We know where we stand. There," he pointed to the village, "they had already made a decision. We must quickly lead our captives east, and then let them fend for themselves."

Demenkov didn't ask what it meant to make a decision, but he must have figured it out. He nodded at Ostapko, gave orders to the guards, and when the captives rose, they immediately rushed them along the road to the east.

Chapter XVI

The sky changed the color of the clouds to be darker and denser, hanging lower than before, white and jagged, making the entire surroundings gray as if by the touch of an evil wizard's wand.

They moved slowly, not yet untied the bound hands of the captives.

Janek carefully surveyed the steppe grasses stretching to the horizon. Their end was faded into gray. Something bothered him, maybe it was the changing weather, or maybe the seventh sense that had warned him several times before, though there was no indication that anything might happen to them.

He downplayed the feeling, blaming it on fatigue and changed weather. He had twelve of his and Demenkov's with him. Only Alik and Joshua with three trained soldiers remained in the village, as well as the new ones who were selected to the detachment and given their weapons. Apparently a lot, but the anxiety kept coming back.

He summoned Ostapko.

"Take two horses and look south. Not too far for us to be in eye contact."

"Yes, sir."

Fedor nodded at the riders and they moved quickly, and Janek headed for Demienkov.

"Something bothers me, but I don't know what," he admitted.

"Irrational fears, you must still be tormented by this people's court, but you did the right thing. They judged themselves and there is no point in dwelling on. However, if something is on your mind and it is to calm you down, I will go a bit to Malinova."

"Take two with you and stay alert."

"Anyway, I'll give a sign, but it's definitely exhaustion."

He quickly left, taking the horses with him.

Janek looked around the steppe. Somewhere further to the right, the military tranches began, where he discovered a bunker. Now the grasses, almost as soon as the snow had vanished, swiftly climbed upwards, greening the surroundings and breaking through the yellows of those left over from the previous year. He had always wondered how it was possible for vegetation, torn by winter frost, to survive under the snow and ice.

He turned back. The village has already disappeared. He concluded that he had not heard the shots. Apparently, he thought, Alik waited with his permission until he and the prisoners were out of sight.

Sewek accelerated.

Time passed slowly to the rhythm of the captives' footsteps. Occasionally they gave them sneaky glances, unsure what their guards were up to. Many people thought that this was the last way and they would probably be shot in the steppe, far from the village. It was evident from lowered heads that they had already come to terms with this idea. Few of them said their goodbyes surreptitiously, and the movement of their lips showed that they were praying.

Janek watched it. "How can you be a thug," he thought, "serve the Bolsheviks and at the same time think of God in a moment of fear?"

While he waited for those sent to be scouted, he spoke to some of them. At first, they were afraid to answer, afraid that they might get a bullet for an incorrect answer. Previous experience in serving the Red Guard, he had learned, as the new Russian army was called, taught them to keep their thoughts deep and to react exactly as expected of them. Not so much commanders as political commissars. If someone did not manage to learn it quickly, he died either openly accused of spying, or of not identifying himself with the workers and peasants revolution, which ended in the same.

But when they saw that he was not reacting like their former superiors, they opened up. Maybe not as much as he expected, but they replied. And he asked about ordinary things, about family, where they came from, what they had done before the war. And only when the question of why they joined the army was asked, they suddenly fell silent, afraid that it was also an interrogation, but different, because it was the Polish army, which they had heard about as the greatest enemy of the revolution. However, a few persuaded themselves and said that they had nothing to say, that they had been taken into the troops, and whoever protested was the last thing in his life.

Now he was looking at them, remembering Demenkov's suggestions on what to do with the prisoners. And Alik's words that he is too soft that you have to act like the Bolsheviks, because only this will enforce absolute obedience. And then he watched his soldiers, whom he saved from death in the town, although he did not have to. After all their behavior so far, he was convinced that even in the face of death, they would not betray him.

"Or maybe I'm naive after all?" It occurred to him, but immediately decided that the gloominess of such thoughts came from exhaustion.

***

Demenkov was the first to return.

"Calm down, nothing's happening," he reported briefly.

Ostapko's group was visible in the distance, although the approaching darkness hid the details, transforming them into shifting dark spots on the background of a brighter sky.

He ordered the march to be stopped.

"Comrades Bolsheviks," he said the first two words, wondering what words to choose.

The captives were anxiously staring at him now, fearfully. All conversation ceased, and the silence was broken only by the few sounds of the birdsong.

"You know what's on your conscience. He felt almost physically pleading in their eyes not to tell them the worst. "We have no time to take prisoners, and you are no stranger to what your Cavalry Army does with them."

If the stillness could get even deeper, and the apathy even darker, then it was now. They bowed their heads, accepting the worst. They had experienced the rules of Budyonny's army for themselves before being sent here. Everything was clear to them now; they will be shot soon. One or the other only escaped a sharp sob, something like a groan, but most of them were still silent.

"The Polish army does not kill prisoners..."

Silence.

"So I let you go."

One, the second, and then the other heads began to rise in disbelief at what they heard. This is probably some cruel joke. They waited involuntarily for this Polish commander to laugh and give orders different from what he had said.

"Follow the road towards the village," he pointed at Malinova. "But if I find out that peasants are going to be raped in some way, this time there will be no forgiveness." When they were still unmoved, he urged: "You have heard, you are free. Come on, before I change my mind."

They were still unmoved. They remembered from Cavalry Army how the captives were being set free, they broke up, and then suddenly a battalion of dispersed Red Army soldiers was running over their horses to a pulp.

"Chase them," he commanded the soldiers, and they pressed on, forcing the captives to move.

Still hesitating, they walked very slowly, looking back, ready to scatter and run away. When nothing happened, they moved faster, still glancing back, but at first faster and faster, until finally they started to run along the course in the direction indicated.

"Damn," Janek now remembered that he hadn't ordered their tied hands untied, but it was too late to do it.

He did not hesitate any longer as the little spots on the horizon began to zoom in.

Ostapko was returning and he was not slow, but clearly rushing the horses, as if worried that the prisoners, who had been walking slowly so far, were now running as fast as they could. Within a dozen or so minutes he stopped in front of Janek.

"Commander, some riders," he blurted out. "They're coming."

This information sobered Janek, pushing aside the irrelevant considerations about ropes on the hands of prisoners.

"How many?"

"It's hard to say, because we only watched them from a distance, but some small unit, fifteen of them will be."

"Demenkov, we're withdrawing, but not in a hurry," he ordered. "Prepare a weapon. One to Alik saying let them move."

The designated soldier rode quickly, forcing the horse to maximum effort, and they slowly followed him, scattered into a row to make it seem more numerous from a distance. The ones Ostapko was talking about were already visible and were approaching quickly.

Janek quickly considered the new situation. They must be from that Ukrainian ataman, but why only a troop? Or is it just a peak followed by an entire regiment? Give them a fight or, after meeting with Alik and the rest of the people, go straight to the forest?

It wasn't long before the aliens got close enough for them to be clearly seen. They probably saw them running along the road and clearly sped up, heading towards them, and not towards the departing unit of Janek. At some point, however, they slowed down, as if they had just noticed Janek's group, or they didn't like something about it.

The manner of riding horses vividly resembled the infamous Cossacks; the same style and nonchalance to keep in the saddle.

The characteristic whistling to accentuate the strength was already heard.

He watched them vigilantly through his binoculars, ready to order the horses to turn back and prepare to repel any attack. It all depended on what they would do now; they will come to the captives or make a turn on them.

For now, however, they continued their direction, reaching the Bolsheviks. Seeing new ones, they started to stop, not knowing who it was and what to expect from them. Maybe it even occurred to them that this new Polish branch and the life they were spared was an empty promise.

There was no point in driving further towards the village. They were far away, but not far enough to be a safe distance. You could see a few jump off their horses and start questioning the escaping ones. They pointed something to Janek's ward.

***

"From the horses to the round, lay them down and prepare them to repel the attack," he said a quick order as he saw the aliens mount their horses and rush towards them.

Now the situation sped up and changed from moment to moment. The attacks could have ended tragically for them.

At first, the others rode slowly, almost as if they were walking, and then they sped up sharply at the guttural command, forcing the horses to full gallop. Already during the ride, they developed into a line.

Sabers flashed in their hands.

"Aim and shoot on orders, wait for now, do not panic," he ordered when the horses, forced to lie down on the ground, formed a makeshift rampart. Soldiers were kneeling behind them, hands on shoulders. They showed no nervousness, which calmed him down.

He drove into the center of the circle, forced Sewek to lie down, and summoned Demenkov to do the same with his, right next to him.

"Your task is to eliminate anyone who breaks in," he quickly tossed him in the final custody. "I'm counting on your eye."

"Sure," the lieutenant was focused and quickly grasped the adopted tactic.

"We have to hold it until Alik arrives, but they seem experienced soldiers, Cossacks, I think."

"I think so too."

The others did not slow their horses, lashing forward and approaching quickly. They were clearly visible now, despite the gray that had taken possession of the evening. At a distance of no more than fifty meters, without any visible order, the unit broke through, leaving the shaft in the direction, and several moved sideways to attack the Poles from three sides.

Janek waited for them to come closer for the fire to be effective. At this point, the people driving straight seem to have disappeared from their saddles. Tilted to the side, almost glued to the horse's sides, they held the saddles with one hand to impress and confuse their opponent. He knew it from the stories of his grandfather and Vasily and he remembered how the Caucasian insurgents dealt with it.

"They are by the side of the horses, watch carefully..."

He waited a moment longer.

"Fire..."

The first volley sounded, followed almost immediately by a second.

The legs broke under the two horses hit and rolled over the head. The other riders returned to their saddles just as the third volley was fired.

Janek noticed that the firefight did not turn into a limp shooting, which proved that his soldiers did not panic and were measuring accurately.

There were shots on the right and left too, but the Cossacks still missed their horses, though at one point one climbed in the saber-cutting stirrups from above and then fell off his horse. The rest, without slowing down, walked around their rampart. They tried to fire from the saddle, though with little effect, as if only trying to distract from those who were attacking from the front.

They were pushing low, leaning on their horseheads, trying to get inside. The first rider climbed his horse and jumped over the soldier kneeling next to the horse, cutting his saber at the same time. He instinctively covered himself with a rifle and it saved his life. A fraction of a second later, Demenkov's rifle rang and the Cossack fell to the ground, and his horse braked sharply next to Janek, nervously twitching his hooves in place and unable to decide what to do without the rider's orders. He was the only one visible against the grass; he was spinning in a circle, whining, shaking his head, but he remained in place, pulling his noses towards the lying Sewek. It is not known what was going on in his head, but after a while he did the same, knelt on his front legs and lay down himself, recognizing that if another horse did it, it must be so.

The Cossacks jumped back after the unsuccessful attack. In the foreground they left five of their own, two dead horses and the one belonging to the one shot by Demienkov. They still did not stand still, just circled in the group, as if agreeing on further tactics and regrouping.

At one point, one broke away from the group and headed towards where they had come from. This worried Janek. He realized the man had been sent for reinforcements. He quickly pointed it to Damienkov, but the rider was too far away, or maybe it was already too dark, and he was lucky because the bullet missed him.

He was already disappearing into the gray of the evening when suddenly a shot fired from the steppe and the rider fell off his horse.

***

This single shot came as a surprise to both Janek and the Cossacks.

Suddenly they stopped spinning and all heads turned in that direction.

And then astonishment turned to stupor from both sides.

New riders have literally grown out of the grass. Until now, they had to keep their horses on the ground and watch the fight going on. Or maybe even earlier, because when he was releasing the captives, he did not notice them. Neither Ostapko nor Demenkov when they returned. If they could disguise themselves so well, they must have been much more dangerous and experienced than the ataman's people.

From his position, Janek, despite the binoculars quickly put to his eyes, could not recognize them. He only saw horses with black-uniformed riders rising from the grass. They may have been Cossacks, but in strange uniforms it was disturbing that they had not intervened so far. Or maybe some Bolshevik detachment, but the skills of ordinary soldiers did not match the Cossacks.

So who?

"On the horse," he ordered.

He wanted to be ready for any eventuality. If it is an enemy, they will have to flee; too many of them. Alik was still not in sight. Why he's so whining? Or maybe they are similar in the village too?

He tried to stay calm and react carefully, but this sudden change of situation disturbed him and caused him more than anxiety. "Take it easy, just take it easy," he repeated to himself, assessing what was happening in the foreground and forcing himself to judge rationally.

"Be ready," he warned his own. "Set aside, and if you are ordered to flee, run as if the devil himself would pursue you."

They just nodded that they understood the seriousness of the situation. Warmed up by the recent fight, now they looked proudly at the Cossacks and this new opponent. They did not give up, they did not suffer losses, and this made them feel strong and confident in their abilities. Everyone calmly checked their weapons and recharged them.

He counted the new ones quickly. There were fifteen of them, if he had not made a mistake in the gray light that had engulfed the steppe for good.

"Stepan, who could it be?"

Demenkov was watching them through the binoculars too, and you could see from his expression that he had no idea.

They approached as if they were in no hurry. So far it has been difficult to judge whether they were targeting the ataman people or them. They acted as if they were just watching the fight and not going to take part in it.

"I once met such black uniforms in the 5th Alexandrian Hussars Regiment of Her Imperial Highness Alexandra Fedorovna," he said slowly. "I also heard about a similar one in the Kornilov Naval Regiment, but who are these, God knows, I don't know."

"They act as if they are up to something."

"I think so too."

"Watch out, boys," he said to the soldiers. "Don't shoot without orders, don't let your toes itch, but your arms at your shoulders."

***

The black riders were already approaching the group of Cossacks, but they hadn't even turned a millimeter in their direction, and no head had even turned to greet them.

They stared straight ahead at Janek's group, not even rushing to a walk, literally following foot by foot.

Suddenly the leader gave an order and in his hands appeared sabers raised on the forearms.

And then something happened that neither the Cossacks nor the Poles had foreseen.

The horses, literally on the spot, turned ninety degrees and immediately went into a gallop. Without a word of command, at least heard in Janek's position.

No less surprised were the ataman people who did not react, and when they did, it was too late.

The black guards fell on them in a split second, and in a minute no one was riding their horses.

This maneuver was so unforeseen that Janek only reacted by modifying his previous order:

"Don't shoot, wait..."

Three blacks jumped off their horses to check if any of the Cossacks are still alive. Without a word, in two or three times they plunged their sabers into the lying bodies and jumped onto the saddles.

The sabers disappeared in the scabbards.

***

They started to reach to Janek's group. As before, very slowly. When they were no more than twenty meters away, the one in front raised a hand, the others stopped, and he rode closer. He stopped and just stared. Not on soldiers, not on Demienkov, but on Janek.

"How did he sense who was in charge?" It occurred to him.

The nervousness disappeared somewhere and there was peace.

What are they up to?

The other was silent for a moment, then he looked at the soldiers and the rifles held at his shoulders.

"Well trained," he said shortly in Russian.

"Not as well as yours," Janek also replied in Russian, not taking his eyes off him.

At that moment, the voice of the rushing riders came from behind.

"Stepan, ours?" He did not turn around, ready to give the order to shoot at any moment.

"Ours."

Black's commander smiled.

"Good tactics," he praised.

Out of the corner of his eyes, Janek saw that Alik, who was in charge of the succor, had quickly placed the soldiers in such a way that a group of strangers could be taken in a semicircle. These, however, did not pay attention to it, on the contrary, they clearly relaxed, exchanging some observations among themselves and joking.

"We were silent, and now it's time to know each other," the blacks commander smiled even wider.

After his first words, Janek caught something, rejected it as irrelevant and only now did he realize what it was. It was not a Russian. He spoke Russian, even smoothly and with great knowledge of the language, but there was a strange note in it.

"A troop of the Polish army," he said this time in Polish, stressing the second to last word.

Surprise crossed the man's face. He was still silent, but it was evident that he was considering what he had heard.

"How's that Polish?" He blurted out. "They haven't come yet."

"And yours? Bolsheviks? People of Ataman Grigoryev? Or maybe the Ukrainian army?"

Silence. Black's commander showed him debating whether to reveal the cards.

"Not one of those fools," he said, but said nothing.

Janek reacted, trying to make his words as cold as he could.

"If not this one, what kind of "scum"?"

Black visibly pouted, but then laughed out loud.

"And also the jaunty, though so young, we are from the ataman Caucasus."

He wanted to ask another question, but something told him to hold off. He had heard this or a similar nickname somewhere before, because it couldn't have been a name.

After a moment he remembered two names from the courier letters he had taken over and used it now. He just did not remember whether he was called the Caucasus or Kazac in the letter.

"Caucasus, you say, and Jaworski is also you?"

Surprise flashed across the man's face once more.

"Well, well, I mean..." he paused, as if not knowing what to say, then added: "Ataman Caucasus is one thing, and Jaworski's unit is another, sometimes we cooperate. We, alone, without authority, he takes care of Count Józef Potocki and his court in Antonin as the base."

"And this," he pointed at the Cossacks lying behind their backs, "is this the result of this cooperation or your showcase?"

"I think we'll get along, you have to meet the ataman," he said enigmatically, still smiling.

Janek watched the eyes that mirror of the soul, in which it was difficult to hide his true intentions. And those eyes of the black commander were serene now, but when he showed the killed Cossacks, for a split second they suddenly hardened, turning to steel.

"Perhaps, but..." He paused, not knowing whether to tell him, then decided, watching him closely.

"In a moment, the companions of these," the movement of the hand on the dead, "will appear here."

"We beat the messenger."

"They'll come anyway, it was just an advanced squad. They are coming already."

"That's for sure?"

"I guess so. Go back to yours, not enough..."

There was a small commotion behind him, and immediately after that Alik drove up to Janek, who leaned over to Janek.

"They're coming, I think it's time to finish our chatter."

He turned around. Alik pointed south.

"I sent a watch when we were driving here, he came back and says that at least the regiment is dragging."

Janek made a quick decision. Indeed, this is not the time for diplomatic talks.

"I guess it's not the time, they are already close, and how is your family?" He asked the black commander who had already been approached by one of his men.

Wachtmeister Kuźma Koryatovich, and you?"

Janek introduced himself and once again saw the surprise in his eyes. He just tilted his head and asked:

"Do you have a relative..."

"You can see them now, finish it," Alik urged him, and without waiting for an answer he spurred his horse and began to give orders.

"It's Mr. Koryatovich, you probably won't be going anywhere," Janek felt excitement and at the same time a strange calmness. With these people, whoever commanded them, the fear of the Bolshevik or Makhnovist advantage ceased to be so terrible. As long as they were who they said they were. "Hold on to us just in case."

Another horse rode up to the other one and briefly reported something.

"Mr. Jan," the smile disappeared from the commander's face and his face suddenly hardened, "I think we will. I also sent a watch, the Makhnovist regiment is coming, but probably mixed up with the Bolsheviks. Lots of them. I suggest..."

He did not have time to finish when the Cossacks appeared, no more than four hundred meters away, galloping towards them.

"Do you have a machine gun?" Asked Alik quickly, who rode up to him again.

"A little trouble, because we found another one, we quickly made a tachanka for it, that's why it took so long. There is no cast."

It surprised Janek, but also made him happy. He turned to Koryatovich:

"Do you have anyone who knows how to operate a heavy machine gun?"

He immediately turned to the back and shouted two names.

"Łyżko and Felsztyn," he introduced them as they drove up. "You are following the orders of the commandant," he pointed to Janek, who quickly explained that he had two soldiers serving one, though not this age, and an additional heavy machine gun, which was not staffed.

"We can make it where is this toy?" the first of them rejoiced as if he got an extra salary. "Me and Felszyn were in the companions of the machine guns, I was a feldfebel, he was also, but before the war, we didn't forget."

He handed them over to Alik, and to Koryatovich he said shortly:

"Set yours as you see fit, but you'd better stick to me. It's good to have an experienced soldier with you."

He simply nodded without resistance and began to give orders to his deputy.

The Cossacks had already approached a distance of about 200 meters and stopped. Soon more joined the spy. Janek did not count them, but at first sight there were over a hundred. He looked at his own and drove up to Alik:

"Place the machine gun forty meters away, and let the rest of them line up in front of them so they won't see them. And shoot only on my orders."

He swept the foreground once more. He had an idea of how to get out of the situation, even though the opponent was outnumbered.

"Mr. Kuźma," he turned to Koryatovich and presented him with his plan.

"It can work out, our way." He just laughed and disposed of his men.

Now forty horses stood in front of the Cossacks in two lines. The blacks behind Janek's soldiers, moving behind their backs from left to right and from right to left, constantly on the move, so that from a distance it was impossible to count how many there were in reality. Only the first line stood still.

He gave the order to Demenkov, and he took command of the horses.

Now it was only necessary to skillfully provoke the Cossacks.

***

He gave Demienek his final orders, and he retired to Alik, who was in charge of setting up the machine-gun tachankas.

All that remained was the smooth execution of the mock attack.

Demenkov had already given his order, and the first line walked towards the Cossacks. There were hoots and characteristic whistles on the other side.

The first line was followed by the second and at the end by Koryatovich's blacks. Slowly at first, gradually accelerating. They were not more than a hundred meters from their opponent when they started, galloping right away.

Janek clenched his fists involuntarily. If only Stepan did not overpay, and if the soldiers obeyed the order.

He raised the binoculars to his eyes. The greyness had yet to pass into the next phase, but darkness was already lurking and full darkness should be present at any moment. Next to Koryatovich, with binoculars to his eyes, he carefully followed the whole action. Seemingly calm, but Janek noticed clenched jaws.

At one point, the Poles from the first line stopped the horses abruptly, the second line and the blacks ended up standing in one row. And almost at the same time, everyone raised their rifles and began shooting at the oncoming.

Too early, thought Janek, assessing the situation, but it immediately occurred to him that Demenkov was closer and that he calculated the distance precisely.

The first firefight knocked a few riders off their horses, but the rest continued to rush at the Poles with their sabers stretched out in front of them, without slowing down.

Another one, this time more precise, and a dozen flew to the ground. Third, more killed.

And after that the Polish unit suddenly turned in place, simulating panic in the ranks and was now running in retreat with literally Cossacks on their tails.

"Get ready," he shouted to Alik, who was circling between the tachanka.

The Cossacks were no more than thirty meters behind the rumps of Polish horses when they were already reaching the place where the barrows were standing. With a coordinated maneuver, they split into two groups, revealing the foreground to the heavy machine guns. And immediately they turned back, creating an additional line of defense, immediately opening fire on the oncoming traffic.

Now machine guns started making the first Cossack ranks a real havoc. The horses collapsed, the riders rolled to the ground under the hooves of those following them, tried to turn back few times, they ran into them speedily, trampling them mercilessly. The horses, sensing the situation, screamed in terror and tried to brake on their own, but it was too late for that. Machine guns hacked mercilessly at the riders and their steeds, giving them no chance. Those who avoided the bullets and made their way to the other side, found themselves on the wall of the shooting Poles. None survived.

The back ranks of the Cossack pack, seeing what was happening, started to turn back, but not directly backwards, but to the sides, to be a more difficult target for the Polish tachankas still firing steel.

"We divide ours in half and finish them off," Janek threw to Koryatovich and without waiting for him to understand he rushed to Alik. The latter immediately understood what was going on, ordered the black commander, and in a matter of seconds two groups jumped on the sparse Cossacks escaping the fire.

Janek rode up to the first tachanka, shouted an order and the same to the second. Now both shotguns fired straight ahead, at those few who jumped in panic, they ran backwards, collecting a bloody harvest among them.

Within a few minutes the machine guns fell silent. The steppe darkened, only the horizon was a tone brighter, and in the distance a mass of infantry was visible in the distance, running towards the battle. Fortunately, the distance was long, so they couldn't endanger the situation.

The troops chasing the Cossacks began to return. Several riders were injured, but no one was killed. Janek realized that in a direct fight the situation would not be so happy for them. The surprise and the trick helped.

Koryatovich drove up. He had to take part in the pursuit of the Cossacks, because he was still holding a saber stained with blood.

"Mr. Kuźma, the commander does not rush into the fight, but coordinates it," he said a tart remark.

"I'm sorry, Mr. Jan, but when I see them, I can't help myself."

"Measure for the future, because you are responsible for your people."

Koryatovich gritted his teeth, ran a rag pulled from his saber over the edge of his saber, looked at them critically and slipped it into its scabbard.

"You're right, the Caucasus Ataman tells me that too, but..." He paused, and his expression changed, squeezed by the memory of pain. He sighed deeply, clutching his saber hilt. "The Cossacks killed my whole family, my wife, parents, sisters, brothers and even small children... When I see them, something confuses my mind and I stop thinking. Sorry again." This time he lowered his head and fell silent.

Janek looked at him, surprised by the openness of his expression.

"Because, Mr. Jan," Koryatovich spoke again, wanting to clarify the matter to the end. "It isn't about the Cossacks, because we have a dozen or so in the unit, but about those who supported the Bolsheviks and the Makhnovist. And not everyone did, and each of my friends lost someone. Those from the Makhnovist region, though they pretend to be a different nation, murder in the same way as the Bolsheviks. Atamanshchins..." He didn't finish, just waved his hand. "And what's next? Should I go back to my own?"

"And far from them?"

"I don't know where they are now. The ataman sent us to make contact with you."

Janek looked at him surprised.

"I don't really understand."

"And because, Mr. Jan, we have our people everywhere and they reported that there was a unit circulating here, but not a gang, because they were defending people, something like us, the ataman ordered to check who are they."

"You don't know where they are?"

"We made an appointment in Kozie Rogi in three days, it is a small village far to the east."

"You can go back, but I don't know if it's safe," he pointed to the horizon and the incoming regiment, now hidden in the darkness. "I'm afraid that they are pulling towards the west," he fell silent, remembering the words that had been said at the beginning of the acquaintance. 'You mentioned that it is too early for the Polish army."

"We have information, obtained from Bolshevik couriers, that Poland is reborn and chased the bandits allied with the created Ukrainian People's Republic, but they prepared a great offensive and are now dragging our people."

"I admit that I don't understand. Is it with those of the Makhnovists, this people's republic?"

"No, no, they're different. The Makhnovists established their state somewhere between the Dnieper and the Azov Sea, and once they cooperate with the Bolsheviks, and sometimes they go for sabers. And this Ukrainian People's Republic is different, closer to us. There was an alliance between them and the Poles, and they allegedly chased the Bolsheviks from Kiev together."

"Wait a minute, is Poland reborn?" Janek's throat tightened. He knew nothing, sewn in his wood, no information reached him, because where did it come from? Now he understood the information contained in the intercepted correspondence.

"Well, yes, Mr. Jan, but they are far away, and we are here, like the old parties in the January Uprising," he fell silent, looking carefully at Janek. "My great-grandfather served under yours, Victor, when he was leading the party on the Moskals."

The surprise was complete. Janek did not know the details of his great-grandfather's history, but only what his grandfather and Vasily told him sometimes. Now, though he still wanted to talk, he had to concentrate on the current situation.

"You have to decide what to do next, and I will be glad to see your commander when the opportunity is available. And now the Bolsheviks or the Makhnovists, one devil, will see this pogrom and will not forgive us, we must hide in the forest. I suggest your unit do the same. It's night and it isn't known what is lurking in the steppe and how much of this stuff is crawling here. Later, my people will lead you through the forest and you will leave in a safe place. What do you say?"

"Reasonable proposition, I suppose, let's go with you."

***

While they were talking, Alik gave the order to catch the Cossack horses that were hanging around in the area and collect all weapons. Mindful of Janek's teachings, he chased his people, whom

Koryatovich's black hussars willingly joined and they were already combing the field of the recent battle.

It was already completely dark and collecting the weapons did not go as fast as Janek wished.

"Alik, let them come back. Give the order quickly and send a joint patrol of Mr. Kuźma's hussars and ours, let them check where the Bolsheviks are and what they are doing. Just be careful, though they probably won't see much in this darkness."

It was only now that he realized that, busy with organizing the defense, and then fighting, he had not noticed where Sheba had gone. She was nowhere around. Concerned, he scanned the immediate surroundings and sighed when he did not find the body of the wolf. He was afraid that she might have been hit by random bullets. He concluded that when the shooting broke out, Sheba simply ran away. He felt sad, but it was better than dying.

Within a dozen or so minutes, horses came from the field, leading the captured ones, laden with weapons.

Janek gave a sign and they headed towards the forest. He intended to settle the guests on the island where Alik was training. He sent two new ones to the villages to notify the peasants of what had happened and to warn them that the Bolshevik-Makhnovist army was approaching.

"What else?" He wondered. "How will they react when they see the Cossack corpses? Will they go in pursuit? Probably yes, because they will not allow themselves to leave an enemy unit behind. Who will they take them for, the Polish army or partisans?"

They drove into the first trees when suddenly a shadow appeared from the bushes and rushed towards Sewek. He just screamed happily, but a commotion arose among the hussars following him. "Wolf, wolf," he heard voices and simultaneous clang of repeated weapons.

He jumped down quickly screaming: "Don't shoot! It's ours!" and after a while he was tugging Sheba's fur, who licked his face with joy, whimpering softly, jumping on his shoulders and squeaking as if she was complaining, and at the same time cutting her ears towards strangers.

The horses snorted at the sight of her, nervously ventilating her scent and kicking their hooves.

"It's a surprise, you even have a wolf, a real Vakho," he heard the admiring voice of Koryatovich, who tightened the reins of his horse tightly so that it would stand still. "No wonder that in the stories of peasants you command the Wolf Regiment."

At first, Janek did not pay attention to his words, but in the next one he was surprised to find in the master's mouth an unknown Caucasian term for a wolf. He made a note to ask about it later.

He jumped on Sewek, and Sheba lined his side, still keeping a vigilant eye on the strange horses and strangers, and showing them her fangs.

"We're going, we'll talk later," he said to Koryatovich. "Just keep your own people away, because you will upset the wolf," he laughed, and then they began to plunge into the forest.

Chapter XVII

The Hussars were due to leave the next day, but news from the scouts changed plans.

A Bolshevik regiment was already setting up a camp near the forest, and the first units of another, the Makhnovists, judging by their slightly different uniforms, were already joining them. They spread over a large area, erecting fortified posts from the side of the forest. The scouts counted about twenty field guns and six armored cars. In addition to the infantry, there were also four cavalry squadrons with no less than four hundred sabers.

Janek questioned the scouts carefully, wanting to count the soldiers. He consulted the calculations with Koryatovich and Demenkov. They determined that they probably had four battalions against each other, divided into several companies, so together more than 1,200 soldiers of the same infantry. The approaching regiment of the Revolutionary Insurgent Army of Ukraine probably numbered the same and now occupied the area east of the Bolsheviks.

"They will not forgive, they will go into the forest and try to kill us, I don't see it well," Demenkov commented calculations. "We'd better run, they'll kill us like flies."

"You are right, you are right, but theoretically," Koryatovich did not seem to be concerned about it and looked at Janek, curious about his opinion.

"Stepan is right, it is not for what they have built posts on the side of the forest and it is not why they stopped here. Handing over a battle to them is suicide, they will hijack us, and the losses are not counted, as I think. Our only advantage is the knowledge of the forest. And for flies, Stepan, we are not hunted by firing cannons. Besides, they don't know how many of us there are, they'll be careful."

"Well, knowledge of the area where they will not be able to hijack us," repeated the hussar satisfied with the assessment.

"There is also a problem with the excess of horses, so I think..." Demenkov was still skeptical. "Maybe get rid of them? Let go loose, because we have neither fodder nor grooms to take care of them, they will only slow us down."

"You are partially right," Janek thought intensely. "But we will always have enough time to let loose, and so they will carry additional ammunition and supplies.

They began to develop a defense plan, its supplementary version if it failed, and to designate assembly and backup points if the situation changed. Janek was in charge of the conversation because of his knowledge of the forest. He drew Koryatovich a map with characteristic points, perhaps not as precise as military staff posts, but precise enough to facilitate orientation in the wooded area. He's also assigned Alik to guide him when he comes to bounce after the first fight.

"Gentlemen," Janek stretched, feeling tired. "Let's do it. To fortify the island, the heavy machine guns on the island are to have crossfire, cut trees to knock them down as we retreat, what am I to tell you, maybe we have a day to prepare for my. And after that rest, sleep, only the guards are to keep their eyes and ears open, and the scouts, the constant observation of the Bolsheviks. Aha, Stepan, now you are wachtmeister when Alik goes to the hussars. All clear?"

"There are few of those resting," Demenkov muttered, which brought a smile to Koryatovich's face, who, however, kept the comment to himself.

***

Janek left the soldiers bustling about and went to his cave. He didn't mention the commander of the black hussars. He wanted to be alone for a while. He had to think about a few things, and the new acquaintance did not want to ask about the few words that escaped him in the course of his acquaintance.

He wondered why such an experienced soldier obeyed him so quickly without questioning any orders. After all, the man had much more practice in warfare and was older, and he was just a grub that had to suddenly grow up. And who was this mysterious commander of his, portrayed as the Caucasus ataman, whom he did not mention? Peasant or noble? How many sabers are in his party, and why was a small group of only fifteen horses actually sent here? Although Koryatovich mentioned that in order to establish contact, he also slipped out that they had spies located in the villages. These, in turn, certainly provided good information, although maybe...

He remembered the term Wolf Regiment. It was greatly exaggerated, because it was not even a squadron, but only a unit and a small one at that. On the other hand, peasant tales have always exaggerated all information, both good and bad for them. They must have known that there was an armed man in the area who did not like the Bolsheviks, and that he had never been seen, except for Sheba, who was conspicuous, and the last incident in the village when they attacked the soldiers, a legend was added.

He had to read carefully the intercepted courier service once more. There were fragments in them that he only glanced over, considering them to be insignificant, although they could have been of greater importance.

He left the coil in his stable, and Sheba, who was going to the cave with him, ordered him to guard the horse. The wolf was surprised by the command, poked him with his nose to change his mind, tried a few tricks with lying on his back, wagging his tail, jumping on his shoulders and licking his face, but Janek persisted. He knew that if an alien appeared here, the wolf would attack and the mere sight of him would cause such a commotion that he would hear it in the cave.

***

He began with unread papers found at commissar Harpan in the town. He was definitely the most important there.

...Following the orders of Comrade Trotsky and in the light of bringing the revolution westward in order to join the revolution of comrades from Germany, the increase in the number of troops must be increased as soon as possible," wrote some Vyacheslav Menzynski, who signed himself as the deputy head of the Cheka. "Thus, it is ordered to recruit to them people who were trained to command such masses of the army. To restore to service, even by force, under the slogan of defending the homeland, trained former tsarist officers, equality of the people, but control their actions strictly not only through the commissioners, but also their own, trusted and devoted people...

He flipped through the documents, picking out the most important fragments. They showed and confirmed that statehood was reborn in Poland, which caused his heart to beat faster. He remembered the longing conversations between his grandfather and Vasily about it.

In the following, a note about a certain Piłsudski, underlined in red: The Council of Soldiers' Delegates in St. Petersburg appointed this son of a bitch a commissioner, but this scab did not take advantage of our proposal and began to form a puppet Polish government.

Several documents dealt with organizational matters.

Order to transform the Red Guard into a Workers-Peasants Red Army. And another one, who said that the identification marks for the commanders of divisions and regiments as well as for ordinary soldiers were being restored. A red star is introduced for the soldiers of the entire army, and if possible with the addition of a hammer and a plow as a symbol of the workers and peasants army. They should be worn over caps or braces. Commanders must have them sewn onto the left sleeve. Below, triangles, squares or diamonds represent the formations.

He did not understand any of this, but he was beginning to understand that the Bolsheviks had created their own army, based in large part on the terror of politician commissars and tsarist officers and non-commissioned officers who were still experienced in battle. Hence Kluyev - he was beginning to understand it now - retained his rank of lieutenant colonel, although he had political officer Babel by his side. And he headed the emergency regiment... Wait, wait, how was it? Всероссийская чрезвычайная комиссия по борьбе с контрреволюцией, спекуляцией и преступлениям по должности. Well, the name itself testified to everything, the All-Russian Extraordinary Commission for Combating Counter-Revolution, Speculation and Abuse of Power could do anything, it was the master of life and death of everyone who stood in its way. Good for themselves, abuses of power and two thieves who, robbing courts and murdering, collected gold and valuables for themselves. But why, while serving in Budyonny's Cavalry Army, were they just sent to the emerging front that was to move to Poland?

Some flyer with the words of Comrade Lenin. As he realized, he was the leader of the Bolsheviks. And the words quoted on it, encouraging to fight against Poles: *These parasites that have sucked the blood of the people for so long must know that neither freedom nor equality will give them back their lost wealth, which will go safely into the hands of the workers. Wherever the bourgeoisie rules, it does nothing to the toiling masses.*

Finally, he left himself a document addressed directly to Babel, with bold red writing on it: *Confidential. For his own hands.* Unsealed.

Wonder if he was deliberately held by Commissar Harpan. He broke the wax and began to read. It was signed by the commissioner of WCzK, Jēkabs Peterss. He flew over the text and started over, because he thought it contradicted what he had already learned. At the beginning, Peterss recalled that the army was headed by Lev Trotsky, because Lenin had no idea about the military. And then that he is Babel's former companion, from the time of the underground, Lejba Davidovich Bronshteyn.

What was the significance of this reminder? Is it a call to order or a warning? He didn't understand the author's intentions, but a wordplay like that probably served something.

He delved into the text as he read another note. In it he emphasized that Lenin too often allows himself to be called Trotsky *that bastard* or even talks about it at WCZK meetings: *Judas Trotsky.* At the end it was the most interesting. In a veiled calm, Peterss made it clear that Lenin was now needed for the revolution, but after joining his German comrades *firm steps will have to be taken with regard to Comrade Lenin.*

Further on, an even more intriguing fragment, in which it directly referred to Babel and Kluyev. Here Janek felt more confident, because he knew who he was talking about:

Maintain good relations with Lieutenant Colonel Kluyev, favor him, let him have you as a friend and confidant. Support him in dealing with this traitor of revolutionary ideas, Nestor Makhno and his Revolutionary Insurgent Army of Ukraine. The time will come for them as well, but only after entering Polish territory and dealing with its bourgeois government. If, however, Kluyev starts to suspect something, you must, comrade, remove him without delay, but quietly so that it does not get to his brother..

Whose brother? He was beginning to understand where the Bolsheviks had dual power, looking at each other's hands and meticulous, even bordering on persecution mania, controlling, regardless of the position he held.

His eyes were starting to stick to themselves.

For a moment he wanted to go back to the island, but - he excused himself - Alik is there and if something starts to happen, he will certainly let him know. In person or through Joshua or Fedor who knew the location of the cave. He wanted to rethink Koryatovich's words, but the dream turned out to be stronger.

***

It was dawn when Sheba awoke him.

She disobeyed the command and ran into the cave, now licking his face and clearly letting him know something was bothering her. So instead of yell at her he praised her, looked outside, but the forest was still sleeping peacefully. The wolf, however, was still a little tense, fawning, but after a while he became tense and listened to something.

Janek has got used to the fact that Sheba does not act like that without a reason. She must have heard and felt something. Had they moved? Probably not, because even if they tried very hard, you would hear soldiers breaking through the forest. So maybe they launched a scout?

He took his rifle and revolver, then, on the cave's threshold, he backed away and reached for his bow and quiver of arrows. He mentally sneered at himself that now such an archaic weapon would be of no use to him, but he did not disregard his old habit and shrugged himself back.

The first steps were directed to Sewek, but he gave up immediately. Sheba's behavior had to be for reasons. For his own peace of mind, he decided to check the direction from which the Bolsheviks could theoretically come. He kept his eyes on the wolf all the time. He knew that before he could see or hear anything, she would be the first to know about the danger.

And so it happened when he did not walk more than a thousand paces.

The she-wolf growled softly, bristled, and pointed in the direction with her mouth.

They could be scouts, it flashed through his head as he removed his bow and tossed the rifle over his back.

Now he doubled his caution, taking his steps gently.

After about fifty yards, he heard them. A word, an order, not entirely whispered, but still incomprehensible. Taking advantage of the tall ferns that grew here densely, he hid in them and came closer. In front of him was a small cut through a stream where trees grew less frequently. He stopped listening. Sheba lifted her tail in an unmistakable sign that the danger was just around the corner.

He didn't have to wait long. A bent soldier emerged from behind the plump clones, followed carefully by another and another.

Nothing happened, the three looked around and began to slowly move forward. After a while, the bushes shuddered farther to the right, and hence three came out. They agreed without words, just with a wave of the hand, and they followed the former without haste.

He waited with them in front of him. Something told him to back off and take no chances. He chased away his thoughts and continued to watch the soldiers. He did not know if they were only six or if there were more, and they only formed the backbone of the reconnaissance.

He felt a growing tension, but not nervousness. The fact that he had scouts in front of him confirmed that the command of the Bolshevik regiment had no intention of leaving behind an enemy unit.

After a long while, patience was rewarded.

The six did not walk more than fifteen or twenty paces, farther to the left of him, as a dozen others emerged behind them, more confidently following the first. Each of them had a rifle in their hands, guiding it carefully from left to right, but - as he noticed - they were not as tense as the first ones. And probably less experienced, because they exchanged some comments.

"All of them, or some more," he wondered. "Why aren't they following the wider bench, only focused? Lack of experience or do they have a greater sense of security?"

He waited a dozen more minutes, watching in which direction they were going. He concluded that they probably did not have a specific purpose, but only the task of checking whether the enemy was hiding just behind the first trees or somewhere beyond.

What now? Let them penetrate the forest further? How do they accidentally get to the lake and see the island? Even the stupidest commander orders to penetrate her immediately. What to do?

The second group slightly changed direction and, to Janek's surprise, headed towards the ferns in which he was hiding.

Not good, a thought flashed through his mind, but he didn't move. Maybe they will change the route, and if not, he will have to react. He got into it himself. He didn't like it, but he didn't have time to back down. The ferns, however large they may be, are not trees, and any backward movement will make them twitch, which will surely get the scouts' attention.

Only now did he thank himself for taking the bow.

The soldiers approached without changing direction. Now he could only hear them, not wanting to lean out. Certainly they were not the people of the forest who watch where they put their feet on an expedition. The crunch of broken twigs was getting closer.

They could be no more than several meters. After the sounds he realized that they were already walking among the first ferns, not trying to avoid them somewhere to the side. He could perfectly hear the rustle of branches rubbing against uniforms.

Now or never.

He has to make up his mind.

He made a decision quickly, though somewhere in the back of his head appeared an irrational fear. Until now, he had dealt with single couriers, now there were many more of them. More importantly, he wanted to counter the gaps with the rifles of the soldiers. He could have used the Winchester, but the flight of the arrow was silent, and that - he consoled himself - should be his advantage.

So it was not the best choice, but it offered a chance to surprise the soldiers.

He reached gently for the quiver.

Taking a deep breath, he waited a moment for adrenaline to seize him and his inner peace to dissipate.

He placed the first arrow on the bowstring and continued to wait, hoping that they would be headed elsewhere.

He felt Sheba on his side tremble impatiently, rubbing against him, waiting for the command.

However, the soldiers were getting closer.

They did not change their march.

He had to do it to survive.

He took another deep breath, let it out slowly, and gave himself a moment to listen for the direction of their march.

They were almost on top of him.

Now...

He got up just enough to maneuver his bow and arms freely.

The first arrow hit the closest one who opened his eyes in surprise and froze in terror. She pierced his neck, taking away the possibility of warning his comrades.

Similarly with the second one, when the arrowhead sank into it, and with the third, who began to suspect that something was wrong, but did not have time to do anything.

He crouched down, controlling the rising panic, prepared more and waited for a fierce rifle butt.

But nothing happened. All he heard was the surprised exhortations of the others and quietly asked questions about what was happening.

He renewed his attack.

Quickly rising over the ferns.

This time he saw as the comrades of the shot lowered their rifles, looking around and trying to understand the situation.

Subsequent arrows left the string and only then did the first rifle respond. Probably a reflex reaction to uncertainty and fear of a situation they did not comprehend.

He realized that they still did not see him, did not look in his direction, and at all, looking mostly at the branches of the trees and pointing the barrels of their rifles there.

He crouched down. Time to step back. He must distract them.

He indicated Sheba the direction, then blinked what to do. He didn't want her to be shot, but only to cause confusion.

The wolf ran through the bushes towards the soldiers.

A dozen seconds later he heard the scream of the first attacker, followed by even louder, full of terror: "Волк!, волк!, За помощь!, спасение!"

And already from several sides someone was shooting, someone else was screaming in the sky, and the silence that had been preserved so far turned into a tumult and chaos full of terror and panic.

Taking the moment, he fired more shots, then whistled at Sheba and, even more bent, began to quickly retreat to the rear. He leaned out once more, glanced at what was happening in front of him, and hid behind a thick hornbeam, the outgrowths of which were perfect hiding.

Here Sheba caught up with him, pleased with herself, but still with her hair bristling.

"Let's get out, lead," he ordered her and headed for Sewek's stable. He had to inform his people about the Bolshevik reconnaissance, although they probably heard the shots anyway.

***

"Now they know that we are in the forest," he gave a short report to Alik after arriving on the island, but instead of a comment in response, he only tapped his forehead.

"Da, however, it has its advantages," Koryatovich remained calm, and judging by his expression, he had his own opinion on Janek's expedition. "You have once again confirmed the legend of the Wolf Regiment, and contrary to what is believed, they are diligently collecting information on each partisan unit. And that is a plus for us. Most are simple people with an atavistic fear of wolves. They will be afraid when they enter the forest. As I suppose, they will not let the scouts go anymore, but will prepare a massive attack so as not to give even the largest pack of wolves a chance. For my taste, we can expect it tomorrow at the earliest, and in two days at the latest. And the first thing they'll do is fire the artillery into the foreground before the infantry goes to attack."

"Which means our scouts shouldn't be sent too far?" Janek wanted to make sure that he understood correctly the wachtmeister's argument.

"Exactly, but we don't know how far the fire will be. I wouldn't risk it, it's a pity for the people and I'd rather move them to the area near the lake."

"So it was decided, but," Janek hesitated for a moment whether he was right, "I would like to provoke the direction of the attack on the lake and the island. Here they will fall into a trap. I'm just afraid that they won't attract those poles with them."

"No, not really, in this thicket, pulled by people and even horses, it would only slow down the march."

"I'm so proud," Demenkov said, "that if they decide to attack, it will be only a preventive or a final measure."

"Good point," Koryatowich scratched his nose. "If they have an old tsarist officer as their commander, it will only be a show of strength and an attempt to drive us as far as possible. He will realize that the mass in the forest does not matter. If, on the other hand, there is such a party, he will order our complete liquidation. Anyway, we will be forced to fight and at some point to retreat to a safer area."

"So, we established it," Janek ended the meeting. "Alik, scouts forward, but close. But not so much that they immediately had the lake behind their backs. Two people on watch. And it would seem that what happened to those with whom I stumbled. Maybe send Ostapko with Fedor if he feels better already?"

"Mr. Pohorecki has hunted, he knows the forest, and Ostapko has peasant sense, so they will succide," Alik smiled for the first time, and Janek only understood the gesture at the beginning of the conversation; the friend was simply afraid for him.

"Wise Wolf," Koryatovich leaned towards Sheba lying at Janek leg, trying to stroke her.

The hand was not halfway to her head yet when there was a warning snarl.

"Mr. Kuźma, you absolutely want to lose your fingers," Janek laughed. "She is better than the Bolsheviks, with her the word trust often has a double meaning."

"I see, I see, but I repeat, a wise wolf, rarely a dog would obey an order like she did." The wachtmeister looked at Sheba with delight, his eyes sparkling with true admiration.

Janek saw Sheba's reaction more than once. She tolerated those around him, but allowed none to become familiar. The only thing that surprised him at first was that she only allowed Alik to puff the fur, clearly treating him as a second master. "Strange," he thought.

***

Until the end of the day, nothing happened. Fedor and Ostapko returned from the reconnaissance. They found a few dead bodies with arrows still stuck, which they meticulously removed from the bodies and brought to Janek, which surprised him.

"I just thought it was a sign, a symbol for a good future," explained Pohorecki, blinking his eye and pointing at Ostapko. "Let the legend grow, and he will probably create it among us, because he was very impressed. And that will come in handy, because we won't miss them soon. Oh, in those ferns there was another one with a torn throat, you have an extra point for Sheba's account. Koryatovich is right when he says that fame is more powerful than cannons. We have the Wolf Regiment," he laughed. "And by the way you are crazy to attack armed soldiers with your bow. I think you took over some traits from your great-grandfather Victor, because your grandfather said that he didn't know fear either."

Janek was surprised that the Pohorecki family spoke of the old times. After all, as he remembered the story he heard from Vasily, Panteleimon Pohorecki, Fedor's grandfather, was a tsarist officer, but the past was now the least important. "Interesting," he thought, however, what the report sounded like, after all, the latter had fought as an officer on the side of the Moskals.

Suddenly he missed a time when his only concern was whether the hunt would be successful. For a moment he returned to the moments when life had seemed so carefree in retrospect. For the stories of his grandfather and Vasily, for Maruchna's pancakes, for his mother and sister Ania, sent to the family near Lviv, and even for Hapka, for whom he followed his eyes because of the thick, black braid to the waist and her black eyes staring at the young master, when they sometimes joked, and not infrequently absorbing the swaying beautiful breasts under a linen blouse...

"Janek, what are you so proud of," Alik snapped him out of his memories. "Come to the peasants, they are waiting, they argue where to put those machine guns, so that there is the best fire."

"Machine guns? Who?" He hasn't quite come back to reality yet.

"Łyżko and Felsztyn are arguing with our old ones, Alesiey and Siemion, about places and everyone is wiser. In the end, they decided that the "colonel", that is you, was to judge, and they came to me with it."

"They could not immediately see me?"

"They could not, you are now like Wernyhora to them."

"Come on, this fairy tale is already starting to irritate me, a little more and I will believe in it myself."

"I will remind you who you are, now come and judge. And the legend, remember what Koryatovich said, gives people courage."

Chapter XVIII

They came at dawn, while the mists were still heavy towards the ground, huddling bushes and tree trunks in their feathery tentacles.

Scouts spotted them.

They moved slowly, in absolute silence; even their shoes were tied with some rags. They seemed to be ghosts caused by old beliefs. There were so many of them that it gave the impression that it was the forest that had suddenly started wandering. Almost a soldier next to a soldier, silently moving forward step by step, staring diligently at the boughs above their heads and into the fog, as if for fear that a pack of bloodthirsty, furious wolves would suddenly spring out of it.

According to Janek's instructions, the shooters did not shoot. Noiselessly they withdrew and notified Alik. The latter sounded the alarm and checked the posts where the soldiers were sleeping.

They were ready. They were waiting for them. Everyone knew who they were subordinate to in the hastily truncated platoons, what to do when an order was given, and how to behave when a fight broke out.

Janek was only afraid that the Bolsheviks might walk around the lake, which they could do if they were outnumbered. So far, as reported by subsequent scouts, they were approaching in one wide bench. It was difficult to judge how many there were, but from a few hundred to maybe even over a thousand.

They certainly did not know about the lake and the island.

"You will have to stay there until the side, one-man posts alert you that the enemy is walking around the lake," Janek analyzed the situation again, thinking aloud in the presence of Demienkov and Koryatovich. "And then retreat along the already marked path, grouping in the designated reserve "A" or "B" point, located even deeper in the forest."

"The peasants are determined," the lieutenant has just returned from the tour of the outposts. Somehow he couldn't bring himself to call them soldiers. For him, a real army, these are the former tsarist troops with drill, regulations, charges, uniforms and all this envelope, binding before the war and in time. Although he appreciated the militancy of Janek's and Koryatovich's units, he showed no dislike of anyone, and even admired their bravery during the clashes with the enemy, but in the vocabulary they were still only peasants, armed, but peasants. "It seems to me that those in your village are concerned about the fate of the families left there, but - I must admit - you instilled a drill in them in a strange way, and that matters now."

"As I can see, the lieutenant is still skeptical and dreams of returning to the tsarist regime," laughed Koryatovich. "They are better because they believe in a commander who showed them how to fight, who impresses them and shows respect. And in your army, the basis was washing after the murder, sticks for the slightest offense and contempt for the peasant."

"You sound like a socialist."

"No, Mr. Stepan, realist..."

"Come on, we have more important matters on our heads than verbal scuffles," Janek silenced them by raising both hands up. "We are sitting on the tip of the fuse and it depends on the efficiency of our people whether we raise our heads safely, and you are ready to fight here."

They looked at each other askance, but fell silent.

"The situation is not very comfortable for us, because, as Stepan already put it, they can hijack us and they will not even feel it," he continued. "What do these dozens of shotguns mean when hundreds are attacked by us? So we absolutely need to do exactly what we have planned; drag them into a trap, crush as many as possible, and withdraw without loss. They are to remain uncertain about how many of us there are and the fear of the forest."

"We've already talked..." Demienkov began, but Janek interrupted him.

"It doesn't hurt to recall, though. And now, gentlemen, to the wards."

"And I?" Alik usually stood at the side of the conference and did not speak.

"We're starting, so send designated people, let them provoke the others to attack, and then quickly withdraw to us. A couple of shot heads would be enough, don't let them charge."

***

The fog still lingered, delaying departure.

Koryatovich was standing in the pulpit next to Janek and was thinking about something.

"What are you thinking about? Can we make it?"

The wachtmeister was silent for a moment, staring at the forest.

"I remember the fight at Antonin, when the Bolsheviks sent great forces on us, because they were fed up with the actions of Jaworski, whom you asked about earlier."

A different tone of voice than before. Janek glanced at him and saw this commander of the black hussars from the first moment he met, right after his men slaughtered the attacking Cossacks. Later, as if he had changed, he turned into an observer who sometimes only gives good advice, an almost good uncle. And now it was the same again, emanating authority, menacing and dangerous. He wondered if it was good or bad, but since he was still with them, then probably nothing would be a threat on his part.

"He provoked the Bolsheviks?" He referred to his statement, not wanting to ask directly about the mysterious ataman who was on his mind.

"The Lord sewn in the woods does not know what was happening there, and it is difficult for him to understand," it was not the first time that he heard such an opinion about himself, so he did not deny it. This reproach was upsetting him, perhaps because it was true.

Koryatovich was silent, thoughtful, then inhaled deeply and shook his head as if he were conducting an internal discourse with himself.

"When the Bolsheviks took a coup, various armed bands arose, using weapons, many of which were at hand. And also various party militias, including the Bolsheviks, the remnants of the Eserians, anarchists, Socialist Revolutionaries, Mensheviks and others. Everyone incited the peasants and workers, because in the chaos they felt like a fish in water and it was convenient for them. Judgment to the landed gentry began, the first robberies of manors, although at first the townspeople did not move. And then came, like an avalanche, a wave of mad hatred; Even court horses and cattle were mutilated, and even ancient park oaks were cut down. Eventually, when it turned out that they were unpunished, and regular units joined the revolt, widespread murders began. The landlords, brutally slaughtered by their own peasants, were completely helpless."

He fell silent, his chest heaving, and his eyes flashed lightning towards the forest.

"The earth, Mr. Jan, has run down the river with the blood of thousands of innocent families. Panic and helplessness, and the ubiquitous slogans of revenge against bloodsuckers and exploiters. In the family estate of Jaworski, he told me about it, Cyganówka near Kamieniec Podolski, all his servants, from the oldest to the children, and even the home inventory were slaughtered."

"From what Demenkov mentioned, there weren't many of these Bolsheviks at the beginning, so why this hatred?" Janek had heard these arguments before and was still intrigued by how suddenly a state ruled by law and order could collapse so quickly, and normal social ties could be rejected.

"There were a lot of crazy people from the revolution and strange parties, but under tsarism they were kept in check. And when the Bolsheviks took power..."

"And Okhrana, because thanks to her the tsar had..."

"I cannot understand that either, but even the aristocracy was lost. Do you understand that Grand Duke Kirill Vladimirovich had a red flag displayed on his Petrograd residence right after the Tsar's abdication? And another, Nicholas Mickalovich announced: The collapse of autocracy will finally bring salvation and greatness to Russia..."

"They are guilty of themselves," Janek muttered to himself and asked: "Nobody defended themselves? It is inconceivable."

"Well, inconceivable, and that is why, when the tsarist hussar captain, i.e. Jaworski, appeared in Volhynia, when he formed a detachment and began to defend the courts against the blackness, people partially breathed and the peasants began to fear his revenge. He hung troublemakers, burned red villages, became the terror of the Bolsheviks. They even offered an exorbitant bounty on his head. And when that didn't work, they sent a whole regiment to Antonina, equipped with machine guns and two armored cars. Firepower. Our units were then together, Jaworski and ataman, but a fight with the entire well-armed regiment? It was then that the ataman quarreled with Jaworski, but we faced them together anyway, you never leave your friends."

"I suppose it was hard?"

"An understatement, as it can be here," he extended his hand towards the Bolshevik troops approaching somewhere in the borough. "The armored squadrons gave them an advantage, and we had no weapons against them. Rifle bullets bounced off the iron armor without doing any harm to them, and they spat out machine guns like rain. Death began to take a toll among us, and the people terrified by the avalanche of fire began to withdraw."

Janek listened eagerly. It was a real battle, one that he could only read about in novels about the war with Khmelnytsky, not his driveways. So he tried to listen carefully, because it might have given him some good idea to use in the one that was about to take place here in the forest.

"Jaworski ran into a combat amok," the wachtmeister continued. "The Ataman wanted to try some trick, regroup, but the other was not listening. He turned his people around, shouted that they were not allowed to run like sheep, and he did, he had authority, you must admit. Our ataman did the same, although ours were underdogs and retreated in the ordinance, without panic. And something happened that had no chance of success; a veritable attack of losers. This fury surprised the Bolsheviks so much that their attack broke down, and then they panicked..."

He paused once more, but only for a moment, and something like a smile lit his face.

"We captured these two deadly battleships, we sore thats, but there were also plenty of dead and wounded among ours. Even Jaworski and the ataman were injured. It was especially hard for Jaworski, because he was the first on the line and the first to push himself under the bullets, as if he wanted to die. When they carried him after the battle, because he could not hold on to his horse, the doctor counted several wounds on the head itself and another number on the whole body. A miracle that he survived."

"You mentioned that they had an argument with the ataman?" Janek directed the question.

"Well, after the battle we went our way further west, and he stayed with his men in Antonina to defend Potocki's estate, who provided him with weapons, horses and board."

"What was that about?"Janek asked further.

Koryatovich shrugged as if it were obvious.

"About the strategy of the fight. Ataman argued that with such a small number of our people, we need tactics, not a fighting trial, and Jaworski argued that honor, open fight and so on. They could not agree, and the ataman after the battle, I saw it myself, he bent over and prayed over each of ours, he felt sorry for everyone, be it a nobleman or a peasant, who was killed. He did not blame Jaworski for biting in all directions, an eye for an eye, because our unit also took its toll on peasants' gangs. But that he did not respect human life as we do."

"I can guess..." Janek suspended the words for a moment. "I suppose you told me this not without reason?"

A sour smile answered him.

"Our ataman likes to say that the determination of the soldier is more effective than the mindless mass led into battle, because the mass has no reason, and the desperate soldier thinks and fights for ten. And so I thought it might be worth passing on to you. Because you're struggling, people may not see it, but I can see it."

Janek looked at him carefully and took a chance.

"Mr. Kuźma, I have a feeling sometimes, and don't laugh, it was born here in these woods, when I had to grow up rapidly."

He looked at Janek and, despite his fears, nodded seriously and only muttered:

"Our ataman also has it and always works, but I have not experienced it."

"And I have, and now something in our situation bothers me, but I cannot specify what."

"It's just like me, although," he joked, "you won't find any visions at me."

They both laughed, which eased the tension in the air.

"I don't know why they did not cover the forest with a flood of fire, but only let go of the foot."

"The same is bothering me," confirmed Janek. "And I can only compare it to a witch-hunt, but this is probably already oversensitive."

"Hopefully, Mr. Jan, hopefully."

***

They remained silent when the roar of weapons heard from the depths of the forest. Initially, only single shots, but immediately after that a violent butt from several dozen or maybe more rifles. After a while, the forest was boiling with fire.

"It begins, I go back to my men," Koryatovich breathed a sigh of relief and walked away quickly.

Janek would prefer to have him with him, the experience of the old soldier would be useful when making decisions, but they had previously agreed that he himself should coordinate the fight. Koryatovich even insisted on it, although he also promised to be careful about everything.

He got down from the pulpit, saw Alik giving an order to one of the soldiers, and walked over to them.

"What about the scouts?"

"They're not back yet, but they should be here soon."

He looked at Janek and added:

"Don't worry, they had strict orders and they certainly followed them. I gave them Ostapko for the boss, and Joshua went with them too. He took on vigor, he changed, for a Jew he is bloody fighting," he laughed. "This isn't our fearful old Joshua who got pissed off by Fedor one time."

"Did you hear that rifle thunder in response?"

"Before the others started shooting, ours were no longer there; two for each and a return. They will be soon."

"Send them to me right now. I need to know what they saw."

"No problem, as soon as they come back."

He went to the position of the heavy machine gun, manned by the people of Koryatovich, Łyżko and Felsztyn. They both had cheeky expressions."

"We have the middle and left side of the lake, Colonel, and your men are the middle and right," they reported smug and confident in what to do. "Let the plague try to get into the water, we run and cut, but as commanded by wachtmeister Alik, bait and then hit. And only on his orders."

"Okay, boys, but no risk. Bolsheviks can have machine guns too, so if you start shooting, they can target you."

"Colonel, the wachtmeister predicted it, and we have two spare positions. If anything happens, we change right away, they won't get it."

"Can you do it, when it's time to evacuate?"

"And why not, it's not a tank, we take on the back and walk," they poked each other with their elbows.

He moved to the second position and the conversation was repeated. This machine gun was operated by Vasily and Igor, aged peasants, who said that they had been in the war with the Chinaman and knew how to use machine guns. During the trial with the Cossacks, they behaved perfectly, but Janek, looking at their furrowed faces, had doubts whether they would be able to physically manage during a possible retreat. The machine gun with the stock was not light, and there was also ammunition. He asked them about it, but the answer was supported by laughter and a sense of strength and confidence.

"We, Colonel, are old, but our brains are not weak, only our strength missing," Vasily's face beamed with complacency. "We agreed with Ivan, the miller's son, because he is young and strong. It will help to carry this iron, for him it is only half a bag of flour."

He remembered the face, it was Joshua's friend. He was big, and the stocky figure guaranteed that he would manage.

One of the soldiers came running and reported that the scouts were back.

"Task done," Ostapko's face radiated with joy. "We gave them a hit and they didn't figure out where we were shooting."

"Fedor is good, almost like a poacher, what he tried on, the Bolshevik was already flying to hell." Joshua was in a similar mood, but the word poacher Ostapko flicked away with his eyes.

"Apparently," said Janek quickly, "he has illegal hunting on his conscience, which was punishable by prison before the war."

"Good," he praised all five, and remarked a fleeting remark, "And after all this, maybe Fedor will accept the work of a forester at the manor, just as good as that."

Ostapko widened his eyes in astonishment.

"The commander is serious?"

"Seriously, Fedor, but the war will probably continue, and when it's over, your job is provided. Now to the platoons for positions. And don't take risk."

He also stopped Ostapko and asked him about the number of soldiers, weapons and other things he had noticed.

"On mine, they were going like for a condemnation," Ostapko spoke slowly, carefully choosing his words, concerned that Janek was drawing his opinions. "Somehow in fear, that's how I saw it."

At the same time, there was something about Fedor's attitude that caught Janek's attention. As if he was trying to hide something.

"Ostapko, what are you hiding?" He asked directly looking into the eyes, but the latter escaped them to the side. "Talk, this is not the time for secrets. Do they keep cannons? They have machine guns? Whatever you saw?"

He started shifting from foot to foot, then straightened as if resigned.

"Because, commander, we did not obey the order."

"Whose?"

"Wachtmeister Alik."

"It means?"

"Because he ordered, two shots and run."

"And?"

"And I thought to myself that it is worth getting know more and that's why we didn't come back right away."

Janek looked at the peasant carefully. This is yet another time when they themselves showed the initiative. He should have praised him for it, but it was contrary to the discipline Alik instilled in them.

"You got it?"

"Well, we got one who broke through and we quickly questioned him, but he was injured, so it was impossible to get him here."

He didn't go into how they did it or what they did with him. He was more interested in what they got out of the soldier.

"What was he saying?"

"Not much, Commander, only that Commander Piotr Kluyev is leading the attack and that they have sent two regiments to attack, but not all of them. The reserve moved ahead of them, still at night, but where, he did not know."

"Kluyev?"

"It struck me too, but it was probably the same surnames."

"Maybe, but be careful the second time, such a failure to obey if they catch you, you know."

"I know, but there was no danger, he went on us, so we..."

"Okay, okay, an order is an order, but thank you, this information will be useful to me. Now to the platoon."

He quickly tried to remember that a fleeting thought was somewhere in the back of the brain. Kluyev? Kluyev? Where was it? He wanted to abandon the memory of himself, especially since the first shots of his soldiers rang out as a hidden thought popped out. He already knew. It was in the letters of the couriers he shot in the village of Pohoreckie. Kluyev wrote to his brother Piotr that he had received new orders from Felix Edmundowich Dzerzhinsky and that the original plan had not changed, but they should be careful, because Vyacheslav Mienzynski, Dzerzhinsky's deputy, was up to something behind his back with Ukrainians and Jews, and this could prevent the implementation of their plans.

Piotr Kluyev? Now he understood the scale of his attack. Somehow he had to find out that his brother died at the hands of those who are hiding in the forest and claiming to be the Polish Army. He just wanted revenge. Hence the unprecedented scale of the attack. And that means you have to be double-minded. Who knows what else this Kluyev came up with? And - now it occurred to him additionally - where did he send the reserves?

***

Buchak Lake was relatively narrow and oblong in shape. It looked more like a swampy river basin than an independent body of water. About halfway down was the island. "Could," Janek began to consider it seriously, "Kluyev sent these extra men to walk around the lake, and when they were busy fighting the attackers straight ahead, would they attack them from behind?"

He quickly found Ostapko, ordered him to take three people and check the immediate surroundings of the place and the routes by which they were to retreat. He wanted to be sure that they were safe from this side.

"Just do your job quickly and check it well, something I do not like that night sending part of the unit into the unknown," he instructed, and Ostapko immediately understood the importance of the information he had brought earlier.

The shots were getting more and more intense. On the part of his people, there were much fewer of them, even sporadic, because they were commanded to aim well, not shoot just for the sake of shooting. One shot, one dead enemy, he repeated to them as soon as the alarm went off.

The name of the Bolshevik commander was constantly on his mind. What task did they have with their brother? The letters showed that both of them were directly subordinate to some Dzerzhinsky, and he was probably an important person in the leadership of the Bolsheviks. There is a rivalry in it, and judging by another letter addressed to Commissioner Babel, friction and the limits of mutual influences intertwine in the struggle for power.

He got to where Alik was. This gave him an account of the situation. The soldiers were already walking to the edge of the forest, and some of them tried to enter the lake and look for a place by which they could reach the island. They realized that the bottom was not deep, but a swampy one, so they looked for a ford where the ground was hard. They left a few bodies in the foreground, but they did not give up, but put fire on the island, which, with the number of attacking rifles, sent an almost uniform wall of steel towards them.

"For now, our machine guns are silent, we'll wait until they move the bench," Alik felt perfectly in the role of the defense manager. "Our people are only supposed to shoot occasionally, so as not to discourage them and," he pointed at the corpses lying by the water, "they have a good eye. Certainly, at this distance, it is only the best."

"And Stepan where?"

"As usual, this one has climbed onto a tree and is waiting."

"For what?"

"He said that when the commissars showed up, or maybe one of the commanders, he would target them, and let them deal with the masses, as he calls them "peasants"," Alik laughed. "He is a good guy, but he never lose these tsarist habits."

"Fedor was also like that, until he got hit in the ass from the Bolsheviks."

"He got this one too, but indeed, maybe not so much."

The bullets sowed the branches of the trees, stripping them of leaves and smaller twigs. "A little more, and each of them will be so packed with iron that they will start to break," it flew over Janek's head.

He withdrew from the fortified pulpit. It was much quieter downstairs, although here too, you could hear individual cartridges that broke through the trunks. You had to be careful and move tightly bent to the ground.

From the side of the lake he heard the loud "Hurray". Apparently there was an attack.

He listened, and it was not a few minutes before one of the machine gunners spoke. He rumbled steadily in response to the Bolshevik attack. Hurray still sounded, but less militant.

He sends them to certain death - Janek noticed about the Bolshevik commander and headed for the rear part of the island, where they were to evacuate through the designated ford. Yuri and two other soldiers were watching over the crossing. Seeing Janek, he assumed a basic attitude.

"They haven't come back yet," he asked about the scout sent.

"No, be quiet here, sir, but we are on guard. I sent one forward. He is sitting in a tree and looking, how are things?" He was calm, but it was evident that he would rather be with his direct defenders rather than be stuck here idly.

"This is an important position because if they came from behind you know what would have been, so keep your eyes and ears open because you're defending our ass."

"I know, wachtmeister Alik explained it to me exactly," Yuri sighed. "Just silence here, and there…" He didn't finish, shrugging.

"I said, this is an important place for us and it is very good that you sent someone further into the forest, it is praised," he praised him and these words clearly pleased Yuri. "When they come back, straight to me." He said while leaving.

***

Within a quarter of an hour, Ostapko reported after his return.

"Something is happening at the edge of the lake," he explained, still out of breath. "On the left and on the right, we noticed troops hiding in the thicket. They walk slowly so as not to see them, but in some time they will bypass the lake and then they will find us."

"How many?"

"It is difficult to measure, and we did not want to approach, there was no order, but probably a lot."

"Okay, get back to your post."

He found Alik and Koryatovich and informed them of the possibility of attacking from both flanks.

"It's a pity, because here we chop them like grain," the hussar commander worried. "In this situation, however, I suppose we must withdraw while the time is right."

"These are our heavy machine guns at the end, so they won't find out," suggested Alik.

"I don't think we have a choice, start the retreat."

Individual platoons began withdrawing from their positions and sending them out of the island through the ford on the other side of it. This was done without haste, and in order to ensure that all weapons and ammunition had been removed. The soldiers were reluctant, because their well-secured positions protected them against bullets shooting from the shore, and at the same time they themselves effectively offended the attacking Bolsheviks. So they reluctantly descended from them, but since there was such an order, they did not argue with him.

After an hour, only the heavy machine gun crews remained on the island, and they continued to check the enemy, effectively suppressing any attempt to break through to the island.

At one point, long bursts of machine guns responded from the opposite side. It was inevitably a sign that the Bolsheviks had pulled up their machine guns. Janek gave a signal and the last people were evacuated.

When they joined the column waiting for them, they made their way to the designated "A" point. The scouts moved forward as well as to the sides to spot any forward detectors of the Bolsheviks. Although the previous reconnaissance had informed that they were still far away, Janek prudently preferred to insure himself. If he were in command of the Bolsheviks, he would have sent a few horsemen for long-distance penetration, but whether this one did, he did not know.

Still in moments when he had nothing to look after, some anxiety returned that he had missed something. Some stray thought could not break out of the depths of consciousness to show the reason what was wrong. When he talked about his feelings with Koryatovich before the start of the fights, it seemed to him that this suspicion was on the verge of spreading from the depths of his brain, but no, it was still there and was tiring. He re-examined the situation and the steps taken; nothing could threaten them, he saw everything.

He put off the tiring deliberation and took care of the current affairs, although the truth was only to go deep into the forest. For his destination, he chose a rather remote area, more to the east, where he had reached only a few times in the past, when he forgot himself while hunting while chasing the chosen game. There was a stream that spilled over a small clearing and vanished somewhere as it turned south. The forest was denser and wilder there, which made it possible to hide in it, but also to defend, if some Bolshevik troops got so far behind them. The latter possibility was unlikely, but he did not rule it out. "But what if," he thought of the Bolshevik commander, "he has some people who are familiar with the forest, and they will lead the soldiers in their footsteps."

"Pensive, as always." A relaxed Koryatovich rode up to him. "Perhaps you wish we had withdrawn too quickly?"

"No, better sooner than later, and in direct clash, we could have lose some people. Mr. Kuźma, let's face it, there are a handful of us, and we cannot afford frills like the tsarist guard, chest forward and with the orchestra on the enemy. For stupidity, too."

"Do not be offended, I only want to talk, because what to do. Those far away, scouts are circling and I'm bored."

"I'm not offended and I didn't want to offend you, but there is something I don't like about this whole situation."

"Oh, yours again."

Janek looked at the interlocutor, his cheerful face and thoughts circulating in his head disappeared somewhere. Maybe he is just tired of being responsible for people, he has too little experience in this type of fights, hence these vague visions.

"I'm just saying that, because everything indicates that by the time they find out that we are no longer on the island, and those who walked around the lake will reach the place where they probably wanted to catch us, we will already be far away."

"Oh, I like it, a bit of optimism does better than a woman."

Janek laughed at such a conclusion. It was good to have an experienced soldier by your side.

***

They had been going deep into the forest for an hour. The scouts returned with information that the Bolshevik troops encircling the lake from the mainland had already joined together and began shelling the island from the other side. They weren't risking a direct attack, and they probably wondered why no one was responding to their fire.

Janek calmed down, took the lead and showed the way in the thicket. The horses slowed down because in some places it was difficult to get through the area densely overgrown with bushes and between low hanging limbses. After some time, they drove into a more accessible part of the forest, where the trees grew less often, and then they accelerated.

"We are probably behind the lake a few versts, they lost us," Alik rode up to Janek.

"I think so, it's hard to judge here. How is the mood among our people?"

"Perfect, but they wish we had pulled back so quickly."

"We have more luck than sense. With such an overwhelming force, the miracle only prevented anyone from perishing."

"But there are a few injured, but nothing serious. Where are we going? Do you have a specific place?"

Janek nodded and described the clearing with the stream, indicating the direction.

"If anything, you'll hit the place."

"What? Are you going somewhere?"

"No, not that, it's better for a few people to know the location, something is telling me..."

He did not finish when the tangle in front of them, overgrown with creeping juniper streaked with club moss and pear, suddenly came to life and flashed all the way like thunderbolts. A fraction of a second later, the thunder of a rifle salvo reached their ears and a wave of bullets sowing the area reached them.

The surprise was complete.

Instinctively, Janek just shouted: "Dismount!"

And he was on the ground alone, retreating backwards. A commotion arose in the line behind him; snorting of horses terrified with a bang, some cries and curses of the wounded. After a while, Koryatovich's voice, supported by Ostapko and Sedenkov, broke through:

"Horses behind the trees! On the ground! Hide yourself!"

Janek hid behind the trunk, and then quickly emerged from behind it. He saw rifle barrels retreating into the thicket.

"What the hell!?" Koryatovich crawled to him, just as confused. "Whom did the devil bring here?"

Through the branches of the bushes, they tried to spot the enemy and understand the situation.

"It's probably not a devil, Mr. Kuźma," Janek had only just unblocked his earlier feelings in his head. His suspicions against the facts showed him the plan of the Bolsheviks. "The attack on the island was a pretense, or rather just a campaign. They fooled us and now they are making flanking maneuver. Before us are probably those units that left at night, what Ostapko squeezed out of the prisoner of war. Neither must they have some foresters who brought them here."

"But how the hell did they know where we were going? We have a traitor?"

"It occurred to me, too, but it probably wasn't possible. He would not be able to contact those in front of us."

"So, only that commander of theirs remains, how is he? Kluyev, not as stupid as I thought. He must have experience fighting guerrillas or he wouldn't have had the idea."

In silence they watched the bushes among which the enemy soldiers were hiding. After the first volley they gave no sign of life, but Janek suspected that it was just another maneuver. Something occurred to him. He crawled back and found Ostapko.

"Would you be able to make reconnaissance?" He asked, not expecting that he would agree to it willingly. The situation was dangerous, a mission on the verge of desperation, because it was difficult to tell what territory the Bolsheviks had taken. They had time to disguise their positions well.

"Why should I not be able to, Colonel, I take..."

"Wait, not so fast. We have to check if we hit the forehead of the ambush or the banks, and if this silence does not mean that they are trying to surround us. This is important."

"Yes, I can move in the woods, you know. I'll take two men more, and if I can, Joshua also has a knack, although he's a Jew, but he's proven himself. I'll give him three savvy and let they examine the other side."

"Just remember, without charging, your life is more valuable to me than information."

"No problem, sir, I remember you scolding me for taking this prisoner of war."

"They took the prisoner of war, I had the information at hand and I did not understand anything of it," thought Janek bitterly, and instructed Ostapko once again:

"Go on and get back quickly. I need to know where they are located and if possible how many of them."

When Ostapko disappeared into the thicket, he surveyed the positions taken by the soldiers. Koryatovich's cuirassiers turned out to be more experienced, it was worse with his people. He rearranged them, found new positions so that the whole would form a unified front, and they would not be an easy target if they were to attack them.

On the side of the Bolsheviks, something was happening, but only some movements were heard, but not visible.

"They are regrouping," Koryatovich reached him. "I sent two of my own, they looked as much as possible and came back."

"Me too, but they have to check the sides."

"Right, I didn't think. What now? Are we waiting?"

"So far, yes, but you have to be ready to maneuver."

They continued for a while, considering various options for withdrawal. However, none of the ideas guaranteed one hundred percent success. Janek crawled away and found Sedenkov, which Ostapko had left because he had been shot in the arm.

"How are you doing?"

"Perfect," the Ukrainian made up for it, although it was obvious that he felt a wound.

"Good, take a few other injured and withdraw all the horses. Mold them so that in the event of a retreat they would be ready, and the direction..." He considered whether to continue holding the goal they were striving for. He figured he would and pointed him to the northeast. "More or less there, but don't go too far, we don't know where the Bolshevik pickets are."

After two quarters of an hour, Ostapko returned from the reconnaissance and shared his observations. It turned out that they stumbled upon the brink of a long Bolshevik ambush.

"I don't know how many there are, but judging from the line they cast, probably two or three hundred."

"Not more?"

"I'm not sure, Colonel, there may be an additional hundred, it is difficult to judge because we did not ask," Ostapko joked. "Just by the noises, but there," he pointed in an undefined north-east direction, "it seems rather empty. I checked myself, but it was on the edge, about half a kilometer. Only single soldiers, many more on the line, maybe a hundred or two hundred meters from us."

Janek wondered. If the line of the Bolsheviks was stretched, the commander of them probably waited for the first shots to draw the others to this place and only then proceed with the general attack. It was time to act. And distract the Bolsheviks.

A quick consultation with Koryatovich. After that, they designated ten of Kuźma's soldiers as more fired, who would carry out a mock attack in a place farther west, bind with fire for a few minutes, and retreat even faster.

The rest were informed that they were to wait for a firefight, but to fire sporadically, as if all their forces had been focused at that point. One machine gun was also taken there. The task of the staff, and they chose Łyżko and Felsztyn because of their age, was to cover the enemy with fire. Janek realized that it would be mainly a more psychological effect, because the trees would effectively protect the people under fire. The intensified fire was only meant to pull the enemy down there, while they would retreat along a fixed route.

Koryatovich also pushed his hussars to the fore, because they were to take over the liquidation of the few who formed Bolshevik pickets on the edge. For safety, Janek added ten more, wanting to be sure that the attack would bring full success and that no one would stop them. He appointed Demienkov as commander, and a hussar from Koryatovich as his deputy.

Everything now depended on coordinating actions.

Chapter XIX

The first volley, then another, and single shots, followed by the rumble of the machine gun.

"Okay, the boys started," concluded Janek while carefully observing the bushes on the opposite side.

He did not have to wait long. Rifle fire rang out straight ahead.

His soldiers, as he had commanded them, responded with only the occasional fire, as if there were only a few.

He stared at the enemy positions, pressing the glasses of the binoculars so hard that he felt pain in his eyelids. They weren't attacking yet, but after a while he noticed that a movement had begun between the bushes and a voice of commands. He waited to see if they would run to his position, but no, they only flashed between the trees, probably heading to a place where you could hear the heavy rumble of the Polish heavy machine gun.

He breathed in, the trick seemed to be successful. The Bolshevik fire in front of us diminished until finally only single shots sounded, which proved, however, that not all of them had left their positions.

He gestured to a nearby soldier who was about to take orders for that position.

"Let them bale out, quickly," he said.

He ordered his own men to cease fire. The Bolsheviks must have had the impression that they had withdrawn from their position.

He realized that the Bolshevik commander of this section probably had left some of the soldiers in their place. And that worried him. He was afraid that if he was right, now convinced that he was leaving the position, they would try to check it out. And they will attack. If they broke through, they would cut off the planned evacuation.

After a few minutes, the suspicion came true.

The junipers twitched, and the silhouettes of the Red Army soldiers appeared in the foreground. They came out cautiously from behind the bushes, leaning low, closely observing the place from where they had been shot until recently. They moved slowly, literally step by step, as if investigating whether the forest would suddenly come alive with a volley of fire. When nothing happened, they started firing themselves, more to encourage themselves than to hit anyone. Behind them appeared several differently dressed figures with rebels in their hands, loudly urging those walking in front of them to run. Janek quickly recognized them by their black jackets; these were the commissioners of the Cheka.

One of the soldiers probably could not stand the tension and stood uncertainly, looked around, then suddenly turned back. He didn't manage to take a few steps when the police officer who followed him shot him in the chest without hesitation.

"So this is what their attack looks like," flashed through Janek mind.

He waited for all the bushes to leave. There weren't many of them, but still many more than a handful of his men.

"We have to get them as close as possible," he thought intensely, gritting his teeth and praying silently that only one of them would not break off and start firing without orders.

The Bolsheviks walked more and more boldly and accelerated. When the first of the line was no more than fifteen meters from the soldiers hidden behind the trunks, Janek shouted:

"Continuous fire! Kill the bastards!"

They waited for this order and the first volley literally swept the front of the charge. Subsequent shots began to decimate the others. The Bolshevik reaction was immediate. If they had continued to charge, they would certainly have broken through. But they panicked and the screams of the commissioners were of no avail. They did not even fall to the ground, which professional soldiers would have done, but turned and despite the Cheka officers shooting at them, they started running backwards as fast as they could.

"Kill the commissioners!" He tried to shout over firefight, while in one move he pulled his Winchester from his shoulder and searched the foreground for the one who shot the first retreating soldier. He had already noticed him almost at the edge of the bushes, when the first one was running, running to hide. He didn't aim long. He squeezed the trigger and, with satisfaction, saw his target swing his arms violently in the air, his legs buckled beneath him, and his body plunged into the ground.

The firefight lasted another minute.

"Hold your fire!" He said, when there was no one else in the foreground. "Prepare to retreat and set out quickly to the retreat line of ours, the rest to the horses!" And to Joshua lying nearby: "You stay and watch, and when they are at your height, you go with them, only without whining."

It flashed through his mind, where is Sheba, who was lying next to him when the first shots starts, but when he chased her away, showing the forest, she immediately disappeared into the bushes.

He decided to wait for the men marking the attack to show up. He wanted to close the retreat, confident that everything was going exactly as he had planned.

Within a quarter of an hour the first soldiers showed up. He signaled Joshua to pick his own and join them.

Suddenly he was chilled to see the three soldiers carried on their coats. Wounded or killed. He ran up and asked the leading hussar what had happened.

"Sergeant Alik took a bullet and two more of ours," grunted, pressing his right hand to the left hand, red with blood. "The Bolsheviks also had their machine and when they chopped, ours got shot."

"Are they alive?" It didn't get to Janek what he heard.

The Hussar just nodded in response and hurried forward.

"Alik, god, Alik..." a panicked thought ran through his head that he might have lost his friend and an iron band tightened his chest.

***

The retreat went smoothly. Scouts from the rear reported from time to time that the Bolsheviks had not followed suit. They even ventured deep into the woods, into the recent struggle, to confirm their first observations and brought the reassuring news: Bolshevik troops are retreating towards the lake.

Koryatovich took over the command, seeing Janek's condition.

And all this time he was with Alik, for whom a kind of stretcher was made for two hussars, and it was suspended between the horses. Like the others, he did not regain consciousness. The bullet hit him in the chest and it left his back. He's lost a lot of blood. They didn't have a doctor, and that could have killed all three of them.

Janek rode alongside as if in amok. He couldn't gather his thoughts. All the time he saw a smiling friend who was not supposed to be in the mock attack, but he was eager to fight and even accused Janek of deliberately trying to protect him. He must have gone himself, he wanted to take part in the battle. And now he lay unconscious, paler than snow, and only groaned as the horses crossed their protruding roots, throwing them away on a stretcher.

"Mr. Jan, we have to reach mine, we have a doctor there and as soon as possible, the better," Koryatovich remained calm and explained patiently, trying to pull Janek out of his apathy. "You are leading, because the forest is foreign to me, and as soon as we get there, they have a greater chance of survival."

Janek looked at him blankly.

"Mr. Jan, start to think like a commander," Kuźma raised his voice, and seeing no reaction, he leaned over to him, grabbed his shoulders and shook him vigorously. "You rebuked me, now do it for yourself and for them," he pointed to the wounded.

Only now did the words hit him.

He looked blankly at the commander of the hussars and said quietly:

"He is my friend, like a brother, and now..."

"Now it's up to you how soon we get to mine." Koryatovich continued to speak calmly, although it was evident from him that he was not indifferent to the condition of the wounded, but also worried about Janek's condition.

By force of his will he held back the tears from his eyes. He realized that the hussar was right, and he had to start thinking rationally. The breakdown and the lamentation that Alik is dying in front of him will not help him. He sighed deeply, shook his head, looked once more at his friend's deathly pale face, and with the last remnant of his will he tried to pull himself out of his apathy. He knew the forest, maybe the rest of it not so well, but he was able to lead the entire squad faster than anyone else. Maybe they'll get to the doctor sooner, maybe these three can be saved.

"You're right, I'm sorry," he finally stammered out.

A smile appeared on Koryatovich's face.

"Well, finally, I was afraid that it would fall on my head. Lead me. And you have a hard time when the first friend is killed, you are not the only one in this situation."

"He's still alive, don't bury him," he said sharply in response, but then regained his composure and asked more calmly: "Where can your people be?"

The Hussar was silent for a moment considering something in his mind.

"We have a point of contact in such a small village, Verhnie Bilka, and our contact will know there."

"Is that somewhere in the east? By the forest or in the steppe?"

"To the forest not far away, not even one verst. A few versts away is the town of Ostrow, and far further Żitomir, from where the road to Kiev leads, God knows, how far away, but this is where the strong red outposts begin."

"And this Bilka is free from the Bolsheviks? They already have commune?"

"Poverty and misery, who would like it. It belonged to Mr. Bogunowicz, a not very wealthy landowner, but he looked after the people in the village as much as he had himself. At some point the Reds sent a commissioner there with three henchmen, they hanged the heir at once, despite the protests of the peasants. The hearing from them was lost."

"How's that?"

"After killing the heir, the locals did not like them. And when right after that they began to requisition their small supplies for the winter, they themselves asked for..."

"Nobody looked for those?" Janek quickly took the hint.

"When we got to them, the ataman thought that it was the peasants who had attacked the court. And he wanted to hang it, but one of Bogunowicz's servants told everything as it was. He suggested to the peasants that they should elect from among their supposed commissar and when the reds came, they were to demonstrate that they were in favor of the authorities. And if they asked about the others, nobody saw them."

"It worked?"

"Yeah, so far. Only once a squad of reds came, saw a poverty, praised a red rag hanging outside, and drove away."

***

They traveled east all day, slightly twisting north. When darkness fell, they stopped. Nobody sang, and nobody talked, as is usually the case after the battle. Half of the people were injured, and apart from Alik and the hussars, four of Janek's men were in serious condition. So as soon as the sun began to wake up, he ordered the horses to be groomed, and they went on.

In the middle of the day, they reached the place where Janek had ordered a stop, and together with Joshua, Koryatovich and one of his hussars they went south to find out if it was far to the boron border and to determine where they were.

It took them almost two hours.

The forest, initially dense, became more transparent as you drove, but partly overgrown with thick bushes that they had to look for passages and even to turn back. Later they drove into the part dominated by beautiful beeches. They grew so densely next to each other, literally just a few meters away, that in some places it was difficult to break through individual trunks. Their branches, grafted above, formed a uniform, dense strip of green in places, which made the sky disappear, and the tangle of branches and leaves hanging above the ground created a gray, even dark corridor.

The place was so gloomy that even the horses had their ears lowered and the bridles had to be kept short to prevent them from turning back.

They had to slow down hard. Fortunately, the ground was devoid of bushes and formed a thick, sagging layer of fallen leaves. There were no forest sounds here, as if even the birds were avoiding this gloomy place. A perfect place to hide, if someone was chasing someone here - Janek was watching the surroundings with interest. There was no such natural ephemera in the part of the coniferous forest he knew.

After some time, the landscape changed dramatically. The island of beech trees gave way to ashes and oaks, it got lighter and the bird trills returned. Soon they drove to the edge of the forest. They stopped their horses, carefully examining a steppe covered with tall grass through binoculars. There were no buildings as far as the eye could see.

"I think we should go here, I remember this place because of this lonely oak," Koryatovich pointed to a lonely tree growing next to the forest, a real, enormous titan among the others, over fifty meters high with a huge crown and a trunk so thick that only a few people could embrace. "And you Nikolai, do you know the area?" He turned to the hussar driving by.

"Yes, commander, I think so too. It's a mother tree, I also remembered it. And to Verhnia Bilka, it seems, only one verst."

"So we come back for ours," Janek commanded. "But we have to leave someone here, so that they will be aware of it, Mr. Kuźma?" He turned to the hussar.

"A good idea. Let them stay here, he pointed to Nikolai and Joshua, and we'll soon get ours. By the time we get there and we come back, it will probably be getting gray and we will be invisible in the steppe."

"When we are gone, look around and find out how far to the village," Janek ordered. "Just be careful lest anyone spot you, Joshua."

***

The picket posted by Demienkov noticed their return. Janek immediately asked about the condition of Alik and the hussars.

"I think not so well, Colonel." The soldier reported without playing with delicacy. "Wachtmeister Alik probably worse, and ours a little better, but I'm not a doctor."

Janek accelerated Sewek. The expedition to the edge of the forest had distracted his mind from his friend, and now his fears for his life had returned with all the violence.

Alik lay quietly on the grass. Fedor sat next to him, cooling his burning forehead with a wet cloth.

"How is he?" He asked, jumping off the horse.

"I don't know, I don't know myself, once he seems to be in worse condition, it seems to be getting better again, because his breathing seems to be calmer, and then again not good. Have you found the village?"

"Not yet, but Koryatovich claims that we left well and that it's not far from there. We're going."

They placed the wounded on a sling between the horses and set off. This time they rode faster because they knew in what direction. They did not retreat, as before when they found densely overgrown, impenetrable shrubs, and they avoided them.

Janek was driving alongside Alik all the time, anxiously looking at his friend. Koryatovich took it upon himself to lead the column and, contrary to what he had said earlier that he did not know the forest, now he perfectly avoided obstacles, so that they moved without stopping.

It started to turn gray as they reached the edge of the woods. Earlier, they had spotted them, left here men, and Joshua told everything to Janek at once.

"They were right, this village is about one verst ahead, but we only looked from a distance. There seems to be peace and quiet there. Nobody else in the steppe showed up."

Janek ordered a stop and immediately drove up to Koryatovich.

"Mr. Kuźma, we are waiting here, and you will send someone to the village right now, preferably three. When they find out that your branch is nearby, let two go there and one to us with a message."

"I intended so, I have already appointed, they are already moving."

Three horses immediately emerged from the forest and immediately headed in the direction indicated by Nikolai, letting the horses gallop at once. All that was left was to wait for the message.

Koryatovich set up posts. He forbade the unbending of the horses, and only ordered the loosening of the girths.

"A hard rest?" Janek asked seeing these precautions.

"The fact that they did not see anyone does not mean that we are completely safe, I prefer to be assured."

Janek did not comment. The hussar probably knew what he was doing.

***

An hour later one of the scouts returned. He brought with him a soldier dressed in a similar black uniform like the Koryatovich hussars. He immediately went to the commander and reported something. Kuźma called Janek.

"We are lucky, they are nearby, but where exactly, I don't know, they went to them. And this is Mikhail. There is a small squad of ataman in the village, they gave them a guide. They have the task of monitoring the dislocation of the Bolshevik troops, if they showed up, because further, at the height of Zhitomir, they would be drawn to a fair, a whole lot. Infantry mixed with cavalry. The ataman is probably planning to nibble on them."

"How long can they show up to the doctor?"

"I don't know, we'll see mine come back."

Janek returned to Alik. The Hussars, as if expecting a visit from a strict commander, examined their weapons and uniforms. They had to respect their ataman. Seeing this, Janek's people followed their example.

The sky darkened. The steppe took over the evening. There was silence all around. The wait was taking longer.

After almost an hour, if not longer, the detectors signaled the approach of some riders. They were not yet visible, but there was the sound of a large number of horses in the air. Koryatovich went to the fore to see who it was and whether it was an unmistakable Bolshevik detachment.

In less than a quarter of an hour they approached. These were the ataman people with the envoys. They drove into the forest without a word. Silent commands were given and they quickly deployed so that they would not be visible from the steppe during the day.

"Where are the injured?" A voice heard nearby.

It was their doctor. Like the others in uniform. He was accompanied by two soldiers carrying large leather bags.

"Two, here," Janek called him and pointed Alik. "It's the worst with him, he got a bullet in the chest, she went out through the back, he didn't regain consciousness," he blurted out in one breath.

"Make a curtain," the doctor ordered, and when it was ready, two kerosene lamps were lit behind it, which illuminated Alik and the newcomer, who had already examined the wounded, then gave an order, the soldiers opened the bags, and he began to cut the bandages.

Janek stood to the side watching his actions. He felt the tension. He wanted to ask about the condition of his friend, but seeing that the wounded was treated efficiently by a doctor, he only waited for his verdict. The latter clucked something under his breath, a curse escaped him, but he continued his work. He pressed his fingers around the wound, brought his face up to it and sniffed it, then cleansed it. He demanded some drug, and when he was served, he gently drenched it on the dressing, placed it on the wound, ordered the soldier to hold it, and the other to turn Alik sideways to get to the exit wound. Here he repeated the sniffing and also put on a bandage. And after that he sprinkled both wounds, reached for the bandages given to him and professionally tied them around Alik.

"Will he be alive?" Janek could not stand it and asked.

The doctor just looked at him now and looked at him for a moment.

"You dressed him well, nothing rots, the wounds are clean, reasonably clean, I have given him what he need, and will he live? My lord, it doesn't depend on me anymore, but on the strength of his body. You can be a cautious optimist."

"For a doctor, a very imprecise diagnosis." Janek suddenly felt angry that the person he was counting on so much answered him with generalities. "There is no infection?"

The doctor smiled this time.

"I can see that it's someone close, but I will reassure you, no infection. It looks worse than it actually is. I gave him something to help him sleep better and disinfected him. Let us be of good cheer. Where are the others?"

Janek indicated the place where the wounded were.

The doctor did not move from his place but ordered Alik to be moved to another place and another wounded to be brought to him by the screen.

"Colonel, the commandant is asking to see you. An unknown hussar appeared next to him."

"Where he is?"

"He is waiting for you, I will lead you, please follow me. He's with Captain Koryatovich, down there in the woods."

"Captain?" Janek noted in his mind with surprise. He hasn't revealed anything to what rank he is, and his soldiers were silent too. This is strange.

He followed the hussar, wondering who this mysterious ataman was. As far as he could see, there were at least three hundred horse riders with tachankas in the woods. Maintaining this amount at the rear of the front, practically on enemy territory, had to require excellent practice in this type of operation. And not only strict discipline among the soldiers, but also their attachment to the commander and full confidence in him.

They plunged deeper into the forest, where they set up a hussar camp. There was silence and you could only hear them talking quietly, joking and telling each other stories. There were small fires, each on the side of the steppe, sheltered by small screens. The horses stood next to the spreading treptuchos, field canvas mangers stretched on pegs, in which they had been given their fodder. Full discipline, order, everyone knew what to do. Janek admired this order. It was not an ordinary partisan unit, it was a disciplined army.

"Or maybe it is some regular unit of the Polish army, sent to the rear of the enemy," he began to wonder when a tent lit inside appeared behind a clump of bushes.

"The colonel will wait, I will report your arrival," the hussar said it politely, but firmly.

In front of the tent there were two armed men, supported by rifles, which did not go unnoticed by the increasingly surprised Janek. Even here, in the middle of the forest, the canons of safety were preserved, although nothing could have happened.

"The commandant requests your presence." The Hussar left the tent and held the entrance wall.

"Well, then I'll see this ataman," thought Janek, and it occurred to him that the name of the commander was more suited to a warlord than a regular army.

He entered the tent squinting his eyes.

Koryatovich was sitting on a stool made of branches, and in the back, a man with his back was standing, dressed in the same uniform as the rest of the hussars.

"How's the doctor?" Kuźma spoke, his face showing amusement. "Bandaged?"

"Yes and said to be of good cheer. That hussar of yours, who took care of the wounds first, did a good job. Wound clean, no infection."

"He helps Lieutenant Jerzewski, our doctor, and I borrowed him for my trip to you. You never know if such an almost medico will not be useful."

Janek looked at him with his back, but as he continued, he replied to Kuźma with a sneer:

"As I can see, you didn't leave anything to chance, and you hid some trinkets."

"I did not hide anything, I did not inform about the skills of my hussar, because there was no need."

"And the rank of captain was also unnecessary?"

This time, Koryatovich laughed loudly, then said to the reversed man:

"I say you he is cheeky."

At that moment, the man turned, and Janek's knees buckled.

He looked and did not believe what he was seeing.

Before him stood his uncle Vakhtang, Vasily, embarrassed. A thousand thoughts flashed through his mind, regret that they had left him with his grandfather, joy that he was alive, love and resentment at the same time. He couldn't utter a word, and there was a lump in his throat. His legs were weak and he staggered.

***

Before he could react, Vasily jumped up to him, wrapped his arms around him tightly, and pressed him against him.

"My little Vakho, I was so afraid for you," he only whispered, and you could heard affection in his voice.

They lasted for a while, then Vasily pushed him away from him at the shoulder length, and Janek was surprised to see that his uncle had tears in his eyes.

"Your grandfather and I were so worried about you, we asked God to watch over you every day," he whispered.

"Grandpa is also alive?"

"He is alive, alive, but he left with the unit, he will probably come back in a few days. The Bolsheviks are constantly sending new soldiers to the Polish front, it is becoming dangerous even here, on the sidelines."

"Why did you leave me?" Janek's regret returned and when the first surprise passed, he blurted out a question full of resentment.

"You guys talk here and I will go around the posts," Koryatovich got up and, without waiting for their reaction, left the tent.

Vasily pointed him to the stool, sat down on his own and was silent for a long time, gathering himself up and looking carefully at Janek. And this one waited patiently for explanations. Anger combined with regret, which he felt a moment ago, escaped curiosity, which then happened, and with a warm feeling of joy that he sees his uncle, whom he had buried with his grandfather somewhere in the depths of his soul.

"The events got out of hand then," Vasily began, choosing his words carefully, as if he were not sure if Janek would understand their importance. "We had information that the Bolsheviks were concentrating their troops in Belarus and Ukraine and were pulling towards Poland. We also had contact with emissaries of Polish intelligence who were to investigate the situation on the side of the Reds..."

"So suddenly they found our manor house?" Janek interrupted him unceremoniously suspecting that he was deliberately changing the subject.

"No, no, it was not a coincidence. I have to go back in time."

"But..."

"Listen patiently..." Vasily held up his hand.

Janek remembered more than one conversation during which he impatiently demanded explanations, not wanting to know the reasons, and then this gesture made him know that he had to listen to the explanations until the end. He felt like before, when he was teen years and his uncle's stories were his window to the world and this was his saying: "You can only take shortcuts through the field, and in important matters, the whole path is important."

"From the time when the Supreme National Committee was established in Kraków, still in the underground, we had constant contact with them. And your grandfather was independently in touch with an old acquaintance from our youth, from Sofia, with Oskar Hranilovic von Czvetassin. He was a military attaché, and was in fact head of the Balkan Group, Austrian intelligence. And we had good contacts in the Caucasus, so you understand."

Janek listened, but not quite carefully. He cared little about some of his grandfather's and Vasily's affairs, which they kept secret. The only question was what happened?

"When the committee began to form Polish legions at the beginning of the war, it was General von Czvetassin who became the head of the Nachrichtenabteilung AOK, the headquarters of the Austrian intelligence in the field," Vasily saw Janek's scattering thoughts, but he did not interrupt. "He supported the creation of Polish formations. And because his friend Piłsudski was to be at their head, the cooperation was good. Thus…"

"I hear that name again. Who is that?"

"It would be a long story, but…"

"Vasily, forgive me, this is not what I mean, but about your twisted secrets." He blurted out regretfully, raising his voice. "You have never initiated me into anything, so why now?" And he repeated, "What happened that you left me?"

"Well… I just wanted to clarify, because you asked about these emissaries, but if you want, I cut it short. We did not initiate this because your grandfather did not want to. He thought there would be a time for this when you grow up, then we'll let you in. He sees you as a little boy all the time. He did not succeed with your father, so… Never mind, and these emissaries warned that the Bolsheviks were gathering armies to attack Poland."

"You? There a few mansions around!"

"Together with your grandfather, we organized a network of informants and routes for couriers."

"Spies? Come on, was there little war in your life? Two old gentlemen..."

"Polish intelligence needed someone in the field, far in the east, and somehow it turned out..."

"It's not very credible, after all I saw you every day, I would notice something."

"We worked in complete secrecy even from our loved ones, that is, you, your mother and father."

"And Dad, do you know anything about him?"

"Your father... Let your grandfather tell you himself. You expect too much of me."

"Secrets again. How do you passed the information, our court is so far away."

"Before the war, we had constant contact with the Headquarters of the Third Polish Military Organization in Kiev."

"What is this creation?"

"Too much to explain to you again, maybe someday, when we have more time."

Janek snorted, but Vasily didn't react.

"It was, in short, a conspiratorial organization with intelligence units in Ukraine, Belarus and Lithuania. Later, we also kept in touch with Major Ignacy Matuszewski, head of the Intelligence Bureau of the General Staff of the Polish Army."

"Stop, my head is bursting with this excess of information," he felt the pain piercing his head, increasing with each utterance of his uncle. "One thing I know now that I was a fool, I did not notice anything, and you were having a great time." He blew his cheeks like a child, then exhaled slowly to suppress his nervousness and hemicrank. He didn't want to act like a spoiled child, but the growing bitterness was stronger than his will.

"Janek, I wouldn't call it a great time," Vasily also took a deep breath, and a frown that was hard to interpret on his face. He experienced this meeting very much, and from the very beginning it did not go as he had imagined it many times. But there was nothing he could do but try to explain what had happened. So he continued in the tone of a confident man.

"The outbreak of the war between the oppressors of Poland gave a chance to regain independence. However, for this to be possible, Piłsudski had to have good and verified information."

"You mentioned that he was the general's friend, von Czvetassin?" Janek regained his composure and tried to keep asking questions in a calm tone, although he knew Vasily could sense it. "I hear that name once."

They both played hard. Neither wanted to show that there was a softening in the middle of both souls unworthy of the commanders, that they would gladly throw themselves around each other's necks, that they started this meeting badly and did not know how to stop it.

"Too much to talk here, too," Vasily changed his tone and said it softly. "Piłsudski is our old friend. He chaired the Polish Socialist Party. At one point, he made contact with the Austrian intelligence, Kundschafts-Stelle, because in his opinion this increased the chances of an effective fight against Russia. Probably then they met."

"But we are far away in the borderlands, he's probably in Warsaw, how did you pass on the information?"

"I can not say too much, but by various means, and even by radio secret intelligence."

"These are the wires on the poles?"

"Also, one day I'll explain."

"Every now and then I hear it.

"Really, it's too long to talk, and I have a few more things to plan," Vasily spread his hands in an excuse. "I'm not expeling you, god forbid, but on my head when the Russians revolve around..."

"Are you blowing me off after so long separation?" Janek felt a rush of regret to his uncle. He so missed talking to him and the advice he was giving and is now expeling him out.

"No, Janek, there will be time for talks, but..."

"Then tell the end why you left me?" He only managed to repeat the question again.

Vasily sighed heavily, shook his head in resignation that he hadn't avoided an answer, and looked him straight in the eye.

"As I said, we did not expect the situation to change so quickly, although we knew about it from the retreating Germans. Do you remember that Oberst Günter Alleberger, commander of the separate squadrons of the cuirassier regiment, who stayed with us? He has provided us with confidential information that Germany has signed a secret agreement with the Bolshevik government. Under it, the Reds began to take over the territories previously occupied by the Ober-Ost army."

"So what? It didn't concern us."

"It did, but not directly. At that time, German and Austrian troops occupied a large part of Russia. They even took Lugansk, the capital of the Teutonic republic, Donetsk, they were even in the Crimea, entered Rostov-on-Don and approached St. Petersburg. And for us it was so important that when they entered Ruthenia in the spring of 1918, they disarmed the Polish units fighting on their side in the east by order of the supreme command. Not all officers liked it, but you know for yourself that the order is sacred to them. This is how we met Jaworski, whom Captain Koryatovich had already told you about."

"Why did you leave me?" Janek repeated the question like a mantra.

Vasily glared at him, like a little child who doesn't answer. However, he smiled, took out his pipe, stuffed it with a smoke and lit it. He was clearly delaying his reply. Finally, he muttered something under his breath and continued.

"You must understand that the situation was too much for us," he repeated. "You were supposed to hunt a few grouse on the road, and after your return, we were to evacuate to the Pohorecki manor, and from there together with him to the west, to reach the Polish troops. And here it turned out that suddenly a special regiment of the Cheka appeared. We only managed to evacuate. Grandfather even wanted to stay, look for you in the forest, but..."

There was silence. Individual words reached Janek, he began to understand what had happened, but still felt regret.

"Why did Maruchna stay at the manor? Do you know what they did with her?" He remembered bitterly the image of her death, and the shock he had felt when he found he didn't know what happened to his grandfather and Vasily. "And in the village they raped and killed Hapka, they hanged the chairman Kuźma together with the mayor, Fedka and that Ivashka..." He fell silent, because a sudden wave of regret tightened his throat and he could not make his voice out. He was aware that he was acting like a little boy who had a toy taken away, but he couldn't help but let the complaints out of him.

"I know some, I guess some. All I can say is that when we left our service on the Polish side, we came back and we were looking for you all the time. At first, to no avail. No sign of your sinking underground. We used the entire network of informants we had created before this to get even the slightest information about you. Only after some time did we hear information, loose, sometimes exaggerated, about someone who supposedly works here.

Jaworski's people were also looking for us. It took a long time. At one point, a few fleeting rumors lifted our spirits. And later, from a few captured Bolsheviks, we learned that their couriers had disappeared in mysterious circumstances, though perhaps it was only desertion. It was rumored that it was acting like a phantom of some Wolf squad, and while we took it for peasants' tales, it suggested that someone..." He paused, puffed the smoke slowly, as if collecting his thoughts, then continued. "We started to feed ourselves hoping it might have something to do with you. We assumed that although you are young, we trained you well, so you survived and you are hiding somewhere."

Janek did not ask any more. He sat in silence digesting what he heard. He still wanted to ask questions, but his reason made it clear that Vasily, in command of such a large force, could not spend all of his time on him.

"Now go to your brother and see if he has improved and I will do more work. I'll find you later and we'll talk more." Vasily said quietly.

Janek got up, looked at his uncle's tired face and smiled at him first, letting him know that he understood.

He turned and was already touching the exit when suddenly Vasily's last words, "Go to brother," echoed in his head like an unexpected cannon volley.

***

He froze in place, the words sinking into his brain with resistance. Which made him unable to decide whether to leave or to step back immediately.

At first he took them as a metaphor, but Vasily had never said that about Alik. He always used the term "friend", yes, just like that; "You and your friend", "You together with a friend", "If both of you and your friend are beaten equally, you will understand" etc. The words "colleague", "boy", "he" were never mentioned, only "friend".

He turned to see the consternation on his uncle's face. He felt that something was wrong, that his word escaped him, and now he quickly thinks about how to get out of the situation and come up with a plausible lie or downplay the situation.

"Now will you explain it to me or lie to me?" He asked quietly and calmly, not stressing any of the terms.

Vasily looked at him silently, clearly examining what to choose. They continued like that for a while, then he pointed Janek to the stool on which he had been sitting so far and again, this time nervously and in a hurry, emptied the used tobacco from the pipe, poured a new one, lit it, and then put it aside, as he didn't like it.

"All because of Sylwester sneers." He rarely spoke of grandfather by his first name. This was the second change. He only ever used "grandfather". The name, if Janek remembered it well, fell so sporadically that at that moment he could not even remember when.

"Vasily, stop with these secrets, I'm not the boy who just has fun in his head anymore. Too much has happened, I've grown up and I'm tired."

"I know, I know, but for me…" He paused.

The silence fell so deep that they both could clearly hear each of them breathing deeply, as if they were getting ready to jump from very high.

"Okay, let it fall on me." Vasily finally cut it off. He reached for the pipe that had been put away and lit it again. This time he blew out the first puff of smoke more calmly, taking his time, gently nailed the chimney with a rammer and put it in his mouth.

"You probably sometimes thought why your father, who also did not love Moskals, stayed in the army, while Hryhor Pohorecki, due to his father's service on the side of Moscow, that is, grandfather Panteleimont, returned to the estate immediately after receiving his officer skills and managed it calmly."

"You mentioned something to me when you told about great-grandfather Victor and his party in the uprising, but I don't know what that has to do with my dad. Pohorecki's grandfather served the Moskals, he was an enemy who even received the lion's share of our fortune as a reward."

"Yes, yes, but not really. This is the official version. In fact, they knew Victor, they were even friends, although their views on Moscow and Poland were different. It was Panteleimon, after the fall of the uprising, when the repressions began, he vowed to the authorities on Victor's behalf that he was a calm man and did not put his hand to "this mob". He risked a lot, and that was a secret to both families."

"You were supposed to be talking about Alik."

"I'm on it." His face brightened, as if he had broken internally because he had been released from secrecy. "When your father was young, like every little kid, he used to go to the countryside, play around and enjoy his life. Victor decided to temper him, because the years were passing, and he and your grandfather were eliminated from the set right away. Because, as he used to say, we had too much conspiracy and too little thinking about the future. And he invented Miss Jadwisia, the daughter of Dunin Churylov from Podole, with whom they met during the uprising and became friends."

"You mean mom?"

"Not right away, because it got very complicated."

"Mom so pretty, which could..."

"And it could, because that villainous Andrius seemed to be eagerly moved to her uppers at once, but he did not change his habits. He was like that, and Victor was tearing his hair out, because in him he hoped to donate his fortune. But when it turned out that he had made a child to Pruzyna, and the beast was indeed very seductive..."

"Wait a minute, how is it Pruzyna? Jefrosinia's daughter wet nurse?"

"Well, yes, just hers. He even wanted to marry her, his head was buzzing, but it was immediately grandfather and Victor who effectively knocked it out of the head, but don't ask how, because I won't tell you, you would lose respect for your father. And they made him marry your mother right away." He paused, smiled to himself, smoothed his mustache, and snorted. "Your father was bad, because you were born much earlier than planned by the Lord God, if you know what I'm talking about, Alik is the first, but you soon after him."

Janek stared at him, trying to systematize what he heard. He wasn't sure what his uncle was so happy about, but when he was lost in his memories, his humor visibly returned.

"Then Panteleimon arranged that Hryhor and Andrzej were sent together to study in St. Petersburg, to the Nikolaev Cavalry School. Hryhor returned after getting his polishing skills, and his father stayed in the army. It was Victor's decision, and on his deathbed, he made himself swear that his grandson would not bring him any shame and that he was to stay in the army until Pruzyna was out of his head."

"But Alik has a father, this Vanka?"

"Indeed, because we married the girl right away, and Vanka got a piece of land, easy?"

"This…"

"That's why Alik grow up in the manor with you. This is how we made it up with the full acceptance of Jefrosinia." He paused, scratched his head, and then ran a hand across his face. "Andriush is like a son to me, and after your grandmother's death your grandfather could not cope, and probably some of the blame for his actions falls on me. Then I swore to myself that I would bring you both up as it was done here in the Caucasus, and grandfather agreed. Oh, the whole secret. You and Alik have the same blood, and what about Pruzyna?"

The roofs of the tent suddenly opened, a soldier burst in and, on the threshold, quickly blurted out:

"Commander, something is happening in the camp, you are urgently needed."

***

Vasily reacted immediately. Janek ran after him.

Deep within the camp, about fifty yards from Vasily's tent, there was a commotion where he had left his soldiers.

"There was a wolf, the horses started to scare, there was a mess, our people wanted to beat him right away, but the colonel's men stood up in his defense, and that's how it started," explained the out of breath hussar who informed the commander.

The image that emerged did not bode well for anything good. Vasily's soldiers surrounded the Janek's ones, while both aimed their rifles at each other. The strangest thing was that behind Janek's soldiers stood his Sewek, and beneath him, Sheba, showing her fangs. The horse positioned itself to the soldiers so that it could kick its hind legs against anyone who tried to approach. He clearly defended the wolf, who stood in a half squat bristling, carefully examining the surroundings.

"Stand back!" Vasily gave an order. "What is going on here?"

A sergeant, whom Janek had seen earlier talking with Kuryatovich, stepped out of the row, giving him an account of what had happened in his absence.

"I don't really understand, Commander, this is unnatural," he ran a hand across his face in frustration. "Suddenly this wolf appeared, oddly enough, I did not see anything like that. He fell in, stormed through the camp, as if he was looking for something, and when he saw the commandant's horse, he immediately hid under it, and this one, even stranger, began to kick and defend access to the wolf. My men wanted to stab him, the wolf is a beast, but the colonel's men stood up for it and that's how it happened."

Vasily listened intently, and an understanding smile crossed his face.

Janek immediately ordered his people to withdraw. At the sight of him, Sewek screamed happily, and Sheba threw herself on his chest, whimpering softly with joy.

"Your?" Vasily asked calmly and then added, "Now I understand why they were talking about the Wolf Ward." He shook his head as if he did not believe what he saw. "Now you are the real Vakhtang, you must tell me how you got it. I recognize Sewek, but how did you convince him not to be afraid of the wolf and still defend it? This is against nature, but as you can see, nature is not always right. Unbelievable."

Janek's soldiers, when the situation was over, lowered their weapons and began talking to those of Ataman, sharing stories, joking and laughing every now and then. The tension that eased, released, and eased from both sides.

Vasily watched closely at Sheba, who was standing by Janek's leg, rubbing against him, her mouth pointing upwards.

"What's his name?"

"Sheba."

"Damn it, we'll talk, come to the tent."

Chapter XX

A week had passed. Koryatovich proposed to divide Janek's unit temporarily into two groups and add his cavalrymen to them as instructors.

"Let them learn, watch our people, such exercises will be useful for them in combat," he explained. "Some of yours, Mr. Jan, are, frankly speaking, of little value in the fight, fresh enthusiasm and not a bit of experience, because one shoot or two is nothing, without sophistication, and mine are old stagers."

So it happened. Officially, Janek appointed Damienkov as the commander of one group, and Fedor Ostapko in the other. Alik, constantly supervised by a doctor who was recovering faster and faster, was to be his deputy. Joshua, whom Ostapko had to help, and Sedenkov, received the honors of sergeants, although Kuźma mocked this division, mocking that there were more charges in a small unit than people. And because he said nothing without a reason, he immediately commissioned his thirty men to him permanently. At first they did not accept it with joy, but the name itself, which immediately caught on and the legend created by the people of Janek, the Wolf's Troop, did its job.

Vasily initiated Janek, together with Koryatovich, into their plans and the situation. Their informants reported on the movement of Bolshevik troops, but this was only fragmentary news. Here, on the edge of the forest, they were safe, but further south, whole regiments stretched west, where heavy fights with the Polish army were said to take place.

He also told him what was new to Janek, that so far, they had kept in direct contact with the commander of the Volyn Front, General Aleksander Karnicki, and it was thanks to him that the previously loose partisan unit was transformed into the official 1st Eastern Far Reconnaissance Regiment. It was from the general's staff that information was received that there were talks in Taganrog, for which Karnicki was delegated, because he personally knew General Anton Deniken, commander of the White Armed Forces of the South of Russia. They also received information that the negotiations unfortunately ended in a fiasco, the tsarist general did not intend to tolerate a free Poland and made no secret that he would not allow the existence of the Ukrainian state, which Piłsudski supported. The result was that the Poles began to talk simultaneously with the Bolsheviks, who willingly declared to give Poland both Lithuania and Belarus.

"You know, fighting is one thing, and secret talks are a completely different thing," Vasily laughed, commenting on Janek's question what this really meant. "It's probably about future borders, and Deniken is a stupid fool to the Bolsheviks who agree to anything, and then they'll probably deny their promises and do their job anyway. Wait, I'll show you something." He started looking for some document in the papers and explained it at the same time. "This is a copy of the instructions to August Boerner, he was in this negotiating group in Taganrog, and sent to us by Karnicki when we asked worried if we were to cooperate with our eternal enemies, the Moskals. - Oh, I have it, listen to what Piłsudski wrote and you will have an answer to your question:

Both the Bolsheviks and Denikin have one thing to say - we are a power, and you are dead. In other words, in soldier's language: choke, fight, I don't care, as long as Poland's interests are not involved." He paused and commented: "You see, he's a revolutionist, a patriot, but also a politician who knows what's going on and what the mess is all about." His eyes rolled over the text and he continued reading: "And if you get involve anywhere, I'll hit. If I am not hitting you anywhere and anytime, it is not because you do not want to, but because I do not want to. I disregard you, I despise you. You are in the hands of the Jews and German Junkers, I do not believe you, your human species." He paused and concentrated on one sentence, which he strongly emphasized: "We cannot talk about any diplomatic... relations because their basic condition is faith and discretion, and you do not deserve one, you do not know the other, you betray civilization, your own country and each other..."

"I do not understand any of this, but for sure I will never become a diplomat," said Janek, to which Vasily just laughed out loud.

The day went by not only talking about politics, but also learning the theory of combat, which Vasily had never discussed with Janek before. Sometimes, with a unit of several dozen horses, they went into the field and there Janek, in command of him, tested the new, acquired skills in practice. After some time, Vasily confessed that he felt like a schoolboy, terrified by the enormity of knowledge he did not know.

"It's gonna be fine, it's in your blood, you just have to wake Grandfather Victor's genes from sleep." Vasily patted him on the shoulder and muttered to himself, "Good boy, he's gonna be a useful man."

All the time they were waiting for the return of grandfather's unit, which had set off for a distant reconnaissance. The information they could have obtained would confirm or contradict what they had from the informants. Vasily was concerned that they weren't coming back yet, but though he didn't show it. Janek sensed it but did not comment.

Sheba became the mascot of the entire regiment. Admittedly, she was not to be fooled by anyone, and when one of the soldiers tried to stroke her, she showed her teeth, but she enjoyed great attention anyway. Immediately a story was written that since there is a wild wolf on their side, no Bolshevik would be able to cope with them.

At first, she was similarly distrustful of Vasily, watching him closely as he approached Janek, tilted her lips to show her fangs, but did not react. At the end of the week, to the surprise of Vasily and Janek, apparently made her decision. When Vasily sat up tired, she approached him carefully and placed her snout in his lap. Friendship was made.

***

The next week was spent on intensive exercises in the maneuvers and tactics of individual units. It was about perfecting their command in case the commander died. This was nothing new for Vasily's men, but Janek's soldiers learned a lot.

At that time, Vasily was also sending small reconnaissance troops into the field more and more often. Each time farther and farther from the place where they are stationed. Janek noticed, although he did not mention it, that he was more and more concerned that his grandfather was not returning, as the agreed date of return had long been exceeded. It bothered him that he was also giving no sign of life through the messengers, as they usually did when the mission was extended.

The scouts only returned reporting the increased movement of Bolshevik troops west and southwest. This suggested that they were probably going to places of high military concentration.

Towards the end of the week, pickets, far from the forest line, signaled some movement of a group of horses on the horizon, clearly headed towards the forest.

An alarm was raised in the camp.

When they approached, the grandfather's unit was recognized, but as if more in number than he had left.

When the returnees drove into the trees, the faces of the soldiers showed fatigue. Many of them had bandages on, which showed that the trip was not a smooth ride. Strangers dressed in various uniforms were also noticed in the group, which was immediately noticed by the welcoming members of the Ataman group, which caused comments.

The exhaustion of the arrivals was also evident in their horses, which made their sides sharply walking with their heads bowed low.

Grandfather was the first to enter the trees, preceded only by a scout, and without dismounting from the saddle, he immediately began giving instructions to non-commissioned officers.

Vasily and the captain were waiting for him.

"Leave it Sylwek, Koryatovich will take care of everything, you are barely alive," Vasily greeted him with relief, forcing him to descend to earth despite protests that he was okay.

They did not embrace each other, but only greeted each other with a shake of the hand.

Janek, watching them from the side, noticed how much emotion there was in this seemingly cool gesture; a firm hold, careful examination of the face, holding the hand a little longer than required by the situation and a gentle smile that appeared after a moment on both faces.

They had known each other for so long that they did not have to waste time on unnecessary words.

They stayed like that for a long moment looking at each other in silence, until Vasily broke it first.

"I have a surprise for you."

Grandfather just looked at him curiously.

"You don't ask what kind?"

"I know, I know, are you ready to go? You must give mine at least a day to rest because we have tripped a few times and they are exhausted. I admit, too."

"And the new ones? Is it enlistment or freed?"

"Rescued from the POW camp, which we found... Brave boys, have already proved themselves, now they will be useful to us when we break through."

"How many are there?"

"Almost a hundred, unfortunately some of them died when we clashed with the Bolshevik regiment."

"They have different uniforms?"

"Oh yes, because some of them are prisoners of our army, and some are Ukrainians, the survivors of Petliura's troops... But, but, you were talking about a surprise. Did you get a new liqueur somewhere? I'd like a drink."

A broad smile spread across Vasily's face.

"Almost. Turn around."

Tired, he was doing it slowly. At first, he did not recognize his grandson in uniform. He just glanced over him, looking for something else. And then suddenly his eyes widened with surprise, and only a short one escaped from his throat: "Oh God!" And despite his exhaustion, he jumped forward as quickly as if he had suddenly become twenty years younger and before Janek could react, he was already hugging him and slapping him on the back whispering touched: "It's you, really, it's you..."

Vasily watched them silently, emotion flashed across his face. Finally, he sighed deeply.

"Enough caresses leave him Sylwek, he's already a big boy," he joked. "We're going to the tent, you have to eat and tell everything, how it is there and what is going on." And to the Koryatovich standing next to him, who secretly rubbed his face as if a drop of rain had fallen on him: "Feed the people and water the horses, and then group the new ones among our units, ask, and you know what to do, I don't have to tell you..."

***

Another week of stationing in coniferous forest has passed. Janek spent long hours with his grandfather, telling him in detail what he did after the Bolsheviks entered, how he acquired and raised Sheba, about Sewek, how he created his unit, how they went to the hiding place to get a gun, and about other moments that shaped him. He did not ask about Alik and his father. He figured what Vasily had told him should be enough. Perhaps someday, when the war rush becomes just a memory, he will come back to the topic.

Vasily's and grandfather's plans to move as quickly as possible failed because the doctor, Lieutenant Jerzewski, did not agree, who commented on the condition of the wounded who returned with their grandfather and made it clear:

"These men will follow you everywhere, because they are faithful to yours, but their condition is such that they will only hinder the march."

Janek participated in the meetings without really realizing why the question of getting on the road quickly arose. Vasily asked about it, and he showed him the papers that grandfather's unit had obtained.

"Very important, they show the places of concentration of Bolshevik troops, and more importantly, the directions of the marches of individual divisions," he picked between papers to get a briefcase with a broken seal from under them. And here's a rarity, a secret new code, a cipher for their messages. This has to get to our command and coders as soon as possible."

"And your lines you told me about?"

"Now destroyed. We have to break through the front and we are looking for a place where it will be real."

"We're on the outskirts, can he take advantage of it? The road is longer, but..."

"You're right, but we have nearly seven hundred horses, they'll notice us sooner or later, and we have a long way to cover."

Janek digested his words, wondering if he could help. Earlier, when the others were debating maps, he had not spoken, but he had an idea.

"Vasily, how many wounded do we have who would delay the march?"

"According to Jerzewski, out of fifty or maybe even more are not suitable for riding. Why?"

"We can leave them."

"Here? No point, they would be lost. The Bolsheviks are walking in a larger and larger bench, and eventually they will swarm with them."

"Not here, there is a place deep down so gloomy that you dread... venturing there. And there you can place the wounded. A day's journey, maybe not the whole day, but sure that no red squad will get there."

Vasily went back to the maps, shaking his head and muttering something under his breath. Janek came out in front of the tent and ordered Koryatovich and grandfather to be brought.

When they arrived, he immediately turned to the captain.

"Mr. Kuźma, you were coming with us, please show this place on the map... You know which, where horses we had to keep there short."

At first, he frowned, not really comprehending, but then his face lit up.

"Oh, that devil's forest. It's indeed a very gloomy place, we didn't even hear the birds." He leaned over the map, staring at it carefully. After a while he looked up. "As I suppose, and I guess our young man, who always has good ideas, has probably solved the question of the wounded?"

Vasily just nodded without taking his eyes off the map.

"It does indeed seem to be the solution to our problems," Koryatovich continued, drawing his words slowly. "You won't find anything on the map, but it's here somewhere," he pointed. "If we leave the wounded in this devil's forest with medical assistants and supplies, no one will find them, there is no possibility. And we..."

"We can go back through the forest almost to the manor, also nobody will see us," finished Janek. "We will gain, although the ride may not be fast, but we know the route."

Vasily and grandfather looked at each other, smiled, then bent over the map again.

***

On the same day, the camp was packed and the troops plunged into the forest. Janek led along with Koryatovich, searching for places that could be passed quickly.

They reached the gloomy forest at dusk. Here, Vasily ordered the camp to be set up and the premises prepared for the wounded. Soldiers who had seen more than one looked around uncertainly, not feeling well in such a strange and gloomy place. It was agreed with the doctor which of the wounded should stay. Among the selected ones was Alik, who had not yet fully recovered, but protested so violently that Janek succumbed to him. The more that he promised Vasily and his grandfather that he would take it upon himself to reveal to Alik that they were brothers. Both older gentlemen, seasoned from an early age, when they fought against the Moskals in the Caucasus, in this case lost their courage and evaded this duty. He decided to do this while making his way through the forest. For now, however, there was no time.

Medical assistants and a dozen able soldiers were added to the list of those who were to stay with the wounded. Janek suggested that they should be those who had already dealt with the forest, or at least were not afraid of it. He appointed Ostapko as the commander of the "hunters", to whom he had promised earlier that when the war was over, he would accept him as a forester at the manor. Fedor, who had been notified at first, was glad, but then he grunted.

"I know, this is a responsibility and an order, but Commander, I would prefer to be with you, because Fedka must be missing, and nothing here, boredom," he tried to explain.

"Do not grumble, I have no one who would know the forest, and it is not known if we will return soon, an experienced hunter will also have to guide them. God forbid, and this is war, Fedor, it will happen that winter will find you here, only you can cope and follow the trail, as if on the path. Come on, let me sketch for you where it is best to look for grouse and coarse game."

Immediately after that, grandfather called Ostapko and officially, next to Koryatovich, would appoint him a sergeant of the Polish Army. And when the latter's eyes widened, expecting some command, not a promotion, he patted him on the shoulder.

"I know from the commandant, I mean my grandson, that you were bravely and showed courage where others lacked it, and you also helped people, then you deserve Fedor. Besides, you are a good scout, you can direct people, then you will be useful to the lieutenant I am leaving here as commander. Just remember that the NCO rank obliges and congratulations, Sergeant, and keep it that way for the future."

Immediately after that, Ostapko found Janek and boasted about his promotion, which he was very proud of. Janek pretended that he knew nothing and also congratulated him.

Grandfather gave the last instructions, then went to talk to the wounded, informing them that they were staying. At first, they objected that they would be able to continue.

"You're safe here," he said, briefly running his eyes over their faces. "You have to recover, it's important to me. Your current state would only hinder our march. We will be back, but when that happens I have no idea because this is war and anything can happen. I leave lieutenant Buczacki and sergeant Ostapko for the commander, there is to be order, no whining and frolics. If we do not come back, and the situation requires it, you create a separate unit and God willing that we meet quickly somewhere there."

The next day, dawn had yet to lighten the sky as they moved on. The silence of the left behind them, who only waved to the departing ones, said goodbye, and they replied throwing them into space that they would probably see each other soon.

Vasily gave Buczacki his last instructions, reminding them again, because they'd already managed everything the previous day.

"Don't worry, I'll take care of people as I should," the lieutenant said it with a stony face, which showed, however, a certain regret that he did not go with the others. "You just wish..."

"Waldek, someone has to stay here, and you seem the best for it. You have a father who was forester, you know the forest, you are a good commander, and you also have a knack for unconventional action. This Ostapko is a good man, and having him as a sergeant, you will have a real hand. He knows the forest, he has been trotting, so he will be very useful here. I also feel sorry that I have to leave an officer like you, because probably your caution would be useful on the way, but I will give someone else, and he will waste my people. Come on."

***

It took them almost a full day to reach the place where the Bolsheviks had ambushed them. The traces of fighting were still clearly visible, especially in the trees scarred with bullets. Even more strangely, they did not bury their fallen after the battle, but just threw them in one place. The bodies were already decomposing, and the stench was afar.

"They don't even respect the dead," Koryatovich only muttered under his breath.

Janek immediately proposed to dig their grave, but grandfather strongly opposed it. He explained that it would take too long, and that carrying a decomposing corpse could cause the soldiers to become infected with deadly venom.

They made a short pasture, loosen the girths of the horses and fed them with oats from their hands, without setting the treptuchos. Grandfather's soldiers listened to the stories of those who fought here, and the fact that each was appropriately exaggerated made an impression on the audience.

During the course, Janek showed Vasily the places where the skirmishes took place and told the tactics he had adopted at that time. The latter praised the prudence, but also commented on some of the moves as too risky and suggested other solutions that could be effective at that time.

One thing that has disappeared is the weapons of the dead. Stranger for Janek, some of the fallen were without shoes and uniforms, which Vasily immediately explained to him that many things are missing in the red army, and thus the living take them away from the dead after the battle.

"Supposedly a great state, quite well-stocked during the war, the warehouses were full of equipment and sorts, and when the Reds took power, suddenly everything started to be missing," he explained with a shrug. "Only paradoxes. The former officers now serve in their army, lead the masses to war, although not so long ago their main slogan and promise to the people was precisely to stop the war and return the workers and peasants home. It's hard to understand."

After a short rest, they moved on. Koryatovich was leading, and Janek drove up to Alik and waited until the whole column had passed them.

"What's happening? Why are we staying?" He asked as the last horse passed them.

"I want to tell you something, although it's difficult, but it has its advantages and I personally enjoy it in a way."

"You got an idea again? Come on, grandfather and Vasily are in charge and have more experience."

"It's not that... It's about you..."

"You want to send me ahead? I'm happy to go and see what's in the village."

"It's about the family."

Alik looked at him closely and shrugged.

"Mom, you know that she died, Vanka drank to death, and grandma... did you find out something?" His face turned gray when he suspected that he would not be able to find her again when he returned.

"No, no, it's more complicated, and only now Vasily told me while you were lying down after the shot."

"Grandmother..."

"Let me tell you, because I don't know how to express it either, and your grandma must be alive."

"So what?"

Janek looked at him carefully. He had been a friend of him not so long ago, and now he did not know if their relationship would suddenly cool down. Although in the countryside it was not uncommon for the heir to have children outside of weddings, but he only heard about it when his grandfather's guests at the liqueur sometimes threw something, talking with laughter about their neighbors.

"You are my brother."

Alik laughed.

"I know, we are like brothers, but..." Suddenly he realized what he had heard and in what sense.

"Did they tell you?" He asked softly, expressing his surprise.

"Yep, Vasily."

There was silence. They rode side by side without looking at each other. Finally Alik stopped his horse.

"Janek, my mother told me that before she died... She did not want to leave without revealing it..."

"And Grandma?"

"She raised your dad like a son, and she probably knows it, but you know how tough she is, she didn't tell me anything, and after my mother died, I didn't ask."

"How will it be, brother?" He gave him an uncertain smile.

"For the life of me, I don't think I know. So far I haven't told you anything, because what will it change? We were always together, and Vasily, remember, he beat us the same way when we messed up something. I get it now. And... Janek, is your grandfather now my grandfather?"

"It looks that waIy, and Vasily..."

They both burst out laughing, and then they bent down on their horses and embraced each other.

***

The closer they were to Buchak Lake and the island where they resisted Brother Kluiev's regiments, the more cautious they were. The scouts were driving ahead of them, but in the end grandfather ordered a stop and sent a small detachment to a distant reconnaissance. Janek offered to command them, which caused resistance from grandfather and Vasily that it was an unnecessary risk.

"Nobody knows that part of coniferous forest as well as I do," he explained to both, frowning arrogantly. "I'll go and take my people, that's for sure. And Sheba can sense strangers from a distance, if they'd come across." Seeing their expressions, which he knew that no argument could convince them, he said defiantly:

"And I'm taking my deputy, brother, I mean, if you know what I mean." And without waiting for their reaction, he walked away, leaving them confused.

Vasily and grandfather looked at each other, surprised by his reaction.

"Something tells me, Sylwek, that old apple in our eyes has become hardened," Vasily commented, wincing in a fake smile.

"As a matter of fact, it's not a kid anymore, but it comes with a character like Victor's, fighting cock and stubborn, but in a way it's my fault."

"Not yours, ours and the situation that slipped out of our hands, but who could have foreseen, you know, we discussed it more than once."

They came to the place where Janek gathered those who were to go with him. He gave his last orders, then turned his horse, stopped in front of them, saluted, then turned around Sewek, stood at the head of the squad and signaled to start.

"He has a knack, but that's how we raised him," Vasily said sentiently. "And sooner or later experience will be useful to him. But when I think about what he had to go through when we were gone, my heart breaks."

"Not only you. He will always be a little kid to me. Over the course of this year, however, we lost something as he transformed from a boy to a man."

"Now we'll be afraid for him even more, and we can't help it. We are already very old horses, Sylwek, there is nothing to cheat. Look at our boys we've gathered in the ward. They see us as great and infallible commanders whom they trust and nothing is terrible to them, and I see a lot of doubts when I make a decision. In the Caucasus, somehow everything was easier and simpler then."

"We were as old as our youngest soldiers. Now we weigh the decisions and then we did not think about their consequences. By the way, I mean what they will do after the war. Now they have learned warriors, what will they do with their lives when there is peace? How will they find themselves?"

"Some will probably become professional soldiers, and some, like those from Janek, will return to their roles, but they will still heal the wounds after what they saw and suffered... Well, enough of this, we are falling apart, and," he joked, "we can't befit as great commanders."

They both reached for their pipes, stuffed them and lit them.

As they stood pondering, one of the NCOs approached.

"What's up?" Grandfather noted that he had assumed a basic attitude, but his eyes were laughing as if he couldn't help but be too happy.

"I dutifully report, Commander, that this idea of wachtmeister Alik makes sense. The boys are just trying to make it happen and they like it too."

"What idea? I don't know anything."

"He with the commandant Janek ordered to keep in a secret until they left, so we didn't tell."

Vasily looked at grandfather and he looked at him, but they didn't comment. Their grandson was also beginning to enjoy great respect in their regiment.

"What is this idea?"

"Please follow me, we'll show you."

He led them on, where the soldiers discussed something hotly, twirling around the horses and strapping something to the saddles. Koryatovich stood beside them and was driving them.

"Mr. Kuźma, what have these hotshots come up with again?"

"They came up with it quite well, but whether it works, we will see after leaving the forest," he pointed them to a structure resembling a platform connecting two horses on each side. "They came up with the idea of the inverted tachanka, as they called it. The idea is to put a machine on it so that it can fire forward."

Vasily stepped closer, pecking under his breath, then climbed onto the tachanka, perched behind the machine gun, and began shaking his head.

"When it starts shooting, the horses will panic."

"We'll put rags around their ears, a sack with holes on their heads, so that they could only look ahead. After all, they got used to fighting and screeching."

"What's the purpose, because I don't understand?" Grandfather also looked at the construction unconvinced to it.

"Janek invented it, and Alik, because he has a flair for construction, outlined what it should look like. Recently, I talked to them that the tachanka is useless during a charge, something else during an escape or a standstill. They said they would come up with something and we have a tachanka that can be fired forward."

"It shakes while driving, neither aim nor effective fire, not to mention driving the horses. No sense."

"There is something to it, though," Koryatovich was more optimistic about the idea. "Imagine the charge. We don't have any combat vehicles, so only sabers remain. A sudden attack, it works, but when we go for entrenched soldiers, it's worse. And here not only the bench of horses pound on them, but also shower them with a hail of bullets. Fire from such a tachanka does not have to be effective, it is important that the shooter fires regularly, the most important psychological effect here."

"There is something to it, but will it work?"

"I'm not able to answer this question, but it is worth a try."

"Well, I think Janek remembered reading about Greek times and chariots," laughed Vasily. "How do you manage it?"

"There is a rider on one of the horses, and the horses' heads are connected with a girth.

"You said, Sylwek," Vasily turned to grandfather, "that we missed the transformation of our butterfly, and here it is, it went in the right direction. We feel sorry here, and he thinks and works out how to strengthen our strength. Let's not waste any time, let's go through the maps again."

*   *   *

Janek raised his hand and the unit stopped. In front of them, not more than a few hundred meters, there was a lake hidden in the forest. He got off the horse and gave instructions to continue walking, leading the horses. He glanced at Sheba at the same time how he was acting, but the wolf showed no concern.

They reached the ford. The neighborhood seemed peaceful, yet he did not neglect his caution. For a long time he and Alik looked through the binoculars of the bushes on the island and the birds soaring above the treetops. There was no indication that there was a man hiding in the thicket.

"Okay, there's no point in standing there, you have to get there," he decided at last. He gestured to the two soldiers.

"Alik, you stay and if something happens, you give me support," he said shortly.

They entered the water, preceded by Sheba, who happily jumped over the water. She still did not signal any danger. After a few minutes they reached the shore of the island, and here they carefully, hiding behind the trees, went deeper. It took them several minutes to find it empty. Janek ordered the others to be summoned.

The Bolsheviks did not destroy the fortifications that were once built. Apparently, only as they ran, they surveyed the place of resistance and went on. Janek and Alik who accompanied him climbed one of the platforms and surveyed the neighboring shore to which the first ford led and the beach where so many enemy soldiers had died. This time the dead bodies were removed, possibly buried somewhere nearby.

"I'm going now," Alik suggested, pulling the binoculars away from his eyes. "But I don't think they've left any guards here. They were sure that their ambush would work and there would be no one to come back."

"Who will go, I will decide in a moment, but I think you're right."

Alik elbowed him on the side.

"Don't be like that, it's my turn and don't insist," he winked at Janek. "After all, I'm older than you by a few months and you do not have to babysit me like a younger brother."

They both smiled. The word "brother" made them feel warm, and at the same time resulted in even greater closeness. However, Janek remembered that he was in charge of the unit and took responsibility for the safety of every subordinate, including Alik.

"Okay, go, just be careful, but take two with you."

They came down from the pulpit. They sent soldiers on to her and the others to insure the crossing. Just before entering the ford, Janek ordered Sheba to cross the river first. She willingly jumped into the water and, as before, did not signal anything disturbing. Alik and his bodyguards were right behind her. Soon they reached the beach and entered the forest, and after a few minutes one of the soldiers signaled that the road was safe.

Janek called those on the platforms and without waiting for them he crossed the ford. As he waded through the water that reached the horse's belly, memories filled him the first time he had discovered the island. So much time had passed, so much regret that they had left him, so much fear that he would conceive and how he would manage, and then, when he was on the brink of collapse, fate bestowed on him Sheba, creating a new thread of life for him and giving him a four-legged friend.

He shook his head, noting that he was no longer the young man from last year that he had coped, saved Alik, Joshua and the others. He felt proud and grateful at the same time to Vasily and his grandfather that they had raised him to deal with this situation.

"There's no one, nearby at least." Alik, who emerged from the trees, snapped him out of his thoughts. "I think we can safely go to the edge of the forest and orientate ourselves there. Countryside or mansion?"

Janek shook himself off the memories, but the thought that came, was not cheerful. He must do something to Sheba when they reach the steppe and begin their way with the entire regiment towards the front. She must stay in the forest. But how do you explain it to her?

"Why so bleak?" Alik noticed his expression. "Memories?"

"That too, but I'm wondering what I'll do with Sheba. She can't come with us."

"With a regiment? It's a real problem, she can die when it comes to fighting."

"Yeah..."

"Why don't you leave her in the cave? She knows the place, she won't feel so alone."

"But she will miss me."

"She will be, you will too, but what to do, at least she will be safer. And when we come back, maybe you will see..." He paused, then laughed aloud and finished, "Grandchildren."

Janek looked at him without comprehending, then he understood and also bursted out laughing.

"You're crazy, but nature will probably do its job. Let's go, lead."

They walked, trying to make as little noise as possible and carefully surveying the surroundings. In the front line of the trees from the beach, the ball marks were still distinct, but the farther away there were fewer of them. They found the bones of three horses, guessing that when they fell from their wounds, they were killed and peeled of the flesh so that the food would not be wasted. However, no dead soldier, as in the battlefield deep in the forest. On the other hand, in one place, not so distant from the beach, they found an artificial mound built in a small clearing and guessed that the dead were buried here.

"This reminds me of those tranches where you found that officers' bunker." Alik scratched his head with his hand. "Remember, we also found bones there. Surely, when the Russians or the Germans were moving forward or escaping, they didn't have time to burial either."

"After the war, if any traces of the dead remain, they will have to be buried."

"It depends whether Poland, Russia or Ukraine will be here. What do you think?"

"This isn't our case and enough of this sadness, we have a job to do, not whining like old women." Janek interrupted the conversation, suddenly irritated by the nostalgia that overwhelmed them when they reached the island.

Without waiting for Alik's reaction, he chased Sewek and went forward.

***

After reaching the forest line, they dismounted again and covered the rest of the way to the last trees on foot.

There were three large red flags in the village and a large red star painted on the council building. There were no soldiers, only the inhabitants were busy with their lives. It crossed Janek's mind that the residents had changed their views, but immediately remembered his own instructions he had given to the new village administrator, Tymek, to hang out red rags and pretend that the revolution had also reached the village. Only this can cause - he explained - that when the Bolsheviks come, they will not pick on them. And not a word about the People's Court and what happened.

He hoped they did exactly as he commanded them. May it be so.

"I was just thinking, what did those freed by you do?" Alik did not take the binoculars away from his eyes, carefully scanned house after house. "Because that's what they saw, how we fought with the Cossacks, and at the same time you let them go, which they wouldn't do with us. And they probably have not forgotten that you put these few thugs on trial."

"I don't know, I mean it too, maybe it was a mistake, but I don't do it for Pythia, and now it's too late to worry about it," Janek still felt an inner nervousness which he was trying to control. "Look over there." He indicated the direction of the fourth cabin from the council headquarters. "They are probably some commissioners?"

For a long moment they watched the three riders dressed in black jackets, characteristic of Cheka. The first one spoke with Tymek, who was pointing to the west, where there was a ford in the river. The questioner merely nodded his head and galloped on, no longer scolding anyone.

"They don't look like pointers, maybe they are following the troops that have already passed," Alik considered aloud.

"There is nothing to stand here, we have to go back to the track," Janek made the decision, realizing that the steppe is more important than the countryside, because if there are any troops drawn through the region, it is this way.

They withdrew deeper into the forest, towards more east. When they got to the place from which Janek used to go to the old trenches, they left their horses among the bushes as before, reaching the forest border already on foot.

There was a lot of traffic on the way. The infantry was running in long columns, but what was striking was nothing like the old tsarist formations, marching in a uniform order; loose mass without a clear division into divisions, companies, battalions or regiments. Sometimes the clusters are more numerous, other times less, stretched out into one long human serpent, one hundred to two hundred meters wide.

The motley was dressed in various uniforms, as if no one in this army paid any attention to it. At the front of each group rode their commanders with accompanying commissars. Both groups stood out from the soldiers. The former were mostly dressed in tsarist field uniforms, blouses with a collar, in breeches reaching to leggings with fur coats on their heads, but with a red star sewn on. The latter in black leather jackets, which particularly emphasized their uniqueness in the crowd. On the other hand, ordinary soldiers most often wore sweatshirts put on over their heads, kept from the war period, and on their rears, instead of backpacks, sacks and sometimes blankets thrown over their shoulders. Some of them, which distinguished them in their gray mass, imposed on themselves garments stolen in manors, effectively eliminated after the troops and lords had passed through.

Janek made a note of it in his notebook to later give a detailed account of Vasily and grandfather. He considered them important, because it was the officers who were dangerous because they had experience from the war period behind them. However, he did not notice, as long as the distance was not a trick, any special awards for the charge, and this fact seemed to him important. Such a commander had less chance of successfully leading soldiers on the battlefield. The elimination of commanders could cause panic among the ranks suddenly deprived of orders.

Horse commissioners kept flitting between the columns, driving it forward, then returning in the opposite direction. From time to time there was a disciplined formation, slightly better dressed and keeping the military drill. It was between them that they noticed tachankas with shot puts and horse-drawn field cannons.

Not all were equipped with rifles, but the ones he saw were a jumble of brands that had once been the equipment of various armies, until recently at war with each other. From the Russian Mosins, through the English Lee Enfield and SMLE, the French Lebel and - Janck was surprised to see them - the characteristic Japanese Arisaka. Probably all of them - he guessed - must have come from prey or even withdrawn from the warehouses of decommissioned weapons. Only once, at the police officer who was driving closer to the forest, was noticed by a modern Gewehr 98 Mauser, which he had obtained on a courier some time ago.

"I don't know weapons the way you do, but I don't think they are the most modern army," Alik muttered to Janek.

As if to deny it, there was a murmur of engines from a distance. Within a dozen minutes, four combat vehicles known to Jan from the war period, when a separate squadron of the cuirassier regiment of Oberst Alleberger were hosted, showed up. These were tall, green-painted Daimlers with two round turrets. They reminded of agricultural machinery enclosed with metal sheets, which was also emphasized by the sound of their engines, like an overheated threshing machine. Armed with three machine guns, they were a formidable weapon on the battlefield, where their appearance during the war often caused panic among the Russian infantry. Where from here? Captured? Armadores with red stars painted on their sides and surrounded by several dozen riders pushed forward, ignoring the marchers and separating them into two benches. As the soldiers passed, they cheered for some of them, greeting the crew sitting in the hatches.

"Maybe they are not well armed, but you see, they have armored cars, and I would not like to meet them during the charge," Janek wrote down his observations all the time. "And when such a mass, even if badly armed, falls, it is difficult to stop."

"Koryatovich's Hussars and the rest of the regiment have only the best weapons, maybe this mass is not so terrible."

"The most important, as Vasily says, is not the weapon, but the training, and a good rifle at the same time, this is a chance to defeat even more numerous opponents. When I look at them like that, I wonder how my grandfather like our idea did."

"Compared to those armored squadrons, it was stupid, but when I look at that red army, it was pretty good," Alik said philosophically.

Chapter XXI

After returning to the camp, Janek immediately looked for Vasily and grandfather. They were sitting in a tent above the maps, putting various stamps and arrows on them, some of which had question marks.

He gave a detailed account of what he saw adding his comments about the role of the commanders and the various weapons.

"And that would agree with information from others," they said shortly, then Vasily explained:

"We sent several recon teams to pick you up in different directions, and they all confirm that something is going on in the west. The Bolsheviks mobilized everyone who was at hand. The armament is actually not the best, but there are also troops, it seems, with front-line experience, and we care about them."

"In the direction of interest to us, the regiments of Budyonny's army were noticed, well-armed, disciplined, and therefore very dangerous for us." Grandfather completed the information. "Most of them are still stationed in the Caucasus, but apparently they are hastily downloading them here. Admittedly, as it seems, they are the outskirts for the time being, the first units, but they cannot be underestimated."

"How do you know?"

"Come on, we've taken orders."

"So, what, too much risk to push yourself further?" Janek asked impulsively.

"It's not that," Vasily nodded, not disaffected by the tone of the question. "Look." He leaned over the map and started pointing to different points. "Here we are, their equipment supply line runs through the road, but mainly in the human mass, and this is where Budyonny's troops are already operating. Cramped, like at an annual fair. We will go out and be spotted right away. We will engage in skirmishes with some, others will come and crush us. And here," he showed on the map the eastern part, "Gai-Khan's cavalry is operating and is almost touching Budyonny's cavalry. Not a happy situation."

Janek narrowed his eyes, wondering if his thoughts were worth anything in this situation.

"I don't know who Gai-Khan is, it's like Budyonny?"

They looked at him carefully. They forgot they knew little.

"Cruel and bandit, just like Budyonny, only Armenian. His troops do not like taking prisoners. Wherever they appear, dead bodies and ashes remain."

"I thought so and..."

They waited silently, letting him develop his thoughts.

"...And I am so proud that we have to go at night, and some of our people dress in Bolshevik uniforms. We have these red rags of theirs pretending to be banners here somewhere. It may not completely hide us, but every cat is black at night."

"Nice idea, we have already considered it." Grandfather smoothed his mustache with his thumb, then blew smoke from a pipe between his teeth. "It's just not enough."

"I know, but we don't have to push our way onto the main road." Janek finished the started thought. "If we went sideways, away from them, then if we come across someone, he will take us as his." He leaned over the map and pointed to the region more to the northwest.

"I'm glad that you think like us." Vasily smiled. "And if the ideas are similar, there is a chance of survival."

"Survival?"

"You see, boy, those Bolshevik ciphers we have already acquired that we mentioned to you are very important to the military. We must break through at any cost, even at the cost of large losses, to deliver them. They can not only save the lives of many of our people, but also give us a chance to win. Information has more value than cannons. That is why we want so stubbornly to break through the front."

"I get it, but once again about our disguise." Janek was thinking about his idea all the time. "When we meet those from Budyonny, we are the foreground of this Gai-Khan and vice versa. We can maneuver anyway. I do not suspect that the commander of any unit noticed."

"Boy has right." Grandfather was blowing smoke from the pipe, clearly pleased with the grandson.

***

They left at dusk. Initially, they continued on their way through the forest, and when they reached a place far west of the track after two hours, the scouts were the first to emerge from the forest. When they returned, they brought the good news: There were no enemy troops in their direction.

"For now, luck is on our side." Grandfather muttered to Janek, while Vasily controlled the previously determined dislocation of individual units.

The latter asked for him and Alik to be released for a few hours. When Grandfather raised his eyebrows in surprise, he explained that it was about Sheba, which he had to leave in the wood. And he wants to do it in his former hideout, so that the wolf, longing, does not run after them.

"In the field, when we break through, she will not survive," he explained, but Grandfather just waved his hand that he understood.

"Go, but come back to us quickly."

While the regiment drove on, they turned south, heading for the former cave.

***

When Janek and Alik and Sheba running next to them disappeared into the trees, Vasily made a sign and the regiment moved on.

At the beginning of the cavalcade, a group dressed in Russian uniforms was placed. At its head rode Vasily dressed as a commissioner, accompanied by one of the deputies in an officer's uniform. Several soldiers held red flags on long poles. After them, three tachankas with heavy machine guns surrounded by a dozen or so riders. A small break and the remaining groups between which the remaining tachankas and wagons constructed according to Janek's idea were placed. Scouts were sent forward and sideways.

No one was encountered until dawn. Janek and Alik came back. The first one was sad, distracted, in the cave where he has left Sheba. He wasn't sure if he would obey the order to stay and look for it when he wasn't coming back for a long time.

"Don't worry, she understands it," Alik consoled him as they mounted their horses, and a wolf's mouth was sticking out of the cave entrance, staring at them carefully if they wouldn't change their mind.

They quickly caught up with the regiment, after only two hours. It was located in the steppe, in a place where the lower ground was covered with a few trees, creating a small grove. Here Vasily ordered a rest, though neither the horses nor the soldiers were tired yet. The location was good because they were inconspicuous from a distance, although it was not possible to hide several hundred horses completely. Detectors were deployed, and three troops were sent for long-distance scouting. The others rested.

Vasily, like his grandfather, was concerned about Janek and Alik, so he stopped the march with the commander's silent consent, under the pretext of penetrating the ground ahead.

The scouts returned after more than two hours. To their left, nearly thirty kilometers away, they noticed a cavalry encampment about a regiment. The other groups did not come across anyone.

Despite the increasingly warming sun, steppe awakened to life very sluggishly. On the one hand, the rays warmed up nature, but on the other hand, the mist rising above the grass heralded a possible change in the weather.

"If it holds up, we can move during the day." Grandfather announced, watching the sky closely. "I think it's going to the rain, although it can bypass us and go sideways."

The soldiers were not woken up on the assumption that they would not leave until noon, when the aura was completely crystallized. Only the watchmen, who had been pushed even farther west, were given increased attention. And it was they who, an hour later, signaled the enemy reconnaissance in the strength of a strengthened unit or company, aimed directly at them.

A silent alarm was ordered, and a hundred horsemen were sent north at once. Their task was to circle that oncoming from the direction they had come from and catch those who would break through if there was a fight. Grandfather decided to seize the opportunity and get information.

"If you fail to get something out of them in a conversation, you will have to liquidate them." The intention, especially its second part, was unambiguous, which surprised Janek.

He had seen his grandfather in the moments when he made decisions, but not in a combat situation and confrontation with the enemy, and so clearly ruthless. He himself released the Bolsheviks, not deciding to shoot them, although others had suggested it.

He remembered Vasily once telling him how his grandfather's actions in the Caucasus as the commander of Imam Shamil's personal guard had repeatedly saved the life of the ruler of the Caucasus Imanate from Russian attacks. For reasons unknown to his environment, Shamil entrusted the management of security to a young Pole. Not only a foreigner, but also a different religion. And he believed him immeasurably until his death. And later he enjoyed similar trust in the son of the imam, Jamal al-Din, who was trying to restore the state of Dagestan that had been liquidated by the Russians. During this period, grandfather and his uncle Vakhtang met. The latter commanded the Jamal's artillery unit, also composed of Poles, refugees from the tsarist army.

Janek did not fully understand these complicated connections and reasons for serving the "Muslim warlord", as the Russians called him. The more so because, according to Vasily, Poles also fought in the tsarist army against the imam and his son.

He always promised himself that he would ask his grandfather or Vasily exactly about it, but it somehow happened that he never asked about it. Now he had seen the experience of both giving orders in practice.

The camp prepared for the visit froze, marking a lazy rest, although there was no soldier who would not keep a weapon at his disposal. They were positioned so as not to block a possible line of fire.

Janek was excited. When in the past he had to make decisions himself, emotions disappeared under the influence of adrenaline and responsibility for the decision. Now it was different, though he was quickly analyzing the situation involuntarily, considering if nothing had been neglected.

Kuryatovich, standing next to him, smiled at his excitement.

"Take it easy, young man, the ataman knows what he's doing."

"And how will they find out and..."

"And one will break through?"

"Exactly."

"No chance, so we sent a security squad to the outskirts so that none of them break through."

"What about prisoners?" Janek was bothered by this issue.

"Well... They would do the same with us. This is a war, my young lord, not a court ball," he ironized. "They are not old Moskals, cruel, but respecting at least a bit of the law of civilization. It is ruled by completely new ones, made for that time, ruthless, Bolshevik, subordinated to one goal only. You saw yourself what was left of the courts and villages through which this scoundrel had passed, only the corpses and ashes."

When Janek was silent, noting this unspoken answer and not fully convinced of its rightness, Kuryatovich noticed it and added:

"I told you about Jaworski. He, too, at first thought that as soon as he said a few mongers, the rest would get scared and the situation would calm down. But it was not so, new ones were appearing in their place, and the lawlessness continued to rage. The mansions continued to go up in smoke, and their inhabitants, regardless of their age, adults and young people, women and children, were murdered in a cruel way. The whole Podolia was on fire. Then he changed his tactics, which for the pogromists became a day of final judgment. He turned the torturers into victims. The villages of guilty of the conflagration went up in smoke, and the leaders of the attacks were hanged without mercy. He responded to cruelty with cruelty, and harm to harm. A cruel warlord, one could say, but such actions immediately took effect. Such fear fell on peasant gangs, they began to fear revenge so much that only then the murders and attacks stopped. Well, at least partially. Turning the other cheek is good in religion classes, not in war."

***

The tachankas were moved to the sides of the grouping, masking them with rim bags and pawning the carts with horses. Seen from the side, it seemed to be the usual pasture of another troops of the army. A spar with red flags hung on the ground was stuck in the ground.

In less than half an hour, the first rider emerged from behind the distant mound, followed by several more. They stopped, looking through the camp for a long moment through binoculars. And then one of them turned back, probably with a report to the commander.

Still nothing happened for the next twenty minutes. And after that, around a hundred horses emerged from behind the hill, led by a characteristic tandem, commander and commissar.

At the sight of this, grandfather made a sign and three previously selected Cossacks set out to meet them from the camp. They walked calmly towards the oncoming traffic, then stopped halfway and waited for the others to come.

"Who is this?" Janek asked Koryatovich.

The riders did not differ in any particular way from those he had already seen. The same military blouses pointed hats with stars on their heads, and sabers jangling to the rhythm of the horses' steps by the sides.

"I don't know, but we'll probably find out soon."

The commander of the new arrivals headed for the messengers, exchanged a few words, then gestured toward where Vasily was sitting with his grandfather in the commissioner's black jacket. He nodded, then signaled that they should stay where they were, and he and his political commissar headed for the makeshift table on which the maps were laid out, vodka with a jar of pickled cucumber for appetizer, and a few glasses were placed.

As he got closer, he hesitated for a fraction of a second, murmured something to the four horse riders walking with him, and then he and the commissar who accompanied him jumped off the horses. They walked over to Vasily.

Janek watched the scene from a distance, curious to see how the conversation would go, but it was too far away to hear anything. He could only infer from his gestures which direction he was going. One of the security officers left for the company standing no more than fifty meters. Those of the horses did not get off and it did not look like it. They were vigilant. It was obvious. Their commander of the rota was talking, but judging by his head turning in all directions, he was making an assessment of who he was dealing with. He picked up the glass Vasily offered him and emptied it in one gulp. He laughed, threw something into space and burst out laughing. Vasily replied similarly and refilled the glasses both dumped quickly.

"I don't like that they do not order to get off the horses," Janek muttered.

"Oh, what, they're up to something," Koryatovich narrowed his eyes as he watched the speakers. "It looks like they are old freaks and they want to lull our vigilance."

He leaned back to the officer behind him and gave a few commands. The latter listened attentively and calmly retreated to one of the tachankas. He paused for a moment, as if to talk, then moved on to the next one.

At the same time, the cavalry of the arrivals did not stand idle, but slowly but clearly began to move to the sides. They came in fours in a row, now they have doubled that number to eight and were constantly expanding the front of the division. And at the same time, literally step by step they approached the place where their commander was drinking another glass. They did it so discreetly that if Janek hadn't been watching them closely, he probably wouldn't have noticed it.

"Mr. Kuźma, I think they're getting ready to attack," he said softly to Koryatovich. "They're widening the front."

He looked in the direction of the newcomers, stared for a moment, narrowing his eyes, then nodded his head and ostentatiously stretched.

"I go to my people, and you go to yours and prepare them. It will begin in a moment."

The conversation at the table continued in a seemingly friendly atmosphere. At the same time, the newcomers moved further apart, forming no longer a straight line of the first ranks, but a half arch around the head of the camp. The reins of the loose horses have now been removed.

Janek watched these movements tensely. Orders for Alik and Demienkov have already been issued. Some of his men hid behind horses with rifles ready to fire. The others continued to mark their rest, their hands on their arms. They were ready. He glanced at the others. Only his men seemed to know what was coming. Only a closer look at the individual groups made it clear that this was not the case. The camp, a moment ago full of slack, now froze, as if a mysterious force had stopped the frame of the film. Everyone waited for what would happen.

Somewhere from the other end of the camp, unnoticed two groups of horses emerged to protect the tachankas. Slowly, without haste, they departed and then parted, one to the south and the other to the north. At some point, both stopped, as if unsure whether they would take the right direction.

And then the rota commander got up, spoke some words to Vasily, laughed, and Vasily got up and answered him in a similar tone.

End of the meeting.

The commander of the newcomers, together with the commissioner, approached the horses kept by their subordinates, climbed up to the saddles without haste and quietly rode away.

Slowly, very slowly, but when they were half their distance, they suddenly galloped, just in front of their cavalry they turned abruptly and headed for the camp.

It was a sign to the others who were just waiting for it.

The attack has begun.

A hundred sabers suddenly flashed in the sun and a violent charge was launched, reminiscent of a rapid attack of wild boars on unsuspecting hunters. Only that, contrary to the Bolsheviks' plans, they were prepared for it.

Over a hundred riders had to cover just a few dozen meters. They had not yet developed a full gallop when the first horses reached the outposts of the camp. And here they were greeted by a volley of those who, in their opinion, should run out of fear, or at least, surprised, not react to the violent assault.

The roar of the rifles merged into a single thunder, and the fired bullets created an invisible wall of steel blades in front of the charging ones. The front line of attackers fell dead before they realized what was happening. At the same time, the rhythmic staccato of machine guns from extended tachankas sounded from the sides, mowing the surprised riders literally like cornfields. Riders leaning forward were not aimed, but bursts were sent at the attackers, at the tangled mass of horses and people.

The surprise was complete.

The following rows, seeing what was happening in front of them, tried to turn to the sides and leave the shed at once, but here too they were hit by fire from the camp. From its depths to the front, the others moved rapidly, creating a front that was impenetrable. Horses with riders fell dead or injured at the feet of others, there was a tumult and unmanageable crush. Some drove places to others, fell out of their saddles hit, and horses suddenly deprived of leaders panicked trying to get outside.

Few managed to break out of the trap, and now, low, bowed on the horses' necks, they raced in the direction from which they had come. They did not go far, because suddenly a hundred companies sent earlier to the north stood in their way. They had no chance of escaping backwards or to the sides, where the area was defended by deadly tachankas.

It was maybe ten minutes, maybe just a little more, when the last rider was dead.

The shots ceased.

Dozens of mounts and a hundred dead or badly wounded Bolsheviks lay in the field.

***

Only the rota commander survived. He was immediately taken for questioning, and it was no longer a friendly conversation.

Janek immediately checked whether anyone in his unit was injured and cooled down the euphoria of the victory. He explained that this is just a foretaste of what really awaits them. And then he delegated people to collect weapons from the fallen. It turned out that the Bolshevik unit was perfectly equipped with modern Gewehr 98 Mauser rifles, and many had, apart from sabers, also nagant pistols, which was a phenomenon for the Bolshevik army.

Further on, beyond the hill and invisible from the camp, the Bolsheviks left hidden three tachankas equipped with heavy machine guns, but only with their staff and without any protection. Perhaps they did not want to flaunt each other with shotguns, and more likely, they set them up here as a line of a possible retreat if the attack on the camp failed and they had to withdraw. Their crew of three soldiers on a tachanka made a mistake by not observing the surroundings. She moved away from the wagons to follow the course of the battle, which they were sure would be successful. It ended, but it was tragic for them. They were spotted by the mounted company sent by my grandfather to secure the direction. Before they could react, they were chopped with sabers.

Apart from the commander of the Bolsheviks, the few of his soldiers who survived were also questioned. It was not seen whether they were injured less or if they were dying. Janek, although persuaded by Koryatovich to participate in these interrogations, excused himself under the pretext that he would do a long reconnaissance with his people in the direction from which the Bolsheviks came from. The old hussar, although he guessed the reason, did not comment on the refusal and allowed him to leave.

They followed the traces left by the others from the camp. The grasses were tall, but the dents and fairly distinct footprints after a hundred horses had walked were clear. They followed them, and groups sent sideways and forward penetrated the countryside.

"You did not want to look at the interrogations, but you can believe me that they would not play with us in the opposite situation," Demenkov, riding by Janek, sensed his mood and the reason for the excursion.

He said the same thing as the hussar before, which made Janek suspect that he had been instructed by Koryatovich to look after the young one. He didn't react, although he felt angry that Vasily and his grandfather, probably their initiative, continued to treat him like a child who needs to be looked after all the time.

"It's not that, Stepan, I just don't like violence, although I realize that it has to be so now."

"You can't, you can't. A bit of weakness, an impulse of human pity, and then the consequences not so difficult to predict. This is war, Jan, you will get your hands wet when do your laundry."

They rode on in silence, each lost in their thoughts.

Every now and then Janek stood in the stirrups looking for those sent for reconnaissance. He knew there was no reason to worry, but every time Alik was out of sight, an irrational anxiety for him crept into his head.

The first three of Ostapko came back. For a dozen or so kilometers to the west, she could see nothing. No traces of troops moving anywhere nearby. Only two hours later a group of riders appeared on the horizon. Alik was returning, penetrating the region further to the south and, due to the possibility of encountering enemy reconnaissance, took ten soldiers with him.

"Empty, but there are signs that the military was moving," he reported shortly after arriving.

"What took so long, you only had..."

"I know, but we saw those tracks and I wanted more information. We've gone quite far, over twenty versts, but nothing. They must have been coming some time ago or we'd probably have spotted them."

"You mean, infantry?"

"Mostly, judging by the tracks, but with wagons and cannons. What do we do, keep going or are we coming back?"

"Little useful information. We don't know where they came from," he pointed behind himself. We are going, three more hours following the tracks and if we don't see anything, we'll turn back."

This time they rushed back to the camp to be there before the evening.

***

Joshua, whom Janek had left in the camp, met them because he was hit in the arm during the fight. Admittedly, it was harmless, but it was supposed to rest and heal itself. He was nervous and distracted. When asked what was happening, he angrily said:

"Criminals, bandits, however..."

Janek thought at first that this was his comment about the interrogations, but Joshua added immediately:

"Do you know what they were doing? Go to the ataman, he will tell you himself."

He and Vasily found grandfather discussing something with Koryatovich, bent over the maps.

"How's your foray?" They asked him, and on his grandfather's face he saw the relief that the grandson had already returned.

"Almost twenty versts to the north and south, and much more to the west, and only traces of infantry with carts and guns, but no contact. These traces in the southern direction, nothing in the north, that is, the Bolsheviks must have come from the south."

"Sometimes appearances are deceptive and you have to look under the lining," Vasily muttered, pointing to an area on the map. "It was a special company of long-distance reconnaissance of the Golden Horde of Gai-Khan."

"I've heard that name before, but I don't remember the details. Is that the bandit like Budyonny?"

"Well, you are right, the same one. Now he commands Kawkor, the 3rd Cavalry Corps, but the Bolsheviks prefer to call it the Golden Horde because it arouses greater fear associated with the Tatars. So far, and this was politely sung by the commander of the rota, the whole corps not so long ago struggled with the army of General Denikin somewhere in the Caucasus, but they had already received new orders and headed for the Polish front. As a spearhead, they sent a reconnaissance company to identify the area and several regiments from the 10th Cavalry Division."

"What if he was lying or hiding something?"

Vasily and his grandfather looked at each other, then shrugged at the same time, the former saying briefly and firmly:

"He wasn't lying."

Janek did not ask where this certainty came from, only guessing how the interrogation had gone.

"And what? I'm not asking where this guarantee comes from, but there is a long distance to us from the Caucasus. If they have Deniken's troops on their heads there..."

"Denikin... But if, as you prefer, such a reservation, then if our "talkative" commander was telling the truth, they were given orders to deploy north of Budyonny, far north, almost on the border with Prussia, to weaken our front."

"Deniken or Denikin, a little difference, I mean..."

"You need to know the enemy, because in a moment he can be your ally," the grandfather laughed, interrupting Janek's thought.

"Did you know him?"

"I didn't know as much as I met. Interesting figure. His father was a major in the tsarist army, and his grandmother was Polish, as far as I remember, née Elżbieta Wrzesińska."

"This is the one who did not get along with Piłsudski on the Polish issue?"

"The same as you can see, blood ties do not play a role."

"Brought up as Russian, also stupid."

"Don't judge him so easily. At home they spoke in Russian and Polish. During the war, he was the chief of staff of the commander-in-chief, so he is not stupid, but has priorities other than Piłsudski."

"And nothing from Pole."

"It's also not like that. The Bolsheviks, as far as I know, swept Kerensky so much that they persuaded him that General Kornilov was preparing a coup d'état, and he ordered his arrest."

"Wait, because I'm already lost. Who is this Kornilov and what has to do with Denikin? Do you have to start every explanation with the end?"

"Not every story is a simple. It was the commander-in-chief of the army after the tsar's resignation."

"Was he? What does it have to do with Denikin?"

"He supported Kornilov during his conflict with Kerensky, they also locked him up in the fortress in Bychowo. There he was released by the soldiers of the Polish I Corps, who were guarding this stronghold. They equipped him with the documents of a Polish officer, gave him a Polish name and from there he got to the Don, where he formed the Volunteer Army. And after the death of Kornilov, he became its commander."

Janek looked at his grandfather with admiration and amazement. How did he get such precise knowledge, when they were sitting at the court all the time, far in the borderlands, and no information from the world, or at least such, reached here.

"Now tell me the sparrows chirped about it," he said sarcastically that he had touched another secret he had no idea about. "Where did this knowledge come from?"

They looked at each other, and grandfather just spread his hands in a silent comment on something that seemed obvious.

"We told you, but you didn't listen." Vasily cut in on the conversation this time. "We coordinated the intelligence activities and organized a meeting between Piłsudski's representative and Denikin. Yes? Hence, if you would add two and two, you would get the result. Simple?"

He paused, looking at Janek with a smile, then, seeing his expression, he reflected and added:

"Regarding the general's stupidity, as you kindly called it my youth, do you know that he almost took Moscow? He took Donbas, the whole of central Ukraine with Kiev, he reached Orzel, and if he had reached an understanding with Piłsudski, there would be no problems with the Bolsheviks today."

"Moscow? What happened that he did not succide?"

"He got a spank from them because the Poles refused to secure his rear and flanks and rushed him all the way to the Caucasus. So he is not stupid, he is full of his strength, and you do not judge someone according to your sympathies and his achievements. He made wrong assumptions about what happens to everyone and paid heavy for the mistake. Although, on the other hand..." He paused and looked meaningfully at grandfather. "He doesn't think so. What, as you can see, is not easy."

"It isn't, because we do not have complete information, but we can only guess." Grandfather explained before Janek asked him. "General Karnicki, I do not know if we have mentioned to you before, and he was the chief negotiator with Denikin and we sent him reports from the field, he believed that Denikin was willing to leave Poland's borders, but those from before 1815, i.e. very limited. And his deputy, Major Przeździecki, directly warned Denikin that if he did not grant us the borders we want, he must take into account the fact that we will remain neutral towards the movements of the Bolshevik troops. And this will result in them hitting his flanks, which he cannot handle. We can only guess the rest."

"Okay, sorry, I went astray in Russian's opinion, but you raised me yourself so that I do not love them. What did you get out of this commander?"

"He wasn't sure of that, but by the time they started going here Denikin was already losing and backed away. And this allows us to guess that the entire body of Gai-Khan will soon be here, if it is not already nearby. He was subordinated to General Mikhail Tukhachevsky, appointed commander-in-chief of the army that is to take the revolution to Germany, where the Bolshevik revolt is also allegedly taking place."

"So, as I understand it, by Polish territory."

"He finally understood," Vasily laughed, this time aloud, and reached for his pipe.

"This is why you was so hurry to deliver the ciphers you acquired to the Polish army. Couldn't you all say it all at once? Plain and simple? After all, I will not run around and spread the word."

"And if you were in the hands of the Bolsheviks, and the interrogator cut your belly with a knife, gouged out your eyes, cut your fingers, then how do you think you would be silent?"

Janek looked at his grandfather in amazement. He never considered the fact that he could fall into the hands of the Bolsheviks. Images from a deserted village came back to him. This made him realize that there is a war going on, and the fate of everyone who takes part in it is unpredictable.

"Joshua was nervous when we got back." He changed the subject. "What happened?"

"We questioned the few who survived a bit and told us what they did. And it turned out that they had burned alive about three hundred Jews in a town whose name they had forgotten. In the synagogue where they spent them with their whole families and set them on fire. Oh, yes, just to pass the time."

"And?"

"They were shot. At my command."

***

For the next few days they moved north-west without meeting any Bolshevik troops, which pleased grandfather with Vasily, but also caused anxiety.

"We hit a gap between them," they considered on one of the stops, delving into the maps and discussing the further route.

"It's probably good, we will pass unnoticed," commented Janek, listening to their reflections, but Vasily immediately made him realize that he was wrong.

"If we miss, it means that we move on the edge of larger formations, and when we come across them, it may not be funny, because they will appear from both sides."

The reconnaissance sent to the sides brought information about abandoned villages, partially burned and corpses found there. The enemy troops were nowhere to be seen, only traces of the march of a large number of troops.

Grandfather was getting more and more concerned. He ordered the pace to slow down. Janek suggested a deep foray and - which surprised him in the context of the previous reservations - he was granted permission. The situation must have been extremely disturbing for both commanders, since they immediately showed him the maps and the direction he should penetrate.

"We have some woods here," Vasily showed him the spot on the map, "and we'll stop here. You have two days, it's a long time to orientate, but don't delay, come back as soon as you notice something. Here, look, we have the town of Orsha on the left, here flows the Dnieper, here the important river Kropivna and ravines leading to the Dnieper. You can hide in them as if something was happening. Further, far further, there is the big city of Vitebsk, but you have to sneak this way," he showed on the map and made himself repeat the names of small villages on the outskirts.

Janek took with him some of his soldiers and twenty experienced cuirassiers, who were unexpectedly joined by Koryatovich.

"Well, yes, they had to give me a wet nurse," commented Janek impulsively, turning to Alik, but he did not protest. However, his pride in entrusting him with scouting was undermined. But immediately he realized that this time it was not what he thought about it and his hurt ego that mattered, but the safety of the entire regiment.

"Would you like to be alone again?" Alik, noticing his expression, smiled sardonically, then clapped him on the shoulder. "They are nervous, it means that the matter is really serious. And when you are sent with Koryatovich, they must be hoping for your luck."

"For what? You goofin'..."

"You see, you react nervously. Something is in the air. I overheard grandfather saying to Koryatovich that you have to rely on your ideas and your luck, because standard actions do not help. They really are concerned."

"Me too," admitted Janek, "because I feel that something is getting ready, you know, my stupid feelings."

They left at dawn the next day. The entire squad was equipped with distinctive Bolshevik caps in case of encountering enemy scouts, and those, Vasily assumed, would also need to penetrate the area. Koryatovich was wearing a black jacket and was supposed to be a squad commissioner.

By evening they reached the village of Szubki. It was abandoned. In the center, the corpses of several men and women were swinging on a few makeshift gallows. Immediately behind it, they stumbled upon a forest complex and continued to use its cover, turning more southwest. In the evening they reached another village, Sobola, and here the view was similar. There was three bodies on the gallows, a few burned huts and no one alive, not even a cat or a dog. They stopped for the night without lighting a fire. Before the first rays of sunlight illuminated their surroundings, they continued on, turning more north. They found another village between two forest complexes, also abandoned, this time without the corpses and the visible presence of soldiers here.

"The villagers are probably hiding in the woods," said Koryatovich.

Janek just nodded that he agreed with him.

Until noon they saw no signs of an army's march, but as it grew dark, scouts sent forward brought word that they were probably reaching the enemy's rear.

"Fresh traces of horse droppings," reported one of the cuirassiers. "In my eyes, a few to several hours."

"How many?"

"If we spotted the tracks well, there will be twenty horses, but there are also other tracks and..." He paused, as if not knowing how to describe it.

"I will tell you,"-Ostapko, who accompanied him, was bolder. "In the bushes we found two dead bodies stabbed with sabers.

Naked, without outer clothes only in gaiters, but in my opinion, they are not peasants, but some lords, because they are different, better."

"Yeah, they weren't peasants." The Hussar returned to his speech. "Because, sir, it was strange, we started looking around and by chance, Ostapko found it. Show it, brother, because they are similar to ours."

Fedor reached into his puffer jacket and took out a piece of tin and handed it to Koryatovich. It was clearly a badge of some formation, but different from the well-known. There was a skull on the background of a black cross, and the whole thing was painted on two crossed swords.

"It doesn't look like Bolshevik," Koryatovich grunted, looking at it from both sides. "Maybe she really belonged to those killed, but where did the Germans come from?"

"What kind of Germans?" Janek became interested, also carefully examining the badge.

"Two years ago, maybe three, I saw them, but the Bolshevik revolt broke out, the war is over," Koryatovich muttered to himself, not answering and calculating something in his head.

"Mr. Kuźma…"

"Oh, sorry, I arranged it so and it turned out that it was impossible."

"For God's sake, don't start like a grandfather, from the end."

"Oh, yes, who is with whom... I saw the regiments of Totenkopfhusaren, the Hussar Assistant Brigade from Gdańsk years ago. They transferred them at the end of the war from the French front here to the borderlands. They had such characteristic black fur hats with a large skull. Maybe it's their badge? But what would they be doing here now? In captivity with the Russians? I also saw Totenkopf on the caps of General Lavr Kornilov's regiment. It is unlikely, although it is possible, that it was their regiment, which made its way to Prussia, but... Probably not, because they would not abandon their only and chopped ones."

"We know something, but..." Janek wondered, "did they only use such symbols?"

"Sure no, but I don't know anything else."

"Then why did your hussar say similar to ours?"

"Because we have our badge, two sabers and a skull on it."

"How do you get it? I have not seen."

"Because not everyone gets it, only the one who distinguished himself in the fight."

"We have some information, and by the way, you must show it to me when you return. But now we must move quickly in their footsteps."

"Mr. Jan, I don't think it's purposeful."

"Mr. Kuźma, absolutely on purpose. If they butchered two soldiers, something tells me it's important to see what's behind it."

"Your gut feeling again," Koryatovich waved his hand in resignation. "So far, it worked, maybe this time, but we have to hurry, because we promised the ataman that only two days, and this one will end."

They didn't discuss any more. They sent two pairs of horses to the sides, with three scouts ahead. They themselves followed Ostapko to the corpses and traces that the one with the hussar had found.

***

Within an hour the first scouts sent westward returned. After driving eight versts, they came upon a squad that stopped to rest in a grove at the foot of the hill.

"They did not push any further, but watched them from this hill," reported Ostapko, worried. "They are the Bolsheviks, maybe twenty horses, maybe a bit more, it is difficult to count, because some of them went among the trees. They don't look particularly fighting, maybe we would..."

"Relax, Fedor, don't be too wise, that's what others are for." Janek stopped clear emotions. "Did you see anything else?"

"I think they have prisoners."

"You think?"

"You can't see that well from a distance, even through binoculars."

"They have prisoners or not?"

Ostapko looked at the hussar, the same with whom they found the corpses and the badge. He just shrugged and stammered out:

"Well, Commander, in my opinion they have, but not so many, a few, maybe a dozen. In uniforms, it seems, but not Bolshevik."

"And what are you so incompatible?" Koryatovich interrupted. "One this, one that, saw one and not the other?"

They lowered their heads trying to hide something.

"Fedor, as for confession, what happened?" Janek stared at Ostapko.

"Commander, I wanted to sneak up, and he objected. I would have done it, the trees from the side reached the hill and you could, but he threatened to go away, so I only walked a bit and came back, as Waśka wanted."

Janek looked at Koryatovich, who could barely suppress his amusement, then assumed a serious expression.

"And if something went wrong, you, Ostapko, would not be such a daredevil. Waśka," he pointed to the hussar, "may have saved your ass and thank him for it. I know, I heard from the commandant that you like such frolics, but sometimes you don't think with your dick, but with your head, Ostapko, your head, and not only about yourself, but also about other morons. I make myself clear?"

"Yes, not with a dick, Captain," he blurted out, but then he reflected and stuck to his opinion: "It was possible to get closer there, really," seeing Koryatovich's gaze he quickly added.

"Although probably Waśka was right, because you never know if wolf does not get your ass."

"And our entire unit can be brought, or at least part of it?" Janek became interested in the topic of hiding behind trees while descending the hill.

"Yes, sure, but maybe not everyone, like me. Lord knows, I know how to approach the game, as quietly as a wolf, and they," he pointed to the other riders, "rather like a badger in heat."

"Then rest for a while, and when the others come back, I'll call you," he gave the order.

When they were alone, he asked Koryatovich about his assessment of the situation.

"If only twenty, it'll be easy, but you'd have to get close to them unnoticed. And if they do have prisoners, we'll learn from them about the situation, because they've taken them captive somewhere. It's worth a try, but let's think about it more carefully than your "dick"."

"I'm glad you're not like your hussar…"

"He was right, I will defend him here."

"Probably yes, but I know Ostapko. He can approach a hare before it notices that someone is tearing it by the ears. He's a born poacher, he's experienced, and yours… Well, maybe he was right, if Fedor had get caught, it would have been a problem."

"Oh, common sense, not bravado."

"But I think we can do that," the idea has already caught in Janek's head. "We will go out on them, so that they can see us from a distance, slowly, as if we were not in a hurry. And some of the best shooters will be sent earlier with Ostapko. We'll give them time to come in for a shot and we'll distract them. What do you say?"

"It's quite good."

Half an hour later the rest of the scouts sent sideways returned. Within a few versts, there were no signs of any foreign troops. Janek gave the orders carefully discussing the tactics. The shooters selected by him were the first to set off with Ostapko. Some time after that, the rest of the unit moved, not hiding, even ostentatiously demonstrating that they were going.

***

The others saw them from afar. Immediately they led the horses out of the trees and mounted them. They did not seem worried, but you can see that they knew the drill, or maybe they just wanted to demonstrate that they were vigilant. They faced the group of approaching riders, in a loose pile, ignoring the sides.

"If I'm counting well, twenty." Janek threw to Koryatovich. "And there are ten on the ground at the edge. They must be the prisoners."

"And I think so. I can't see the others among the trees, but they've tied one of them to a branch by their hands and it seems to be hanging."

"Where?"

"Behind that big hawthorn. I thought it was some kind of rag, and this is a human."

"I wonder if he's still alive."

They approached the standing walk, not letting the horses accelerate. They felt that something was going, because despite the pulled reins they tried to change their steps, and when it failed, they shook their heads nervously, snorting or lifting them high and pulling the noses towards the strangers.

Koryatovich raised his hand and the squad stopped. They were no more than forty paces from the Bolsheviks now. The others did not react. Only after a while, seeing that the visitors had no intention of moving, who had been sticking to the rear so far better dressed than the others, he decided and drove among his people. He gave an order and they slowly moved towards Janek's unit.

"This one is in charge, I take it on myself," Koryatovich muttered under his breath and hurried as if inviting the Bolshevik commander to an interview.

The latter saw it, gave another command, and his men stopped, and he pushed himself forward.

Janek glanced at the trees on the right. He did not notice his people, but some branches twitched slightly despite the lack of wind.

"They are ready." He mentally thought pleased.

When Koryatovich and the Bolshevik commander were separated by a distance of no more than three meters, Janek raised his hand to let the shooters know, held it for a moment, then abruptly lowered it. His hand had not yet fallen on the rifle butt as shots fired from the trees, and Koryatovich, forcing his horse to jump, climbed into the saddle and almost cut off his opponent's head with one stroke. At the same time, those who followed Janek, so far pretending to be bored, suddenly transformed and made use of their rifles. Before the shots died out, they leapt forward at the utterly surprised Bolsheviks.

The others didn't stand a chance.

The fight lasted no more than a minute when twenty dead soldiers littered the ground.

"Cut off the hanging one and see if he is alive," Janek gave an order to Alik, pointing to the hawthorn, and he himself headed towards the prisoners.

They didn't really know how to react. Some got up, and the rest, apparently, did not have the strength for it and only rose on their knees. They stared at Janek, but seeing his Russian uniform, they did not speak, although a part of his face showed both surprise and hope.

"Who are you?" He snapped the general as he drove up to them.

The faces changed. Surprised by the Polish language, they stared at him, a grimace of disbelief and an uncertain smile on their faces.

"Prisoners of war, Polish prisoners of war." One of them, maybe thirty years old, said the first.

"Where from? What formation?"

The respondent looked carefully at Janek, assessing who he was dealing with and asked the question himself.

"Is that a Russian military detachment?"

"I asked you something, Mr. Military. Your uniforms are weird."

At that moment Alik came up to him and whispered softly:

"He's alive but unconscious. They beat him and he looks like a chop, but I don't think they broke anything."

The prisoners carefully watched what the newcomers were doing with their colleague. When they saw that their companion had been cut off and laid on the ground, and the medical assistant meticulously examining the unconscious, they breathed visibly. And the one who spoke first smiled with obvious relief.

"Lieutenant Kawęcki from the Death Cavalry of the Volunteer Cavalry Squadron of the 1st Army," reported briefly.

"Nice hussars who let themselves be taken captive," Janek blurted out.

This time, all the captives' heads rose sharply, then fell back. The words of the unknown commander hurt.

"You're right, it bothers us too," Kawęcki said it quietly.

He was silent for a moment, and Janek patiently waited, regretting his rashness and the words he had said.

"They surprised us when we were on the reconnaissance," the lieutenant decided to break the silence. "They literally showered us with hats. We put a lot of them down, but they kept pushing forward, only firing at the horses, not us, and we finally ran out of ammunition. We defended ourselves against the corpses of horses with only sabers, but we couldn't. That's all. Later, they told us that they had received an order from the command itself to capture us alive at all costs and deliver some Gai-Khan to the Third Cavalry Corps."

"Are you so valuable? Why did they care about you? Gai-Khan murders, takes no prisoners."

"We do not know either, but maybe because our cavalrymen took their toll on the Bolsheviks, because often, on the orders of the command, we operated in their rear causing panic, which made our fight easier. They knew our sign."

Janek frowned and reached into his pocket, taking out a badge with a skull and a bones found by Ostapko.

"Yours?"

"Yes, but..." A shadow of a suspicion that they were being interrogated ran across the face of the interlocutor, perhaps even killing those Bolsheviks who were transporting them was also a deliberate act to extract information from them.

Janek could almost see his suspicions on his changing face.

"Please don't worry." He handed him the badge and explained, "We found them near two saber-chopped soldiers."

The lieutenant looked at him and brightened again.

"Excuse me, they interrogated us, but we agreed with our colleagues that they could kill us and we will not tell them anything. And the others... These are Captain Wasyłko and Light Cavalry Daniluk, they simply killed them for show, to show us what awaits us, if we remain silent."

"But they were supposed to deliver you alive, you said?"

"Vasily overheard the conversation between their commander and the other, probably a second, while they drank. These were not ordinary soldiers, but the Cheka unit. They wanted to boast to their commandant's office that they had obtained testimony from us. And sorry to ask, sir, from what unit, because those uniforms of yours..."

"Bolsheviks know how to dress up, so why not us." Janek spread his hands. "I think we have a lot to say to each other, but our commander, Ataman, would probably prefer to hear it for himself."

Chapter XXII

The rescue of ten prisoners from the hands of the Bolsheviks caused a sensation in the camp. Admittedly, one was on the verge of life, but almost everyone wanted to see the rescued Death Cavalry. They heard about them, and some met the soldiers personally when their commander collaborated with Feliks Jaworski.

"You did an excellent job, although in fairness, you were supposed to be away for only two days," grandfather held Janek in his arms, unable to decide whether to chase him or hug him.

"I know, I'm sorry for this extension, but I couldn't go back when I saw these two dead bodies and Ostapko found a strange badge. Something told me this might be the information you've been waiting for."

"Still... Damn you, Vasily was right, when standard actions fail, you have to be sent." He paused, looking him in the eye, then added tartly, "They say the imprudent is lucky."

"So what are we going to do with them?" Janek flashed the hint and asked immediately.

"For now, we have to question this lieutenant, who proves them, because time is pressing, and then they will probably join us. Be at my place in an hour, and now rest and, most of all, go to the cook, let him prepare something good for you."

Janek was bursting with pride. He did not expect his grandfather to congratulate him in such a veiled manner, although he did it in private, not in front of everyone. His first question, when they arrived at the camp, was: "What about those who were guarding them?" He didn't ask who the prisoners were, though Janek saw Koryatovich and Vasily exchange glances, and the former nodded at the captives.

The killed Bolsheviks were buried in the forest, not on the periphery, but deeper, masking the place. Fourteen horses were fit to ride, the rest had to be finished. Their carcasses were also hidden in the forest. They collected all the weapons, loaded them on two carts that the Chekists had and which also had provisions. What pleased them the most was the tachanka with a cannon and a large supply of machine gun ammunition.

Now Janek went to give orders to the cook, but he, without waiting for orders, had already prepared food for all the scouts.

***

Grandfather with Vasily, Koryatovich, the commander of the survivors, Lieutenant Kawęcki and another, Warrant Officer Dowgiłło, was sitting at the table on which the maps had been laid out.

"We were just waiting for you," Vasily muttered, dissatisfied, but his eyes were laughing.

"Let's start, there is no time." Grandfather added his and turning to Kawęcki, he asked him to shed light on the situation.

He got up and bent over the maps. And then he showed various points, commenting on them, pointing to the characteristic topography, the probable dislocation of the Bolshevik and Polish troops.

"This, Colonel, has information about a week ago, before we got into their hands." He cautioned when he finished.

According to his information, they had been very lucky so far not to come across enemy troops. The Gai-Khan Cavalry Corps operating in the region numbered almost five thousand horsemen, including two battle-hardened cavalry divisions drawn from the Urals and Kuban, and an infantry brigade of about seven hundred riflemen. According to the testimony of the prisoners, whom the Death Cavalry had previously captured, the corps was extremely well armed. There were about a hundred heavy machine guns and almost thirty cannons in stock.

"The most important thing is that they are all experienced soldiers, real killers, and not those from round-ups who are dragging to Warsaw," he summed up. "It won't be easy with them, unless the Colonel comes up with a trick."

He sat down and waited for further questions.

"We have this young colonel from unusual walks." Vasily laughed pointing at Janek. "But you and your people have already found out about that."

Kawęcki looked at him, then at Janek and it was clear from him that the age of the indicated person did not agree with the charge, but he did not comment on it.

"Tell me, what the situation of our people is and what is happening?" grandfather called the crowd to order.

His expression was focused. He twirled his mustache nervously with his fingers, then nodded his head to himself, pulled out his smock and lit a pipe. Janek guessed that the situation presented by the hussar was not the best for them.

"When we were leaving the camp, ours were getting ready to attack in the direction of Babruysk," interjected Ensign Dowgiłło. "General Stanisław Szeptycki was in charge of the whole grouping, but he was not entirely sure if he could do it."

"Why and how do you know that?" Janek saw hesitation.

"This is my territory, I helped with the plan. And the general was not sure of the attack, because there aren't many of ours, and the Bolsheviks are swarming."

"What was the purpose of the operation? It is a small town. Do you know anything about it?"

"Their 16th Army is occupying Minsk. Orders came to take the city, because it is a large railway junction. And ours less than the others."

"It means?" Janek took over the interrogation of the ensign, seeing his grandfather's approval.

"We had, I mean, planned to hit an even smaller town, Mołodeczna first. The general had only two rifle divisions at his disposal. It was promised that the units of Greater Poland Group would strengthen us, but when we set off, they were not there yet, so the success of the attack was debatable.

Janek leaned over the map, thought for a moment and said:

"If I had planned it, I would have gone first to the Zasław - Papiernia - Białorucza line, and then to Minsk, but it is indeed a difficult journey without cavalry."

"The general said the same to the staff."

"Then we have to consider what tactics to choose." Grandfather leaned over the map too. "The best solution seems to be going to the line shown by Janek. These are the outskirts of Gau-Khan's army, we should deal with them, and then straight on... Well, exactly in which direction?"

Lieutenant Kawęcki got up and indicated the region on the map without hesitation.

"Here are ours. If we manage to break through Białorucz, we will reach them."

"We will go from their rear, they do not expect, this is our plus." Janek analyzed the map, coming to the conclusion that the plan had a chance of success. The final decision, however, was up to grandfather. He was in charge here, and based on his experience, he will make the decision. "Although there are railroads to Bobruisk and Minsk, they can get reinforcements, but when they do, we'll be a long way off."

Grandfather was nibbling on his pipe, glancing at Vasily to see if he had anything to add, and when everyone was silent, waiting for his decision, he said briefly:

"Gentlemen, we have an outline of the plan, and now let's consider its implementation."

***

They left before dawn, preceded by scouts. The tachankas were placed on the sides, in front of them they put out carts invented by Janek, which could fire straight ahead.

Tension was felt throughout the regiment, not yet in combat formation. Everyone, from the ordinary private to the officer cadre, from the least experienced to the old veterans, realized that they would have to break through the front Bolshevik troops, that they could suffer heavy losses and now their fate would depend on the decisions and experience of those in charge.

The closer to the front, the more traces of fighting appeared. Crumbles, tranches, carcasses of horses, and not infrequently the unburied corpses of soldiers and wrecked equipment, ranging from damaged guns to burnt armor. When noon was over and the sun was scorching hard, the first sounds of clashes, rifle shots, the screech of heavy machine guns and the throaty rumble of heavier weapons began to reach them somewhere in the distance.

They sped up, and at one point the grandfather stopped the column. For a long time he analyzed the murmur of the clashes that seemed to be coming from all directions, even from the direction they had come from.

At one point he gave a signal and they moved on.

The regiment quickly moved further north, but not far enough to lose touch with sounds over the horizon.

"Did they circle us or what?" Janek asked Koryatovich who was riding next to him. He wasn't sure how to interpret the sounds of fighting that could be heard from them.

He looked from side to side, listening more than looking for anything.

"No, Mr. Jan, only part of the clash is, and the rest is a resonance, reflected somewhere in the hills. It is difficult to orientate; therefore the ataman maneuvers us so that we are on the verge of audibility."

"Is there a difference?"

"I don't know, but Mr. Vasily certainly is. He has already led us safely out of trouble several times. He has hearing, like a real wolf."

On command, the regiment tightened its ranks, and the scouts kept jumping in all directions to return immediately with reports. So far, in the border of several versts, they did not notice anything disturbing, and only verified the reverberation creeping across the steppe.

Until the afternoon they accelerated, then slowed down, turning north, then turning south after some time, all the time keeping the target direction to the west. As it neared dusk, somewhere in space they still heard their murmurs of clashes, but now more distinct from the latter.

"Change the line-up," Aide-de-camp Vasily said in passing, sneaking past the troops, and continued without stopping to deliver orders.

"Is it already?" Janek felt like the adrenaline was starting to flow in him.

"I think so, somewhere they are fighting on the line Zasław - Papiernia - Białorucza," Koryatovich was staring carefully at the map he rented. "Time for a change and at a gallop, Mr. Jan, as was scheduled, your squad pushes the tachankas forward, to the center, and good luck."

Without waiting for a reply, he spurred his horse up and rode quickly to his hussars, who were already turning into two parallel wedges, extending backwards like a battle battering ram, leaving a space in the center. The gap was filled by Janek's soldiers, whom Alik and Damienkov were setting up. No rush. They had practiced it before and now they did it efficiently and without unnecessary questions.

***

The leaders gave a sign and the entire formation immediately headed south-west, to Białorucz, from where the sounds of fighting were the loudest. The horizon was throbbing with one thud of gunshots, and it was impossible to tell whether it was rifles, shotguns, or guns; one murmur, like the sound of a thousand drums merged into one ominous sound. Only the darkness, far beyond the line of sight, flashed over and over, as if a storm had stood over it, throwing lightning all the time.

They were not speeding up yet, still riding at a walk. Scouts in the strength of the squad were sent ahead, followed by another, who was to additionally insure him.

Nothing happened for half an hour, and then another passed, and only then, when the sky was already deeply darkened, getting ready for the night, they came forward from over the horizon, rushing what the horse jumped.

Janek did not take the binoculars away from his eyes, trying to find the details in the engulfing gray area. When he saw galloping riders, the sudden tension and uncertainty that had so far grown in him disappeared somewhere. He knew the feeling. Now it was all settled; without maneuvering in the field, avoiding meeting the enemy, sneaking sides. The Jaworski's people assigned to him pulled the reins of their horses harder, and Lieutenant Kawęcki, who was riding next to him, crossed himself, reproaching: "Finally, God." Ensign Dowgiłło followed him closely, raising his eyes to the dark sky and whispering softly but with clear relief: "Merciful Lord, at last."

He was counting scouts involuntarily to form an image of a clash after their condition. Because they must have undoubtedly encountered an enemy. Some rushed to protect those who had been injured and, though hesitantly, still clinging to the horse's backs. He noticed two figures slung over the saddles, but they fled so quickly towards grandfather that he couldn't tell who it was.

In less than ten minutes Koryatovich galloped in.

"Mr. Jan, we are going to the very center of the fight," he said and wanted to leave, when Janek asked:

"How many killed and who do we have in front of?"

Koryatovich stopped his horse.

"Fortunately, none are killed, but a few are injured."

"And those brought?"

"For a brief interview."

"So, Mr. Kuźma, who's ahead of us?"

"Probably ours are fighting the Gai-Khan cavalry division and the infantry. We do not know any more details. Scouts went to the outskirts, where they saw nearly two hundred killed, prisoners and civilians. They clashed with a company there."

And he was gone.

Tension rose, but at the same time, among the soldiers who heard this exchange, so did the rage and the desire for revenge against the barbarians murdering the defenseless.

"Mr. Kawęcki, find out more," Janek ordered the lieutenant, who quickly galloped back.

He had been gone no more than ten minutes when he returned.

"They chased me to come back to you, but I know something. Before us, the Second Regiment of Legions clashed with the Bolsheviks. They are still defending themselves but are slowly surrendering to the front. They are infantry, and against them they probably have the entire 10th Ural Cavalry Division, several times more numerous and well-armed. The colonel ordered to speed up, because they would be destroyed on sabers."

They sped up.

Now the entire regiment formed a battering ram whose task was to unexpectedly punch into the enemy's rear and tear the front apart.

Horse's hooves, kicked off the ground, made one steady clatter. At the same time, the sounds of the fighting ahead became clearer.

Janek signaled to Alik that the banners should be ready. He had discussed it with his grandfather and Vasily earlier.

"What will we do when we join the fight and our people start shooting at us as well?" He asked a question that was bothering him. "Somehow we have to let them know, or we will fall into a double fire."

They admitted he was right, because they were busy planning the attack and did not take this into account.

"What do you suggest?" Grandfather, as usual, did not enter into the discussion and waited for ready-made proposals.

"Push on the forehead, but close and protect my tachankas, a few flagships. You have them, I saw them, especially the one with the big white eagle. It should be visible despite the darkness. And select the protection of the banner from peasants with a shrill voice. Let them scream that it is the Polish army that the others, that is ours, would not shoot at them."

"Do you have someone in charge?"

"I think that lieutenant Kawęcki is best suited, and his men are best suited to protect the banner."

"How much do we have?" Grandfather turned to Vasily without commenting on the idea, which clearly convinced him that it was worth considering.

"The one with the eagle from the uprising and two new ones, but these are more white and red flags."

"Do it, the idea is real, although at night..."

"I also suggest," Janek interrupted him, "that the ten-man unit should not get into a fight, but rush as fast as possible in order to forestall them."

"Not real," Vasily responded this time, grimacing. "This is..."

"Hold on." Grandfather stopped him and asked Janek: "How do you imagine it?"

"Chaos will arise, it will be dark, they have a chance to break through. Difficult task, but doable."

"Do you have someone you could recommend for this task? Damienkov?"

"No, he's a Russian after all. I thought more about Fedor, to whom I would give Ostapko and eight more. All must be in uniforms that distinguish them from the Bolsheviks."

"Okay, I agree, but warn them this is a near suicide mission."

"Almost like ours," Vasily added sentiently, and smiled knowingly at Janek.

***

They passed no more than a verst when they encountered the first enemy troops.

These were the ones that were withdrawn to the rear after many hours of fighting due to numerous losses and exhaustion. Operating in this section, the 10th Cavalry Division, drawn from the Urals, had spare battalions and some of them had not yet entered combat. Their leaders could afford it, rationally using the luxury of multiple advantages. Moreover, the Polish lines could not withstand repeated, fierce attacks. Now they were moving backwards, leaving more and more dead. Admittedly fine and still biting off, but their end was only a matter of time.

They gave the Bolsheviks no chance.

Before the others could ask who was riding, Koryatovich's hussars pushed forward and struck unexpectedly. Grandfather forbade the use of cannons and rifles, so as not to prematurely indicate that someone was operating on the rear of the red, but the surprised Russians, resting next to the horses, were deprived of any possibility of defense. The cavalry emerging from the darkness were mistaken for the next Ural cavalry units on their way to the battlefield. By the time they realized it was enemy cavalry, by the time they jumped up to fight and grabbed their weapons, they were already falling under the blows of the sabers. The fight lasted no more than a dozen or so minutes.

The regiment slowed down, then stopped.

Janek has come to mind some time ago an idea taken from stories about old fights with Tatars. He had it before his eyes all the time, but only now, looking at the lightning-fast clash, he crystallized. He threw two words of explanation to Alik and immediately pushed him to Vasily asking for permission to proceed. Without waiting for his return, he ordered Damienko to have his squad catch the mounts that had survived the encounter and now ran around, stunned and riderless. About forty were brought in soon.

"And what are you thinking about, Mr. Jan?" Galloped from grandfather Koryatovich with Alik.

"Do you remember, Mr. Kuźma, old tales about Tatars? You probably know them too. When they wanted to surprise the enemy, they let go of the horses with their tails on fire. Under the influence of fire and pain, they panicked and charged blindly forward without looking where they were going, but further from what was causing them pain. Such a rushing flock caused quite a stir in the ranks of the opponent."

"You want to fire horses' tails?" Koryatovich's eyes widened as he looked at him in disgust. "Fear God, Mr. Jan, it does not befit, although this is a war. We are not Tatars. They are just poor animals!"

"I do not want to fire their tails, but ropes with dry grass attached to their saddles. The horses will be okay, but frightened by fire and smoke, they will be the first to attack the Bolsheviks. Before they know what's going on, they will get under the fire of our cannons, which will increase the panic and increase the chances of reaching our unit Fedor with Ostapko."

"Crazy, real madness, not honorable, but..." He paused and looked at Janek somehow strangely, he recalculated something in his head and after a while added: "go". Just fasten yourself on those ropes, because there - he showed the direction where the battle was going on, "it is raging and there is no time."

***

It did not take long to prepare the ropes and bunches of the dried grass. They soaked the latter with vodka to make them burn better.

When they were ready, the order came to move forward again. At first walk, then they quickly went into a gallop, because you could already see the front, flares of shots and you could hear the calls of cavalrymen of subsequent Gai-Khan units, preparing to attack the Polish front.

They pressed in silence, and the beat of the horses now seemed to be a rising tide that the Bolsheviks should hear. The tension reached its maximum, but the troops in front of them, staring only at the Polish front, did not react yet. The gallop of nearly six hundred horses was nothing to the loud clatter of weapons, defending and attacking.

It was dark, but not so dark that the darkness would mantle the details. It was a steppe, and there was never absolute darkness there. If anyone heard a horse approaching and saw the riders' silhouettes emerging from the gray surroundings, it never occurred to him that it might be someone other than his own.

Janek had a revolver in his hand and a saber in the other. He didn't have to guide Sewek with the reins, just a slight pressure on his knees for him to react.

The ranks of the attackers were getting closer.

He raised his sabers up, signaling Alik and his soldiers who were holding torches. At the same time, he turned to Fedor and Kawęcki, who were riding next to him.

"It's time for you!" He shouted, and they just nodded, jumped back and took over the lead of their troops.

A bunch of dried grass, hooked at the ends of short ropes, caught fire at once. The horses rushing ahead of them began to turn their heads nervously, and when the stench of smoke hit their noses, they saw the flames rushing forward like crazy, wanting to instinctively escape from the fire.

The entire regiment was galloping now, preceded by the horses fleeing from them. In many places the grass of the steppe was seized by the burning flares, hitting the ground every now and then and fueled by the rush of air, which gave the impression that all of a sudden hell had opened the gates and poured out into the darkness, scratching the darkness of the night with bloody claws and leaving long lines on the ground fire.

They could already see the fighting front and the Bolshevik troops circling before it. They attacked not in formation, but in loose stakes, then rushing forward, then marking the attack, then finally retreating to close lines, and in a moment to move the bench together on the defenders.

The front line was attacked by infantry which, unlike the cavalrymen, moved slowly but relentlessly forward. The soldiers rushed forward, fell to the ground under the influence of the defenders' fire, then, torn by the urgent orders of the commissars screaming behind them, stood up and ran forward again.

Janek didn't even notice when Fedor's squad broke aside and disappeared into the darkness. He heard a humming noise nearby, only glanced at the unfurled banner.

He signaled and the barrows, which had been silent until then, started a murderous fire, spitting out hundreds of cartridges.

The soldiers leaned over the horse's backs. The sabers went up.

They were pushing like a storm now.

Without any shouts so characteristic of Russians, in silence, they gazed only at the Bolsheviks who had not noticed anything yet.

Horses crazed with fear galloped ahead, leaving long lines of fires in a burned steppe behind them.

***

The surprise was complete.

The Russian troops, noticing the commotion in the rear, stopped their attacks and began to turn back to orient themselves in the new situation and recognize what was happening.

Dozens of horses running away from the fire fell out of the darkness on them. Behind them flew fireballs creating a glow that increased their size in the darkness and recalled in peasant soldiers the memory of old tales about a god, Swarog Ogonija, who threw lines of fire on the ground, vindictive and cruel, from whom there was no escape.

Panicked mounts attacked them in fractions of a second without looking where they were going, as long as they were only further away from the flames behind them. Some hit the cavalrymen, knocking them down in a rush, others attacked the obstacles with their hooves, and if they did not break their legs and emerged victorious from the fight, they rushed forward, this time falling between the infantry, causing more and more confusion and panic that inflicted on the cavalry mounts.

Before the Bolsheviks cooled down, a steel angel of doom flew from the darkness in the form of projectiles thrown by the heavy machine guns of speeding tachankas. They mowed dozens of riders and their horses. As if that was not enough, from behind the wall of darkness, like another doomsday angel, preceded by lines of burning grass, riders in foreign uniforms suddenly appeared, cutting down the surprised cavalrymen like cornfields.

This was too much for the hitherto fearless fighters of the infamous, cruel Tenth Cavalry Division.

The survivors of the first horse attack and a series of heavy machine guns, and later sabers, plunged into a limp run, not looking at which direction they were taking, just further from what was beyond their imaginations. They collided with each other, trampled each other, making their retreat difficult, and it was hard for them to attack anyone or create a common defense front. The commissars, so dangerous to their subordinates, gave up the thought of fighting at once, if only to run as far as possible from the unnatural phenomena of fire horses and the wall of missiles behind them.

In an instant, the world went mad on the previous front lines.

Nobody was in control of what happened anymore, and nobody wanted to explain. Everyone just wanted to save their life.

After the first attack of the horses and the red conflagration right behind them, the infantry disintegrated, throwing back or panicked, dropped their weapons and rushed towards the Polish lines. Be far from what was terrifying in its pronunciation and could not find a rational explanation. The panic spread faster than the hens in the steppe. They did not care that they became an easy target for Poles who were also surprised by the situation, that they were faced by the enemy they were attacking a moment ago, so as to escape as far as possible from the incomprehensible phenomenon that evoked an atavistic fear of the unknown.

*   *   *

Janek tried to coordinate the attack, but in the chaos that arose, among the clouds of dust on the trampled grass and in the darkness, it was not easy. He only glanced back and saw the figures of the mount's bench emerging from the shadows, storming forward and repelling the few attacks of those Bolsheviks who had not managed to slip aside.

The shots stopped in front of them and he guessed that the legionaries had been informed by Fedor's group that they were facing an attack by Polish cavalry. On the side, however, groups of the part of Gai-Khan's cavalry began to appear, which noticed the break in the front and was ordered to close the hole. Not exposed to the attack that terrified those in the Polish regiment's charge section, they were now trying to join the fight.

Fortunately, the Bolsheviks also could not find out in the dust storm who was attacking and from what direction. Therefore, individual units tried to break into the fighting section. But here they were broken by speeding cavalry. The increasing confusion meant that no one was in control of events anymore. And when the voices of "Attack!", "To the Bolshevik" were heard from the front, and soon after that the legionnaires jumped forward, no one knew what was happening anymore.

Janek saw in front of him a rushing horse with a characteristic hat, who at the sight of him suddenly veered the horse's run and swung his saber.

He bounced his blade, leaned over, and used his momentum to slash across the other's chest. Without slowing down, he galloped on, the corner of his eye only registering that the rider had fallen off his horse.

Another equestrian emerged in front of him and he had it at the end of his saber when he saw a uniform different from the Russian one.

"Pole! Pole! Pole!" He heard the voice of the other, braking sharply.

He did the same, and before asking the other said, "Who's in charge?"

"Here, me, but the whole regiment behind me."

"We must coordinate the attack, because the Bolsheviks will find their bearings, order of the command."

Janek did not ask who had given such an order, what was the command and what was it about, but when he noticed Alik he handed him over to stop the attackers in their place.

It was not easy to stop immediately the cavalcade emerging from the darkness, the speeding horses and their riders, before whom Janek suddenly appeared cavalrymen, so far rushing at the forefront, and now trying to stop the entire regiment. Some flew on, slowed down and returned, others flashed by and only after several dozen meters did they realize that others were turning back.

It was still pending the attack when grandfather appeared next to him, followed by Koryatovich.

"What's happening?"

Janek pointed at the stranger cavalryman without a word.

"Lieutenant Jabiński from the 15th Uhlans' Regiment," he reported immediately and quickly added: "We had only just arrived at the front and we were informed that ours were breaking through the Bolsheviks and..." He paused for a moment, then added quickly, though hesitantly: "that - excuse me - but there is some demon of fire death in front of them, whatever that means."

"Why did you stop your attack?"

"The commander will explain, he is on his way, and we are from the 4th squadron, because the rest went to Minsk and Borysów. Here it is, our Captain Marjan Drouer," he pointed to the emerging group of cavalrymen.

The others rode up saluting.

"What situation?" Grandfather did not even introduce himself and without waiting for the newcomers to react, he quickly said to Janek:

"Take your people and the tachankas and secure the northern section, and you, Koryatovich, the southern section." And before Janek pulled the reins, he said to him: "Vasily is wounded, he was shot in the chest, I sent him with people somewhere behind the

Polish lines, I hope they broke through." And turning to the arrived captain: "How many people do you have?"

"Report about two hundred, waiting on the line with the infantry."

"Get me the legionnaire commander here, now." Grandfather said to one of the officers. And to the captain: "There is a chance to break the Bolsheviks, but we must attack immediately, while the turmoil continues. You comes under my command."

***

It was not yet dawn, although on the horizon the sky was brightening, glistening with bright red ribbons cut by a duvet of pale blue inclusions. The battle was over. The Tatar division of Gai-Khan, not knowing what forces had attacked them from the rear of the front, evacuated, surrendering the rear and escaping to the east. The remnants of the infantry abandoned by their own were captured.

An officer came from the staff of general Szeptycki, asking for grandfather to come. He left the regiment under the command of Koryatovich and went to the council. The officer, Captain Mieziński, hastily explained on the way that the Polish troops were preparing to attack Minsk and that the headquarters of the "Jaworczyk" commander who had helped capture Babruysk and crashed the Russian counterattack that was going to retake the city. And that only distracting Bolsheviks are taking place here, because they are pushing a whole lot directly towards Warsaw, and it is said that General Rozwadowski's staff is preparing something to stop them.

"In a word, it is not good, but general Szeptycki will explain everything to you," he added and after a while, staring at Ataman, he stated: "I think it will be a joyful meeting with Major Jaworski, because he is asking about you all the time," he added and after a moment: "And our boys on the commander-in-chief's staff, those from the intelligence service, want to meet you too." He paused, and when the Ataman did not respond, he said, "So far I have heard rumors about your regiment, but it seemed to me that these are only fairy tales for sustaining the spirit, as it happens, and here you yourself. I'm honored to meet you in person."

Chapter XXIII

Janek, immediately after the fighting had ceased, went to Koryatovich. Grandfather had not yet returned from the headquarters and, having deployed the entire regiment, he had nothing to do but wait for orders. He wanted to find the field hospital and see what was going on with Vasily, because anxiety for his uncle tormented him more and more, and fear for his condition did not allow him to wait idly after the fighting had stopped.

"Mr. Kuźma, nothing is happening, maybe I will look for my uncle, I suppose I can, I will not break any orders?"

"Sure, sure, but where the hospital is, I don't know, but maybe the legionnaires know something." He looked at him, his expression tightened and his brow furrowed. "Be prepared, Mr. Jan, for bad news, because the wound was severe and he was taken unconscious by the boys from the battlefield. I don't even know if they broke through, I don't know anything because I didn't see them later in the camp and they didn't check in, which is strange. So I'm worried myself, and so is your grandfather, but... Go, go while it's still calm, and don't worry about the troop, Alik and Demenkov are here, we'll be fine."

He quickly jumped onto Sewek and headed west, where a regiment of legionnaires was located. On the way he asked about the hospital, but no one knew where it was located. Only one of the ensigns showed him the direction to the youngster visible in the distance.

"There, sir, they set up it, but you have to drive up from the west, there is such a narrow road there and it is about three hundred meters to the old forester's lodge."

He speeded Sewek up, confused by the uncertainty that Vasily was there. Now it occurred to him that he should nevertheless find the three in the regiment who had taken Vasily from the battlefield and ask them. Why haven't they checked in so far? This hospital so far? They could have taken him elsewhere, maybe there are two hospitals, maybe...

He scolded himself for the doubts, but he didn't want to go back and only speeded Sewek up towards the forest.

He found the track easily, as did the forester's lodge with makeshift tents. Below them, on makeshift beds made of branches, lay the wounded, between which the nurses bustled. There was a faint smell of blood and various medications in the air. The whole thing was completed by the sight of ubiquitous bandages, soft groans and flies hovering in whole swarms over the tarpaulins. And sisters running between the lairs with syringes and armlets of bandages. Many of the wounded lay on the beds, staring blankly at the linen ceilings of the tents, indifferent to what was happening in their surroundings. Somewhere he heard a call for water, and on the side someone was playing the harmonica softly as if nothing happen.

The sight hit him so hard that he stopped his horse, just watching, adjusting his eyes and nerves, and mentally struggling with his mounting anxiety for Vasily. The night battle made itself felt with weariness, which he only realized now, for his eyes stinged as if someone had sprinkled sand on them. On top of that, there was nervousness and uncertainty that made me feel a growing headache.

"Buck up." He mentally reminded himself that he hadn't learned to smoke a pipe, as Grandfather and Vasily did when things were getting out of hand or difficult decisions had to be made, and which supposedly allowed him to collect his thoughts.

"You came to see whom?"

He twitched involuntarily when an unexpected voice came from his side.

He turned around.

A young nurse in an apron smeared with blood and a handful of fresh bandages in her hands was looking at him with a smile.

"Some soldier, and he was touched, he did not taste blood?" She joked, tilting her head to the side.

"No... I... I mean... yes," he blurted out, unable to gather his thoughts at the sight of the phenomenon of the girl's beauty.

Because this one was more than pretty. Black hair escaped from under the cap, and her eyes were green and large, framed only by dark circles that showed fatigue. The clash of her smile with the blood on her apron and all around him unexpectedly upset him.

"You should make up your mind, because I have to go now, and I can help."

"Please, I'm sorry, I thought, it's all so... I'm looking for Vasily?"

"Every second here is Vasily, military man, Janek, Misha, Antoś and others. Some indecisive gentleman and this outfit, a strange uniform, as if not ours, not Polish." This time she gave him a distrustful look.

"I mean..." He stuttered again. "I'm looking for Colonel Vakhtang, Uncle Vasily for me," he blurted out quickly, fearing that he would cause a racket and explain nothing.

"Oh, you should start with this from the beginning, as if you had never seen the hospital." The nurse's smile widened again. "You must be from those who saved our legionnaires and broke the front, even we heard here." This time she looked at him curiously. "He is conscious, even though he was in such a condition that Dr. Jareński thought that before he bandaged him, he would give up his spirit. He got the bullet out of him, I assisted him, and he didn't want any anesthesia, even though we wanted to give him. Tough as not a man, because you guys..." She laughed. "I'm kidding, I will take you, but leave the horse in front of the tents, because it will bring some pestilence."

He stared at her eyes, which were also laughing now with her lips, and felt relief at the news of Vasily.

"And the cavalrymen brought him. Have they left already?"

"No," She waved her hand, clearly amused. "Each of them was also injured, the doctor immediately ordered them to give morphine, because they wanted to come back. And now they sleep like children when he operated on them. They also had such strange uniforms."

He jumped down from Sewek and tied him to a tree.

"My name is Lila and you?"

"Janek."

"And this uncle of yours is not like you, he is darker. And that name is so strange."

"It's not a surname, it's a Caucasian first name, Wolf, it means in ours."

"Are you from the Caucasus? Far away."

"No, but too much to say. Have you been here for a long time?"

"No, but actually, yes. For almost a year, when they announced in Lviv that our army needed nurses, I applied immediately."

"It's a difficult job, no experience..."

"No, before the war started, I attended the Lviv School of Nursing. When the fighting broke out, it was closed, but I already had the knowledge and worked in the General Hospital. I even thought about transferring to St. Vincent de Paul in Kraków, but in this turmoil, you probably know yourself, I stayed in Lviv."

He listened to the melodic accent and found that for the first time in a very long time, this young girl made a similar impression on him as the late Hapka from the village. Except that the other one was different, and this one... Well, what this one had such that he listened to her words, as at a concert, and the small figure, her hair, eyes, smile, made him stiff. He mused and quickly explained that he hadn't seen the girl in a long time. A living girl.

***

Vasily was seated and apparently flirting with the nurse on the bed. There was no indication that he was injured and the bullet had just been removed from his chest. Janek had not seen him such amused for a long time.

"And this is that dangerous Vakhtang that everyone is worried about?" He came up from the headboard, not sure if it was right to fall into Vasily's arms or to keep a steady distance.

"Shiver me timbers, my Janek!" His uncle tried to jump up at the sight of him, but the pain in his chest did not allow it, and neither did the nurse who stopped him at once.

"And I was talking about heavy surgery." Sister Lila laughed and immediately rebuked girl sitting on the bed: "Krysia, let the colonel rest. Let them say hello, because you can see that they would like to hug each other, and it is not appropriate with us. Come on, I'll come see the wound later."

And they were gone, because from the other end of the room, from behind the partition, came a corpulent man who looked more like a butcher than a doctor. He saw the sisters and motioned for them.

"Why didn't you let me know you were alive? Everyone is worried about you."

"Everyone, you're exaggerating," Vasily beamed, holding Janek's hand. "Your grandfather was already here and he came back to the headquarters. They have a problem there, because they are getting ready to attack Minsk and they have to plan it well. You know, regiments from Greater Poland have come, we already have the strength. And an order came from the commander himself to do it as soon as possible. I'm only worried about how to escape here, because I will not leave the regiment only in the hands of Sylwek and Koryatovich. How is it, have you already counted the losses? Big?"

"Don't think about it now, you need to recover, but not as much as you predicted."

"Bravo, kid, this is your merit and your absurd but effective ideas."

"What are you talking about, Vasily, if I were in charge, I'd be making mistakes."

"Do not be so modest. Grandpa visited me with this commander, General Szeptycki, and he also appreciated it. He even laughed that the old tacticists had to be taught by a youngster like you. But, what's up, where's Alik?"

"I left him, someone has to help Damienkov and Koryatovich, and I also have to come back soon."

"You don't have to, before the staff decide something, Grandpa will come here."

Janek remembered what the legionaries he had spoken with after the battle had said unofficially. Those about moving the entire Bolshevik army to Warsaw.

"With this Warsaw, is it true? Do you know something more?"

"How do you know that?"

"It's hard to be deaf, since the legionaries are talking about something, and those from that regiment of uhlans only confirmed it. Apparently, a powerful army is pushing forward and ours are retreating in all directions. So many rumors, but what is it really like? Oh yeah, those ciphers of yours will help something?"

Vasily laughed but had a coughing fit and spat blood into the napkin next to it.

Janek, seeing this attack, started looking for a nurse, but Vasily stopped him. He was silent for a moment, recovering, then asked him to bend over him.

"I don't think I'm going with you," he whispered and tried to smile, but only a grimace came out.

"I can see it, I will let the doctor know."

"Come on, he did what he could, and the hole in the lungs is not so little thing and it will not heal right away. And this is not real hospital."

"So maybe…"

"No maybe, I will leave, but I really will not go with you. Now listen. You are to listen to your brother-in-law, that is, to your grandfather like never before. Understand? This is no joke, this is a war, but not like it is in the east. Here the bullets take a sharp harvest."

Janek looked surprised, because Vasily had never spoken to him like that before.

"I always listen, but you mainly raised me, because my grandfather used to go somewhere. You are like him to me, I only have two, not counting my mother. Father, I doesn't even know where he is, and you…" He paused, because now he was getting the term he had heard earlier. "Did you say brother-in-law?"

He looked at Vasily closely, at his pale face and his lungs moving as he fished for air and bloodshot eyes. He got up quickly and, ignoring the protests, Vasily ran to where he had seen the doctor. He opened the curtain. Another operated patient was carefully removed from the table and placed on a stretcher.

"Doctor, something is happening to my grandfather, he is spitting blood!" he exclaimed.

"It's that young colonel from that colonel, Vakhtang, that you took the bullet out of his lungs," Sister Lila, standing next to him, explained quickly.

The doctor gave her some command in Latin, and she reached into the shelf taking something out, and he immediately headed for Vasily's bunk.

"Oh, Colonel Caucasus, you are making trouble again instead of resting." He muttered and placed the stethoscope against the patient's chest.

He listened for a moment, then nodded and let sister know, who took his forearm, felt for a vein and gave him an injection."

"What's with him?" Janek asked, not knowing what was going on.

"Nothing, nothing, he just strained the wound, and it's unhealed, it is wrong this way, but this is a real wild animal, and he will be good, as long as he has peace." In one stroke the doctor muttered and then added: "But, my lord, do not upset him, he will fall asleep in a moment and let him rest, because then I cannot guarantee that he will get out of this."

He nodded to sister and they walked away.

Janek dipped a napkin in the vessel of water, squeezed it out and gently wiped Vasily's sweating face.

"My Vakho, sorry, I overestimated my strength." Uncle whispered softly. "I'm going to fall asleep, they probably gave me opium or morphine, or maybe some other filth."

"Say nothing, the doctor ordered you to rest."

"Hush, I know better than medico what to do."

When Janek tried to argue, he waved his hand at him to keep him quiet.

"I have to tell you because this is our last secret with Grandpa. He is indeed my brother-in-law, because he has a wife, there in the Caucasus…" He paused, closed his eyes, and after a while, only by force of will, opened them and continued. "Tamriko… They fell in love… Tamriko was my sister, they got married, and when the Russians captured our fortress, Akhaltsikhe, they slaughtered all the inhabitants… Tamriko died as well. Later grandpa couldn't… It doesn't matter… So you are also my relative and you have grown, to our pride, into a brave Vakho. Grandpa was afraid that he would raise you to protect you from danger, to be a mollycoddle, because he loves you too much, so he commissioned me to train you. Oh, our last secret… Now go now, because my eyes…" This time he was silent for a long time, and then without opening his eyes, he added: "And remember, listen to your grandfather, because the biggest battle with the Russians is about to come, but grandpa will say you… And watch out, my Vakho, because…"

He didn't finish and fell asleep.

www.ingramcontent.com/pod-product-compliance
Lightning Source LLC
Chambersburg PA
CBHW060210030726
47499CB00004B/985